SISTERS in CRIME 3

Berkley Books Edited by Marilyn Wallace

SISTERS IN CRIME
SISTERS IN CRIME 2
SISTERS IN CRIME 3

SISTERS in CRIME 3

Edited by
Marilyn Wallace

BERKLEY BOOKS, NEW YORK

SISTERS IN CRIME 3

A Berkley Book / published by arrangement with
the editor

PRINTING HISTORY
Berkley edition / August 1990

PRINTED IN THE UNITED STATES OF AMERICA

Quality Printing and Binding by:
ARCATA GRAPHICS/KINGSPORT
Press and Roller Streets
Kingsport, TN 37662   U.S.A.

For Steven, Debra, Nathan, Becky, and Zachary,
with love
(Now will you come back?)

Contents

Foreword

This summer a reader confessed that until she'd seen the first volume of *Sisters in Crime* she hadn't realized that so many American women were writing mysteries. As she handed me the book to sign, she added with a grin, "And they're all still alive!" Alive, indeed, and producing crime fiction that is testimony to the fact that the mystery-writing family isn't limited to our talented British sisters (Agatha Christie, Dorothy Sayers, Ruth Rendell, and P. D. James, for example) and American brothers (such as Dashiell Hammett, Raymond Chandler, Robert B. Parker, and Ed McBain), all of whom provide many hours of wonderful reading.

Most of the stories in this third volume of *Sisters in Crime* appear in print here for the first time. Readers have commented on the diversity of subject and style in these books; still, it has been curious and marvelous to watch each volume develop its special personality. The first volume tended toward psychological suspense, the second volume toward humor and satire. In this, the third volume, several stories examine social conflicts in contemporary America. That two of the stories (Susan Kelly's "The Healer" and Karen Kijewski's "Katfall") begin with a similar premise and explore different outcomes is intriguing—but not at all surprising.

A few things have remained the same through all three volumes: some contributors are members of the organization Sisters in Crime while others are not. And the stories are arranged in alphabetical order, according to the author's last name.

Many of the writers have received such awards as the Edgar (the Edgar Allan Poe award, given by Mystery Writers of America, Inc.); the Anthony (named for the late writer/critic Anthony Boucher, awarded at Bouchercon, the annual mystery convention); the Shamus (also given at Bouchercon, by Private Eye Writers of America); the Agatha (awarded at the Malice Domestic convention); and the Macavity (awarded by Mystery Readers International).

Once again, I'm pleased, proud, and enriched to have the opportunity to work with so many fine writers—and to have their stories to entertain and inform me.

　　　　　　　　　　　　　　—Marilyn Wallace
　　　　　　　　　　　　　　San Anselmo, CA
　　　　　　　　　　　　　　December 1989

Mary Jo Adamson grew up in Illinois, went to school in Iowa and California, lives in Colorado, and writes mysteries featuring Balthazar Marten, a former New York City policeman who works with partner Sixto Cardenas in Puerto Rico. Enlivened by the richness of two distinct cultures—and the occasional clashes when they meet—her novels (with titles from Shakespearean quotes) include Not Till a Hot January, A February Face, Remember March, April When They Woo, *and* May's Newfangled Mirth *(one of eleven crime novels listed among the notable books of 1989 by* The New York Times*).*

In "Arts and Crafts," a husband, never satisfied with the canvas of his life, tries to manipulate his wife's vision, too.

ARTS AND CRAFTS

by Mary Jo Adamson

"BUT, JACK, IT is amazing! She lives in the middle of a garden in one of those glass houses, you know, to grow things in—"

"Greenhouses," he replied, dumping his cigarette into the half-empty coffee mug, reaching for the aspirin bottle next to the salt shaker.

"Greenhouses," Rosa corrected herself before rushing on. "Not a big one, but a small one just for flowers, but now she has built a room in back where she cooks and sleeps. She rents out the brick house in front, and she lives all winter on the money she makes from that and what she grows—"

"Is this some sort of a pitch for getting a house of our own?" he asked sourly, swallowing the aspirin with the orange juice in his wife's glass.

"No, no, no. It is just that I have never seen such a garden. Very pretty, but so . . . useful. Not just vegetables, but herbs, and sunflowers bigger than plates, and queer flowers that look like weeds. She says she makes medicines of those—to heal people. And sne teaches courses, um . . . survival courses she calls them, so that people lost in the wilderness would know how to live by eating plants. Even trees.'' Her enthusiasm gave a bronze vibrance to Rosa's dark eyes. As she talked, her slim brown fingers made bridges between sentences, plucked words out of the air. ''You can eat juniper berries. They smell like gin. I tried one and it did not taste very good. But still, in the winter, if you were very, very hungry . . . And you can boil the green needles of the spruce and make a tea that has much vitamin C. Even coffee from dandelion roots. And—''

''Just regular coffee,'' he said, shoving his mug across the table toward her. Rosa got up quickly and poured the dregs into the small sink, picking the butt out of the strainer and putting it into the trash basket. Then she rinsed the mug carefully with scalding water before adding the hot coffee. She didn't mind the American kind, but she still missed the rich Puerto Rican coffee, each time brewed fresh. That made from dandelions might not be too bad, she considered. She'd tasted the leaves, which had been boiled and chilled for salad, and she'd thought that, with the right dressing, they'd be nice. Setting down the coffee before him, she crossed the small kitchen and peered in the ancient Frigidaire to see what she could fix him for breakfast. Satisfied, she continued talking, her mind filled with what she'd learned. ''You can make dough from the insides of hemlock trees.''

''Hemlock's poison. Don't know your Plato, obviously. Neither does she. Socrates was forced to drink it. It paralyzes you.''

Rosa sat down, thought, and then shook her head. ''But I am sure that is what she said. That the Indians here made bread from the hemlock tree. It is easy, sometimes, to mix up the good plants and the bad. Like the lilies. She does these lovely drawings to show the differences and watercolors them. She is very careful about telling her students what not to do. She makes these penny whistles for children out of reeds, and she said you had to make sure—''

He had lit another cigarette and was motioning for the ashtray on the counter. Rosa got up and handed it to him. ''What was I saying? Anyway, her name is Birch.''

''Bitch?'' he inquired, raising a mocking eyebrow.

''Birch,'' she repeated. It was going to be one of his bad days. And so soon after the move, too, Rosa reflected sadly. Usually after they'd settled into a new city and he enrolled at a new college, he would be filled with energy, and be less irritable. But they'd only been in Boulder now for six months, and already he'd started drinking late with one or two of his fellow art students. On the rare occasions when she wasn't working and he was at home in the morning, she tried to catch his interest. But he interrupted her, making little jokes of his own, deliberately misunderstanding everything she said. When he returned late at night, she shrank from talking to him. Then his anger exploded at her, the words cutting like sharp metal fragments.

She wanted so much to tell him about this woman—so odd-looking and so beautiful. Her long hair was red-gold, like the edges of the rising sun, and her eyebrows and lashes were so white that they were as invisible as if they'd been seared off. Her eyes were only an impression of blue. The skin of her face and arms was pinpricked by brown freckles. But what had most impressed Rosa was Birch's knowledge and her self-containment. Given a problem, she imagined Birch would look inward. Her own mother and her friends in Puerto Rico, discussing making the food stamps stretch, drew together like a flock of multicolored doves in Paloma Park. Rosa had always assumed it was the only way to solve things.

She glanced up at the kitchen clock—it was already ten-thirty. Today she was working both lunch and dinner shifts at the restaurant. She would have to leave soon. "An omelet?" she asked Jack placatingly. "A sandwich? There is chicken."

He picked up his cigarettes and disappeared into the bedroom without a word. He kicked the door shut behind him. She propped her elbows on the wobbly-legged card table on which they ate their meals and ran anxious fingers through her heavy black hair. They'd always stayed at least a year in each place, two in Boston where his family lived. But these signs were not good, and Rosa desperately wanted to stay in Boulder, Colorado.

She and Jack had met when he was in the Navy, stationed at Roosevelt Roads, the big base on Puerto Rico's east coast. Her mother had always said, "As pretty as you are, Rosa, marry a sailor, have some security, get off the island." It had always been her mother's dream to move to America. Rosa wondered later if her mother could have imagined how large and lonely the country was when you traveled through it.

But when the eighteen-year-old Rosa saw Jack Kilkenny,

she'd have gone gladly to the waterless mountains of the moon with him. He had dark hair, brows, and lashes, but eyes as changeable blue-green as the Atlantic. She was so proud to be his *novia*; all the other Puerto Rican girls were envious, seeing her walk beside Jack in his smartly pressed uniform. He talked with an angel's tongue, telling her how beautiful she was, how happy they'd be.

But once they were married and back in Boston, his hometown, he'd not been happy. He'd first enrolled as an art major at Boston University, but he was impatient with required classes, saying they weren't relevant for artists. He'd transferred to the University of Massachusetts, but had argued with his professors, saying they were fossils, unable to appreciate the boldness of his new approaches. He set up a studio of his own in an abandoned warehouse, but he found the light was wrong. Then he said it made him nervous living near his parents, who were pressuring him to settle down. He and Rosa began their odyssey. She could always find waitressing jobs in the university towns where they landed.

If only, Rosa thought forlornly for the thousandth time, if only she could talk to Jack like the Anglo women students, knowing the large words thrown about, knowing what it was to be an artist; she would understand his problems and he would surely be happier. She'd taken an art appreciation extension class when they'd lived in Boston and she'd liked the instructor very much. But the lectures taxed her English, and Jack had ridiculed both the text and the teacher. She'd quit going. Besides, she'd taken to working long hours because the moving was expensive.

Not only did Rosa hate moving, she loved Boulder. She had dreaded winter on the East Coast and then in the Midwest, where the gray skies descended, sealing off the sun for months. But here the daily sun in a sky of Caribbean blue sparkled the snow and then melted it on the street, leaving it pristine on the Flatirons and the distant mountain peaks that rose above the city. The town was only medium-sized, although swelled by twenty thousand University of Colorado students, every one of whom seemed to Rosa taller, healthier, and blonder than the next.

The older residential sections of Boulder looked just like the pictures of America she'd seen in grade school textbooks: the houses of smooth, scrubbed brick with white wooden porches shaded by thick-trunked trees. Children ran on green lawns. Bicyclists pedaled through the quiet streets.

Now that it was summer, the elegant pedestrian mall in the heart of town was bustling. People strolled past planters filled with marigolds and petunias or chatted with friends in sidewalk cafés. She loved to window-shop in the expensive clothing stores and Indian art galleries, in the little shops that sold hand-knit sweaters, handwoven skirts, as well as in those that displayed crystals and geodes.

"Craftsy crap," Jack had scoffed. "Bunch of New Age nuts here. Psychics, rebirthers, past-life specialists! Not to mention all the life-and-growth-empowerment pushers, thinking they know how to live." Rosa didn't quite understand, but everyone seemed very excited and interested in what they were doing. She liked hearing about it. All her regular customers told her earnestly about their ideas, urging her to read this book, attend that session, join this group.

And Rosa was happy working at Mama Sofia's. Not only were the wages good, but the old widow had given Rosa and Jack one of the two small apartments upstairs very cheaply. Rent was very high in Boulder. It was a family restaurant, although the students crowded in, too. Privately Rosa marveled that they could down so many of the Mexican dishes filled with the searing jalapeño peppers. She liked the refried beans, but she'd thought the customers would also enjoy the Puerto Rican red beans cooked with ham, onions, and sweet chili peppers and seasoned with cilantro, oregano, and garlic. Her mother had always said Rosa was a genius in the kitchen, that her dessert flan tasted not like an eggy custard with brown sugar topping, but like a sherry-tinted cream cloud that would make Spanish angels weep with envy. Rosa would have also liked to include on the menu her *caldo gallego*, that rich soup of ham, white beans, *chorizo*, cabbage, and greens. But she'd been afraid that Mama Sofia would misunderstand, would think it a criticism if she offered. Mama Sofia was a very good cook, Rosa thought, and she knew that only the freshest of ingredients were used at the restaurant.

Because of that, Rosa had met Birch. Mama Sofia clucked at the price of fresh herbs at the supermarket—three little leaves for one dollar. The widow was saving for her retirement to the hot winters of Mexico. When the tall, pale Anglo appeared with cheap bunches of cilantro, basil, oregano, thyme, and fennel, Mama Sofia was delighted. Also, Birch sold clusters of garden flowers for the tables: lilies of the valley, sweet peas, daisies. She came every Thursday, but yesterday Mama Sofia had run short of needed spices and asked Rosa to go to Birch's.

In the bright greenhouse that was her living room, Birch was perched on a stool before a long wooden counter, cutting fat bulbs from the ends of the stems of delicate deep-blue flowers. A heap of darker brown bulbs were next to her elbow. "Here," she said, offering Rosa one of these. "I roasted these with pine needles last night in my stone pit and I'm storing them for winter. Did you ever eat a lily?" Rosa crunched into the bulb cautiously and swallowed, surprised at how much she liked the nutty taste.

"A treat, isn't it?" Birch smiled. "The Indians fought wars over the rights to collect camas. They were careful to dig them up in June and July, though, when they could see the color of the flowers. Those with blue ones are edible; those with white flowers are quite poisonous." She'd slid off the stool and brought another pot with a showy, white, bell-shaped flower. "But this lily, the sego, is white and very good to eat. Its bulbs saved the Mormons in Utah from starvation."

"But how did you learn all this?" Rosa asked, looking in envious wonder at the lush plants in the sun-filled room.

"From other people, from books." She looked thoughtfully at Rosa, who was staring at a glowing fuchsia bougainvillea that reminded her of her home. "Stay a minute," Birch said. "I'll get some of my homemade mint tea. Herbal teas are expensive, but mine costs almost nothing. Give mint an inch of your garden and it'll try for eight yards."

As they'd chatted, sipping the aromatic beverage, Rosa had felt for the first time in America as though she were with a friend. And—Rosa so wished she'd been able to tell Jack before he stomped out—Birch had offered to help her start her own garden. Rosa got up from the card table and, for the fourth time that morning, peered out of the small kitchen window at the dry sandy ground in the back of the restaurant. Rough crabgrass struggled there now, and some determined crawling weed with small white flowers, but she could envision wide-bellied peppers, plump tomatoes, crisp lettuce.

Last night, Mama Sofia had been pleased with the idea. "Every year, Rosa, when Rafael was alive, we talked of putting a patio there with outside tables for customers. But we never did. Now, a garden—that would be excellent. You understand, I cannot help. The arthritis in the knees. But maybe in the winter we can put some of the plants on my sun porch upstairs. And, if you plant chili peppers for me, I will help with some expenses.''

But, Rosa reflected as she excitedly clattered down the stairs to work, it wouldn't cost much. In return for help in Birch's burgeoning garden, she'd been promised compost, cuttings, and advice. Between the two shifts today, Rosa would have two hours off and she planned to start right away.

Each night, over the next few weeks, Rosa submerged her protesting muscles in the claw-foot bathroom tub, and tried to stay awake long enough to go over what she'd learned that day. "A wide margin of cracked oyster shells around the garden will keep out the slugs," Birch said. "And might keep out the neighborhood cats who'll enjoy your fresh dirt. Put the mint in buried coffee cans so it won't overrun everything else.'' She made suggestions for next year. "Plant clematis along the base of this old chain-link fence—you remember the dark purple flower on the sides of my house? Someday it will cover the fence beautifully. Tomatoes go where they'll catch sun all day. A whole bed of the different parsleys—cilantro, especially, because it's expensive to buy fresh. Big clumps of Shasta daisies in back because they don't need good soil and make nice bouquets for the tables.''

To Rosa's disappointment, she'd severely limited what could be planted this year. "Colorado's growing season is just too short. You're much too late for corn, but zucchini sprouts fast. You'll have to be inventive about recipes using them. Otherwise, your patrons will boycott. At the end of the summer, people here stand on street corners desperately trying to give away their summer squash.''

Rosa had little chance to talk to Jack. She'd slipped into exhausted sleep before he returned at night. She left fresh fruit and cereal for his breakfast each morning and then hurried down to the garden. Occasionally she saw him peering at her from above as she and Birch bent down, noticing the new leaves. She could tell by the set of his shoulders that he was angry. When Birch looked up mildly, he'd glower at her. Rosa would wave at him, hoping he'd come down and inspect their progress. But he only turned away and disappeared down the outside steps toward campus.

At Birch's garden and greenhouse, the two women usually worked in companionable silence, picking out the yucca seeds, harvesting yampa roots for specialty stores, drying leaves for spices, making oils and tonics for sale in the health food stores that abounded in Boulder. But Birch always explained what they were doing. "Fresh willow bark makes a great tea, and it has a chemical structure like aspirin. Valerian is a natural antiseptic. The Indians used it on wounds."

On some days, gathering plants for Birch's classes, they searched through fields of grass and chose examples from along the canyon streams. "Look at these three tall plants with white flowers, Rosa. They all belong to the parsley family. But the wild carrot is so pretty that English courtiers wore it as living lace. Cow parsnip has fatter flowers, thicker stalks, and the Indians ate the leaves and stalks when they were tender in the spring. But look at the flower umbels carefully on this one. And," she said, cutting open the thick stem, "this is hollow inside, with horizontal chambers. This is the one you never use for whistles. It's water hemlock, and it's as dangerous as poison hemlock. Maybe more so, because it doesn't smell as bad. Poison hemlock smells dusty and strong, like mouse urine, so grazing animals avoid it. But water hemlock looks a lot like cow parsnip. The hemlock *tree*, of course, is a friend." She added musingly, "To me, living is doing what you love, but sometimes I think survival is the art of knowing what not to do."

Just as Birch predicted, the zucchini crop was abundant, and Mama Sofia looked at the piles of green squash in alarm. Rosa began to smile. "Let me try," she said. The largest ones she sliced in half, scooped out the centers and added chicken, cream sauce, mild peppers, and jack cheese. Others she cored, stuffed with link sausage, and covered with spicy tomato sauce. She filled some with ground lamb and spices and sliced them into rounds. Soon "Rosa's zucchinis" were much requested by the regular customers. With Mama Sofia's encouragement, she branched out into the savory soups and chicken stews of the Caribbean. Soon thereafter a new waitress appeared and Rosa stayed full-time in the kitchen.

"Bring us some coffee, Rosa," Mama Sofia said one afternoon after the lunch rush, lowering her bulk into one of the booths. She fixed her old walnut eyes on the young woman's face. "This morning I talked to Alicea Ortiz's son, who is a lawyer. I told him in a year I want to go home to Mexico to live. He has an idea. You take over the restaurant. Send me so much money every year. He says if I trust your head and your heart, and I do, then we save the bank's interest on a mortgage. We do it all on paper. If you pay on time, you will end owning the restaurant. If you do not pay, I take it back. In the meantime, I will teach you all I know.''

As Mama Sofia talked, even Rosa's breathing became shallow, so she would not miss a word. She could only smile and nod, nod and smile. The old woman added, ''I heard your husband go upstairs. You talk to him, take the evening off.'' On the way up, Rosa's sandals barely touched the creaky wooden stairs.

Jack was standing before the sink, running the water to get it hot before adding it to the cup with instant coffee powder. Without turning, he said, ''We're leaving.'' He didn't see Rosa's horrified face or hear her strangled gasp. ''I'm not going to be admitted back to the program in the fall. Stupid, jealous bastards!'' He slammed the thick mug so hard on the sink edge that the coffee crystals flew over the counter and onto the floor. Then he turned and glared at Rosa.

It had taken her a minute, but now she was smiling. ''But you do not have to care about them now, Jack. See here.'' She described Mama Sofia's offer, ending triumphantly with a new idea. ''You can have her apartment—with its sun porch—for a studio. You know more than these professors, I am sure. Make your own art. We can put it on the restaurant walls. Perhaps, if you like, you can sell it. Or—''

''No.'' He'd pressed his lips together so thinly that the word barely escaped. Then he released a torrent of words that drowned her. ''You want me, *me*, to put my art on some bean eaters' walls? What do you think—that I'm some sort of commercial hack? And you, Rosa, you're a . . . a half-wit. You want to spend your life cooking? You want to be a cook? God, I can't believe it!'' He almost danced with rage. ''Art, Rosa, *art* is what's important. And art is painting—the works of men like Gauguin, van Gogh, Picasso. You're just like . . . these Philistines here! Well, we're leaving. You hear me? We'll go take a look at Oregon. Start packing.'' He strode out of the kitchen, his footsteps crunching on the spilled coffee powder.

Rosa sank down into one of the plastic chairs, pressed her trembling fingers together between her knees and swallowed painfully. Then she groped across the table for a pencil to begin the long list of things to be done before moving. She tried to gather her thoughts. She could get boxes at the nearby liquor store, but she'd need the special ones to pack Jack's bigger canvases. Perhaps the art supplies store on Pearl Street. Their small savings would be just enough to reach the new town. She would have to hurry then to find another waitressing job. Was it Oregon where it always rained? Mama Sofia would have to be reminded to water the lettuce, just coming in so nicely.

Pushing back the chair, she went to the window so that she could keep in mind all the garden chores that would need doing after she was gone. Numbly, she stared down at the fruits of her labors. The tears began, running unhindered down her cheeks. Suddenly, in the midst of the leafy frames, she spied a ripening tomato. Even Birch had not thought she'd have tomatoes, but each day Rosa had whispered words of encouragement to the plants. Now one was burgeoning in the sun. And there'd be others. And she knew what she was going to do.

Turning back to the table, she tore out a newspaper ad that was mostly white space. On it she scrawled, her fingers still unsteady: "I am sorry, Jack. But I cannot go." Then she picked up her small purse and went quietly down to the street.

An hour later, figuring it was time enough for Rosa to accept the idea, Jack slid his cigarettes into his shirt pocket and returned to the kitchen. When he read the note, his first furious thought was that someone whose handwriting was semi-illiterate was an idiot to believe she could run a restaurant, order the liquor and the food, manage the employees. He'd point *that* out to her. How could she think—Rosa had always been so sensible. She'd been brainwashed. That was it. He'd have to set that Bitch Birch straight, too.

He planned his actions. Now that it was after five—only alcoholics drank before five—he'd grab a few quick drinks, go to her greenhouse, and tell her a few home truths. Rosa was *his* wife, and he wanted no interference. Especially, he thought, as he slammed the apartment door so loudly that it echoed in the restaurant below, from some magical-thinking New Ager who'd probably impressed his gullible wife with tea-leaf reading.

It was later than he planned when he arrived at the address Rosa had long ago posted on the refrigerator. And he was angrier than when he'd left home. With each vodka gimlet, he'd grown more incensed at the woman's meddling. It had occurred to him that this Birch must have some scheme. Why else was she being so helpful? Maybe she was going to wangle a piece of the restaurant while Rosa did all the work.

There was a dim light in the room built onto the greenhouse, which was still basking in the setting sun. His thunderous knock caused the flimsy frame door to fly open. "Birch," he bellowed, and when no answer came, he barged into the glass enclosure.

He shouted again, but there was no movement from the back, and he wheeled around and strode to the west-facing garden, then stopped, taken aback by its singularity. He saw no familiar flowers—no cheerful geraniums or hollyhocks. The sun, withdrawing behind the mountains, silvered the saber leaves of spiky plants, growing next to spiny cactus. Whole sections of white, fleshy-leaved flowers. Odd, blue-violet, saucer-shaped blooms topped slender stalks; erect plants, as thick as stout poles, were crowned with sticks of densely packed· yellow flowers. A quarter acre, he judged, trying to focus, and he didn't recognize one plant. He wondered if Birch were back there behind some of the six-foot varieties. Somehow he wanted to avoid going along the flagstone paths. Those plants made him think of a Hawthorne short story, "Dr. Some-Italian-Name's Garden" where poisons grew. He'd wait inside, he decided. She'd have to come home sometime.

The glass enclosure smelled of green growth and rich earth. Desk-high, the wooden counter was jumbled with plants in pots and plants in vases, books, drawings and, next to his elbow as he pulled up a stool, a child's set of cheap watercolors. He shoved some of the stuff aside and peered at the drawings. There were three sketches, one of each of what seemed identical plants with white lacy flowers in water-filled mayonnaise jars above the half-finished pictures. Each was carefully detailed, and its characteristics listed in flowing calligraphy. He snorted and shoved them aside. "Crap," he said aloud. *Anybody* could be a draftsman.

Pulling out his crumpled Camel pack, he ripped open the top and saw only two cigarettes. He lit one and jammed the used match into a tiny pot with one struggling leaf.

He drummed his fingers impatiently on the thick plank countertop. Where in the hell was she? Standing up, he stumbled and kicked the stool viciously. Then he giggled. He picked up one of the lacy plants and stuck it in the jar of another, then switched the other two. That stalk was thicker; she'd get mixed up and make a mistake. He dribbled water on the third drawing, pleased at the black ink's smearing.

He sat back down, lit his last cigarette from the end of the first and ground the butt beneath his heel on the tile floor. He wished he'd thought to buy more, as well as a half-pint of vodka. But he'd damn well wait. His glance lit on the paints. He wet the watercolor brush in a jar and smeared a glob of black in the clear yellow. Pleased, he mushed red into the white, then added green. He stuck the cigarette butt into the blue square and yawned. Maybe, he considered, he'd just run out and pick up some more cigarettes and that vodka. No, she might return, see what he'd done, and leave. Maybe even Rosa had come and gotten her and they'd gone someplace. Be just like his wife to not think of him. He couldn't wait to see their faces when he cut loose and told them what *he* thought.

Twirling one of the white flowers in its jar, he realized the stalk was hollow. Like a reed. He pulled it out and peered at its dripping end in the faint light from the back room. Peeling it back, he thought it'd make a fine whistle. He blew on it. The taste was acrid, but he broke off that section and tried another, narrowing its end. He sucked slightly and blew again. A thin pipe-of-Pan sound. A few more tries. Not bad, he thought; he was a virtuoso, even on weeds.

Without getting up, he stretched and looked to see if anyone was coming down the path. The house on the front of the lot had no lights on. Outside, the garden was almost dark, and the plants inside and out seemed to be pressing nearer him.

He closed his eyes uneasily, and then put his head on folded arms. A little nap, maybe; she was bound to come soon.

A bit later, he awoke with a start, not sure where he was at first. His head ached and his feet had gone to sleep. But they felt more numb than he'd ever recalled them feeling before. He pinched his calf, but it was as if he'd squeezed a stone. His panicked finger probed a rigid thigh. Leaning on the countertop, he pushed up wildly, but his unwilling legs collapsed beneath his weight. As he fell, the drawings fluttered down beside him. He could see the smeared word *hemlock* in the light from the kitchen, and he remembered then Plato's description of Socrates' death. He'd only read the beginning and end of the

Dialogue and skipped all the boring stuff in the middle, but he recalled that the jailer had apologetically asked Socrates to move so the poison could take effect . . . or was it to lie still? Desperately, he scrabbled for a fingerhold on the tile to pull himself forward. But he could only inch along. The cold seemed to reached his groin in seconds. Sweating, he thought of the stilling of the heart muscle. And the lungs. He gulped for air, still trying to crawl toward the open door. He shouted again and again, but he realized no one could hear. Birch had probably told her tenants to leave. Must have been a plot, he thought furiously. That was it. A plot.

Dying, he was obsessed with the idea that somehow the crafty bitch had known. . . .

*Marcia Biederman calls on her experience as a journalist to
write about how ordinary people, caught up in extraordinary
circumstances, rise to meet the challenges that confront them.
In her first novel,* The Makeover, *a secretary uncovers some
shady business in the company for which she works. In* Post
No Bonds, *Grace Stark, housewife-turned-bail bondswoman,
takes over her husband's business and in the process discovers her own unsuspected talent for sleuthing.*

*In "Listen and Listen Good," a newly arrived Chinese
student decides that in America actions sometimes speak
louder than words.*

LISTEN AND LISTEN GOOD

by Marcia Biederman

THE TEACHER HAD designed a lesson especially for the Chinese students again, so Fan Chu was in the third stall of the ladies' room, throwing up.

"Oh, there you are. I see your shoes." Who could be talking to Fan in English? She would have to answer in English, but what would be correct—"Yes, I am," or "Yes, I do"? Fan mumbled something and pulled the lever. The toilet had a nice noisy flush.

It was one of those Hong Kong girls, waiting outside the door for her. "It's over," said the girl. She was speaking Mandarin now, but with a heavy Cantonese accent. "The teacher sent me for you. The break is starting soon. Then you have to come back for the quiz."

Fan went to the washbasins to rinse her mouth. The other girl followed, parking her big handbag on a sink corner and rummaging through it for equipment.

"There's going to be a memorial service tomorrow. Three o'clock," she told Fan while squeezing hair gel onto her fingers. "Haven't you seen the posters?"

No answer came, but the girl was too busy lubricating her hair to notice. She worked on each strand until it was shiny and messy enough to suit her. Fan remembered her name now: Ngoot Kyin. She was one of three Hong Kong girls in the class who called themselves Jennifer.

The rest room door opened with a bang, and a group of young Hispanic women came in, shrieking and talking in their language. Fan moved away to let them at the mirrors.

The hall outside was clotted with breaktime activity. A line of African students waited to feed correct change into the soda vending machines. The Cypriot boys, moist and nearly naked in their tank tops, had formed their usual knot around their countrywomen. Fan threaded her way back to Room 715, where she and her classmates sat four hours a day, five days a week, while the reading, writing, listening and pronunciation teachers took turns teaching them English with varying degrees of efficacy and patience.

Here was the reading teacher now, striding down the corridor on those big feet of his, stirring up a breeze that set the memorial service notices flapping against the walls. He must be rushing toward his special afternoon class (extra fee) that prepped students for the Test of English as a Foreign Language so that they could hatch from this incubator and take regular college courses. Fan smiled at him, and the reading teacher smiled back. Fan was very good at reading, top of the class. She was genuinely glad to see this teacher and also glad that he was rushing past.

But now the reading teacher had stopped, and he was pointing at Fan's arm and talking.

"Sorry," Fan picked out of his rush of words, and "your brother."

Fan said "Yeah, yeah" very fast, two syllables shoved close to each other and identical in pitch, like a back-door bell. It was what she always said when she couldn't think of the English. The reading teacher moved on, and Fan twisted the black strip of cloth around her arm so the safety pin wouldn't show.

In the classroom she maneuvered past the cart holding the television and the VCR to take her preferred seat at the inside back corner. Some Japanese students filed in from the break. That was all right; they never spoke to her. But behind them was the listening teacher with her can of Diet Coke.

"Fan!" she said.

Fan smiled. "Yeah, yeah," she said, her fingers straying to the armband as if to hide it.

Something, something, Sorry, said the teacher. Something, something, Quiz.

"Yeah, yeah," said Fan. This time the words burst out on a gust of released breath. It was fine. The teacher was not sorry about Fan's brother. She was sorry that Fan had missed the lesson and wouldn't be prepared for the quiz.

The other students trickled in, and one was chosen to pass out the quizzes. It was going to be all right. Pencils and paper. Reading and writing.

But, no. No, no. The teacher was standing in front of the VCR now, gripping the remote control in a two-hand hold.

"One more time," she said. Her thumb was on the search button, squeezing it relentlessly, sucking images of tanks, soldiers and Chinese students across the television tube.

Fan lowered her eyes. The quiz stank of the ditto machine fluid that was always on the teachers' fingers. She tried not to read, but the blurry purple English words wagged at her.

I. What happened last week in Tiananmen Square?

II. Read the paragraph. Then select the correct words from the following list to fill in the blanks: *protest, tank, kill, casualties, slaughter, massacre.*

"Guess," said the teacher. She was standing right over Fan.

A lot of time must have passed, because some of the students were sitting with their hands folded, waiting for the papers to be collected.

"Guess," the teacher repeated, as she always did when she talked to Fan. She knew which students were weakest at listening. "If you don't know, guess."

The teacher moved away, but her eyes stayed trained on Fan. Fan lifted her pencil, and at the bottom of the paper she traced the three Chinese characters that moaned from the posters announcing the memorial service.

Loss. Mourning. Anger.

Foot pain. Beauty careers. Cockroach traps. The posters on the subway car walls rarely got more than a glance from Fan as she rode to Manhattan and her after-school job, but today she studied them like texts, as if to make up for the ruined quiz. One by one she vanquished them with her reading skills, identifying the main ideas, figuring out words from context, cracking their codes.

She left the train still puzzling out one of the tricky ones, a warning from the mayor about window guards that began "Children Can't Fly." The sense of it finally came to her as she settled down at a table for her customary late lunch at the Salad City restaurant. Why, it was beautiful, almost like poetry! How nice it was to read, how much nicer than trying to understand the refrigerator hum of spoken English vibrating through the crowded restaurant.

Lifting her Styrofoam teacup, she savored her victory over the subway placard, and in that moment some words ripped through the hum, loud and insistent like a buzz saw.

"I'm going to kill them. Watch. I'm going to kill them."

Fan had heard it correctly. She was sure. That's what the man at the next table was saying.

His companion was not so clear, mumbling as he chewed on sesame noodles and cottage cheese. What strange combinations Americans chose from the salad bar.

The first one leaned forward over a hot meatball sandwich and steaming coffee. And his voice—that was hot also.

"I'm going to slaughter them." And again the repetition that gave Fan two chances to understand, like the audiocassettes in listening class. "Slaughter them."

She stood up and bent down for her umbrella and book bag, then gathered up her cup and her paper plate, still laden with uneaten pork and rice. Much as she tried to perform these operations with a minimum of fuss, her elbows and hips refused to cooperate. They kept knocking against the neighboring chair and the hot-food man who wanted to kill.

For there was no chance of mistake. The voice coming from his broad chest and large head was like the voice on the clearest of the language tapes. And his words were the words of the quiz: *kill* and *slaughter*.

As she plied her way down the narrow aisle of the restaurant to the wastebaskets, the English around her congealed into jelly. But when she crossed back to walk to the door, the voice reached her like the first sounds heard by a swimmer after water clears from the ear.

"They'll be screaming."

It was almost four o'clock, a bad time to dash past Grand Central and the knots of pedestrians outside it, but soon she

was turning the corner of Third Avenue and East 43rd to enter
Good Luck Gifts. It was good luck indeed: Mrs. Wu was busy
with a customer or else surely she would have given Fan a
scolding for her few minutes of tardiness.

The door to the office in back of the store was ajar. Mrs.
Wu's sister, the bookkeeper, must have gone out to use the
bathroom at the Burger King. Fan sat down and started on the
pile of work that had been left for her. As usual, there was too
much to do in these short hours, but they refused to let her
work more than three afternoons a week. However, as Mrs.
Wu continually reminded her, a person with a student visa and
no green card was fortunate to have any job at all. And this
one was so convenient to the Number 7 subway—the Orient
Express, as Americans called it—which connected her with
school and home in Queens.

The bookkeeper came back and grunted a greeting. There
had been no mention of granting Fan a day off, not even last
week, when the news had just come and the black armband
was fresh. The sister and Mrs. Wu were Taiwanese and seemed
to take almost a dim delight in what had happened.

The two hours dragged in their usual way, with the bookkeeper occasionally grunting orders at Fan and complaining
about her slowness. On a good day, she might chat with Fan a
bit about Chinese movies. The chats were a welcome relief
from the tedium, even though the bookkeeper's taste ran to
melodramas and Western-style action films, while Fan preferred the purer Chinese cinema, particularly the starkly realistic works directed by Xie Jin, with their brave heroines.

But today the bookkeeper spoke only about the rain of the
last few days, complaining that it was aggravating a pain in her
leg. Fan found these complaints curious. The accounts showed
that the rain had improved the store's sales by increasing demand for umbrellas, and the bookkeeper, who owned a share
in her sister's store, had surely profited.

By the time Fan emerged from the office, most of the store
lights had been turned off, but a last-minute customer was still
in the midst of making a purchase. Mrs. Wu's keys were dangling from the door lock. Fan could have used them to let
herself out, but rather than risking the proprietor's ire, she
decided to wait until the sale was rung up. She stood out of
the way, near the side wall of the store, where various types
of merchandise hung from hooks on a pegboard.

"Sorry," Fan heard the customer say. "Trouble . . . China."
"Oh, we from Taiwan," barked Mrs. Wu in that bad English
grammar of hers. "Taiwan and China *very* different."
Fan, who had been staring idly at the items on the wall,
selected the most expensive one, a plastic travel raincoat pack-
aged in a small zip-up pouch, and slipped it into her book bag.

The memorial service was held in the lobby of the school's
main building. All the Chinese students were there, gathered
around the symbolic casket. Cafeteria-bound Americans
swerved past it, snapping their fingers to the sound of their
Sony Walkmans or gawking.

Fan took her place in line and laid a flower on the casket.
"Jian Ping," she whispered, as if her brother were in there
listening.

"There's a meeting after this," one of the Jennifers whispered to Fan. "We're going to do something about it."

Fan's eyes were too blurred by tears to see where they were
leading her. She was dimly aware of riding in a car, sandwiched in a backseat with four others as the windshield wipers
made pitiful shrieking sounds. The driver turned off the highway at the Kissena Boulevard exit in Flushing, not far from the
apartment she shared with another girl. Oh, well, at least she
could walk home from here.

About a dozen people piled into the living room, finding
seats on the stained rug or on milk crates. Fan recognized one
student who was from Shanghai and another from Xi'an. The
others were from Hong Kong.

A boy with electric-shock hair and a motorcycle T-shirt,
fitting so snugly into his beanbag chair that surely he must live
here, introduced himself as Walter Lo and announced that the
meeting would begin. He said that money was needed to help
the leaders of the Tiananmen Square protest escape from the
country.

"But that's already being done," someone protested from a
corner milk crate. "I just gave fifty dollars to the Chinese student organization in Manhattan."

"Ah, but how can you be sure where that money goes?"
said Walter. "Weren't the officers of that organization appointed by the government?"

A murmur went through the room.

"Raise money for us, and you'll see the fruit of your ef-

forts," said Walter. "In a few weeks some of the bravest of
the Beijing student leaders may be sitting here—right in this
room!"

And whatever would they think, reflected Fan, taking in the
Bruce Lee posters on the wall and the spots on the carpet.

Questions were hurled at Walter. He stretched out a palm
for silence.

"We are in touch with a group in Hong Kong who have set
up an underground railway. Even at this moment people are
being brought out."

"And we are still continuing to spread the truth about the
massacre," said another Hong Kong boy, this one wearing the
kind of oversize American eyeglasses that made people look
like insects. "We need money to keep sending news articles
to fax machines on the mainland."

Better not to send anything, Fan thought. She herself had
stopped writing to her parents and sisters. They would all be
under investigation because of Jian Ping's activities, and letters
from America would cast more suspicion. She must stand alone
now.

A collection was taken, and the meeting dispersed. Fan rose
to leave, but the boy called Walter tapped her on the arm,
touching the strip of black cloth.

"Stay," he said in a low voice. "Some of us have something
more important to discuss."

Everyone left except Fan and the insect-head boy, who appeared to live here also. Walter motioned for Fan to follow
them down a hallway and into another room. She averted her
eyes from the two narrow beds covered with American cloth.

Walter was opening a bureau drawer now. The other boy
protested in Cantonese, but Fan was too tired from a day of
English classes to try to follow them.

"Look," Walter commanded.

The drawer was full of handguns, five or six of them.

Fan averted her glance, which fell instead on a framed picture of a nude woman on the bureau top. She looked back at
the guns.

"We're going to take them into Hong Kong," said Walter.
"They're loaded and ready to go, and we've got plenty of extra
cartridges. It's all planned. Your brother will be avenged."

"Why do you care?" Fan blurted out, and the tears, released

from their temporary confinement, flowed down her face. "It isn't your country."

"It's my people," Walter said, and his face became hard and metallic under his spiky hair. "Stop mourning. Get angry."

The listening classes were going better. The teacher had tired of showing news clips, and today they watched a tape of *I Love Lucy* instead. Fan laughed and laughed as the lady walked over her sofa and armchairs, trying to escape her angry husband.

Her good spirits continued after school, as the Number 7 train drew into the 33rd Street and Rawson station just as she arrived on the platform. It swept her into Grand Central early, with plenty of time for the salad bar.

She was spooning up some snow peas at the big metal food island when those same two men came in, the cottage cheese and noodle eater and the man who had said such terrible things. But was he really so menacing? Fan, who had missed numerous items on the *I Love Lucy* quiz, now wondered if she had heard correctly. She dawdled over the scoops and tongs of the salad bar until the men had filled their own plates and found a table.

They sat against the wall this time, so it was a simple matter for her to seat herself at the neighboring table. She opened her fresh copy of *News for You*, the simplified English-language newspaper that was distributed at school every Thursday, and pretended to read.

"I'm going to slay them, I tell you," said the man with the clear voice, slathering mustard on his sandwich of pink, raw-looking meat.

Slay. Where had Fan heard that word before? She looked down at her copy of *News for You* and saw the headline: CHINESE ARMY SLAYS STUDENTS. The weekly newspaper, always behind, was only now reporting the massacre, and Fan dropped her fork as her eyes fell on the photograph of the tank column.

"Come see it," the man was urging his friend. "Tonight. You've got to come this time."

Fan tried to look only at the paper. "Innocent," said someone quoted in the article about China. "They killed innocent people."

"They won't know what hit them," said the man, and he

dictated a Manhattan address to his friend, all numbers. To Fan Chu, the bookkeeper's assistant, numbers were the clearest words of all.

That evening Fan could hardly wait to leave Mrs. Wu's shop. In Flushing she got off at her usual stop, but walked in a different direction.

She found the garden apartment complex she wanted without difficulty, but which was the right apartment? She spent a half hour crisscrossing the courtyard and reading doorbell labels before she found the name she wanted. She was wearing the travel raincoat she had stolen from Mrs. Wu. Before ringing the doorbell, she shrugged her shoulders inside it, hoping it would act as a talisman.

Walter's eyebrows rose when he saw her. He asked her in and gave her tea in a cracked white cup. The roommate seemed to be out.

"I want to see the guns again," she said. "Are they still here?"

"They're here," said Walter. "We have to wait until the school term ends before we start carrying them in. But why do you want to see them?"

"Just to know they're here," said Fan, and she racked her brain for something else that would please him. "Just to know that my brother's death will be avenged."

Again, the walk to the bedroom. Again, the open drawer. Fan noticed that the beds weren't made this time. No one had been expecting company.

He let her look, then leaned forward to close the drawer, but she caught his hand and began to stroke it.

"You're so brave," she said, and she placed her hands on his chest. He looked surprised, then pleased. The picture of the nude woman was to her back, but she felt its presence watching the falseness and hesitation of her own movements. If only she had watched more movies of the type that Mrs. Wu's sister favored!

But it was all right. His arms were around her now. She waited until he was weak and lost, then she worked one of her arms free.

"Hey, you mainland girls have to learn how to kiss right," he said. She giggled.

There was the sound of a key in a lock.

"Damn," said Walter, releasing her. "Someday I'll have a place of my own."

It was only after she ran out the door, nearly colliding with the roommate, that she realized the travel raincoat was perfectly transparent. The gun was sitting in the right front pocket for all the world to see. But it was dusk, darkened by a light drizzle, and no one noticed as she transferred it to her pocketbook before catching the subway to the city.

She rode all the way to the end of the line, to Times Square. The address was west of there. Ordinarily Fan would have detoured several blocks south to avoid the prostitutes and the pushers and the porn shops, but today she walked past them with her head up. A drug dealer hissed something incomprehensible to her, and she felt complimented that he thought she might buy drugs from him. And why not? Hadn't she robbed Mrs. Wu? Perhaps the plastic raincoat made her look more "overseas," as they said in Beijing, more American. And the kiss with Walter Lo had not been bad at all. Maybe that made her look more American too.

The nearer she got to the river, the quieter the neighborhood became. The pedestrians were better dressed, their voices more subdued. A turn to the right brought her to her destination.

It was a restaurant of some sort, nearly empty. They seated her far from the door. She was afraid to protest: It was important that no one hear her accent. She didn't want to stand out. A waitress came, and Fan pointed to the words *club soda* on the menu. The little table wobbled as she was being served, and some drops of the fizzy water landed on her raincoat like tears. Well, that would be the last of the tears.

The place began filling up with young couples. All of them sat facing a small platform with a microphone at the rear of the restaurant. To the right of the platform was a piano. But none of this interested Fan. She kept her chair tilted to one side so that she could watch both doors of the restaurant, the one that the people were pouring through, and the other one marked with a red exit sign. He would do it soon after he came through the door. Which door she didn't know, but he'd spoken of a door.

His companion from the salad bar was here already, seated near the platform, laughing and joking with a blond woman. Fan tried to keep from staring at him. It was hard to believe he could sit there like that, knowing what was going to happen.

There were no Asian faces in the room, and the English was closing around her like a poisonous cloud. Still, Fan felt at one with these people. *Innocent.* She chanted the word to herself to the rhythm of the music that someone was playing on the piano.

The waitress who had served Fan was approaching again. Fan looked away. Already she had drunk so much club soda that her bladder was full. But instead of stopping by the table, the waitress got up on the platform and grasped the microphone. She signaled to the pianist and launched into song.

So this was a theater of some kind with singing waitresses. The price for the food would be very expensive then, but Fan had no intention of paying, no more intention than she had of watching the waitress. She kept swiveling her eyes between the doors.

But now the song was finished, and the lights were going down. The exit sign burned like a hot ember over the door below it, which had slipped into blackness. The door in the back had no such marker and seemed to have disappeared. But it was important to see it! "Open," he'd said. "I'm going to open." The piano music changed as she squinted into the darkness. There was commotion and applause, and then—that voice.

Fan turned to see the salad-bar man on the stage, one hand on the microphone pole and the other in his pocket.

And the people at the tables were laughing. Laughing! He had no plastic raincoat. They didn't know what was in that pocket.

Fan opened the clasp of her purse and stood by her chair, unnoticed by the laughing, innocent people. She wouldn't let it happen. He wasn't going to kill them, he wasn't going to slay them. The laughter rose higher and higher as she lifted the gun and took aim.

Lilian Jackson Braun, former journalist, reveals how much fun she's having when she says that she's retired ". . . unless you call novel-writing an occupation." Puzzle-solving Qwilleran and his feline assistant Koko have garnered a large and loyal following of readers (who might differ over who is assisting whom!). Among her nine novels and one collection of short stories are The Cat Who Saw Red *(nominated for an Edgar),* The Cat Who Sniffed Glue, *and* The Cat Who Played Brahms *(nominated for an Anthony).*

In "SuSu and the 8:30 Ghost," a Siamese cat helps two sisters sniff out the truth about an eccentric, wheelchair-bound neighbor.

SUSU AND THE 8:30 GHOST

by Lilian Jackson Braun

WHEN MY SISTER and I returned from vacation and learned that our eccentric neighbor in the wheelchair had been removed to a mental hospital, we were sorry but hardly surprised. He was a strange man, not easy to like, and no one in our apartment building seemed concerned about his departure—except our Siamese cat. The friendship between SuSu and Mr. Van was so close it was alarming.

If it had not been for SuSu we would never have made the man's acquaintance, for we were not too friendly with our neighbors. The building was very large and full of odd characters who, we thought, were best ignored. On the other hand, our old apartment had advantages: large rooms, moderate rent, and a thrilling view of the river. There was also a small waterfront park at the foot of the street, and it was there that we first noticed Mr. Van.

One Sunday afternoon my sister Gertrude and I were walking SuSu in the park, which was barely more than a strip of grass alongside an old wharf. Barges and tugs sometimes docked there, and SuSu—wary of these monsters—preferred to stay away from the water's edge. It was one of the last nice days in November. Soon the river would freeze over, icy winds would blow, and the park would be deserted for the winter.

SuSu loved to chew grass, and she was chewing industriously when something diverted her attention and drew her toward the river. Tugging at her leash, she insisted on moving across the grass to the boardwalk, where a middle-aged man sat in a most unusual wheelchair.

It was made almost entirely of cast iron, like the base of an old-fashioned sewing machine, and it was upholstered in worn plush.

With its high back and elaborate ironwork, it looked like a mobile throne, and the man who occupied the regal wheelchair presided with the imperious air of a monarch. It conflicted absurdly with his shabby clothing.

To our surprise this was the attraction that lured SuSu. She chirped at the man, and he leaned over and stroked her fur.

"She recognizes me," he explained to us, speaking with a haughty accent that sounded vaguely Teutonic. "I was-s-s a cat myself in a former existence."

I rolled my eyes at Gertrude, but she accepted the man's statement without blinking.

He was far from attractive, having a sharply pointed chin, ears set too high on his head, and eyes that were mere slits, and when he smiled he was even less appealing. Nevertheless, SuSu found him irresistible. She rubbed against his ankles, and he scratched her in the right places. They made a most unlikely pair—SuSu with her luxurious blond fur, looking fastidious and expensive, and the man in the wheelchair with his rusty coat and moth-eaten lap robe.

In the course of a fragmentary conversation with Mr. Van we learned that he and the companion who manipulated his wheelchair had just moved into a large apartment on our floor, and I wondered why the two of them needed so many rooms. As for the companion, it was hard to decide whether he was a mute or just unsociable. He was a short thick man with a round knob of a head screwed tight to his shoulders and a flicker of something unpleasant in his eyes. He stood behind the wheelchair in sullen silence.

On the way back to the apartment Gertrude said: "How do you like our new neighbor?"

"I prefer cats before they're reincarnated as people," I said.

"But he's rather interesting," said my sister in the gentle way that she had.

A few evenings later we were having coffee after dinner, and SuSu—having finished her own meal—was washing up in the downglow of a lamp. As we watched her graceful movements, we saw her hesitate with one paw in midair. She held it there and listened. Then a new and different sound came from her throat, like a melodic gurgling. A minute later she was trotting to our front door with intense purpose. There she sat, watching and waiting and listening, although we ourselves could hear nothing.

It was a full two minutes before our doorbell rang. I went to open the door and was somewhat unhappy to see Mr. Van sitting there in his lordly wheelchair.

SuSu leaped into his lap—an unprecedented overture for her to make—and after he had kneaded her ears and scratched her chin, he smiled a thin-lipped, slit-eyed smile at me and said: "*Goeden avond.* I was-s-s unpacking some crates, and I found something I would like to give to you."

With a flourish he handed me a small framed picture, whereupon I was more or less obliged to invite him in. He wheeled his ponderous chair into the apartment with some difficulty, the rubber tires making deep gouges in the pile of the carpet.

"How do you manage that heavy chair alone?" I asked. "It must weigh a ton."

"But it is-s-s a work of art," said Mr. Van, rubbing appreciative hands over the plush upholstery and lacy ironwork of the wheels.

Gertrude had jumped up and poured him a cup of coffee, and he said: "I wish you would teach that man of mine to make coffee. He makes the worst *zootje* I have ever tasted. In Holland we like our coffee *sterk* with a little chicory. But that fellow, he is-s-s a *smeerlap.* I would not put up with him for two minutes if I could get around by myself."

SuSu was rubbing her head on the Hollander's vest buttons, and he smiled with pleasure, showing small square teeth.

"Do you have this magnetic attraction for all cats?" I asked with a slight edge to my voice. SuSu was now in raptures because he was twisting the scruff of her neck.

"It is-s-s only natural," he said. "I can read their thoughts, and they read mine of course. Do you know that cats are mind readers? You walk to the refrigerator to get a beer, and the cat

she will not budge, but walk to the refrigerator to get out her
dinner, and what happens? Before you touch the handle of the
door she will come bouncing into the kitchen from anyplace
she happens to be. Your thought waves reached her even though
she seemed to be asleep.''

Gertrude agreed it was probably true.

"Of course it is-s-s true," said Mr. Van, sitting tall. "Everything I say is-s-s true. Cats know more than you suspect.
They cannot only read your mind, they can plant ideas in your
head. And they can sense something that is-s-s about to happen.''

My sister said: "You must be right. SuSu knew you were
coming here tonight, long before you rang the bell.''

"Of course I am right. I am always right," said Mr. Van.
"My grandmother in Vlissingen had a tomcat called Zwartje
just before she died, and for years after the funeral my grandmother came back to pet the cat. Every night Zwartje stood in
front of the chair where Grootmoeder used to sit, and he would
stretch and purr although there was-s-s no one there. Every
night at half past eight.''

After that visit with Mr. Van I referred to him as Grandmother's Ghost, for he too made a habit of appearing at eight-
thirty several times a week. (For Gertrude's coffee, I guessed.)

He would say: "I was-s-s feeling lonesome for my little
sweetheart," and SuSu would make an extravagant fuss over
the man. It pleased me that he never stayed long, although
Gertrude usually encouraged him to linger.

The little framed picture he had given us was not exactly to
my taste. It was a silhouette of three figures—a man in frock
coat and top hat, a woman in hoopskirt and sunbonnet, and a
cat carrying his tail like a lance. To satisfy my sister, however,
I hung the picture, but only over the kitchen sink.

One evening Gertrude, who is a librarian, came home in
great excitement. "There's a signature on that silhouette," she
said, "and I looked it up at the library. Augustin Edouart was
a famous artist, and our silhouette is over a hundred years old.
It might be valuable.''

"I doubt it," I said. "We used to cut silhouettes like that in
the third grade.''

Eventually, at my sister's urging, I took the object to an
antique shop, and the dealer said it was a good one, probably
worth several hundred dollars.

When Gertrude heard this, she said: "If the dealer quoted hundreds, it's probably worth thousands. I think we should give it back to Mr. Van. The poor man doesn't know what he's giving away."

I agreed he could probably sell it and buy himself a decent wheelchair.

At eight-thirty that evening SuSu began to gurgle and prance.

"Here comes Grandmother's Ghost," I said, and shortly afterward the doorbell rang.

"Mr. Van," I said after Gertrude had poured the coffee, "remember that silhouette you gave us? I've found out it's valuable, and you must take it back."

"Of course it is-s-s valuable," he said. "Would I give it to you if it was-s-s nothing but *rommel*?"

"Do you know something about antiques?"

"My dear Mevrouw, I have a million dollars' worth of antiques in my apartment. Tomorrow evening you ladies must come and see my treasures. I will get rid of that *smeerlap*, and the three of us will enjoy a cup of coffee."

"By the way, what is a *smeerlap*?" I asked.

"It is-s-s not very nice," said Mr. Van. "If somebody called me a *smeerlap*, I would punch him in the nose. . . . Bring my little sweetheart when you come, ladies. She will find some fascinating objects to explore."

Our cat seemed to know what he was saying.

"SuSu will enjoy it," said Gertrude. "She's locked up in this apartment all winter."

"Knit her a sweater and take her to the park in winter," said the Hollander in the commanding tone that always irritated me. "I often bundle up in a blanket and go to the park in the evening. It is-s-s good for insomnia."

"SuSu is not troubled with insomnia," I informed him. "She sleeps twenty hours a day."

Mr. Van looked at me with scorn. "You are wrong. Cats never sleep. You think they are sleeping, but cats are the most wakeful creatures on earth. That is-s-s one of their secrets."

After he had gone, I said to Gertrude: "I know you like the fellow, but you must admit he's off his rocker."

"He's just a little eccentric."

"If he has a million dollars' worth of antiques, which I doubt, why is he living in this run-down building? And why doesn't he buy a wheelchair that's easier to operate?"

"Because he's a Dutchman, I suppose," was Gertrude's explanation.

"And how about all those ridiculous things he says about cats?"

"I'm beginning to think they're true."

"And who is the fellow who lives with him? Is he a servant, or a nurse, or a keeper, or what? I see him coming and going on the elevator, but he never speaks—not one word. He doesn't even seem to have a name, and Mr. Van treats him like a slave. I'm not sure we should go tomorrow night. The whole situation is too strange."

Nevertheless, we went. The Hollander's apartment was jammed with furniture and bric-a-brac, and he shouted at his companion: "Move that *rommel* so the ladies can sit down."

Sullenly the fellow removed some paintings and tapestries from the seat of a carved sofa.

"Now get out of here!" Mr. Van shouted at him. "Get yourself a beer," and he threw the man some money with less grace than one would throw a dog a bone.

While SuSu explored the premises we drank our coffee, and then Mr. Van showed us his treasures, propelling his wheelchair through a maze of furniture. He pointed out Chippendale-this and Affleck-that and Newport-something-else. They were treasures to him, but to me they were musty relics of a dead past.

"I am in the antique business," Mr. Van explained. "Before I was-s-s chained to this wheelchair, I had a shop and exhibited at the major shows. Then . . . I was-s-s in a bad auto accident, and now I sell from the apartment. By appointment only."

"Can you do that successfully?" Gertrude asked.

"And why not? The museum people know me, and collectors come here from all over the country. I buy. I sell. And my man Frank does the legwork. He is-s-s the perfect assistant for an antique dealer—strong in the back, weak in the head."

"Where did you find him?"

"On a junk heap. I have taught him enough to be useful to me, but not enough to be useful to himself. A smart arrangement, eh?" Mr. Van winked. "He is-s-s a *smeerlap*, but I am helpless without him. . . . Hoo! Look at my little sweetheart. She has-s-s found a prize!"

SuSu was sniffing at a silver bowl with two handles.

Mr. Van nodded approvingly. "It is a caudle cup made by

Jeremiah Dummer of Boston in the late seventeenth century—
for a certain lady in Salem. They said she was-s-s a witch.
Look at my little sweetheart. She knows!''

I coughed and said: ''Yes, indeed. You're lucky to have
Frank.''

''You think I do not know it?'' Mr. Van said in a snappish
tone. ''That is-s-s why I keep him poor. If I gave him wages,
he would get ideas. A *smeerlap* with ideas—there is-s-s nothing
worse.''

''How long ago was your accident?''

''Five years, and it was-s-s that idiot's fault. He did it! He
did this to me!'' The man's voice rose to a shout, and his face
turned red as he pounded the arms of his wheelchair with his
fist. Then SuSu rubbed against his ankles, and he stroked her
and began to calm down. ''Yes, five years in this miserable
chair. We were driving to an antique show in the station wagon.
Sixty miles an hour—and he went through a red light and hit
a truck. A gravel truck!''

Gertrude put both hands to her face. ''How terrible, Mr.
Van!''

''I remember packing the wagon for that trip. I was-s-s complaining all the time about sore arches. Hah! What I would
give for some sore arches today yet!''

''Wasn't Frank hurt?''

Mr. Van made an impatient gesture. ''His-s-s head only.
They picked Waterford crystal out of that blockhead for six
hours. He has-s-s been *gek* ever since.'' He tapped his temple.

''Where did you find this unusual wheelchair?'' I asked.

''My dear Mevrouw, never ask a dealer where he found
something. It was-s-s made for a railroad millionaire in 1872.
It has-s-s the original plush. If you must spend your life in a
wheelchair, have one that gives some pleasure. And now we
come to the purpose of tonight's visit. Ladies, I want you to
do something for me.''

He wheeled himself to a desk, and Gertrude and I exchanged
anxious glances.

''Here in this desk is-s-s a new will I have written, and I
need witnesses. I am leaving a few choice items to museums.
Everything else is-s-s to be sold and the proceeds used to es-
tablish a foundation.''

''What about Frank?'' asked Gertrude, who is always genuinely concerned about others.

"Bah! Nothing for that *smeerlap*! . . . But before you ladies sign the papers, there is-s-s one thing I must write down. What is-s-s the full name of my little sweetheart?''

We both hesitated, and finally I said: "Her registered name is Superior Suda of Siam.''

"Good! I will make it the Superior Suda Foundation. That gives me pleasure. Making a will is-s-s a dismal business, like a wheelchair, so give yourself some pleasure.''

"What—ah—will be the purpose of the foundation?'' I asked.

Mr. Van blessed us with one of his ambiguous smiles. "It will sponsor research,'' he said. "I want universities to study the highly developed mental perception of the domestic feline and apply the knowledge to the improvement of the human mind. Ladies, there is-s-s nothing better I could do with my fortune. Man is-s-s eons behind the smallest fireside grimalkin.'' He gave us a canny look, and his eyes narrowed. "I am in a position to know.''

We witnessed the man's signature. What else could we do? A few days later we left on vacation and never saw Mr. Van again.

Gertrude and I always went south for three weeks in winter, taking SuSu with us. When we returned, the sorry news about our eccentric neighbor was thrown at us without ceremony.

We met Frank on the elevator as we were taking our luggage upstairs, and for the first time he spoke. That in itself was a shock.

He said simply, without any polite preliminaries: "They took him away.''

"What's that? What did you say?'' we both clamored at once.

"They took him away.'' It was surprising to find that the voice of this muscular man was high-pitched and rasping.

"What happened to Mr. Van?'' my sister demanded.

"He cracked up. His folks come from Pennsylvania and took him back home. He's in a nut hospital.''

I saw Gertrude wince, and she said: "Is it serious?''

Frank shrugged.

"What will happen to all his antiques?''

"His folks told me to dump the junk.''

"But they're valuable things, aren't they?''

"Nah. Junk. He give everybody that guff about museums

and all." Frank shrugged again and tapped his head. "He was *gek*."

In stunned wonderment my sister and I reached our apartment, and I could hardly wait to say it: "I told you your Dutchman was unbalanced."

"Such a pity," she murmured.

"What do you think of the sudden change in Frank? He acts like a free man. It must have been terrible living with that old Scrooge."

"I'll miss Mr. Van," Gertrude said softly. "He was very interesting. SuSu will miss him, too."

But SuSu, we observed later that evening, was not willing to relinquish her friend in the wheelchair as easily as we had done.

We were unpacking the vacation luggage after dinner when SuSu staged her demonstration. She started to gurgle and prance, exactly as she had done all winter whenever Mr. Van was approaching our door. Gertrude and I watched her, waiting for the bell to ring. When SuSu trotted expectantly to the door, we followed. She was behaving in an extraordinary manner. She craned her neck, made weaving motions with her head, rolled over on her back, and stretched luxuriously, all the while purring her heart out; but the doorbell never rang.

Looking at my watch, I said: "It's eight-thirty. SuSu remembers."

"It's quite touching, isn't it?" Gertrude remarked.

That was not the end of SuSu's demonstrations. Almost every night at half past eight she performed the same ritual.

I recalled how SuSu had continued to sleep in the guest room long after we had moved her bed to another place. "Cats hate to give up a habit. But she'll forget Mr. Van's visits after a while."

SuSu did not forget. A few weeks passed. Then we had a foretaste of spring and a sudden thaw. People went without coats prematurely, convertibles cruised with the tops down, and a few hopeful fishermen appeared on the wharf at the foot of our street, although the river was still patched with ice.

On one of these warm evenings we walked SuSu down to the park for her first spring outing, expecting her to go after last year's dried weeds with snapping jaws. Instead, she tugged at her leash, pulling toward the boardwalk. Out of curiosity we let her have her way, and there on the edge of the wharf she

staged her weird performance once more—gurgling, arching
her back, craning her neck with joy.

"She's doing it again," I said. "I wonder what the reason
could be."

Gertrude said, almost in a whisper: "Remember what Mr.
Van said about cats and ghosts?"

"Look at that animal! You'd swear she was rubbing against
someone's ankles. I wish she'd stop. It makes me uneasy."

"I wonder," said my sister very slowly, "if Mr. Van is
really in a mental hospital."

"What do you mean?"

"Or is he—down there?" Gertrude pointed uncertainly over
the edge of the wharf. "I think Mr. Van is dead, and SuSu
knows."

"That's too fantastic," I said. "*Really*, Gertrude!"

"I think Frank pushed the poor man off the wharf, wheelchair and all—perhaps one dark night when Mr. Van couldn't
sleep and insisted on being wheeled to the park."

"You're not serious, Gertrude."

"Can't you see it? . . . A cold night. The riverfront deserted. Mr. Van trussed in his wheelchair with a blanket. Why,
that chair would sink like lead! What a terrible thing! That icy
water. That poor helpless man."

"I just can't—"

"Now Frank is free, and he has all those antiques, and nobody cares enough to ask questions. He can sell them and be
set up for life."

"And he tears up the will," I suggested, succumbing to
Gertrude's fantasy.

"Do you know what a Newport blockfront is worth? I've
been looking it up in the library. A chest like the one we saw
in Mr. Van's apartment was sold for hundreds of thousands at
an auction on the East Coast."

"But what about the relatives in Pennsylvania?"

"I'm sure Mr. Van had no relatives—in Pennsylvania or anywhere else."

"Well, what do you propose we should do?" I said in exasperation. "Report it to the manager of the building? Notify
the police? Tell them we think the man has been murdered
because our cat sees his ghost every night at eight-thirty? We'd
look like a couple of middle-aged ladies who are getting a little
gek."

As a matter of fact, I was beginning to worry about Gertrude's obsession—that is, until I read the morning paper a few days later.

I skimmed through it at the breakfast table, and there—at the bottom of page seven—one small item leaped off the paper at me. Could I believe my eyes?

"Listen to this," I said to my sister. "The body of an unidentified man has been washed up on a downriver island. Police say the body had apparently been held underwater for several weeks by the ice. . . . About fifty-five years old and crippled. . . . No one fitting that description has been reported to the Missing Persons Bureau."

For a moment my sister stared at the coffeepot. Then she left the breakfast table and went to the telephone.

"Now all the police have to do," she said with a quiver in her voice, "is to look for an antique wheelchair in the river at the foot of the street. Cast iron. With the original plush." She blinked at the phone several times. "Would you dial?" she asked me. "I can't see the numbers."

Dorothy Cannell, who writes about people she likes, behaving the way she'd like to behave if ". . . something thrillingly chilling . . ." happened to her, says that she became a writer to avoid learning algebra—and her fans are delighted that she made the choice. Her first novel, The Thin Woman, *introduced Ellie and Ben Haskell;* Down the Garden Path *featured Hyacinth and Primrose Tramwell; and* The Widows Club, *nominated for a 1988 Agatha, brought the four sleuths together.*

In "The High Cost of Living" a brother and sister are taxed by the consequences of their plan to keep pace with inflation.

THE HIGH COST OF LIVING

by Dorothy Cannell

"THEY'RE NOT COMING!" Cecil said for the fourth time, peering out into the rain-soaked night. The gale had whipped itself into a frenzy, buffeting trees and shaking the stone house like a dog with a rag doll. On that Saturday evening the Willoughbys—Cecil and his sister, Amanda—were in the front room, waiting for guests who were an hour late. The fire had died down and the canapés on their silver tray were beginning to look bored.

"They're not coming!" mimicked Amanda from the sofa, thrusting back her silver-blond hair with an irritable hand. "Repeating oneself is an early sign of insanity . . . remember?"

Her eyes, and those of her brother, shifted ceilingward.

"Cecil, I regret not strangling you at birth. Stop hovering like a leper at the gate. Every time you lift the curtain an icy blast shoots up my skirt."

A shrug. "I've been looking forward to company. The

Thompsons and Bumbells lack polish, but it doesn't take much to break the monotony in this morgue."

"Really, Pickle Face!" Amanda eyed a chip in her pearl-pink manicure with disfavor. "Is that kind?"

"Speaking of kind"—Cecil let the curtain drop and adjusted his gold-rimmed spectacles—"I didn't much care for that crack about insanity. I take exception to jibes at Mother."

"Amazing!" Amanda wielded an emery board, her eyes on the prying tongues of flame loosening the wood fibers and sending showers of sparks up the chimney. "Where did I get the idea that but for the money, you would have shoved the old girl in a cage months ago? Don't hang your head. All she does is eat and—"

"You always were vulgar."

"And you always were forty-five, Cecily dear. How you love to angst, but spare me the bit about this being Mother's house and our being a pair of hyenas feasting off decaying flesh. That woman is not our mother. Father remarried because we motherless brats drove off every housekeeper within a week."

"Mary was good to us." Drawing on a cigarette with a shaking hand, Cecil sank into a chair.

"Brother, you have such a way with words. Mary had every reason to count her blessings. She acquired a roof over her head and a man to keep her warm in bed. Not bad for someone who was always less bright than a twenty-watt bulb."

"I still think some respect . . ." The cigarette got flung into the fire.

"Sweet Cecily"—Amanda buffed away at her nails—"you have deception refined to an art. I admit to living in Stepmother's house because it's free. Come on! These walls don't have ears. The only reason Mad Mary isn't shut up in a cracker box is because we're not wasting her money on one."

"I won't listen to this."

"Your sensitivity be damned. You'd trade her in for a used set of golf clubs any day of the week. Who led the way, brother, to see what could be done about opening up Father's trust? Who swore with his hand on the certificates of stock that Mary was *non compos mentis*? Spare me your avowals of being here to keep Mary company in her second childhood." Amanda tossed the emery board aside. "You wanted a share in Daddy's pot of gold while still young enough to fritter it away."

Cecil grabbed for the table lighter and ducked a cigarette toward the flame. "I believe he would have wished—"

"And I wish him in hell." Amanda tapped back a yawn. "Leaving his money tied up in that woman for life . . ."

"Mary was halfway normal when Father died. Her sister was the fly in the ointment in those days. Always meddling in money matters."

"Hush, brother dear." Amanda prowled toward the window and gave the curtain a twitch. "Is the storm unnerving you? I'm amazed we haven't had the old lady down to look for her paper dolls. For the record, I've done my turn of nursemaid drill this week. Mrs. Bridger didn't come in the last couple of days, and if I have to carry another tray upstairs I will need locking up."

Her brother stared into the fire.

"No pouting." Peppermint-pink smile. "Beginning to think, dear Cecily, that the world might be a better place if we treated old people the way we do our dogs? When they become a bother, shouldn't we put them out of everyone's misery? Nothing painful! I hate cruelty. A whiff of a damp rag and then deep, deep sleep. . . . Oh, never mind! Isn't that the doorbell?"

Cecil stopped cringing to listen. "Can it be the Thompsons or the Bumbells?"

"Either them or the Moonlight Strangler." Amanda's voice chased him from the room. Hitching her skirt above the knee, she perched on the sofa arm. From the hall came voices.

"Terrible night! Sorry we're late. Visibility nil." A thud as the wind took the front door. Moments later an arctic chill preceded Cecil and the Thompsons into the room. Mrs. Thompson was shivering like a blancmange about to slide off the plate. Her husband, as thin as she was stout, was blue around the gills.

"Welcome." Amanda, crisp and sprightly, stepped forward. "I see you've let Cecil rob you of your coats. What sports to turn out on such a wicked night."

Mr. Thompson thawed. This was one hell of a pretty woman. He accepted a brandy snifter and a seat by the fire. His wife took sherry and stretched her thick legs close to the flames. That popping sound was probably her varicose veins.

"The Bumbells didn't make it." Norman Thompson spoke

the obvious. "I told Gerty you wouldn't expect us, but she would have it that you'd be waiting and wondering.

"Our phone was dead," Gerty Thompson defended herself. "Heavens above!" Cheeks creasing into a smile. "Only listen to that wind and rain rattling the windows. Almost like someone trying to get in. I won't sleep tonight if it keeps up."

"She could sleep on a clothesline," came her husband's response.

"Refills?" Cecil hovered with the decanters.

Gerty held out her glass without looking at him. Staring at the closed door, she gave a squeaky gasp. "There's someone out in the hall. I saw the doorknob turn." Sherry slopped from glass.

Norman snorted. "You've been reading too many spook-house thrillers."

"I tell you I saw—"

The door opened a wedge.

"Damn! Not now." Almost dropping the decanter, Cecil grimaced at Amanda. "Did you forget her sleeping pills?"

An old lady progressed unsteadily into the room. Both Thompsons thought she looked like a gray flannel rabbit. She had pumice-stone skin and her nightdress was without color. Wisps of wintry hair escaped from a net and she was clutching something tightly to her chest. A child terrified of having her treasures snatched away.

"How do you do?" Gerty felt a fool. She had heard that old Mrs. Willoughby's mind had failed. On prior occasions when she and Norman had been guests here, the poor soul had not been mentioned, let alone seen. Meeting her husband's eye, she looked away. Amanda wore a faint smirk, as though she had caught someone drinking his finger bowl. Most uncomfortable. Gerty wished Norman would say something. He was the one who had thought the Willoughbys worth getting to know. The old lady remained marooned in the center of the room. A rag doll. One nudge and she would fold over. Why didn't someone say something?

Cecil almost tripped on the hearth rug. "Gerty and Norman, I present my stepmother, Mary Willoughby. She hasn't been herself lately. Not up to parties, I'm afraid. You never did like them did you, Mother?" Awkwardly he patted Mrs. Willoughby's shoulder, then propelled her toward the Thompsons.

Gerty began shivering worse than when she was on the doorstep. "What's that you're holding, dear?" She had to say something—anything. The old lady's eyes looked dead.

An unreal laugh from Cecil. "A photo of her twin sister, Martha. They were very close; in fact, it was after Martha passed on last year that Mother began slipping. She always was the more dependent of the two. They lived together here after my father was taken."

"Sad, extremely sad." Mr. Thompson would have liked to sit back down, but while the old lady stood there . . .

Nudging Cecil aside, Amanda slid an arm around Mrs. Willoughby. "Nighty-night, Mary, dear!" she crooned. "Up the bye-bye stairs we go."

"No." The old lady's face remained closed, tight as a safe. But her voice rose shrill as a child's. A child demanding the impossible. "I want Martha. I won't go to sleep without Martha."

"Poor lost soul!" Ready tears welled in Gerty Thompson's eyes. "What can we do? There must be something."

"Mind our own business," supplied her husband. He was regretting not keeping his relationship with the Willoughbys strictly business. They had been a catch as investors, money having flowed from their pockets this last year.

The old lady did not say another word. But everyone sensed it would take a tow truck to remove her from the room.

"I give up," Amanda said. "Let's skate the sweet lamb over to that chair in the bookcase corner. She won't want to be too near the fire and get overheated. I expect she feels crowded and needs breathing space. Look, she's coming quite happily now, aren't you, Mary?"

"Ah!" Gerty dabbed at her eyes with a cocktail napkin as Amanda tossed a rug over Mrs. Willoughby's knees. "She didn't want to be sent upstairs and left out of things. Being with the ones she loves is all she has left, I suppose."

"Yes, we are devoted to Mother," responded Amanda.

Mrs. Willoughby rocked mindlessly, her pale lips slack, the photo of her dead sister locked in her bony hands.

The others regrouped about the fire. Cecil poured fresh drinks and Amanda produced the tray of thaw-and-serve hors d'oeuvres. Rain continued to beat against the windows and the mantel clock ticked on self-consciously.

"We could play bridge, or do I hear any suggestions from

the floor?'' Amanda popped an olive into her mouth, eyes on Norman Thompson.

"How about . . ." Gerty's face grew plumper and she fussed with the pleats of her skirt. Everyone waited with bated breath, for her to suggest Monopoly. ". . . How about a séance? Don't look at me like that, Norman. You don't have to be a crazy person to believe in the Other Side. And the weather couldn't be more perfect!''

Amanda set her glass down on the coffee table. "What fun! My last gentleman friend suspected me of having psychic powers when I knew exactly what he liked in the way of . . . white wine.''

Cecil broke in. "I don't like dabbling in the Unseen. We wouldn't throw our doors open to a bunch of strangers were they alive—"

"Coward!" His sister wagged a finger at him. "How can you disappoint Gerty and Norman?''

Mr. Thompson forced a smile.''

Gerty was thrilled. "Everything's right for communication. This house—with the wind wrapped all about it! What could be more ghostly? And those marvelous ceiling beams and that portrait of the old gentleman with side whiskers . . .'' While she enthused the others decided the game table in the window alcove would serve the purpose. Amanda fetched a brass candlestick.

"Perfect!" Fearless leader Gerty took her seat. "All other lights must be extinguished and the curtains tightly drawn.''

"I trust this experiment will not unsettle Mrs. Willoughby.'' Norman Thompson glanced over at the old lady seated in the corner.

"Let's get this over.'' Cecil was tugging at his collar.

"Lead on, Gerty.'' Amanda smiled.

"Very well. Into the driver's seat. All aboard and hold on tight! Everyone at his own risk. Are we holding hands? Does our blood flow as one? Feel it tingling through the veins—or do I mean the arteries? I can never remember.''

"My dear, lay an egg or get off the perch,'' ordered her husband.

Gerty ignored him. She was drawing upon the persona of her favorite fictional medium, the one in that lovely book *Ammie Come Home*. "Keep those eyes closed. No peeking! Let your minds float . . . drift, sway a little.''

"I can't feel a damn thing," said Norman. "My leg's gone to sleep."

"The change in temperature! We're moving into a different atmosphere. We are becoming lighter. Buoyant! Are we together, still united in our quest? The spirits don't like ridicule, Norman."

"They'll have to lump it."

Amanda wiggled a foot against his. *Let's see if the old coyote is numb from the waist down.*

"Is anybody out there?" Madame Gerty cooed. "We are all friends here. With outstretched arms we await your coming."

Sounds of heavy breathing . . . the spluttering of the fire and a muffled snoring from the bookcase corner.

"Is there a message?" Gerty called. Only the wind and rain answered. The room was still, except for Norman, who was trying to shake his leg free of the cramp—or Amanda's teasing foot. The clock struck eleven. From outside, close to the front wall of the house, came the blistering crack of lightning. The whole house took a step backward. The table lurched toward the window. For a moment they all imagined themselves smashing through the glass to be swept away by the wind. Gerty went over with her chair, dragging Cecil down with her. The candle, still standing, went out.

It was agreed to call a halt to the proceedings.

"We must try another time." Gerty hoisted herself onto one knee and reached for her husband's hand. "I am sure someone was trying to reach me."

Amanda shivered. "My God, this place is an igloo."

"The fire's out." Cecil righted the chairs.

"Well, get it going again! I'm freezing solid. Someone stick a cigarette between my lips so I can inhale some heat."

"The trouble with your generation is, you have been much indulged. A little cold never hurt anyone. Leave those logs alone. They must last all winter. I am not throwing money on a woodpile."

The voice cracked through the room like another bolt of lightning, turning the Willoughbys—brother and sister—into a pair of dummies in a shop window. Norman Thompson sat down without meaning to, while Gerty resembled a fish trying to unswallow the hook. Otherwise the only movement came from the old lady in the corner. Even seated, she appeared to have grown. Her eyes burned in the parchment face. Glancing at the photo in her hands, she laid it down on the bookcase, tossed off her blanket, and stood up. "There has been a great deal of waste in this house lately." The voice dropped to a whisper but carried deep into the shadows.

"This extravagance will stop. When one is old, people tend to take advantage. It appears I must come out of retirement, get back in harness and pull this team."

Her face as ashen as her hair, Amanda stood hunched like an old woman. She and Cecil looked like brother and sister for once. They wore matching looks of horror—the way they had worn matching coats as children. As for the Thompsons, they resembled a pair of missionaries who, having wandered into a brothel, are unable to find the exit.

"Norman, dear, I think we should be running along; it is getting late. . . ."

"We can get our own coats. . . . Good night!" Husband and wife backed out the door. Never again would Gerty Thompson lift the mystic veil.

"Good night," echoed the voice of Mary Willoughby. "A pedestrian pair . . ." A pause, filled by the banging of the front door. "In future the decision as to who comes into this house is mine. I certainly do not enjoy entertaining in my nightdress, and more to the point . . ." The pale lips flared back. "You, Amanda and Cecil, are uninvited guests here. Don't forget. Whether you go or stay will depend on how we all get on together. A pity, but I don't think either of you can afford to live anywhere else at present. Gambling is your vice, Cecil. The corruption of the weak and indolent. I remember how you never wanted a birthday cake because you'd have to share it. As for you, Amanda, all you're good for is painting your nails and throwing up your skirts." A smile that turned the parchment face colder. "Neither of you are talking and I won't say much more tonight. I don't want to strain my voice. Tomorrow I will telephone lawyer Henry Morbeck and invite him out here—for the record. Your year of playing Monopoly is over. Your father left me control of his money and I want it back in my hands. The capital will come to you both one day, but bear in mind you may have quite a wait." Smoothing a hand over her forehead, Mrs. Willoughby removed the hair net and dropped it in the grate. "Good night, children. Don't stay up late; I won't have electricity wasted."

She was gone. They stood listening to her footsteps mounting the stairs. Finally a door on the second floor closed.

"It's not her!" Amanda pummeled a fist into her palm. "That creature—that monster—is not Mary."

Cecil grabbed for a cigarette, then could not hold his hand steady to light it. "That fool Thompson woman and her fun-and-games séances. She unearthed this horror. We're talking possession. Someone else looked out of Mother's eyes. Something has appropriated her voice."

"We have to think." Amanda hugged herself for warmth. "We gave it entrée, now we must find a way to be rid of it before it sucks the life out of us all. It will bleed the bank accounts dry. We'll be paupers at the mercy of an avenging spirit. We're to be made to pay for every unkind word and deed Mary has experienced at our hands."

"What do you suggest?" Cecil still had not lit the cigarette. "Do we tell the bank manager that should Mary Willoughby ask to see him, she is really a ghost in disguise?"

"We'll talk to Dr. Denver." Amanda was pulling at her nails. "He saw the condition Mother was in last week. He'll know something is crazy. He'll come up with a diagnosis of split personality or . . . some newfangled disorder. Who cares, so long as he declares her incompetent."

"He won't." With a wild laugh Cecil broke his cigarette into little pieces and tossed them onto the dead fire. "He'll opt for a miracle, and why shouldn't he? Is anything less believable than the truth?"

"Do you never stop kidding yourself?" The words were screamed. "We all know who she is, and we know why she has come back. So if you can't answer the question how to be rid of her, kindly shut up. I'll die of cold if I remain in this ice chest. Let's go to bed."

"I'll sleep in a chair in your room," offered Cecil.

"Some protection you'd be. At the first whisper of her night-dress down the hall you'd turn into a giant goose bump." Amanda opened the door. "Remember, she's seeing Morbeck tomorrow."

They huddled up the stairs like sheep, making more than usual of saying good night before separating into their rooms. After a while the murmur of footsteps died away and the lights went out, leaving the house to itself and the rasping breath of the storm. The stair treads creaked and settled, while the grandfather clock in the hall tocked away the minutes . . . the hours. The house listened and waited. Only the shadows moved until, at a little after three, came the sound of an upstairs door opening . . . then another. . . .

Early the next morning Dr. Denver received a phone call at his home.

"Doctor, this is Amanda Willoughby!" Hysteria threatened to break through her control. "There's been the most dreadful accident. It's Mother! She's fallen down the stairs. God knows when it happened . . . sometime during the night! We think she may have been sleepwalking! She was very worked up earlier in the evening. . . . Please, please hurry!"

The doctor found the door of Stone House open and entered the hall, pajama legs showing under his raincoat. Dripping water and spilling instruments from his bag, he brushed aside the brother and sister to kneel by the gray-haired woman sprawled at the foot of the stairs.

"Oh, Lord!" Cecil pressed his knuckles to his eyes. "I can't bear to look. I've never seen anyone dead before. This bloody storm. If she screamed, we would have thought it the wind! I did hear a . . . thump around three A.M. but thought it must be a tree going down in the lane. . . ."

"These Victorian staircases are murder." The doctor raised one of Mrs. Willoughby's eyelids and dangled a limp wrist between his fingers. "One wrong step and down you go."

Amanda's eyes were bright with tears. "Our one hope, Dr. Denver, is that she died instantly."

"My dear girl." He straightened up. "Mrs. Willoughby is not dead."

"What?" Cecil staggered onto a chair that wasn't there and had to grip the banister to save himself from going down. His sister looked ready to burst into mad laughter.

"Your stepmother is in a coma; there is the possibility of internal injuries and the risk of shock." The doctor folded away his stethoscope. "Shall we say I am cautiously optimistic? Her heart has always been strong. Mr. Willoughby, fetch your sister a brandy. And how about taking this photo. Careful, old chap, the glass is smashed."

"She was holding on to it for dear life when she fell . . . I suppose," Cecil said in an expressionless voice.

Dr. Denver stood up. "Get a new frame and put it by her

bed. Amazing what the will to live can accomplish. Ah, here comes the ambulance. . . .''

Two weeks later the setting was a hospital corridor. "Often the way with these will-o'-the-wisp old ladies!" Henry Morbeck, lawyer, ignored the no-smoking sign and puffed on his pipe. "They harbor constitutions of steel. Had a word with Dr. Denver this morning and he gave me to understand that barring any major setbacks, Mrs. Willoughby will live."

Amanda tapped unvarnished nails against her folded arms. "Did he tell you she has joined the ranks of the living dead?"

Mr. Morbeck puffed harder on his pipe. "I understand your frustration. She remains unconscious, even though the neurologists have been unable to pinpoint a cause. Small comfort to say that such cases . . . happen. The patient lapses into a coma from which not even the most advanced medical treatment can rouse him."

"They say Mary could linger for years." Cecil's voice barely rose above a whisper. "She looked older, but she is only in her early sixties. What do you think, Henry?" Desperate for some crumb of doubt.

"My friend, I am not a doctor. And remember, doctors are not God. With careful nursing and prayers for a miracle . . . well, let's wait and see." Mr. Morbeck cleared his throat and got down to business. "Since this hospital does not provide chronic patient care, the time comes to find the very best nursing home. Such places are extraordinarily expensive, but not to worry. Mrs. Willoughby is secure. Your far-seeing father provided for such a contingency as this."

Silence.

"The bank, as co-trustee, is empowered to arrange for her comfort and care no matter what the cost. The house and other properties will be sold."

"Oh, quite, quite." Cecil knew he was babbling. "We had hoped to take Mother back to Stone House and care for her ourselves."

"I love nursing." Amanda knew she was begging.

"Out of the question." The lawyer tapped out his pipe in a plant stand and left it stuck there. "Your devotion to Mrs. Willoughby is inspiring, but you must now leave her and the finances in the hands of the professionals. Take comfort that the money is there. She keeps her dignity and you are not burdened. You have my assurance I will keep in close touch with the bank.'' He pushed against a door to his left. ''I'll go in with you and . . . take a look at her.''

The three of them entered a white, sunlit room. The woman in the railed bed could have been a china doll hooked up to a giant feeding bottle.

''She would seem at peace,'' Mr. Morbeck said.

There must be something we can do, Amanda thought. It always sounds so easy. Someone yanks out the plug and that's that.

Nothing to pull, Cecil thought wearily. She's existing on her own. No artificial support system, other than the IV and no damned doctor is going to starve a helpless old woman.

She has no business being alive, Amanda thought as she gripped the rail. She should be ten feet under, feeding the grubs instead of feeding off us. ''Cecil, let's get out of here.'' She didn't care what the lawyer thought. ''And if I ever suggest coming back, have me committed.''

Alone with the patient, Mr. Morbeck quelled a shiver and clasped the leaden hand. ''Mary Willoughby, are you in there?'' His voice hung in the air like a bell pull, ready to start jangling again if anyone breathed on it. And Mary Willoughby was breathing—with relish. Had Mr. Morbeck been a man of imagination he would have thought the pale lips smiled— mischievously. Eager to be gone, he turned and saw that the woman in the photo by the bed seemed to be laughing back. Mary's twin sister, Martha. Or was it . . . ? Mr. Morbeck had always had trouble telling the two of them apart.

*Dorothy Salisbury Davis, winner of a 1985 Mystery Writers
of America Grand Master award and a 1989 Bouchercon
award, has written twenty novels (including* Death of an Old
Sinner, Death in the Life, *and* The Habit of Fear*) and numerous short stories, some of which were collected in* Tales
for a Stormy Night. *The Cleveland* Plain Dealer *summed up
the feeling of her fans when it was suggested that she* ". . .
should be declared a natural resource. . . ." *for her contri-
butions to the mystery.*

*In "By the Scruff of the Soul," the pressures of small-town
life erupt into tragedy.*

BY THE SCRUFF OF THE SOUL

by Dorothy Salisbury Davis

MOST PEOPLE, WHEN they go down from the Ragapoo
Hills, never come back; or if they do, for a funeral
maybe—weddings don't count for so much around here
any more either—you can see them fidgeting to get away again.
As for me, I'm one of those rare birds they didn't have any
trouble keeping down on the farm after he'd seen Paree.

It's forty years since I've seen the bright lights, but I don't
figure I've missed an awful lot. Hell, I can remember the Ku
Klux Klan marching right out in the open. My first case had
to do with a revenue agent—I won it, too, and we haven't had
a government man up here since. And take the League of
Nations—I felt awful sorry in those days for Mr. Wilson though
I didn't hold with his ideas.

Maybe things have changed, but sometimes I wonder just
how much. This bomb I don't understand, fallout and all, but
I've seen what a plague of locusts can do to a wheat field and
I don't think man's ever going to beat nature when it comes to
pure, ornery destruction. I could be wrong about that. Our new
parson says I am and he's a mighty knowing man. Too know-

ing, maybe. I figure that's why the Synod shipped him up to us in Webbtown.

As I said, I don't figure I'm missing much. There's a couple of television sets in town and sometimes of an evening I'll sit for an hour or so in front of whichever one of them's working best. One of them gets the shimmies every time the wind blows and the other don't bring in anything except by way of Canada. Same shows but different commercials. That kind of tickles me, all them companies advertising stuff you couldn't buy if you wanted to instead of stuff you wouldn't want if you could buy it.

But, as you've probably guessed by now, I'd rather talk than most anything, and since you asked about The Red Lantern, I'll tell you about the McCracken sisters who used to run it—and poor old Matt Sawyer.

I'm a lawyer, by the way. I don't get much practice up here. I'm also Justice of the Peace. I don't get much practice out of that either, but between the two I make a living. For pleasure I fish for trout and play the violin, and at this point in my life I think I can say from experience that practice ain't everything.

I did the fiddling at Clara McCracken's christening party, I remember, just after coming home from the First World War. Maudie was about my age then, so's that'd make a difference of maybe twenty years between the sisters, and neither chit nor chizzler in between, and after them, the whole family suddenly dies out. That's how it happens up here in the hills: one generation and there'll be aunts and uncles galore, and the next, you got two maiden ladies and a bobtailed cat.

The Red Lantern Inn's boarded up now, as you saw, but it was in the McCracken family since just after the American Revolution. It was burned down once—in a reprisal raid during the War of 1812, and two of the McCrackens were taken hostage. Did you know Washington, D.C., was also burned in reprisal? It was. At least that's how they tell it over in Canada—for the way our boys tore up the town they call Toronto now. You know, history's like a story in a way: it depends on who's telling it.

Anyways, Maudie ran the inn after the old folks died, and she raised Clara the best she could, but Clara was a wild one from the start. We used to call her a changeling: one minute she'd be sitting at the stove and the next she'd be off somewhere in the hills. She wasn't a pretty girl—the jutting McCracken jaw spoiled that—but there were times she was mighty feminine, and many a lad got thorny feet chasing after the will-o'-the-wisp.

As Clara was coming to age, Maudie used to keep a birch stick behind the bar, and now and then I dare say she'd use it, though I never saw it happen but once myself. But that birch stick and Old Faithful, her father's shotgun, stood in the corner side by side, and I guess we made some pretty rude jokes about them in those days. Anyways, Maudie swore to tame the girl and marry her to what she called a "settled" man.

By the time Clara was of a marrying age, The Red Lantern was getting pretty well run-down. And so was Maudie. She wasn't an easy woman by any calculation. She had a tongue you'd think was sharpened on the grindstone and a store of sayings that'd shock you if you didn't know your Bible. The inn was peeling paint and wanting shutters to the northeast, which is where they're needed most. But inside, Maudie kept the rooms as clean and plain as a glass egg. And most times they were about as empty.

It was the taproom kept the sisters going. They drew the best beer this side of Cornwall, England. If they knew you, that is. If they didn't know you, they served you a labeled bottle, stuff you'd recognize by the signboard pictures. About once a month, Maudie had to buy a case of that—which gives you an idea how many strangers stopped over in Webbtown. We had more stores then and the flour mill was working, so the farmers'd come in regular. But none of them were strangers. You see, even to go to Ragapoo City, the county seat, you've got to go twenty miles around—unless you're like Clara was, skipping over the mountain.

Matt Sawyer came through every week or two in those days and he always stopped at Prouty's Hardware Store. Matt was a paint salesman. I suppose he sold Prouty a few gallons over the years. Who bought it from Prouty, I couldn't say. But Prouty liked Matt. I did myself when I got to know him. Or maybe I just felt sorry for him.

It was during the spring storms, this particular day. The rain was popping blisters on Main Street. Most everyone in Webbtown seems to have been inside looking out that day. Half the town claimed afterwards to have seen Matt come out of Prouty's raising his black umbrella over Maudie's head and walking her home. I saw them myself, Maudie pulling herself in and

Matt half in and half out. I know for a fact she'd never been under an umbrella before in her life.

Prouty told me afterwards he'd forgot she was in the store when he was talking to Matt: Maudie took a mighty long time making up her mind before buying anything. Like he always did, Prouty was joshing Matt about having enough money to find himself a nice little woman and give up the road. Maudie wasn't backward. She took a direct line: she just up and asked Matt since he had an umbrella, would he mind walking her home. Matt was more of a gentleman than anybody I ever knew. He said it would be a pleasure. Maybe it was, but that was the beginning of the doggonedest three-cornered courtship in the county history. And it's all documented today in the county court records over in Ragapoo City. But I'm getting ahead of myself.

I've got my office in my hat, you might say, and I hang that in rooms over Kincaid's Drug Store. I was standing at the window when Matt and Maudie came out of Prouty's. I remember I was trying to tune my violin. You can't keep a fiddle in tune weather like that. I played kind of ex tempore for a while, drifting from one thing to another—sad songs mostly, like "The Vacant Chair." *We shall meet but we shall miss him . . . there will be one vacant chair.* I got myself so depressed I hung up the fiddle and went down to The Red Lantern for a glass of Maudie's Own.

Well, sure enough, there was Matt Sawyer sitting at the bar advising Maudie on the costs of paint and trimming and how to estimate the amount of paint a place the size of The Red Lantern would need. Now I knew Maudie couldn't afford whitewash much less the high-class line of stuff Matt represented. But there she was, leaning on the bar, hand in chin and her rump in the air like a swaybacked mule. She drew me a beer and put a head on Matt's. Then she went back to listening to him.

I don't know how long it took me to notice what was really going on: I'm slow sometimes, but all this while Clara was standing on a stool polishing a row of fancy mugs Maudie kept on a ledge over the back mirror. The whole row of lights was on under the ledge and shining double in the mirror. Hell, Matt Sawyer wasn't actually making sense at all, what he was saying in facts and figures. He was just making up words to keep old Maudie distracted—he thought—and all the while him gazing up at Clara every chance he'd get. I might as well be honest with you: it was looking at Clara myself I realized what was going on in that room. The way she was reaching up and down in front of that mirror and with a silk petticoat kind of dress on, you'd have sworn she was stark naked.

Well, sir, just think about that. Matt, being a gentleman, was blushing and yearning—I guess you'd call it that—but making conversation all the time; and Maudie was conniving a match for Clara with a man who could talk a thousand dollars' worth of paint without jumping his Adam's apple. I'll say this about Maudie: for an unmarried lady she was mighty knowing in the fundamentals. Clara was the only innocent one in the room, I got to thinking.

All of a sudden Maudie says to me, "Hank, how's your fiddle these days?"

"It's got four strings," I said.

"You bring it up after supper, hear?" It was Maudie's way never to ask for something. She told you what you were going to do and most often you did it. Clara looked round at me from that perch of hers and clapped her hands.

Maudie laid a bony finger on Matt's hand. "You'll stay to supper with us, Mr. Sawyer. Our Clara's got a leg of lamb in the oven like you never tasted. It's home hung and roasted with garden herbs."

Now I knew for a fact the only thing Clara ever put in the oven was maybe a pair of shoes to warm them of a winter's morning. And it was just about then Clara caught on, too, to what Maudie was maneuvering. Her eyes got a real wild look in them, like a fox cornered in a chicken coop. She bounded down and across that room . . .

I've often wondered what would've happened if I hadn't spoken then. It gives me a cold chill thinking about it—words said with the best intentions in the world. I called out just as she got to the door: "Clara, I'll be bringing up my fiddle."

I don't suppose there ever was a party in Webbtown like Maudie put on that night. Word got around. Even the young folks came that mightn't have if it was spooning weather. Maudie wore her best dress—the one she was saving, we used to say, for Clara's wedding and her own funeral. It was black, but on happier occasions she'd liven it up with a piece of red silk at the collar. I remember Prouty saying once that patch of red turned Maudie from a Holstein into a Guernsey. Prouty, by the way, runs the undertaking parlor as well as the hardware store.

I near split my fingers that night fiddling. Maudie tapped a special keg. Everybody paid for his first glass, but after that she put the cash box away and you might say she drew by heart.

Matt was having a grand time just watching mostly. Matt was one of those creamy-looking fellows, with cheeks as pink as winter apples. He must've been fifty but there wasn't a line or wrinkle in his face. And I never seen him without his collar and tie on. Like I said, a gentleman.

Clara took to music like a bird to wing. I always got the feeling no matter who was taking her in or out she was actually dancing alone; she could do two steps to everybody else's one. Matt never took his eyes off her, and once he danced with her when Maudie pushed him into it.

That was trouble's start—although we didn't know it at the time. Prouty said afterwards he did, but Prouty's a man who knows everything after the fact. That's being an undertaker, I dare say. Anyway, Matt was hesitating after Clara—and it was like that, her sort of skipping ahead and leading him on, when all of a sudden, young Reuben White leaped in between them and danced with Clara the way she needed to be danced with.

Now Reuben didn't have much to recommend him, especially to Maudie. He did an odd job now and then—in fact, he hauled water for Maudie from the well she had up by the brewhouse back of Maple Tree Ridge. And this you ought to know about Maudie if you don't by now—anybody she could boss around, she had no use for.

Anyways, watching that boy dance with Clara that night should've set us all to thinking, him whirling her and tossing her up in the air, them spinning round together like an August twister. My fiddle's got a devil in it at a time like that. Faster and faster I was bowing, till plunk I broke a string, but I went right on playing.

Matt fell back with the other folks, clapping and cheering, but Maudie I could see going after her stick. I bowed even faster, seeing her. It was like a race we were all in together. Then all of a sudden, like something dying high up in the sky and falling mute, my E string broke and I wasn't playing any more. In the center of the tavern floor Clara and Reuben just folded up together and slumped down into a heap.

Everybody was real still for about a half a minute. Then

Maudie came charging out, slashing the air with that switch of hers. She grabbed Clara by the hair—I swear she lifted the girl to her feet that way and flung her towards the bar. Then she turned on Reuben. That boy slithered clear across the barroom floor, every time just getting out of the way of a slash from Maudie's stick. People by then were cheering in a kind of rhythm—for him or Maudie, you couldn't just be sure, and maybe they weren't for either. "Now!" they'd shout at every whistle of the switch. "Now! Now! *Now!*"

Prouty opened the door just when Reuben got there, and when the boy was out Prouty closed it against Maudie. I thought for a minute she was going to turn on him. But she just stood looking and then burst out laughing. Everybody started clouting her on the back and having a hell of a time.

I was at the bar by then and so was Matt. I heard him, leaning close to Clara, say, "Miss Clara, I never saw anything as beautiful as you in all my life."

Clara's eyes snapped back at him but she didn't say a word.

Well, it was noon the next day before Matt pulled out of town, and sure enough, he forgot his umbrella and came back that night. I went up to The Red Lantern for my five o'clock usual, and him and Maudie were tête-à-tête, as they say, across the bar. Maudie was spouting the praises of her Clara—how she could sew and cook and bake a cherry pie, Billy Boy. The only attention she paid me was as a collaborating witness.

I'll say this for Clara: when she did appear, she looked almost civilized, her hair in a ribbon, and her wearing a new striped skirt and a grandmother blouse clear up to her chin. That night, by glory, she went to the movie with Matt. We had movies every night except Sundays in those days. A year or so ago, they closed up the Bellevue altogether. Why did she go with him? My guess is she wanted to get away from Maudie, or maybe for Reuben to see her dressed up that way.

The next time I saw all of them together was Decoration Day. Matt was back in town, arranging his route so's he'd have to stop over the holiday in Webbtown. One of them carnival outfits had set up on the grounds back of the schoolhouse. Like I said before, we don't have any population to speak of in Webbtown, but we're central for the whole valley, and in the old days traveling entertainers could do all right if they didn't come too often.

There was all sorts of raffle booths—Indian blankets and

kewpie dolls, a shooting gallery and one of those things where you throw baseballs at wooden bottles and get a cane if you knock 'em off. And there was an apparatus for testing a man's muscle: you know, you hit the target on the stand with a sledge-hammer and then a little ball runs up a track that looks like a big thermometer and registers your strength in pounds.

I knew there was a trick to it no matter what the barker said about it being fair and square. Besides, nobody cares how strong a lawyer is as long as he can whisper in the judge's ear. I could see old Maudie itching herself to have a swing at it, but she wasn't taking any chance of giving Matt the wrong impression about either of the McCracken girls.

Matt took off his coat, folded it, and gave it to Clara to hold. It was a warm day for that time of year and you could see where Matt had been sweating under the coat, but like I said, he was all gentleman. He even turned his back to the ladies before spitting on his hands. It took Matt three swings— twenty-five cents' worth—but on the last one that little ball crawled the last few inches up the track and just sort of tinkled the bell at the top. The womenfolk clapped, and Matt put on his coat again, blushing and pleased with himself.

I suppose you've guessed that Reuben showed up then. He did, wearing a cotton shirt open halfway down to his belly.

"Now, my boy," the barker says, "show the ladies, show the world that you're a man! How many?"

Reuben sniggled a coin out of his watch pocket, and mighty cocky for him, he said, "Keep the change."

Well, you've guessed the next part too: Reuben took one swing and you could hear that gong ring out clear across the valley. It brought a lot of people running and the carnival man was so pleased he took out a big cigar and gave it to Reuben. "That, young fellow, wins you a fifty-cent Havana. But I'll send you the bill if you broke the ma-chine, ha! ha!"

Reuben grinned and took the cigar and, strutting across to Clara, he made her a present of it. Now in Matt's book, you didn't give a lady a cigar, no, sir. Not saying a word, Matt brought his fist up with everything he had dead to center under Reuben's chin. We were all of us plain stunned, but nobody more than Reuben. He lay on the ground with his eyes rolling round in his head like marbles.

You'd say that was the blow struck for romance, wouldn't you? Not if you knew our Clara. She plopped down beside

Reuben like he was the dying gladiator, or maybe just something she'd come on helpless in the woods. It was Maudie who
clucked and crowed over Matt. All of a sudden Clara leaped
up—Reuben was coming round by then—and she gave a whisk
of that fancy skirt and took off for the hills, Maudie bawling
after her like a hogcaller. And at that point, Reuben scrambled
to his feet and galloped after Clara. It wasn't long till all you
could see of where they'd gone was a little whiff of dust at the
edge of the dogwood grove. I picked up the cigar and tried to
smoke it afterwards. I'd have been better off on a mixture of
oak leaf and poison ivy.

Everything changed for the worse at The Red Lantern after
that. Clara found her tongue and sassed her sister, giving Maudie back word for word, like a common scold. One was getting
mean and the other meaner. And short of chaining her, Maudie
couldn't keep Clara at home any more, not when Clara wanted
to go.

Matt kept calling at The Red Lantern regularly, and Maudie
kept making excuses for Clara's not being there. The only times
I'd go to the inn in those days was when I'd see Matt's car
outside. The place would brighten up then, Maudie putting on
a show for him. Otherwise, I'd have as soon sat in Prouty's
cool room. It was about as cheerful. Even Maudie's beer was
turning sour.

Matt was a patient man if anything, and I guess being smit-
ten for the first time at his age he got it worse than most of us
would: he'd sit all evening just waiting a sight of that girl.
When we saw he wasn't going to get over it, Prouty and I
undertook one day in late summer to give him some advice.
What made us think we were authorities, I don't know. I've
been living with my fiddle for years and I've already told you
what Prouty'd been living with. Anyways, we advised Matt to
get himself some hunting clothes—the season was coming
round—and to put away that doggone collar and tie of his and
get out in the open country where the game was.

Matt tried. Next time he came to Webbtown, as soon as he
put in at The Red Lantern, he changed into a plaid wool shirt,
brand-new khaki britches, and boots laced up to his knees, and
with Prouty and me cheering him on, he headed for the hills.
But like Cox's army, or whoever it was, he marched up the hill
and marched down again.

But he kept at it. Every week-end he'd show up, change, and

set out, going farther and farther every time. One day, when the wind was coming sharp from the northeast, I heard him calling out up there: "Clara . . . Clara . . ."

I'll tell you, that gave me a cold chill, and I wished to the Almighty that Prouty and I had minded our own business. Maudie would stand at the tavern door and watch him off, and I wondered how long it was going to take for her to go with him. By then, I'd lost whatever feeling I ever had for Maudie and I didn't have much left for Clara either. But what made me plain sick one day was Maudie confiding in me that she was thinking of locking Clara in her room and giving Matt the key. I said something mighty close to obscene such as I'd never said to a woman before in my life and walked out of the tavern.

It was one of those October days, you know, when the clouds keep building up like suds and then just seem to wash away. You could hear the school bell echo, and way off the hawking of the wild geese, and you'd know the only sound of birds till spring would be the lonesome cawing of the crows. I was working on a couple of things I had coming up in Quarter Sessions Court when Prouty pounded up my stairs. Prouty's a pretty dignified man who seldom runs.

"Hank," he said, "I just seen Matt Sawyer going up the hill. He's carrying old man McCracken's shotgun."

I laughed kind of, seeing the picture in my mind. "What do you think he aims to do with it?"

"If he was to fire it, Hank, he'd be likely to blow himself to eternity."

"Maybe the poor buzzard'd be as well off," I said.

"And something else, Hank—Maudie just closed up the tavern. She's stalking him into the hills."

"That's something else," I said, and reached for my pipe.

"What are we going to do?" Prouty fumbled through his pockets for some matches for me. He couldn't keep his hands still.

"Nothing," I said. "The less people in them hills right now the better."

Prouty came to see it my way, but neither one of us could do much work that afternoon. I'd go to the window every few minutes and see Prouty standing in the doorway. He'd look down toward The Red Lantern and shake his head, and I'd know Maudie hadn't come back yet.

Funny, how things go on just the same in a town at a time

like that. Tom Kincaid, the druggist, came out and swept the
sidewalk clean, passed the time of day with Prouty, and went
inside again. The kids were coming home from school. Pretty
soon they were all indoors doing their homework before chore
time. Doc Sissler stopped at Kincaid's—he liked to supervise
the making up of his prescriptions. It was Miss Dorman, the
schoolteacher, who gave the first alarm. She always did her
next day's lessons before going home so it was maybe an hour
after school let out. I heard her scream and ran to the window.

There was Matt coming down the street on Prouty's side,
trailing the gun behind him. You could see he was saying
something to himself or just thinking out loud. I opened my
window and shouted down to him. He came on then across the
street. His step on the stair was like the drum in a death march.
When he got to my doorway he just stood there, saying, "I
killed her, Hank. I killed her dead."

I got him into a chair and splashed some whiskey out for
him. He dropped the gun on the floor beside him and I let it
lie there, stepping over it. By then Prouty had come upstairs,
and by the time we got the whiskey inside Matt, Luke Weber,
the constable, was there.

"He says he killed somebody," I told Weber. "I don't know
who."

Matt rolled his eyes towards me like I'd betrayed him just
saying what he told me. His face was hanging limp and white
as a strung goose. "I know Matt Sawyer," I added then, "and
if there was any killing, I'd swear before Jehovah it must've
been an accident."

That put a little life back in him. "It was," he said, "it was
truly." And bit by piece we got the story out of him.

"I got to say in fairness to myself, taking the gun up there
wasn't my own idea," he started. "Look at me, duded up like
this—I had no business from the start pretending I was something I wasn't."

"That was me and Hank's fault," Prouty said, mostly to the
constable, "advising him on how to court Miss Clara."

He didn't have to explain that to Weber. Everybody in town
knew it.

"I'm not blaming either one of you," Matt said. "It should've
been enough for me, chasing an echo every time I thought I'd
found her. And both of them once sitting up in a tree laughing at
me fit to bust and pelting me with acorns . . ."

We knew he was talking about Reuben and Clara. It was pathetic listening to a man tell that kind of story on himself, and I couldn't help but think what kind of an impression it was going to make on a jury. I had to be realistic about it: there's some people up here would hang a man for making a fool of himself where they'd let him go for murder. I put the jury business straight out of my mind and kept hoping it was clear-cut accident. He hadn't said yet who was dead, but I thought I knew by then.

"Well, I found them for myself today," he made himself go on, "Clara and Reuben, that is. They were cozied in together in the sheepcote back of Maudie's well. It made me feel ashamed just being there and I was set to sneak away and give the whole thing up for good. But Maudie came up on me and took me by surprise. She held me there—by the scruff of the soul, you might say—and made me listen with her to them giggling and carrying on. I was plain sick with jealousy, I'll admit that.

"Then Maudie gave a shout: 'Come out, you two! Or else we'll blow you out!' Something like that.

"It was a minute or two: nothing happened. Then we saw Reuben going full speed the other way, off towards the woods.

" 'Shoot, Matt, now!' That's what Maudie shouted at me. 'You got him clear to sight.' But just then Clara sauntered out of the shelter towards us—just as innocent and sweet, like the first time I ever laid eyes on her."

I'm going to tell you, Prouty and me looked at each other when he said that.

The constable interrupted him and asked his question straight: "Did she have her clothes on?"

"All but her shoes. She was barefoot and I don't consider that unbecoming in a country girl."

"Go on," Weber told him.

Matt took a long drag of air and then plunged ahead. "Maudie kept hollering at the boy—insults, I guess—I know I'd have been insulted. Then he stopped running and turned around and started coming back. I forget what it was she said to me then—something about my manhood. But she kept saying, 'Shoot, Matt! Shoot, shoot!'" I was getting desperate, her hounding me that way. I slammed the gun down between us, butt-end on the ground. The muzzle of it, I guess, was looking her way. And it went off.

"It was like the ground exploding underneath us. Hell smoke and brimstone—that's what went through my mind. I don't know whether it was in my imagination—my ears weren't hearing proper after all that noise—but like ringing in my head I could hear Clara laughing, just laughing like hysterics . . . And then when I could see, there was Maudie lying on the ground. I couldn't even find her face for all that was left of her head."

We stood all of us for a while after that. Listening to the tick of my alarm clock on the shelf over the washstand, I was. Weber picked up the gun then and took it over to the window where he examined the breech.

Then he said, "What did you think you were going to do with this when you took it from the tavern?"

Matt shook his head. "I don't know. When Maudie gave it to me, I thought it looked pretty good on me in the mirror."

I couldn't wait to hear the prosecutor try that one on the jury.

Weber said, "We better get on up there before dark and you show us how it happened."

We stopped by at Prouty's on the way and picked up his wicker basket. There wasn't any way of driving beyond the dogwood grove. People were following us by then. Weber sent them back to town and deputized two or three among them to be sure they kept the peace.

We hadn't got very far beyond the grove, the four of us, just walking, climbing up, and saying nothing. Hearing the crows a-screaming not far ahead gave me a crawling stomach. They're scavengers, you know.

Well, sir, down the hill fair-to-flying, her hair streaming out in the wind, came Clara to meet us. She never hesitated, throwing herself straight at Matt. It was instinct made him put his arms out to catch her and she dove into them and flung her own arms around his neck, hugging him and holding him, and saying things like, "Darling Matt . . . wonderful Matt. I love Matt." I heard her say that.

You'd have thought to see Matt, he'd turned to stone. Weber was staring at them, a mighty puzzled look on his face.

"Miss Clara," I said, "behave yourself."

She looked at me—I swear she was smiling—and said, "You hush, old Hank, or we won't let you play the fiddle at our wedding."

It was Prouty said, hoisting his basket up on his shoulder, "Let's take one thing at a time."

That got us started on our way again, Clara skipping along at Matt's side, trying to catch his hand. Luke Weber didn't say a word.

I'm not going into the details now of what we saw. It was just about like Matt had told it in my office. I was sick a couple of times. I don't think Matt had anything left in him to be sick with. When it came to telling what had happened first, Clara was called on to corroborate. And Weber asked her, "Where's Reuben now, Miss Clara?"

"Gone," she said, "and I don't care."

"Didn't care much about your sister either, did you?" Weber drawled, and I began to see how really bad a spot old Matt was in. There was no accounting Clara's change of heart about him—except he'd killed her sister. The corroborating witness we needed right then was Reuben White.

Prouty got Weber's go-ahead on the job he had to do. I couldn't help him though I tried. What I did when he asked it, was go up to Maudie's well to draw him a pail of water so's he could wash his hands when he was done. Well, sir, I'd have been better off helping him direct. I couldn't get the bucket down to where it would draw the water.

After trying a couple of times, I called out to Weber asking if he had a flashlight. He brought it and threw the beam of light down into the well. Just above the water level a pair of size-twelve shoes were staring up at us—the soles of them like Orphan Annie's eyes.

There wasn't any doubt in our minds that what was holding them up like that was Reuben White, headfirst in the well.

The constable called Clara to him and took a short-cut in his questioning.

"How'd it happen, girl?"

"I guess I pushed him," Clara said, almost casual.

"It took a heap of pushing," Weber said.

"No, it didn't. I just got him to look down and then I tumbled him in."

"Why?"

"Matt," she said, and smiled like a Christmas cherub.

Matt groaned, and I did too inside.

"Leastways, it come to that," Clara explained. Then in that quick-changing way of hers, she turned deep serious. "Mr.

Weber, you wouldn't believe me if I told you what Reuben White wanted me to do with him—in the sheepcote this afternoon."

"I might," Luke Weber said.

I looked at Prouty and drew my first half-easy breath. I could see he felt the same. We're both old-fashioned enough to take warmly to a girl's defending her virtue.

But Weber didn't bat an eye. "And where does Matt here come in on it?" he said.

"I figure he won't ever want me to do a thing like that," Clara said, and gazed up at old stoneface with a look of pure adoration.

"Where was Matt when you . . . tumbled Reuben in?" Weber asked, and I could tell he was well on his way to believing her.

"He'd gone down the hill to tell you what'd happened to Sister Maudie."

"And when was it Reuben made this—this proposal to you?" Weber said. I could see he was getting at the question of premeditation. Luke Weber's a pretty fair policeman.

"It was Matt proposed to me," Clara said. "That's why I'm going to marry him. Reuben just wanted—"

Weber interrupted. "Why, if he wasn't molesting you just then, and if you'd decided to marry Matt Sawyer, why did you have to kill him? You must've known a well's no place for diving."

Clara shrugged her pretty shoulders. "By then I was feeling kind of sorry for him. He'd have been mighty lonesome after I went to live with Matt."

Well, there isn't much more to tell. We sort of disengaged Matt, you might say. His story of how Maudie died stood up with the coroner, Prouty and I vouching for the kind of man he was. I haven't seen him since.

Clara—she'll be getting out soon, coming home to the hills, and maybe opening up The Red Lantern again. I defended her at the trial, pleading temporary insanity. Nobody was willing to say she was insane exactly. We don't like saying such things about one another up here. But the jury agreed she was a temporary sort of woman. Twenty years to life, she got, with time off for good behavior.

You come around some time next spring. I'll introduce you.

Linda Grant introduced Catherine Sayler, private investigator who specializes in corporate crime, in Random Access Murder, *nominated for a 1989 Anthony. Catherine has a black belt in Aikido, an ex-husband who is a cop, and a lover who is a private eye and unregenerate political radical. In* Blind Trust, *Catherine and company search for a missing banker and uncover a twenty-year-old crime. As Linda Williams, this versatile author writes books and articles about computers, education, and the human brain.*

In "Lady Luck," two sisters play a deadly game in which luck is only one small factor.

LADY LUCK

by Linda Grant

MARTHA MCGRATH STOPPED to catch her breath before walking the last half block to her apartment. It seemed like she tired more easily lately, but at seventy-three, that was to be expected. Cataracts, arthritis, various aches and pains—getting old was not fun. But, as her friend Janet was fond of saying, it sure did beat the alternative.

The bags from the grocery store were heavier today because she'd let her sister Alice talk her into buying three cans of soup and a half dozen eggs. Alice, who was five years younger and in good enough shape to play golf, should be the one walking to the store, but somehow it was always Martha who made the trip.

She chided herself. On a day like today, it was just plain ungrateful to complain about anything. The sun warm on her back, just a bit of breeze, and the fruit trees that lined the streets bursting with pink popcorn blossoms—it was going to be a good day.

She felt lucky this morning. She'd awakened feeling good, the arthritis in her hands had calmed down, and she'd slept

straight through the night. All that was a good sign, as was the
sun and the blossoming trees. And to top it off, it was Thursday, her favorite day.

Mondays were nice because she got her hair done then, and
she always enjoyed chatting with Bernice and the other women,
but the only decent bingo game on Monday was thirty minutes
away by bus. Tuesdays she cleaned her tiny apartment and went
to the library. Sometimes she went to bingo at the hall down
the street, but it wasn't much fun because Louise and Janet
didn't like the caller, so they rarely came. Wednesday was
wash day, which she had never really liked, and the day she
paid the bills and answered letters if any had come during the
week. Sometimes she went to bingo.

But Thursday nights she never missed. Thursday night the
Senior Citizens Alliance ran the game, and the callers were
always good. People came from all over the Bay Area for
Thursday night bingo. She looked forward to it all week.

She walked the last half block feeling good and took the
elevator to her second-floor apartment. She carried the groceries in and set them on the counter, then sat down to catch
her breath.

She frowned at the crowded little room. They called it an
efficiency, probably because if you weren't efficient in using
every inch of space, you'd never fit.

The kitchen was sandwiched into a corner, its appliances no
bigger than those in a child's play house; a small round table
and four chairs occupied another corner, leaving just enough
space for a love seat, an armchair, the television, and one
bookcase. The bedroom was even smaller, and the bathroom
was the size of a closet.

Today was the first of the month, and she'd picked up her
horoscope at the store, but she forced herself to put the groceries away before prying the tightly rolled sheet from its tube.
The darn things certainly weren't made for anyone with hands
like hers. She scanned the "Horoscope for the Month" section
first and then checked the weekly forecasts.

The month begins well when the Sun/Jupiter sextile
makes everything you touch turn to gold. However, be
careful because personal relationships may be difficult. The
new moon in Virgo and your solar fourth house on the

second marks major changes for you concerning a home
or family matter.

"Major changes." Martha sighed. They always tried to make
the horoscopes sound so positive, but Martha knew too well
that major changes came in both good and bad. Her daily horoscope had predicted "important changes in your life" the very
day ten months ago when Alice had called to announce her
intention to move into Oak Grove Retirement Home to be near
her dear sister.

Martha felt a pang of guilt, then of annoyance. She loved
Alice, but she found her younger sister more than a little trying. She checked the clock over the stove. Eleven-fifty. Alice
expected her at noon. She turned the horoscope over and read
the little box for "1—Thursday": "Family relationships may
be difficult today, but expect good luck in the evening."

Difficult family relationships were nothing new. She'd been
dealing with that for ten months. But good luck in the evening
had to mean bingo. She was right about today. Sometimes you
just knew when you were going to get lucky. She could hardly
wait till five o'clock.

Martha decided to change her dress and water the plants.
She put away the dishes in the drying rack and dusted the
bookshelf. Then she took the elevator to Alice's sixth-floor
apartment.

"You're late," Alice announced as she let her sister in.
"Twenty minutes late."

"Sorry," Martha replied. "I lost track of the time." She
looked around the apartment and admired with just a touch of
envy its size and lovely furnishings. Alice's kitchen sat in its
own nook, separate from the large main room where there was
space for their parents' lovely mahogany dining room table as
well as a living room full of furniture. The bedroom was big
enough for a queen-size bed, and the bathroom had both a tub
and a shower.

"I waited lunch for you," Alice complained.

Since lunch was always sandwiches, usually tuna fish, and
some variety of Campbell's soup, Martha felt that *waited lunch*
overstated matters. "It's lovely outside. Why don't we eat on
your balcony?" she suggested.

"Too cold," Alice replied. "Besides, the railing is weak on
one side."

"We'll eat on the other side."

"Oh, all right," Alice conceded grumpily. "For what I pay for this place, you'd think they could keep it in better shape. It's not just the railing—the kitchen faucet leaks and the water pressure in the shower is just awful."

Martha knew all about the water pressure in the shower and thought it tactless of Alice to complain when she had a bathtub and a balcony and Martha had neither. She walked across the room, opened the sliding glass door and stepped out onto the coveted balcony with its view of San Francisco. The bay was a robin's-egg blue, and beyond it, San Francisco had a fairy tale quality, like the Emerald City of Oz, except it wasn't green.

How like Alice to complain about a little wind and a wooden railing when she had all that beauty in front of her. But then she'd always been that way. She'd had everything she wanted, and she'd never appreciated it.

Martha's lips pursed into a thin, tight line as she remembered their childhood. Five years older, she was responsible for anything that went wrong, and with Alice that was plenty. Like the time that a neighbor chased the younger girl out of his yard and she sneaked back and pulled up all his petunias and dahlias. Martha was punished for not keeping an eye on Alice. Alice was excused because she was too young to understand that she was wrong.

Alice was the baby; if she wanted something she raised a fuss until she got it. Martha had learned over the years that it wasn't worth it to oppose her. She still remembered a lovely pink sweater with pearls on it that she'd had when she was fifteen. It was one thing she'd absolutely refused to let Alice borrow. One morning she found it torn and soiled in the muddy gutter in front of the house. Alice swore she hadn't touched it.

"If you want to eat out here, at least you can help me carry things out," Alice fussed.

Martha grumbled agreement. She still remembered the sweater.

Lunch was the usual tuna fish sandwich and tomato soup with weak iced tea. As they ate, Alice held out her right hand to display an impressive ring. "I had Mother's diamond reset for a dinner ring. Isn't it lovely?"

"Very nice," Martha replied, trying hard not to choke on the words. Mother's ring was to have been hers, but Alice had fussed and begged and sulked until Martha agreed to let her have it. It galled her still that Alice had gotten half of every-thing. When it was time to take care of her parents, Martha'd gotten the whole job, but when it was time to parcel out the inheritance, Alice got her half and more.

"You don't use Mama's dishes, do you?" Alice asked for the fortieth time. "I mean you really don't have room for them, and your table only seats two comfortably."

"I am not going to give you Mother's dishes," Martha said forcefully. "So stop bullying me. And I'm not going to give you Grandma's emerald ring or her silver either."

Alice looked taken aback. "I didn't realize I was bullying," she said in a hurt tone. "And I wouldn't think of asking for something you didn't want to part with."

Not much you wouldn't, Martha thought. Alice would keep asking, pleasantly at first, more acrimoniously as time went on. Alice always got what she wanted. And she'd get the dishes, ring, and silver, too, eventually, Martha realized. She should never have let her sister talk her into making reciprocal wills.

Alice seemed to want to make peace. She suggested, "Let's go to the movies tonight. That new comedy they've been ad-vertising on TV is down at the Rockridge."

Martha shook her head. "No, I've got plans."

"Bingo?"

Martha wondered how you pack that much disapproval into two syllables. "I always go on Thursday nights. Besides, to-night is going to be my lucky night." She regretted it as soon as she'd said it.

"Oh, honestly, Martha." It was the same superior tone their mother had used. Martha could remember hearing Alice talk to her dolls that way. She gritted her teeth. "You are so su-perstitious. It's just an excuse for not taking control of your own life. I've always believed you make your own luck."

Martha had noticed that people who had a lot of luck often didn't believe in it. It was as if they had so much that they didn't have to pay attention to it. Alice was like that, born lucky; she'd gotten all the luck for both of them. And she'd always taken it for granted.

What had Alice done to deserve the large apartment and ample bank account? It was Al who'd earned the money. Vern would probably have done even better if he'd lived. It was luck that had brought Alice's husband home from the war and left hers buried in France.

And talk about luck. What else could she call it when Alice's husband died of a heart attack three days after he announced he was going to divorce her? Al told her he was leaving on Monday; he was dead Thursday night. His new honey got zip and Alice got the estate. Now that was luck.

It was only fair, of course. A lot fairer than the fact that Alice got half of their parents' meager estate after Martha had spent twenty years taking care of them. Martha resolved anew not to let Alice talk her out of the dishes or the ring.

"Bingo is a form of gambling," Alice said. "There was an article in the *Good Housekeeping* about how gambling is a disease just like alcoholism. It's an addiction."

"You just don't understand," Martha protested wearily. "I don't go just to win money. It's like a social club, a place to be with my friends."

"I'll bet an alcoholic would say the same about a bar."

Just like Mother, Martha thought. You could never tell her anything. It was because of Mother that she'd started going to bingo years ago, to have a place to get away from the house, to relax and have a good time. But Alice wouldn't understand that. She'd never spent more than an afternoon or evening taking care of Mother.

Alice was still talking. She was well into her gambling-as-a-form-of-moral-weakness speech. Boy, Martha thought, it's sure too bad you don't get to pick your relatives.

"You're *not* listening," Alice complained.

"We've been through this before. You just don't understand. You don't want to understand."

"Is that right? Well, I'll go with you then, see for myself. Since you won't go to the movie, I'll go to bingo with you."

"I don't see why we have to come at five o'clock when the game doesn't start until six-thirty," Alice complained.

"Because I want to get my favorite seat, I don't like to stand in line to get my cards, and I want to visit with my friends."

Alice looked around the hall critically. "Didn't this used to be a supermarket?" she asked.

"Probably." Martha led the way to a chair near the end of the third table from the back and laid her pad of cards on the table in front of it. She tipped the next two chairs against the table to save them for Janet and Louise. Then she took her color daubers from her bag and arranged them above the pads, blue, pink, purple. She considered buying a new dauber, maybe green.

"What are those things?" Alice asked, somehow managing to make it sound like criticism.

"Daubers. You use them to mark the numbers as they're called."

"Why do you need three of them?"

Martha wasn't going to answer that one. She knew what response she'd get if she told Alice that sometimes one color was luckier than the others. She took a tiny ceramic dog from the bag and set it in front of the daubers. She hoped Alice wouldn't notice.

"What's that for?" Alice asked.

"It's my good luck dog," Martha said, her voice challenging Alice to make a crack. Alice had enough sense to keep her mouth shut for once. Martha had considered leaving the dog home, but it was a gift from Janet, and it had brought her luck the day she got it. Nothing was going to ruin her evening.

Martha went to the food counter and came back with a large coke and tortilla chips covered with a yellow gooey mass. "Want some nachos?" she asked.

Alice looked shocked. "Those things are terrible for you. They're just full of cholesterol. And they're fattening." The way she said it she might as well have pointed out that Martha was only an inch shorter but a good thirty pounds heavier.

Martha's mouth squeezed into a tight, thin line. She clenched her teeth so hard they hurt.

"Is this the smoking section?" Alice demanded.

"Yes."

"Do we have to sit here? You know secondhand smoke is just as bad for you as if you smoked that cigarette yourself." Martha didn't particularly like cigarette smoke, but Janet smoked, so she sat in the smoking section. Tonight she'd have sat there even if Janet weren't coming. She considered inviting Julie Grayson, who smoked constantly, to sit with them, but decided against it.

Fortunately, Janet and Louise arrived. Janet took one look at her and gave her a big hug. They exchanged greetings and Martha introduced Alice. The women knew all about Alice; they greeted her politely, gave Martha a knowing look, then headed off for the refreshment stand.

Martha had Alice sit on the side, away from Janet and Louise, so she wouldn't ruin their conversation, but her sister's presence put a damper on everything. Martha couldn't really tell the others about her horoscope, and Alice kept asking stupid questions or complaining about the smoke.

"Sure are a lot of coloreds here," Alice said.

The others looked startled, then irritated. They weren't flaming liberals, but some of those people were friends.

"Look at that one over there, with that sequin cape. Isn't she something?"

Frowns deepened. Clarice wasn't a friend, but she was a regular at Thursday night bingo, and that was her lucky cape. She'd worn that the night she'd won two games. When she won the second one, she'd bought popcorn and Cokes for everyone at the table. She was a nice person.

Conversation was getting strained when one of the volunteers walked by, selling pull tabs. Alice wanted to know what they were. Martha bought five one-dollar tickets and ten fifty-cent ones.

"You peel off the five tabs, and underneath each tab there are little pictures." She pulled off a tab, revealing a row with a bunch of cherries, an orange, and a diamond. "That's not worth anything," she said. She pulled off the next tab and the next. Under the last tab were three bunches of cherries. Martha smiled. "That's worth a dollar."

"Looks just like a slot machine on paper," Alice pointed out. "And it just cost you a dollar to win that dollar."

Martha realized she was clenching her teeth and tried to relax her jaw. "Yes, but if you get three diamonds, you win two hundred and fifty dollars."

"I'll bet that doesn't happen too often."

At last the caller announced the first warm-up game. Alice decided at the last minute that she would play and dashed off to buy a pad of cards. Martha noted with satisfaction that there was a long line.

By the fourteenth game Martha knew that Alice had not only ruined her evening, she was also ruining her luck. She hadn't won a game, and she'd spent fifteen dollars on pull tabs without getting close to a big winner.

The caller announced the last game. She took her last five dollars from her purse and held it up. "Pull tabs," she called.

The volunteer walked toward her. Alice pulled a dollar from her purse and said, "What the heck, I'll take one of those."

Before Martha could protest that she had asked first, the volunteer gave Alice the card on top. She counted out the next five for Martha.

"That's *my* card," Martha said, reaching for it. "I called for pull tabs first."

"Nonsense. She gave it to me." Alice turned her back and began peeling the tabs. She let out a squeal. "Look at that. Look at that. I got the three diamonds."

She held it up for Martha to see. "I won the jackpot," she crowed.

Others turned to congratulate her. Martha sat in stunned silence. "It was my card," she muttered.

"See, I told you, you make your own luck. Now don't be a sourpuss," Alice said. "Tell you what, I'll trade you the card for Mama's dishes and the emerald ring."

"No," Martha snapped. "Never."

The young policeman shook his head as he looked at the broken rail. It was criminal that a building housing old people wasn't more careful about maintenance. Of course, even a young person wouldn't have survived a six-story fall.

"I'm sorry, ma'am," he said to the old woman who sat weeping in the living room. "I know it's no comfort, but I think you could sue the owner of the building for negligence. The wood in that rail was obviously rotten. I guess your sister just didn't see it. Was her eyesight poor?"

Martha looked up at the nice young man. "Well, it wasn't so good. And, you know, she was not as careful as she should have been. She always told me she was lucky. I guess her luck ran out."

*Faye Kellerman proves that someone with advanced degrees in mathematics and dentistry has a multitude of options. Her fast-paced, absorbing mystery series features Sergeant Peter Decker of the L.A.P.D., and his girlfriend Rina Lazarus (*The Ritual Bath, *winner of a Macavity award,* Sacred and Profane, *and* Milk and Honey). *As further proof of her range and versatility, she offered readers the richly textured* The Quality of Mercy, *a novel of Elizabethan suspense.*

In "Malibu Dog," the beleaguered residents of a condominium learn the true meaning of "man's best friend."

MALIBU DOG

by Faye Kellerman

STUBBORN AND MEAN are a lethal combination, a perfect case in point being Conroy Bittune—an old coot of sixty, as skinny and dried-up as a stick of jerky. He was a wiry man with small brown eyes, thin lips, and a mouth full of brown stained teeth. His cheeks were never without wads of chewing tobacco, giving him a stale smell and his scrawny face a pouchy appearance. I've always wondered how he managed to talk and chew without choking. Conroy was retired, having earned modest money doing something for the IRS. He was and always had been short on friends, so no one in the Estates was surprised when Conroy bought himself a companion—a pitbull terrier named Maneater.

I was as close as you could call a friend to Conroy, which meant we were on speaking terms. He and I were next-door neighbors in a condominium complex called The Sand and Sea Estates. The development consisted of one- and two-bedroom boxes built above one-car garages. The units were framed with the cheapest grade lumber, drywalled with the thinnest plasterboard and roofed with layers of tar paper. The interiors were equally as chintzy. The ceilings were finished with cottage cheese stucco and the floors were nothing more than low-pile carpet over cement slab. Who would buy such junk? Fact was the condos were snapped up faster than flies around frogs.

Why?

Not only did the condos grace the golden sands of Malibu Beach, but they were also granted *private* beach rights. That meant residents of the Estates could romp in the blue Pacific without mixing with the *public* riffraff. The units sold for three hundred grand and upward, depending on location and size. Of course, Conroy Bittune's little bit of paradise sat on the choicest parcel of land—a corner spot that allowed a view of the famous Malibu sunsets.

Me? I'm a lowly tenant, paying my out-of-town landlord four hundred a month for the privilege of residing there. I came out to the Estates during one of my college term breaks to visit a friend. I was instantly entranced by the endless horizon, the splashy sunsets, the nighttime sky, sometimes as black as tar winking with millions of stars. Five years later the ocean still has me under her spell. I earn my living as a handywoman, keeping my rent down by doing free repairs on my unit and a couple of others that my landlord owns.

My connection with Conroy was tenuous. One Saturday morning, his sink pipe burst, spewing water in his face and all over his ultramodern compact kitchen. He came banging on my door at seven in the morning, waking me up, demanding that I do something.

Conroy never asks, he demands.

Being an easygoing gal, I took his harsh tone of voice in stride and went next door. The pipe repair took all of five minutes—a loose joint—and just to show what kind of sport I was, I didn't even charge him. He never did thank me, but from that day on, I was the only one in the complex whom he never threatened to sue. We never became friendly enough to carry on a true conversation—the kind with give-and-take. But I would condo-watch his place when he went away on vacation, which was about four times a year.

One Friday afternoon, Conroy showed up at my door, beaming like a new father as he presented me to the pitbull. The dog was white and black, seemed to be molded from pounds of muscle and had teeth like razors.

Conroy spat a wad of tobacco into my geranium box. Still

chomping his Skoal, he said, "Don't need you no more, Lydia." He spat again. "Meet my new watchdog, Maneater."

The dog was on a leash and, by way of introduction, bared his fangs.

"Lookie at this, Liddy."

Conroy smacked the dog soundly across the mouth with a rolled-up newspaper. The pitbull let out a menacing growl but didn't budge. Conroy hit him again and again. The dog never moved an inch. Then Conroy pried open Maneater's mouth and stuck his nose inside the gaping maws. The dog endured the ordeal but wasn't pleased. And Conroy? He just stood there, smiling wickedly.

"Now you try to pet him, girl," he told me.

Slowly, I raised my hand toward Maneater's scruff. The dog snapped so hard, you could hear an echo from his jaws banging shut. Only quick reflexes prevented me from becoming an amputee. Conroy broke into gales of laughter that turned into a hacking cough, sending bits of tobacco over my threshold.

"Cute, Conroy," I said. "You're going to win loads of friends with this one."

"Don't need no friends," Conroy answered. "I need a good guard dog. One that'll attack anyone *I* say to attack. One that'll protect me with his life no matter how I whop the shit out of 'im."

"That's why you bought a dog?" I said. "To whop the shit out of him?"

"For protection, Liddy," Conroy said. "Now, look at this." He looked down at the dog. "Nice, Maneater, let her make nice."

He turned to me and said, "Go ahead and pet him now."

"Once burned, twice shy, Conroy."

"Go ahead, Liddy." His smile bordered on a smirk.

Call me irresponsible, but I reached out for the dog again. This time, he was as passive as a baby, moaning under my touch.

"Amazing," I said.

"Now if *you* tell him to be nice," Conroy said, "it won't mean a thing. He only responds to *my* voice, *my* words. That's what I call a well-trained dog."

"You trained him?" I asked.

"Of course not, girlie!" More laughter mixed with coughing. "I spent six months looking for the choicest breeders, another six sorting through litters to find the perfect pup. *Look* at 'im, girl. Broad chest, strong shoulders, massive forequarters, a jaw as powerful as a vice. Look, *look*!"

I looked.

Conroy spat, then continued. "Before he was even weaned from his mama's tit, I hired the best trainer money could afford. And now he's all mine. Perfect dog for the perfect man."

I gazed down upon Maneater's mug. The pleasure of my company had worn off and he was growling again.

"I don't know, Conroy," I said. "A dog that mean. He could get you into lots of trouble."

"Bull piss," Conroy spat. "You know how them thieves are. They see Malibu, they think money, money, money. Well, let them burgle the other condos! No one's gonna touch *my* property unless they wanna be hamburger."

"I don't know, Conroy," I said again. "You'd better keep him locked up during the day or else there's going to be trouble."

Conroy's mouth turned into one of his evil grins. "Liddy, where does a two-ton elephant sleep?"

"Where?" I said.

"Anywhere he wants," Conroy said. "Get what I'm saying?"

I got what he was saying. But before I closed the door, I reiterated my warning. He'd better keep an eye on the dog.

And of course Conroy, being the cooperative fellow that he was, let the dog go wherever he pleased. The dog tore up Mrs. Nelson's geranium boxes, turned over Mrs. Bermuda's trash cans, and peed on Dr. Haberson's BMW car cover. He chased after the resident dogs and cats—terrified them so badly, they refused to go out for walks even when carried by their owners. Maneater should have been called Bird Eater. He ingested with gusto the avian life that roosted in the banana bushes, chased sea gulls, spraying feathers along the walkways. Whenever he ran along the shore, he kicked sand and grit in everyone's faces.

Since his purchase of Maneater, Conroy had taken many more day trips. When he went away, the dog posted guard in front of the corner condo, not letting anyone get within ten feet of it. Postal carriers stopped delivering mail to neighboring units, leaving letters in a clump at the guardhouse. The gardeners refused to maintain the nearby lawns and planter boxes. Soon the greenery gave way to invading weeds, the grass dried up until it was a patch of straw.

But the biggest problem had to do with the walkway. One of the two main beach access paths curved by Conroy's condo. Technically, you could pass without getting lunged at if you hugged the extreme right side of the walkway. But pity the poor soul who wasn't aware of this and walked in the middle. Maneater would leap up and scare him to a near faint. Most of us learned to avoid the path whenever Conroy was away. But that wasn't the point at all.

Conroy thought it was hysterically funny. The rest of the tenants were livid. They tried the individual approach, knocking on Conroy's door, only to get frightened away by a low-pitched growl and a flash of white teeth. Every time they were turned away, they heard the old man laugh and hack. One of the tenants finally took the step and called in Animal Control. Problem was that Maneater hadn't actually succeeded with any of his attempted attacks. Unless they caught him in the act, there wasn't anything they could do.

So the people of the Estates did what they usually do when at wit's end. They called a condo meeting: *Sans* Conroy, of course.

The complaints came fast and furious.

"This used to be a peaceful co-op until Conroy and his dog came along. We didn't pay all this money to have to be scared stiff by a wild beast or have sand thrown on our backs. This is Malibu, for God's sake. People just don't behave like that here. Something has to be done. And it has to be done immediately. Call the City Council. Call the movie-star mayor and ask him to declare Malibu a pitbull free zone. Call the Chamber of Commerce."

After living in Malibu all these years, we all knew that the local political bodies didn't wield any real power. It was the moneyed ones with their connections downtown who sat on the throne. And since none of us in this development had enough California gold to buy us the ordinance we needed, we were left to deal with the problem on our own.

That left just one recourse. Someone would have to convince Conroy to keep his dog tied up or on a leash. Someone would have to square off with him face-to-face. Someone would be appointed to speak for the group.

That someone was me.

I knocked on his door, identified myself, and Conroy told me to come in.

He was on the floor wrestling with Maneater, baiting the dog with a raw steak. The match was hot and heavy, Conroy all red-faced and panting, saliva and bits of tobacco leaking out of his mouth. Every time the dog would try to get the meat, Conroy would whip him across the back with a blackjack. I hated the dog, but I winced whenever the leather made contact with the rippling canine muscles. Maneater's pelt was striped with oozing red lines, his legs and paws inflamed. The pitbull was *furious*, snapping, growling, digging in with his hind legs as if ready to charge. But he never so much as laid a paw on Conroy. I wondered how long *that* was going to last.

"He's going to maul you one of these days," I said.

"Not a chance."

"I wouldn't be so sure of that," I said.

Conroy stopped wrestling, spat into a bowl and told the pitbull to be nice to me. I went over and petted the poor thing. At last, Conroy threw the steak to the ceiling and gave Maneater verbal permission to fetch it. The dog leaped into the air and caught it on the rebound.

"I'm telling you," I said. "He's going to get you."

"You don't know a thing, Liddy, so quit wastin' your breath. This dog was well trained. I spent two years finding the right breeders. . . ."

He launched into his Maneater pedigree speech. When it was over, I shook my head. "I don't know, Conroy. Seems to me the dog is angry because he's mistreated."

"They need a strong hand, girl."

"But not a cruel one."

"What are you, Liddy? Some kind of dog headshrinker?"

"I know an angry dog when I see one."

"He's supposed to be angry, girlie," Conroy said. "That's what he was trained to do."

"But it goes beyond that," I said. "He's a menace, Conroy. He doesn't just protect, he destroys."

Conroy spat again. "The condo board must be pretty pissed 'bout him guarding the accessway."

And there it was. The famous Conroy smirk!

"That," I said, "but much more. Maneater charges after the local cats and dogs—"

"If the local cats and dogs come too close, he's gonna chase them," Conroy said. "If *they'd* stay away, Maneater wouldn't do nothin'."

"When he runs on the beach, he kicks sand in everyone's faces, Conroy."

"Well, ain't that too bad." Conroy smirked. "How 'bout if I teach him to say 'Scuse me'?" Then he laughed and hacked, laughed and hacked and finally spat. "They don't like sand, tell them to get off the beach."

"They like the sand, just not in their faces."

"That's their problem, Liddy."

"Conroy, the beach belongs to the whole group."

"They got a complaint with Maneater," Conroy said, "take it up with him. Otherwise, tell them to mind their own damn business."

"You're not going to do anything about curbing the dog's behavior?" I said.

"Girlie, I spent hard-earned money on training him to do what he's doing," Conroy said. "Don't particularly feel like undoing it right now."

I was disgusted. I turned to leave, but before I did, I repeated that the dog was going to get him.

And Conroy? He just laughed and coughed.

No doubt about it. We were stuck with the two of them.

I remember the Sunday because it was such a perfect beach day. The sky was cloudless, smogless, a rich iridescent blue and full of gulls and pelicans. The sun was strong, shining on the water like a ribbon of gold. The ocean was just right for swimming—seventy degrees with mild waves breaking against the shore in tufts of soft white foam. A saline breeze wafted through the air. Everyone was outdoors building sand castles, reading or just working on their tans.

We were a funny sight. All of us bunched up on the left side of the beach, tobacco-cheeked Conroy and Maneater owning the right. It didn't seem the least bit fair, but what could we do about it? The inequity had become a fact of life.

Conroy was in perfect form, laughing and coughing, goading

us with kissy noises and rude names. We tried to ignore him, but it was getting more intolerable by the minute.

"You guys are lily-livered pussies. Afraid of Maneater. Lookie here."

He took a towel and whacked Maneater on the back. A gasp rose from our group.

"Here he goes again," I said.

"Why does he do that?" Mrs. Bermuda said.

"Because he's a sociopath," said Dr. Haberson. "And that's a professional diagnosis."

"Lookie here," Conroy teased. "You pussies *couldn't* be afraid of a dog like this."

Conroy kicked the pitbull in the stomach. The dog let out a high-pitched squeal, followed by an angry bark.

"Can't we call the ASPCA?" Mrs. Nelson said.

"He'd just deny it," Mrs. Bermuda said.

"Not if we could show marks on the animal," Dr. Haberson said.

"And who could prove Bittune made the marks?" Mrs. Bermuda said.

"Do something, Liddy," Mrs. Nelson said.

"I tried," I said. "He won't listen." I yelled to Conroy. "He's going to get you one day!"

"In a pig's eye, Liddy."

"Yes, he will."

"Yes, he will," Conroy imitated me. "Just lookie at this, girl."

He punched the dog in the snout. Did it again. The dog started circling him like a hawk around its prey.

I eyed Dr. Haberson, Dr. Haberson eyed Mrs. Bermuda. Conroy was making nervous wrecks out of all of us. The dog was getting more and more agitated—barking louder, baring his teeth.

"You're a bleeping sadist, Bittune!" Mrs. Nelson shouted. "Any second now that dog's going to chew you up!"

With that, Conroy doubled over with big, deep guffaws, followed by his spasmodic cough. His face was flushed, beaded with sweat. "You pussies!" he screamed. "Lookie here!"

He grabbed the dog by the neck and yanked him down onto the sand. Then he picked him up by the front paws and swung him around, huffing and puffing from the effort. The dog was all snarls and barks during the ride.

"Watch it, Conroy," I shouted. "Maneater's starting to foam at the mouth."

"Wimps!" Conroy shouted back, spraying bits of saliva and tobacco out of his mouth. "You weak, itty bitty pussies!"

He put the dog down and doubled over. We expected to hear more derisive laughter but none came.

We waited a couple of seconds, a half minute, a minute. The dog was still snarling. Suddenly everyone became aware that no one was talking.

Finally, Mrs. Bermuda said, "What's with Bittune?"

Good question. Even the dog looked puzzled. Conroy's face had turned deep red and he was jumping up and down.

"A rare Indian rain dance?" Mrs. Bermuda said.

"Figures," Mrs. Nelson said. "Conroy *would* rain on our parade."

"I don't think that's what he's doing," I said.

Conroy was still jumping, his face getting redder and redder. One hand went to his chest, the other to his neck. He seemed to be gasping for air.

I jumped up and shouted, "He's having a heart attack!"

Applause broke out.

"We've got to help him," I yelled.

No one said a word.

"Dr. Haberson," I scolded, "we both know CPR. We've got to—"

"All right, all right," Dr. Haberson said. He got up slowly, brushed the sand from his legs. Meanwhile, Conroy's lips had turned blue.

I ran toward the old man, but was immediately halted by Maneater's growl.

"Nice dog," I tried. "Make nice, nice dog."

I took a step forward and so did he. I took a step backward and so did he.

"For God's sake, Conroy," I shouted in desperation. "Call Maneater off!"

Conroy pointed to his throat.

"You're *choking*?" I said.

Conroy gave a vigorous nod.

His right cheek was empty.

"The tobacco! He's choking on his *tobacco*," I yelled out. "Give Maneater a hand signal."

Conroy flailed his hands in the air. Maneater sat, acting as though the signals meant something. Yet when I tried to approach Conroy, the dog lunged at me.

We were hamstrung. The dog wouldn't let us near Conroy, and Conroy couldn't call Maneater off.

"Hit your chest, old man," Dr. Haberson said. "Try to do a Heimlich maneuver on yourself. Hit your sternum hard! Right here!" Dr. Haberson demonstrated the procedure.

Conroy tried and tried again. Meanwhile, he was turning bluer and bluer.

"Give it another try, Conroy!" I said. "Or just hold the dog off physically."

By then, Conroy was the color of the sky. He fell onto the sand and blacked out, his body shaking as if he were having a seizure. It was awful. Maneater circled his master, licking his quivering arms and legs, nudging his face. But he snarled at anyone who attempted to come within helping range.

Mrs. Bermuda said, "First time I've ever seen a dog protect his master to death."

We tried to tempt Maneater away with meat. We tried to poke him away. We even tried a decoy method, using me as bait. Nothing would lure him away from his master. By the time Animal Control came with the tranquilizing gun, it was too late.

The dog was well trained.

Susan Kelly's first novel, The Gemini Man, *nominated for a 1985 Anthony, featured writer Liz Connors and Cambridge police officer Jack Lingemann.* The Summertime Soldiers, Trail of the Dragon, *and* Until Proven Innocent *continued Liz and Jack's adventures. Consultant to the Simmons College New England Writers' Workshop and to the Massachusetts Criminal Justice Training Council, Susan informs her work with an affectionate skepticism that illuminates the flaws, strengths, and stumblings of a wide spectrum of people at the same time she entertains her readers.*

In "The Healer," Liz Connors must heal herself when she discovers the facts surrounding her physician's death.

THE HEALER

by Susan Kelly

WHEN SOMEBODY MURDERS your gynecologist, that's *news.*

I found out about the shooting death of Dr. Warren Hastings on a cold and dank Tuesday morning in February. Both Boston papers ran articles about the killing—the *Globe* on the first page of the Metro section and the *Herald* on page four.

To say I was stunned by the event was to understate my reaction to it.

I'd always liked Warren Hastings. Unlike some of his predecessors in my medical history, he'd treated me as if I had some claim to be an intelligent adult. Did that make him unusual, or just nice?

Whatever—pretty clearly, someone else hadn't shared my good opinion of the man.

Dr. Hastings died in his office in Cambridge, which is where I live. The city, not the office. My name is Elizabeth Connors. I'm a free-lance writer. My specialty is true crime and law enforcement. I used to be a college English professor, but I bailed out of that racket as soon as the opportunity to earn an honest living arose. I'm thirty-seven years old. I've never been married. I don't live with anyone. I have a dog. I also have a companion. He's a detective-lieutenant in the Cambridge Police Department. He investigates a lot of murders.

He might very well be investigating Warren Hastings's.

I was sure as hell going to ask.

There might be a story in it.

Does that sound cold? I hope not. We all have our own ways of dealing with the violence that blears and smudges our lives. Writing about it is mine.

It wasn't as if I hadn't anything else to write. I had plenty. I was, in fact, working on two articles: one about women DEA agents, and the other about a serial killer who had ravaged western Massachusetts and eastern Vermont for two years. His victims had been elementary-school-age boys. It was a horribly painful piece to write. I'd work on it for as long as I could bear—an hour or so—and then turn, with relief, to the profile of the drug investigators. The deadline for the latter was a lot closer anyway.

I also had a letter from a woman named Demelza Farrell, whom I'd never heard of before she wrote to ask if she could give me some information for a possible article on the sexual abuse of children.

The letter had been sitting on my desk for ten days. Unanswered. It wasn't that I was offended at receiving mail from a total stranger. Like most magazine and newspaper feature writers, I very often get suggestions for article subjects from people I don't know, as well as from editors and friends. Some of them are actually helpful.

The trouble was, I had just recently completed a three-part series on the sexual abuse of children, and I didn't even want to think about the subject for a while. Grappling with the northern New England serial killer was bad enough.

As I left for the police station, it occurred to me that I might be using the murder of Warren Hastings as a convenient excuse to escape, even if briefly, from child-rapists and child-killers.

Jack was just arriving at his office as I was. He had a brown paper bag in his right hand. He grinned when he saw me.

"By God," he said. "I bet I can guess why you're here."

"Pleasure of your company," I said.

"Uh-huh." He unlocked his office door. "That plus whatever I know about the city's latest homicide statistic. Well, come on in."

I preceded him into the office and sat down in the visitor's chair before the desk. He gave me the brown paper bag and then took off his coat and hung it on a hook behind the door.

"You had any lunch yet?" he asked.

I shook my head.

He gestured at the bag in my lap. "Want to split a large tuna sub and some potato chips?"

"Sure."

He sat down behind the desk, although not before removing his suit coat and draping it over the back of the chair. He began rolling up his shirt sleeves.

"Warren Hastings was my gynecologist," I said.

Jack stopped in the act of turning back his left cuff and looked at me sharply. "I didn't know that."

I smiled slightly. "I never had occasion to tell you before today."

"How long have—had—you been going to him?"

I took the sandwich and the potato chips from the bag. "Two years." I began unwrapping the sub. "I switched to him on the recommendation of a friend."

"What friend?"

"Chris Cameron."

He nodded.

"I couldn't stand the jerk I went to before Hastings," I said, ripping open the potato chip bag.

"Not competent?" Jack asked.

I shook my head. "No, I think he was probably an excellent diagnostician. Too temperamental for my taste, though."

Jack took a bite of his sandwich. "How so?"

"He got mad at me for having a narrow pelvis."

Jack paused to swallow. Then he said, "Excuse me?"

"I'm telling you true. He threw the speculum on the floor and pouted that he just didn't know how he could do a proper examination on me."

Jack put his sandwich on a paper napkin on the desk blotter. "Uh," he said, "don't they come in different sizes?"

"What? Pelvises?"

"No, dear. Speculums. Speculae."

I shrugged. "I never thought about it."

Jack rubbed his right index finger over his upper lip. "Liz?"

"Yes?"

"Do you mind if I laugh?"

"Go ahead. I'll join you."

When the hilarity abated, we went back to lunch.

I held out the potato chip bag to Jack.

"Okay," he said, taking a few of the chips. "I can see why you changed doctors."

"Uh-huh." I put the potato chips on the desk between us. "So. All humor aside—what the hell happened to Warren Hastings?"

"Somebody shot him twice in the chest at close range."

"Any idea who?"

"None at all." Jack ate another bite of his sandwich.

"Is it your case?"

"Mine and Bobby St. Germain's and Artie Lorenzo's. And the usual contingent from the state police."

"I see."

Jack finished his sandwich. He balled up the waxed paper wrapper and tossed it into the trash basket. Then he wiped his hands on a paper napkin.

"Since you were one of Hastings's patients," he said, "can I ask you some questions about him?"

I was a little startled. "Sure. I really don't know what I can tell you, though."

"At this stage," Jack said, "any information might be helpful."

"You have no suspects?"

He shook his head. "Don't have much of anything."

"Well, I only saw Hastings a few times." I crunched a potato chip. "But . . . ask your questions."

He took a pad of white lined paper from the top desk drawer and tossed it onto the desk blotter. Preparation for note taking. I didn't think he'd fill up a lot of paper recording what I had to say.

"All right," Jack said. "Why don't you start out giving me your general impressions of Hastings?"

I ate another potato chip, slowly. "Well, the best thing about him, other than the fact that he wasn't a prima donna and didn't get huffy with me 'cause I'm not built like the Callahan Tunnel—''

Jack made a faint snorting noise and compressed his lips.

"All right, sorry," I said. "I couldn't resist that. I won't screw around anymore."

He wasn't quite able to suppress a further snicker. "You're developing a cop's sense of humor. Black.''

"Must be contagious. Okay. Back to Hastings. Other than the fact that he seemed sane and competent, he was . . . '' I made a vague circle with my right hand. "You could talk to him. He was very open and accessible. Simpatico, I guess. He didn't patronize or condescend, either.''

"Sounds as if you liked him a lot.''

"I did. So did Chris Cameron.''

"All right. Go on.''

"Geez, what else. He was a big, fairly attractive guy. Late forties? Early fifties? Something around there. Very fit-looking. But you probably know all that.''

Jack made a wry face. "He didn't look too terrific when I saw him.''

"No, I guess he wouldn't have.''

Jack nodded and put down his pen. The pad before him was blank. He leaned back in his chair, linking his hands behind his head. "I've talked to a couple of other people who tell me exactly what you say about Hastings.''

I finished the potato chips. "Not much of a motive for murder, is there?''

"None, unless somebody was jealous of Hastings's charm and good looks.''

"Which I gather you think at this point is unlikely.''

He smiled. "I'll keep it in mind as a last resort.''

"Who discovered the body?''

"The cleaning person who did the offices. Last night at eight-thirty.''

"Was the office all torn up?''

"No, everything was in perfect order, as far as Hastings's receptionist and nurse could tell.''

"Where was the body?''

"In the chair behind the desk. It looks as if Hastings had been sitting there talking to whoever shot him.''

"Then I guess whoever killed him wasn't somebody who broke in looking for drugs or money.''

Jack shrugged without taking his hands from behind his head. "There were no signs of forced entry."

I deposited the remainder of the lunch wrappings in the wastebasket. "Sounds as if you have a mystery on your hands."

He made another face. "I hate mysteries."

I smiled. "Cheer up. Maybe the villain will stagger in here and confess. It happens."

"Oh, absolutely. And he'll be followed by a delegation from the League of Women Voters wanting to draft me as the next attorney general of Massachusetts."

"Seriously," I said, "not to tell you what you already know, but whoever shot Hastings had a reason for doing it. I mean, they didn't just walk in off the street and pop him for the hell of it. Although I guess those things do happen, too."

"Probably not in this case."

I drummed my fingers on the arms of my chair.

"The two guys from the state police are questioning the other doctors and nurses and whoever in Hastings's office building," Jack said. "Artie and Bobby are doing his personal background."

I lifted my eyebrows. "Anything there?"

"It's a little early to say, isn't it? We *do* know that Hastings was divorced."

"So does that make his ex-wife an automatic suspect?"

"Well," Jack replied in judicious tones, "it *has* happened. Although in my experience, it's mostly the ex-husband who kills the ex-wife. But . . ." He jerked his right shoulder as if there were a bird perched there that he wanted to shoo. "On the basis of what very little information I have about her so far, the former Mrs. Hastings—her name is Elise, if you care— doesn't sound as if she had any grudge against Warren. Not a big enough one to kill him, anyway. The divorce wasn't a bloodbath. She didn't gouge him for a huge settlement or ali- mony, and he in his turn didn't fight her stipulations for child support. Or renege on them afterward. So neither side had reason to be pissed at the other for failing to live up to the agreement they made." Jack leaned back a little farther in his chair. "Elise and the kids live in Minnesota now. Hastings had generous visitation rights with the boy and the girl, which as far as I hear, Elise was scrupulous about complying with."

"Sounds as if you already know a lot about the doctor's personal life," I said.

"Oh, honey. That's just scratching the surface. God knows what Artie and Bobby might dig up in time."

I nodded. In my reporting career I'd overturned a lot of sludgy black dirt on people who'd publicly led Ozzie and Harriet family lives.

"So what part of Hastings's background are you investigating?" I asked.

"At the moment? His finances."

"What about them?"

"He was rich."

"Most established doctors aren't living on the poverty line."

"Sure. But Hastings had inherited money, too. Which he had managed to sock into some pretty good investments. Also, he was a partner in a couple of hot real estate deals here and in Brookline."

"You think there might be something in that?"

Jack gave me a thoughtful look. "What do you mean?"

"I'm thinking what I assume you think I'm thinking. Not to let speculation carry me away, but maybe Hastings found out one of his partners was a crook, and he was going to blow the whistle on him. And the partner killed him to shut him up. Or maybe Hastings was the crook. Or maybe he was overextended and went to the sharks for a loan and couldn't pay up and—"

"There's no evidence of any of those things. So far."

"But you won't rule them out."

"I never rule out anything."

"So I've noticed."

Jack pushed his chair back from the desk. "Would you like some coffee?"

"Love some."

He got up and left the office. I put my chin in my hand and let my mind wander.

A phone rang in the outer office. A pair of detectives, male and female, came through the swinging doors. They were laughing together softly.

Jack returned with two Styrofoam cups. He handed me one. I smiled my thanks. He went back to his seat behind the desk.

"Something just occurred to me," I said.

"What's that?"

"Was Hastings ever sued for malpractice?"

Jack gave me the same sharp glance of interest he'd given

me when I'd announced that I'd been Hastings's patient. "Good question," he said. "Not so far as I know."

"Oh." I chewed my lower lip ruminatively.

"He may have been at some point," Jack added. "If he ever was, I'll find out pretty quickly."

I nodded. "If the plaintiff lost the suit . . ."

"Yes?"

"Well, whoever it was might want to—how shall I put it?—exact the retribution denied her by the courts?"

"Her? Who are you thinking of?"

"Hypothetically?" I shrugged. "A woman Hastings treated whose pregnancy ended badly. In a miscarriage or a stillbirth. Like that. And the courts didn't find Hastings culpable or negligent or however the legal terminology goes. But the woman was still convinced that he'd mishandled her case? Not given her the proper treatment?" I made another loop with my right hand. "It wouldn't even have to be the baby's mother. It could be the father." I paused a moment. "Somebody crazed with grief."

Jack blew out his breath. "Yeah." He reclasped his hands behind his head. "Yeah," he repeated.

"I hope it's not that," I said.

He nodded.

We were quiet. The human silence was punctuated by the backfire of a car on Green Street. The sound reminded me of gunshots in the night, although in reality most gunfire doesn't sound like backfire.

Jack took his hands from behind his head, leaned forward, and put his elbows on the desk. He was still gazing in my direction. But I could tell from his expression that he wasn't seeing *me* any longer.

I let a few seconds pass. Then I said, "Earth to Lieutenant Lingemann."

He gave the minutest of starts. "Oh. Yeah. Liz?"

"Yes?"

"Did Hastings perform abortions?"

It was I who was now a little taken aback. "Abortions?"

"Yes."

I frowned. "I suppose . . . I don't . . . well, sure, he must have at some stage in his career. For whatever reason. A gynecologist would, right?"

Jack made a note on his pad. "I gotta find out if he was ever

affiliated in one way or another with one of the family planning
clinics.''

''I can't help you with that,'' I said. ''I know he was connected with the Commonwealth Memorial Hospital. I imagine
if he performed abortions, he did at least some of them there.
From what I saw of the examining rooms at his Cambridge
office, they weren't equipped for that sort of surgical procedure. It's hard for me to say. It's not a question I've ever faced.
Thank God.''

Jack nodded absently, still scribbling on his pad.

I said, ''I know what you have on your mind.''

''Do you?''

''Uh-huh. You're wondering if Hastings got plugged by one
of the more out-of-control elements of the antiabortion movement. Like the ones who don't even believe that a woman
should abort to save her own life. What kind of mentality is
that?''

Jack shrugged. ''The kind that could decide to kill the doctor
who kills the babies. That could be somebody's logic.''

''Yes,'' I said. ''It could.''

Lunch and talking took up a half hour. After that, Jack had
to go back out on the street. ''Time to try and detect something,'' was the way he put it.

I walked downstairs with him. Outside on Green Street the
rain was a soft but persistent drizzle.

''Anything in particular you'd like for dinner tonight?'' I
asked, raising my umbrella.

Jack smiled at me. ''Whatever you decide is fine.''

''Okay. I'll see you around . . . seven?''

He nodded. ''That's good.''

''Luck with finding out about Hastings.''

''Yeah,'' Jack replied, in somewhat sour tones. He looked
at the dripping sky. ''Beam me up, Scotty,'' he said. ''This
case sucks.''

Does it surprise you that Jack should so fully discuss with
me the details of an open police investigation? It shouldn't. A
lot of cops do the same with their lovers or spouses. A few I
know do it anonymously with newspaper columnists.

Anyhow, Jack's known me long enough to know that I have

the sense to keep my mouth shut about sensitive police business.

At dinner that night he was quiet and abstracted. Preoccupied. He apparently hadn't learned anything more about Hastings's financial situation that would help identify the doctor's killer. Probably Bobby and Artie and the staties hadn't produced the goods, either. Jack would have mentioned if they'd been on to something.

Unusual as this murder case may have been in some respects, it was just like any other in one very important way. If it wasn't solved quickly, it wouldn't be solved at all.

I spent the next few days working on the article about the DEA agents. It went well.

The serial killer piece I set aside. I didn't have a tight deadline for that one anyway.

The investigation into Warren Hastings's death continued. From what I understood from Jack over drinks Thursday evening, it still wasn't going anywhere.

The medical examiner released Hastings's body to his exwife. A notice in both Boston papers said that the funeral and burial services would be private, with a memorial service to be scheduled at a later date.

I wrapped up the piece on the DEA agents Friday afternoon. I had mixed feelings about completing the project. On the one hand, I'm always pleased to have finished something, especially if I'm happy with the kind of writing job I did. On the other hand, now I'd have to work full-time on the serial killer piece.

Not till tomorrow, though. I'd take a break this evening. Maybe have an early dinner out with Jack. Then go back to his house to watch a rented movie on the VCR.

I gave the DEA article a final proofreading, stuck it in a manila envelope, and took it to the post office.

When I got home, the message light on my answering machine was blinking frenetically. The first recorded call was from Jack, telling me that he'd be held up at work and probably wouldn't be free until nine or nine-thirty. So much for my

notion about the two of us going out together for an early dinner. We could still do the rental movie, though, and split a
take-out pizza or Chinese food.

The second message was from a woman called Demelza Farrell. It took me a second to remember that that was the name
of the woman who'd written me the letter I still hadn't answered. The letter about the sexual abuse of children.

Her voice was soft and rather hesitant. What she said was,
"I'm trying to get in touch with Elizabeth Connors. I have
some information for an article she might be interested in writing. My number is 617-555-6722. Thank you very much."

The tape ended and rewound. I stared at the answering machine, frowning a little. There had been no hint of reproach in
either the content or tone of Demelza Farrell's message for my
failure to respond to her letter. Which, of course, made me
feel incredibly guilty for not having done so.

Her muted voice was a cultivated one, educated and intelligent. Not at all like those of some of the crackpots who called
me with what they think are fabulous article ideas.

I let my dog, Lucy, out for a brief run in the enclosed back-
yard. When she came back from her travels, I fed her.

Then I returned Demelza Farrell's call.

I really don't like being rude. And feeling guilty.

And so what if she was going to tell me a story I didn't want
to hear? For a crime writer, that's part of the deal.

The Casablanca is a subterranean bar on Brattle Street behind Harvard Square. A developer has it slated for demolition.
A tragedy, as far as I'm concerned. With its checked table-
cloths and blown-up stills of Bergman and Bogart, the Casa B
is as much a part of Cambridge history as the George Washington elm on the Common. The honor roll of writers and
artists and musicians who passed their nights getting incredibly
drunk on these premises goes on and on and on. . . .

Demelza Farrell had suggested we meet there. Perhaps she
thought the place appropriate for one of my calling. Also, it
was quite dark.

At five-thirty on a Friday evening, the Casablanca was fairly
crowded. I strolled through it slowly, peering through the murk
in hopes of identifying someone who resembled the description
of herself Farrell had given me. I didn't spot anyone who remotely looked like the person I was seeking.

Cruise completed, I grabbed one of the few empty tables left and sat down to wait. Maybe Farrell had been delayed. Or had had second thoughts about talking to me. They do that, sources. A waitress with buttock-length black braids asked me what I'd like to drink. I ordered a vodka martini.

At five-forty, one of the double doors to the bar swung inward to admit a tallish and very slender woman in a tan trench coat. I put down my drink and squinted at her. She took a few tentative steps into the room and came to a halt beside the jukebox. Dark hair parted in the center and drawn back into a loose chignon. Oval face with high cheekbones and small chin. It had to be her. She looked in my direction and I waved. She walked over to my table.

"Elizabeth Connors?" she said.

"Hello." I smiled and held out my hand.

We shook, and she sat down across from me. Unbelting and unbuttoning her coat, she wriggled out of it and let it fall in folds over the back of the chair. She set her purse in her lap.

The waitress reappeared. Farrell ordered a glass of red wine. We appraised each other through the cocktail-hour gloom, she with a bit of wariness and me with considerable curiosity. I don't know what she saw, but what I was looking at was a woman probably in her mid-thirties, with nacreous skin and large, slightly slanted blue eyes. Her mouth was wide and tinted with a deep rose lipstick. She was wearing a brown knit turtleneck dress and a heavy antique gold chain. She was quite beautiful. If I had been a man, I would have supposed—or hoped—that this was my lucky night.

The waitress set a glass of burgundy down before her. Farrell let the drink sit, which I thought was interesting. And different. Usually when I meet strangers in bars to hear their stories, the first thing they do is grab and gulp half their first glass of whatever before they speak. This woman seemed a bit tense to me. But poised enough to control it.

"Thank you for meeting me," she said. "Especially since I'm a total stranger."

I smiled. "To be blunt, you sounded a lot more sensible than some of the cuckoos who call me with what they assume are terrific ideas."

I'd intended the remark to be jocular and reassuring. Apparently it was. I could see her relax. She sipped her wine.

"Demelza," I said. "That's a lovely name. Unusual. Does it run in your family?"

She nodded. "It was my great-great-grandmother's. And a great-aunt's."

"Perhaps it'll get handed on to the next generation."

"No," she said curtly. "I don't think so."

I had made a blunder of some sort. I was silent.

She had another drink of her wine. Then, without taking the customary deep breath or indeed making any other kind of preparatory gesture, she said, "As I told you on the phone, what I want to talk about with you concerns the sexual abuse of a female child."

I tried to be careful about how I phrased the question that followed naturally out of such a declaration. "Do you have a special reason for wanting to tell me in particular?"

She looked at me straight on across the table. "You've written about the subject before. I've read what you've written. I . . . it was well done."

I nodded slightly to indicate my thanks.

"You tried to put yourself in the victim's place," she continued. "That was good, that you did that."

I nodded again, watching her.

"This story I'm going to tell you," she said. "I was the victim."

I drew a long, quiet breath. "I see."

"Do you?"

I said nothing.

"When I was five years old," she said. "My brother started raping me. He was sixteen at the time."

I folded my hands on the tabletop. I had heard several stories like this. I never got used to hearing them.

"It went on for two years," she continued. "Then he went away to college." She lifted her right hand to her face and pushed back a wisp of hair that was beginning to escape from the chignon. "After that, he was only home for vacations. He never touched me again in . . . that way. Maybe he had a girlfriend at school." The hand that she'd used to stroke back her hair twiddled with the stem of her glass.

"Did you tell your parents?" I asked.

"No." She moistened her lips. "My brother told me it was our little secret game we were playing, and that Mommy and Daddy wouldn't understand."

"Did you have any sisters? Were they—?"

"No. I was the youngest of four children. I have three older brothers. *He* was the oldest." She glanced over at the bar, and then back at me. "Could we get another drink?"

I hadn't noticed she'd finished hers. "Of course." I signaled to the waitress.

Demelza said, "Neither of my other brothers ever did anything to me."

I leaned forward a bit across the table. "And your parents had no idea what was going on? None at all?"

She shook her head, somewhat wearily. "No. He only did it to me when they weren't home. If they were out for the evening, say, and he was baby-sitting me and the others."

The waitress came to the table and I reordered.

When the waitress had left, Demelza said, "He didn't do it every time he was alone with me. Just a few times a month. Maybe three. Enough."

A lot more than enough, I thought.

The waitress delivered our drinks and cleared away the empty glasses.

"There were a lot of games he and I played," Demelza said. "He taught me how to"—she paused to sip her wine— "perform oral sex on him. He said what came out of him was special milk. Good for me."

I flinched automatically. She noticed and nodded, as if acknowledging my reaction.

I took a mouthful of my drink.

"Now comes the strangest part," she said.

I looked at her.

"I forgot it all," she said. "It stopped, and afterward, it must have been right afterward, I blanked on it. When he came home from college the first Christmas, he was . . . just my big brother. Nothing else. I had no memory of him and me doing anything."

I hesitated a moment. Then I said, "That's not at all uncommon, from what I understand. The mind can't handle a certain memory. So it buries it. Or transforms it into something else."

She smiled wryly. "Yes. I've read that."

I picked up my drink. "When did the memory come back?"

Her eyes strayed away from my face and focused on something above and behind my right shoulder. "I never dated in high school," she said. "I had friends who were boys, but I never went out with any of them." She looked back at me. "I didn't want to."

"You were scared of what might happen if you did?"

She shook her head as if puzzled. "I must have been. But I didn't know it. That I was scared. I'd just pull away anytime any boy acted as if he . . . liked me more than as just a friend. It was . . . a reflex. To pull away."

"I see."

She rubbed her palms together in a slow, hard, circular motion. "In college, it was the same. I went to a women's school. Even so, there were opportunities to meet men. Dances and mixers and all. My roommates tried to fix me up with guys they knew. I could never . . . you know." She smiled painfully. "I even thought I might be gay. That *that* was my problem. That I was trying to deny my true inclinations or suppress them. Some damn thing." She drank her wine. "It wasn't that."

"No," I said.

"I didn't know what it was," she said. "All I knew was that . . . when I thought about sex and about getting into bed with a man, naked, I—"

"What?" I prompted softly.

"Just thinking about it would make me feel as if I were suffocating."

I nodded.

"After college I went to graduate school. I got a master's in art history." She gave me another small smile, this one a little less pained than the previous one. "It wasn't so much of a problem there, with the men."

"Yes," I said. "Graduate school has a tendency to make people asexual. All the energy gets used up studying or worrying about the job market."

She laughed very slightly. "I see you've been."

"Uh-huh."

"After I got my master's, I got an assistant curator's job at a museum in Williamstown. I was lucky; it was just the kind of work I wanted. I stayed in it for five years. Up until the time I got married."

I raised my eyebrows.

"I know," she said. "I know what you're thinking. Why would a woman who feared and hated sex get married?"

I was silent.

She sighed. "I met Dennis at a party. He was a professor of

fine art at one of the local colleges. He . . ." She shook her
head vaguely. "He was—is—a very sweet person. Very easygoing. We sat together at dinner that night and got to talking
and . . . I enjoyed myself with him. When he asked me to go
out, I agreed. For some reason he didn't repel me or frighten
me. I didn't have that impulse to draw away."

"I see."

"He respected me." She gave me a quirky half smile. "That
sounds so old-fashioned, doesn't it? So nineteenth-century."

"Not entirely," I said.

"Maybe." She sighed once more. "Anyway, it wasn't until
we'd known each other for a few months that he made a pass at
me. I never questioned his restraint. I was just grateful for it."

"What happened?"

She looked down at her glass. "I tried to respond. I thought
I owed him that much, and anyway, I *did* care for him. But it
didn't work."

"And?"

"I guess he was upset. I don't know if he was angry. If he
was, he hid it well. I tried to explain to him how I felt about
sex, that it terrified me and I didn't know why it did."

"Uh-huh."

"I also told him that if he gave me time, I thought I could
get over the problem."

"Yes."

"He told me that he loved me, and that he understood, sort
of. That he'd sensed something, oh, how did he put it? A little
reserved about me. Or shy. I forget exactly what words he
used, but that, he said, was why he hadn't been more, um,
aggressive. He also told me that maybe I should see a therapist." She picked up her glass. "I was so relieved that he
wasn't furious with me that I said I would."

"Yes."

"I didn't. I told him I was seeing someone, and that the
therapy was working, but I wasn't. He was pleased. A month
later I went to bed with him. Two months later we were married." She looked at me. "I really did love him."

I nodded.

"The sex was awful," she continued. "I expected it would
be the first few times, but then I figured after that, that I might
get used to it, and relax—"

"And finally get to enjoy it."

"Yes."

"Didn't happen that way, did it?"

"No."

"What did Dennis think?"

"He didn't know."

I frowned at her.

"I faked it," she said flatly. "After a while, I got good at that. Dennis was delighted." She shrugged. "I guess I thought that *one* of us deserved some pleasure out of it."

I exhaled softly.

"Still," she said, "I thought I could hack it. Make the marriage go. Everything else about it was good. The companionship, the closeness, all we had in common."

"But . . ."

"Yes. I started having the nightmares."

"Oh."

"They started about three months after we were married."

I sipped my drink.

"They were horrible. They . . ." She blinked and shook herself slightly.

"All right," I said. "Don't describe them to me unless you can do it without tearing yourself apart. I can guess what they were about, anyway."

She was quiet for a moment, as if regrouping. "Yes, I guess you can."

"And then?"

"It all started to fall apart." She brushed the fingers of her right hand across her forehead. "It got harder and harder for me to fake . . . you know . . . and finally impossible. It got to the point where I couldn't bear to be in the same bed as Dennis. Finally . . ."

"Finally what?"

"I had to leave him." She paused. "It was a week before our first anniversary. I couldn't stand it anymore. I couldn't even stand him hugging me."

"Jesus," I said.

"It was terrible," she said. "For me. For Dennis."

"He must have been devastated."

"He was," she replied bleakly. "Can we get another drink?"

"Absolutely." The waitress was standing at the drink preparation area at the end of the bar. I indicated to her by smiling and pointing at our glasses that we wanted a third round. I didn't, especially, but I had to keep Demelza company.

"I don't want to talk about the divorce," she said. "Nor the two years after it. I tried to kill myself twice."

"Oh, God."

"I didn't think I deserved to live. I didn't even feel human."

The drinks arrived. "We have some nice cheese and crackers I've just put out on the table over there," the waitress said.

"Thank you," I replied.

She smiled and went off to wait on somebody else.

"The second time I tried to knock myself off," Demelza continued, "they put me in a sanitarium for six months." She laughed dryly. "God, what a crew there was in there."

"The other patients or the doctors?"

"Both." She sipped her wine. "Anyway, while I was making clay ashtrays and shuffling from group therapy to individual sessions, the nightmares stopped."

"Yes?"

"And the memory came back."

"What did the shrinks say?"

She looked at me for a few seconds. "Nothing. I didn't tell them."

"Wha— I don't understand."

"The memory didn't come back in a session," she explained. "Just in bits and pieces. While I was lying in bed at night trying not to sleep so I wouldn't dream."

"But why didn't you tell the psychiatrist?"

"Because," she said, "it would have interfered with what I had decided to do. What I knew right away, as soon as the first piece of memory came back, that I was going to do."

"Which was?"

"Kill my oldest brother."

I sat very still, staring at her.

"They let me out of the nuthouse four years ago," she said. "Pronounced fit and able to return to society. They were, in fact, amazed by how successfully I'd—what do they call it? Reintegrated. Reintegrated my personality." She drank a little wine. "Psychiatrists aren't hard to fool."

"I've noticed," I said, my eyes still fixed on her.

"Well," she said. "I was *not* going to commit a murder the day after being released from a mental institution. That might have been a bit obvious. So I waited. I could do that. I've been leading what's called a normal life for the past four years now. I have a part-time teaching job at a junior college on the Cape. I opened a gallery in Hyannis. It's doing well. I even see one or two men occasionally. Nothing serious, though. Purely platonic.''

I didn't move except to breathe.

"This week I decided it was time. I drove up here from the Cape."

"Please don't," I said.

"Please don't what?"

"Kill him."

"I already have."

I closed my eyes. When I opened them she was looking at me, her face reflective and a little sad. "God," I said. Her expression didn't change, except perhaps to become more remote. I narrowed my eyes. There was something about the modeling of her cheeks and jaw that I was only seeing now, while her features were in full-faced repose. Something familiar.

I leaned back in my chair, very slowly and stiffly. "Farrell isn't your maiden name, is it?"

"No. It's Dennis's. I decided to keep it after the divorce, for a number of reasons."

"The name you were born with was Hastings, wasn't it?"

"That's right."

"And your oldest brother's name was Warren."

"That's right."

"And last Monday night you shot him to death."

"That's right."

I decided I wanted my third drink.

"I have the gun right here in my purse." She patted the handbag in her lap.

"Jesus, keep your voice down," I hissed.

"Why? What does it matter?"

"You want this whole room to know what you did?"

"They'll find out soon enough." Her voice was very low. "It'll be in the papers, after I tell the police."

"You're going to confess?"

She nodded.

I was bewildered. "Then why did you come to me with the story first?"

She looked impatient. "I told you that already. I want you to write about it. My side of things."

"Don't you care that you might spend the next thirty years in the state prison at Framingham?"

She shook her head. "It doesn't matter. I have no life anyway. Maybe I can teach drawing to the inmates."

"Oh, God." I gulped the rest of my drink.

"I did what I had to do," she said. "I'm satisfied. Whatever happens next isn't important."

"*No.*"

"What?"

I sat up straight. "It's important."

She scowled and started to speak.

"Shut up," I said. "You really want to stay in prison till you're sixty or seventy? You say you don't have any life now. What do you think that life will be in prison? Did you like the cell they put you in in the nuthouse? Shuffling around in a little white johnny with paper slippers on your feet? Weaving baskets and being force-fed drugs? All that will seem swell in comparison to prison."

She put her hands to her face.

"If you don't go to the police," I said, "then as far as I'm concerned, we never had this conversation."

She let her hands drop to her lap.

"Do you really *want* to go to prison? Do you think you *should* go to prison?"

"No," she whispered.

"All right."

"What *do* I do?"

"First of all, listen to me." I ran my eyes around the bar. It wasn't crowded now. There were indeed empty tables on either side of us. "Now, this gun you have . . . is it registered to you?"

She looked startled, then shocked. "No, of course not."

"Is it registered to a friend or relative?"

"No."

"Does anyone but me know you have it or have access to it?"

"No."

"Would you care to tell me how you obtained it?"

She looked at me without replying.

I nodded. "Okay. Probably wiser not to. You're positive there's absolutely no way this gun can be traced to you or connected with you or associated with you in any way whatsoever?"

"Yes, yes, I'm positive."

"Good."

She peered at me. "Why? Why do you want to know? What are you going to do?"

"I'm going to get rid of it for you."

The peer changed to a stare.

"You say you have it with you in your purse," I said.

"Yes. I—it's in a paper bag."

"Unloaded, I hope."

"Yes, certainly."

"Excellent. Now, reach into your purse, get the bag out, and hand it across the table to me."

"What?" She glanced quickly, covertly, at the bar. *"Here?"*

"Just *do* it."

She did.

The bag weighed about a pound. I hefted it a moment, grinned at Demelza, and said, in normal tones, "Thanks so much. I've been looking all over for one of these. How much do I owe you?"

Comprehension dawned on her face. She waved her right hand negligently. "Forget it. I had to pick one up for myself. They were running a special."

"Well, I sure appreciate your trouble." I dropped the gun into my shoulder bag, praying that she had indeed unloaded it, not neglecting any possible chambered round. I could hardly check.

Demelza said, "I don't think anyone noticed that."

I shrugged. "Why would they?"

She took a deep breath. "Now what?"

"Tell me how, exactly, you did it." I returned to a whisper.

She put her elbows on the table. "I had no huge, complicated plan. I closed the gallery at five Monday night, my normal time. I drove up here to Cambridge. I called *him* from an outside phone booth in Kendall Square and told him I wanted to see him."

"About what?"

She smiled. "About buying some more property on the Cape. Warren loves talking real estate deals."

"He was willing to see you?"

"Of course." Her tone was ironic. "He was my darling oldest brother. He had no idea I had any memory of what he'd done to me. He even gave Dennis and me a one-thousand-dollar silver tea set for a wedding gift."

"Uh-huh."

She bit her lip thoughtfully. "You know, I sometimes wonder if *Warren* even remembers what he did to me. I've never seen any indication of it."

"A lot of times they rationalize it," I said. "Or tell themselves it's no big deal."

"Mmm." She cocked an eyebrow at me. "I bet even if he'd publicly confessed to it, no one would have believed him. Certainly not my parents," she added bitterly. "Or his professors at medical school or his ex-wife or his colleagues. Oh, no, not Warren. He would never do anything so evil or disgusting. Not him. Not the Healer. Saint Warren the Good who helped all those women with infertility and difficult pregnancies and birth control. God. I think he even advised some of his patients about their sexual problems. Well, he would know what caused them, wouldn't he?"

I forbore telling her that I'd been her brother's patient. And that I liked him. *Had* liked him.

"Let's get back to what happened Monday night," I suggested gently.

"He told me to go to his office. He'd leave the door unlocked. He was going there to catch up on some paperwork."

"So you went to the office. Are you sure no one saw you there? Going in or out?"

"No one saw me."

"Okay. Did you leave anything in the office?"

"Like what?"

"Anything. A newspaper. A scrap of paper. A used Kleenex. A wad of chewed gum in an ashtray. Your fingerprints."

"Nothing like that." She shook her head very definitely. "I was wearing gloves anyway. Thin leather ones."

"The whole time?"

"The whole time."

"All right. How long were you in the office?"

She frowned. "It couldn't have been more than five minutes."

"That's *all*?"

She looked at me strangely. "You don't think I was going to sit there for half an hour and make conversation with him, do you? I did what I did and I left. I walked into his office, sat down in front of the desk, took out the gun, and shot him. Then I got up and walked out."

I clapsed my hands and rested my chin on them. "Are you sorry?"

"That I killed him? No. I'd do it again tomorrow, if I could."

"Okay." I raised my head. "I'll get the check. Then I think we should leave. If we stay here any longer the waitress will remember us. Which is probably immaterial, but why take chances?'' I glanced around for the woman with the black braids. When I caught her eye I smiled and mouthed the words, "Check, please."

I paid the bill. Demelza pulled on her raincoat. We rose together and walked out of the bar.

"One thing," I said. "The police will probably want to talk to you at some point. Don't worry; it's routine. Someone may approach you after the funeral. You *are* going to the funeral?"

She nodded. I was fleetingly reminded of the old story about all the people who'd attended Harry Cohn's obsequies "just to make sure the bastard was dead."

"Okay," I said. "Whatever story you tell the cops, keep it simple. *And* consistent. Last Monday night, you went home after you closed your gallery, fed your cat, had dinner, read a book, watched TV, whatever, and went to bed. But don't be overly specific, like saying that between 8:07 P.M. and 9:16 P.M. you were reading an article about Don Johnson in the March issue of *Cosmo*. You didn't know about the murder until Tuesday morning. All right?"

"Yes."

Out on Brattle Street it was starting to snow slightly. Demelza's raincoat had a hood. She flipped it up over her head.

"Why are you doing this for me?" she asked quietly.

I looked at her for a moment. "You say you've read my articles about sexual abuse of children," I said. "Then you know how frequently the kind of crime that was committed against you gets committed. And you also know how infrequently those guys come to trial. And even if they do, and they get convicted, they get a slap on the wrist. Not all of them, but far too many."

"Yes."

"Well, that's why."

"I see."

I held out my hand. She clasped and held it in hers.

"No matter what happens," she said, "I will never, ever tell anyone that I told you about this. Nor will I ever tell anyone that you took the g—"

"Ssh." I put my finger to my lips. Then I smiled. "I don't know what you're talking about."

She nodded once, a slight dip of the head.

"Before you go," I said, "just let me ask you one thing."

"What's that?"

I inhaled deeply of the damp, cold air. "If I had answered your letter right away . . ."

"Yes?"

"Would you still have . . . you know."

She stared at me with shadowed eyes and immobile face. "Yes. Oh, yes."

I nodded.

"Good-bye."

"Good-bye."

She walked slowly down Brattle and around the bend to Mount Auburn.

I never saw her again.

I'm not going to say what I did with the gun. It's in a place where the likelihood that it'll ever be found is remote in the extreme.

Going home that night, I thought, *I am now an accessory after the fact of murder.*

I called Jack and told him I couldn't see him that night because I wasn't feeling well. No, no, nothing serious. I'd be fine tomorrow. A little touch of the flu. This rotten weather.

Actually, I felt okay. I just wanted to be alone.

Do I believe what Demelza said, about how she'd have killed her brother even if I'd answered her letter right away?

I can't say.

That's one question I don't want to think on too hard.

I'm afraid to go beyond I don't know.

The Cambridge Police Department file on the shooting death of Dr. Warren Hastings remains an open one. Nobody's actively working on the case now. As far as I hear.

Maybe someday I'll tell Jack about Demelza Farrell and what she did.

And what I did.

Maybe. Someday.

Karen Kijewski, winner of the 1988 St. Martin's Press/Private Eye Writers of America award for Katwalk, *shares several significant attributes with Kat Colorado, her Sacramento-based private eye. Both are concerned with friendship, integrity, and independence, and both know the difference between a sidecar and a stinger, having put in their time tending bar. Kat's adventures continue in* Katapult, *and Karen says she has enough stories—and titles—for many more books.*

In "Katfall," Kat struggles to remain loyal to a friend whose behavior raises moral doubts—a real katch-22.

KATFALL

by Karen Kijewski

M Y HEAD ACHED, my mind was fogged, and the .38 Police Special in my waistband dug uncomfortably into the small of my back. I ran to answer the telephone but it wasn't worth it—it stopped ringing before I got there. The man sitting in my office grinned at me.

"Kat, long time no see," the familiar voice said. Fifteen years and it was familiar still.

"Not long enough," I said. He smiled; I didn't. He pretended I was joking; I didn't. I wasn't.

"Hey, Kat—"

"How did you get in, Riley?"

"The door was open."

"Like hell it was."

He grinned again. "I've got a job for you, Kat Colorado, private investigator."

"No."

"C'mon. The past is—"

"No."

"Double your usual fee."

"Get lost, Riley. I wouldn't give you the time of day if I had five watches on." I stared him down. His eyes dropped after thirty seconds and he started to get up. Then Merissa drifted in. She has a way of looking like a mermaid washed up on the beach, helpless, fragile, and singing a siren song you can't quite hear but is nevertheless devastating and irresistible. She's a good friend but we'd been out of touch for a while.

"Kat—oh, excuse me, I didn't mean to interrupt."

"You're not; he's leaving." Riley stared at Merissa, the siren song playing in his ears. I scowled. She smiled. He had a hard time leaving, but he did.

"Who was that?" I shook my head; I didn't want to explain. Riley was right, it was past. Still, hatred takes longer than love to dissolve.

"Kat."

"Hmmm." I sat down at my desk and flipped the computer on.

"I need your help."

"Not wallpaper again?" I waited for the computer to boot up and retrieved the document I'd been working on earlier. It was overdue, it and three or four other projects. I'd left the office earlier on a false alarm and was kicking myself for the lost time.

"Kat."

"Or research. No wallpaper, no research, no gambling junkets to Tahoe."

"Kat, I need your help bad." There was a desperate quality to her voice.

"You must; it's affecting your grammar."

"Badly." She sounded a little frantic. "You'll come to work for me, won't you? Please? Say you will."

"In a couple of weeks. I've got a full schedule now." I indicated the stacks of folders and piles of papers on my desk. The computer prompt blinked invitingly at me. My attention drifted back to it and I finished a sentence on the report I'd been writing.

"I could be dead in a couple of weeks."

"Hmmm?" I finished the paragraph and wondered if I should indent for the figures to come.

"Kat, someone's trying to kill me."

I got it that time. "Kill you?" I have friends who overreact and exaggerate. Merissa's not one of them.

"Kill me," she said firmly. "I need someone to stay with me, to watch after me."

"I'm a private investigator, Merissa, not a bodyguard. If someone's threatening you, call the police."

She shrugged. "They can't do anything, there's not enough to go on. At best they'll suggest I get a restraining order. Big deal." She shrugged again. "All that means is they know where to look first when they find my body." I started to answer but she cut me off.

"No, I need someone with me twenty-four hours a day." I shook my head. "Not for long, Kat. The rest of the week, maybe, just until I finish this story. When it comes out, when it's public knowledge, he's got nothing to gain by killing me."

"I'm not hired muscle, Merissa, I'm brainpower. I can find you muscle if that's what you need." I looked the question at her; she shook her head.

"Come with me to lunch. Just listen. Please." There was a rare note of entreaty in her voice and it caught me; Merissa is one of the least emotional people I know. "Even in third grade you were always the one who helped me. Please." That note again. The siren song.

I went to lunch. I fell for it.

First we got our iced tea and ordered, then business.

"What story, Merissa?" She's a free-lance journalist who specializes in investigative journalism and political exposés. It's the kind of journalism that makes enemies, but as far as I knew, she'd never been threatened before.

"Listen to this." She pulled out a microcassette recorder, snapped in a cassette and pushed the play button.

"You know who this is?" a loud male voice said. Three men in business suits turned around and stared at us. Merissa flushed, turned the volume down to a murmur.

"Who is it?" On the tape Merissa's voice was low, but firm and clear.

"A phone conversation?" I asked. She nodded. "Did he know you were taping it?" She shook her head. It's illegal, but what the hell.

"You know," the male voice stated flatly.

"Alec Howard?"

"I understand," he continued, not answering her question, "that you have been most interested in the work my associates and I are involved in. Your interest is, of course, flattering."

He didn't sound flattered; he didn't even sound annoyed. He sounded cool and businesslike.

"I thought you should know that we would prefer that you direct your attention elsewhere." He paused briefly. Merissa made no comment.

"I have not had the pleasure of meeting you, Ms. Landow, but I hear that you are a very beautiful woman. It would be a shame to lose that beauty, to have it marred or disfigured." Merissa's fine-boned, lovely face was white and drawn. She showed remarkably little enthusiasm for her carefully ordered lunch.

"How unfortunate if you were to be in an accident or to become a victim of random violence." His voice sounded genuinely distressed.

"You're threatening me." Her voice was calm, unrattled.

"Not at all." He sounded shocked at the thought, genial and pleasant. It gave me the shivers. "I am merely expressing concern about your health and welfare. I bid you good day."

She pressed the off button in the middle of a dial tone. "He's threatening me."

"Yes." She didn't need a detective for that. An alert four-year-old could have told her.

"How frightened are you?"

"Very."

"Enough to drop it?"

"No."

"Tell me, then."

"Have you heard of Alec Howard?"

I thought about it before I answered. "He's a high-priced criminal lawyer who takes difficult, last-chance, often largely unsympathetic cases, like child molestation? Better than average record on acquittal for his clients?"

She nodded. "That's the one. I would say he's not generally well liked—"

"Slime ball is the term that comes to mind," I commented.

She smiled briefly, perfunctorily. It was an effort; Merissa doesn't smile much.

"Tsk," she chided me. "Even child molesters and rapists are entitled to competent legal representation. That's the beauty of our system. Anyway"—she shifted gears—"although he is not well liked, he is respected and feared. Or was. There's been talk.'' She looked at me, raised her eyebrows in a question.

I shook my head. "No, I haven't heard it."

"It's just a whisper. People are too cautious to talk openly. And he's slick, very slick. He covers his tracks well." I nodded and waited. The salads came. I started on mine.

"He's always been known for his meticulous preparation and attention to detail. He covers all the ground, interviews every conceivable witness, brings in expert testimony, does extensive background and site research. You name it, he does it. When he walks into a courtroom, he's a formidable opponent. There is nothing magic about it; it's hard work, good courtroom presence, and occasional flashes of brilliance."

I nodded and ate. She looked at her salad and shoved it around the plate a bit, then continued.

"The word now, though, is that he's crossed the line, that he's bought witnesses and perjured corroborative statements, even that he's intimidated, blackmailed, and scared off witnesses friendly to the prosecution. It's hard to find something that can be traced directly to him, he's that slick." She paused, smiled. "But I have—quite a bit actually."

I frowned. "Why would he take chances like that?"

"I don't know. It can't be the money; he's got that. I think it has more to do with power, with the sense of being above the law. It is the temptation to play God in human affairs."

Merissa squeezed the lemon into her iced tea, added sugar, stirred it carefully, then didn't drink it. "The article focuses on that issue, the crossing of that line. Howard, here in Sacramento, is one example. I've also profiled a lawyer in Chicago, one in Miami, one in Atlanta."

Death threats no longer sounded melodramatic or improbable. Take a number. The line forms to the left. News at eleven.

"What makes you think it's Howard and not one of the others?"

"Style. Timing. The voice on the tape. Anyway, does it matter? If it's not him it's someone else. And I need you with me—a friend and a witness, really. That, more than a bodyguard." She looked at me pleadingly and I looked back.

"Please, Kat? It's not as bad as it sounds. Just a few days. I've done all of the research and most of it is written. We'll just hole up somewhere with groceries while I finish. You'll be my peace of mind so I can relax and concentrate on my work."

"Great. Who's going to be *my* peace of mind?"

She smiled at me. "Please, Kat?" I said I'd think about it. We both knew I'd do it. "Thanks," she said softly.

"Damn," I muttered under my breath. She smiled again. I frowned, was graceless and grumpy, finished my salad and iced tea. The waiter offered us dessert but I declined. I'd watched Merissa push enough uneaten food around for one day.

Then she sprung San Francisco on me. "Kat, we're going to the champagne opening of an art show in the city."

I stared morosely at her. "Merissa, we just agreed to hole up."

"I know, and we're going to, but I have to do this. There are people there I need to talk to. I arranged it this way so we could meet publicly, safely. This way no one will be compromised. It won't take long, but it is important."

"When?"

"Tomorrow."

I agreed, but reluctantly.

I went along, also reluctantly. I'd started off smiling but I'd stopped that, too, especially when I discovered I had to dress to the occasion and wear high heels. The shoes hurt. They were Merissa's; I don't own high heels.

At the gallery we each went our separate ways, Merissa looking at pictures and chattering, apparently innocently, with people. I looked at people and at pictures but mostly I kept an eye on Merissa. Finally she drifted over to me and touched my elbow.

"Over there, Kat. That's Howard."

"The short beefy guy with the plaid vest?"

"Yes."

"Okay." I entertained a fleeting, compassionate thought for Chinese women and bound feet. How much worse than high heels. On my way to Howard I snagged a glass of champagne off a waiter's tray.

"Alec Howard?" I smiled as I looked down at him, a good five-nine in two-inch heels to his five-five. He looked at my breasts first, then let his eyes travel to my face. They were bloodshot and bold. The words *slime ball* came to mind again. Already I didn't like him.

"Yes," he leered back. "And who are you?"

"My name's Kat. I'm a fan of yours." I smiled broadly. I always smile like that when I lie.

"Is that so? You're interested in the law, are you?"

"No."

He looked surprised.

"I'm interested in winners: law, sports, business, politics, beauty contests, whatever. It's the winning I care about. I'm not there yet," I said softly, "but I want to be. I read about you in the papers, then someone pointed you out to me today." He smiled, gracious celebrity to fan.

"I was bold enough to come over and talk to you. I hope you don't mind?" I lied, smiling. Usually I have more pride; maybe it was the high heels and a slow process of demoralization.

"No, I don't mind."

"How do you do it?" I smiled sweetly and naïvely, or at least I hoped so. Naïve was only a dim memory for me. At this point, sweet was too.

"A good education, hard work, a willingness to make sacrifices . . ." He went on that way for a bit. I tuned him out. Who wouldn't? Then I interrupted him.

"You sound like a Boy Scout." He looked surprised. "There are a lot of plodders out there who do that. They're not where you are. What makes the difference?"

"Well, well," he said with a grin. "You're not just what you seem, are you?"

I grinned back. "No." I was relieved to be telling the truth again, however briefly.

"What is it, Mr. Howard?"

"Call me Alec."

"Alec."

"It's brilliance and—"

"Alec, darling, do come join us." A diminutive redhead in kelly green, dimples, and cheap costume jewelry latched on to his elbow and claimed him. He smiled at me and allowed himself to be hauled off.

"And?" I spoke after him. He turned.

"Balls. That's what Boy Scouts forget." He turned away, then back again. "And blood."

"Aleeeec," the redhead whined.

"You like the power?"

"No." He shook his head. "It's beyond that, way beyond;

it's become the air I breathe." He looked absolute, unconditional, and serious. "Coming, doll," he said, before she could whine again. He leered and winked at me. He was a slime ball but, I thought, a likable one.

"Kat?"

"Hmmm?" I jumped a little.

"You're just standing there. You spoke to him. What did you think?"

I thought I was out of champagne. "Are you drinking, Merissa?"

"No."

"Not at all?"

"No."

Good. We had a designated driver. I traded my empty glass for a full one as a waiter cruised by. Brilliance, balls, and blood: it was quite a combination. I wasn't sure what I thought. We talked about it more on the drive home from San Francisco to Sacramento.

"Did you recognize the voice?" Merissa asked.

"Was it the voice on the tape, you mean?"

"Yes."

"It could have been."

"You're not sure."

"No. It wasn't distinctive, just a low, masculine voice. Lower than Howard's, actually. Still, it could have been his." I paused. "Did you speak to him, Merissa?"

"No."

"Why not? It doesn't seem like you. Why not confront him and have it out? It's a public place. I was there. You were certainly safe."

"Oh no." She seemed barely to breathe. Her hands tightened on the steering wheel. "I'm too afraid to do anything like that." I looked at her in amazement. She loosened her right-hand death grip on the wheel and ran her fingers through her hair. For a moment she looked about twelve.

"That's why I'm a writer. I can be brave and confrontational on paper, but in person? Oh no!" Her horror was real. "I'm much too afraid for that. It's why I need you, Kat—to deal with the real world and be brave for me." She smiled wanly. "And to protect me from the consequences." I didn't smile.

"You remember? It was like that when we were young." I remembered. I'd fought battles for her then too.

We pulled into the driveway of Merissa's two-hundred-thousand-dollar high-class tract home near Folsom Lake. She doused the lights and started to climb out.

"Wait here; lock the door. I'll look around first." She stared silently at me. "I'll need the house key." I held out my hand. Reluctantly she gave me the keys.

"Kat, is this really necessary?"

"This is what you're paying me for, Merissa," I said gently.

"Okay." She nodded. I got out, moved the .38 from the small of my back, stuck it in the waistband in front, and snapped the flashlight on. It illuminated an area roughly the size of Cleveland. I looked around, found nothing amiss, no sign of disturbance inside or out, and headed back to the car.

"It's all right." I reached out to open the car door on Merissa's side. "You were supposed to lock it," I told her as it opened.

"Oh. Yes. I forgot. You said it was all right, though."

"Now. I didn't know then." She shook her head as if to clear it. I shook mine, too, but for a different reason.

The house was lit up; I'd left the lights on as I moved through and checked it out. I kicked Merissa's shoes off. Too little, too late. My feet still hurt.

"I'm going upstairs to change. Then let's have something to eat." Merissa looked tired.

"Do you have any other plans this evening?"

"Oh no, just to work. I want to finish this as soon as possible. It's wearing me out a bit." I nodded. "A bit" was clearly an understatement.

"Shall I make coffee and look around for something to eat?"

"Yes." Merissa looked pleased and grateful. "I didn't know you cooked, Kat."

"I don't."

"Oh." Puzzled.

"Go on." I gave her a push toward the stairs. "I'll fake it." She smiled weakly.

I found a can of mushroom soup, crackers and cheese, grapes and apples. The soup was heating. I'd finished cutting up the cheese and was starting on the apples when the screams began. They were long, wild, hysterical cries that traveled up and down octaves like crazed mountain locomotives.

I cut my thumb with the paring knife. Fresh blood splashed onto a slice of apple. The screams went on.

It didn't take me long to get upstairs. Or to find Merissa—I
followed the screams. She stood in the master bath in her un-
derwear, pointed at the vanity mirror and screeched.

"Merissa," I called out. She screamed.

"Stop it!" I hollered, over her noise. She screamed. I stuck
the .38 back in my waistband and slapped her face.

Blessed silence.

"Kat." She still pointed at the mirror, hiccoughing and sobbing now. "Look." I looked.

Scrawled across the mirror in bright red lipstick was the
message:

> YOU WRITE
> YOU DIE
> YOU BITCH

The lipstick had been rolled out almost all the way and
jammed into the mirror. It looked like a knife hilt protruding
out of a bloody, fleshy blob. Merissa hiccoughed and moaned.

"Get dressed. I'm calling the cops."

"No!"

"This is serious now, Merissa," I explained patiently. "It's
gone beyond phone threats."

"I don't want the police. I don't want to get into it and
explain and explain. I can't afford the time." She was on an
hysterical edge.

"You can't afford to die, either," I pointed out sensibly.

"I won't. I've got you. Kat, please."

"Get dressed. Let's eat and talk."

"You won't call them?"

"Not until we talk."

"Is dinner ready?"

"Almost," I said, not knowing, hardly caring.

"I'll be right down."

I stared at the lipstick message for a while. It was all caps
but it looked like an adult and literate hand. The strokes were
firm and sure, the spacing even. I didn't like it, not at all. I
went downstairs, turned off the soup—boiling and unappetizing—and finished cutting up the apples. I looked at the blood-
stained one for a long time before I threw it out.

"Can I help?"

"Dish up the soup. Merissa, who has a key to the house besides you?"

"My mother."

"That's it? How about a boyfriend, an ex-boyfriend, your cleaning lady?"

She shook her head.

"Is your mother trustworthy?"

"Oh yes!" She was shocked.

"We're calling the police."

She shook her head. "Eat your soup, Kat." I took a small spoonful. No rush; it was only Campbell's. "Anyway, we can't."

"Yes, we can. We will."

"No. I scrubbed it off the mirror." I stared at her, soup dripping from my spoon. "I'm sorry, don't be mad. I couldn't look at it anymore. I couldn't bear knowing it was there, ugly and threatening. I couldn't work, or eat, or do anything—" I groaned. "Kat, I couldn't even have a shower with it there. You understand, don't you?"

I understood but I wasn't happy. "We can't go to the police now, not without any physical evidence."

"It's all right, Kat, really it is. I didn't want to anyway, you know." She said it softly. I knew. I wasn't happy about that either. "Please understand."

She pleaded with me. I put my soup spoon down and picked up an apple slice. I put it down too; I couldn't get the blood out of my mind.

"I can't stand the thought of interruptions and complications right now."

"Get it straight, Merissa. Death threats in your house *are* complications." I tried to sound tough.

"Don't be mad."

I snorted. I was mad. A little. We ate in silence. "Come on, let's walk the house. If we can't figure out how he got in we've got a problem." That was an understatement on my part. The house was locked up, tight and sound. Every door, every window, was closed and latched.

"Do you ever open the windows?"

"No, I've got air-conditioning."

I nodded, but I wondered about writers who shun fresh air. I headed back to the sliding glass doors on the patio. "Now what?"

I opened the door, went out, closed it behind me. It latched automatically. I slammed it with my hand: hard, carefully, just right. It jumped, jolted the lock out of the track. I slid it open.

"Oh my." Merissa's mouth hung open.

"Yeah. Break-in artists know a lot of stuff like that." I found a sponge mop with a screw-on wooden handle, unscrewed it and dropped it into the sliding door track. It could still be jumped but the door wouldn't slide more than an inch; they'd have to break it.

"That's how he got in?"

"I don't know. It's one way, one possibility. There are a lot of others I don't have a clue about. Where does your mother live?"

"Here in Folsom."

"Let's go."

"No. She lives in a senior-citizen mobile-home park. There's no room, no computer. I couldn't work. We have to stay here."

"My house, then. I've got a computer."

"No, all my stuff, my research, is here. I can't, Kat." Her face was stiff and stubborn. I gave up, but I wasn't gracious about it.

"You hired me to keep you safe and now you're not taking my advice."

"I know." She sighed. "I know. Let's just do the best we can, okay?" The phone rang before I could answer her. It was probably just as well.

"Do you want me to get it?" We walked back toward the kitchen.

She shook her head. "That's all right."

I started clearing away the food we hadn't eaten. She talked. I listened. Of course. It didn't do me any good.

"Yes, this is Merissa Landow. Who? Oh. Oh! Yes, I do, absolutely. No, that would be all right. Tonight? Isn't there any other— No? Okay. How, then? Uh-huh . . . uh-huh . . . uh-huh . . . What? Uh-huh . . . uh-huh . . . uh-huh . . ."

Who would have thought writers could be such boring conversationalists? I thought about it as I stacked dishes in the dishwasher.

"Fine, yes, I'll be there. Good." She held out the receiver, stared at it, then hung it up. I waited.

"I have to go out for a bit."

"No."

"Well, I do."

"What for?"

"To pick up some information from someone."

"On Howard?"

"Yes."

"Who are you picking it up from?"

"He—I—it doesn't matter, Kat."

"A snitch."

"An informant, yes."

I snorted. A snitch.

"It could be very important. Very."

"It could be a setup."

"Oh no, I'm sure it's not. I'm meeting him in a public place."

"Where?"

"A casino on the south shore."

"Tahoe?"

"Yes."

"When?"

"Tonight at ten. I have to leave soon."

"Where?"

"In one of the bars at the Starlight."

"I don't like it. There's no way you can do that and be safe."

"I have to go, Kat. I need this information." Her voice was low, pleading. Her eyes filled with tears. The mermaid; the siren song again.

"Does he know what you look like?"

"No."

"So I could go in your place?"

"Oh, Kat, I *couldn't* ask you to do that." Her voice said that. Her eyes asked me, held out my coat, and walked me to the door. I sighed.

"If I go, you'll be here alone."

"I'll be all right."

"Damned if I do, damned if I don't," I muttered.

"It's okay."

"I don't like it."

"I know." She nodded. "And you're right. If I promise to stay here? You've checked the house out. I'll be all right."

I still didn't like it. Something was wrong.

"I'll close the curtains, leave all the lights on and put the phone next to me. I'll be fine; I can take care of myself." She looked at me anxiously for approval.

I didn't give it. I'd tried before to teach Merissa self-defense tactics but she'd refused to learn. She was about as capable of defending herself as a day-old kitten.

"I can take care of myself, Kat," she repeated, still anxiously. "Really."

I laughed. The only thing she could do was dial 911.

"Really."

"We'd better get started. I'll make coffee; you can take a thermos with you. Do you want some cookies too?"

That was how I ended up on the road to Tahoe: eating cookies, drinking coffee and wondering about my judgment. It used to be better. The drive out Highway 50 is a nice one, scenic. Usually I enjoy it. Usually I'm in a better mood. I figured three and a half hours up and back and another half hour or so to check out and meet the snitch. Four hours. Too long. I stepped on the gas.

The casino was large, brightly lit and noisy. It hummed with the thunk and clatter of slot machines, voices, and the bell-ringing, coin-rattling sound of an occasional payoff. No windows; there are never windows in casinos. Or clocks. When you walk in, you can't tell whether it's day or night. After a while you don't ask, you don't care. It's a world apart with its own time, rules, fantasies and dreams. That's part of the seduction. I headed for the bar where I was to wait. There I ordered a martini with three olives. Those were the instructions.

"Gin or vodka?" I looked at the bartender and shrugged. He looked at me with thinly disguised contempt. The three olives, I guess. Martinis are gin. He knew that; he didn't know I did.

"Vodka." He nodded, his suspicions confirmed. His mouth was okay but the contempt won out in his eyes. "Up." He nodded again and made the drink. I ate an olive off the toothpick. A man slid onto the stool next to me. I didn't look up.

"Say, didja get lucky yet?" I looked up. Polyester sleaze with black, slicked-down hair, bloodshot eyes and a salesman smile. A definite maybe. "Say, whaddaya say we try and get lucky together?" I looked at him for a long time, ate another olive. He leered.

"What do you say we don't." I stared at him coldly, watched him flush, go ugly and leave. Two ladies in their fifties sat down and ordered piña coladas. No. A young guy in cowboy boots and a hangover. Probably not. A blond bimbo with capped teeth, diamonds and aspirations. Maybe. I ate the last olive and gestured to the bartender, who came over and stared at my untouched drink.

"Three more olives please." The bimbo's eyes bounced off me on the way to the cowboy. I sighed. The bartender gave me the olives without a word. His eyes still spoke. The snitch was twenty minutes late.

I stretched and yawned. I hate martinis; I can't stand green olives; and waiting isn't on my top-ten list of favorite things. I did it for half an hour. Then I left.

On the way out I covered myself. I didn't want to be jumped by someone who had fingered me at the bar. Leaving town, I cut through a few parking lots, made some fancy detours, made sure that there was no one on my tail. Pretty sure. I'm not that good at cops-and-robbers stuff.

I played tapes for a while, then turned on the radio. The reception isn't that great coming out of the mountains and the music faded in and out. The newsbreak broke. I started to turn it off.

"Hostage situation in Folsom," the announcer said. The radio went snap, crackle and pop the way cereal never does. "Police have cordoned off—" More static. My hands were clenched and sweaty on the wheel.

"One hostage is believed to—" I went around a curve and it faded. "Also involved is the local personality—" I went around another bend. Shit! I sped up, barely took a curve and slowed down again.

I imagined the worst.

"Update to follow," the announcer finished in a smug, self-satisfied voice. I swore and hurled questions at him. He played music; I hurled obscenities. And none of it got me anywhere.

They played three songs and two commercials. I thought about water beds, cars and hostages. I thought about Merissa, exposés, lawyers and hostages. I thought about changing my job. And about hostages. I was out of the mountains by the next newsbreak.

"Police believe that journalist, Merissa Landow—" Damn. I banged the steering wheel and hurt my hand—a good, solid professional response. ". . . is being held by local lawyer, Alec Howard. It is not known what the motivation is, although

Landow is believed to be writing an article on Howard, who is known for his drinking and womanizing, as well as his legal expertise. Phone contact was initially made, then broken off.'' Damn. I banged the steering wheel again. Not as hard this time. I learn fast.

"It is not known how many hostages are involved. Neighbors reported seeing two women enter the house earlier this evening. At the time of the last phone contact, two hours ago, Landow was believed to be alive and well. Nothing new since then, although the longer a hostage situation goes on, the more hopeful the outcome. Police spokesperson Laura Allen stated that—''

Two hours ago and nothing since then. Damn, damn, damn.

A phone call, the Tahoe setup, Merissa alone with me out of the way. It didn't take a detective to figure out that I was on a wild-goose chase. I felt like the goose: stupid, flying blind. I was on the straight stretch of 50 and speeding. I got off at Scott Road and sped some more. It didn't change anything but it made me feel better. A road sign welcomed me to Folsom and the Snail Race. There were more stop signs than I remembered, a lot more—Folsom was growing up fast. I turned right on Natoma, sped past the city hall, the police department, and Folsom Prison. I was almost to Merissa's house.

The place was crawling with cops, with cops and the curious. I parked a block away and walked up to the barricades. The SWAT team, ninja-suited, was there. It wasn't going to be easy talking my way in. I looked around for a cop I knew and found one. It still wasn't going to be easy.

"Delaney." I had to raise my voice and call a couple of times. He finally looked around, saw me and shrugged. What a pal.

"I'm in this, Delaney." He walked over. "Merissa Landow is a close friend. I was the woman neighbors saw entering the house earlier with Landow. I met Howard yesterday, spoke with him. Landow hired me to protect her. She'd been receiving threats and—''

"Nice job, Kat." Delaney nodded approvingly. "Where were you when all this came down—out to lunch, powdering your nose? Hot date, maybe?" It got to me; we both knew it would.

"Fuck off, Delaney."

He grinned. "C'mon." Grabbing my elbow, he shouldered

his way through a knot of police. We didn't get far. There was a silence and a collective intake of breath as the lights in the house started going off one by one until only the porch light was left. That went off too. I didn't like the symbolism.

A plainclothes put a bullhorn to his face. The door opened slightly. Slowly he lowered the bullhorn. I reminded myself to breathe. The door opened wider and Merissa stumbled out looking white and big-eyed. Howard was right behind her, her right wrist tied to his left. His right hand was in his jacket pocket.

"He's got a gun," Merissa screamed, a loud, strong voice coming out of a tiny, pale body. She started to stumble away but he hauled her back. His hand came partway out of his pocket.

"No, I—" His sentence died there. A SWAT sharpshooter took him out with one shot to the head.

Things went from slow motion to fast. It wasn't necessary. There was no hurry now. Merissa was safe; Howard was body-bag material. None of it was pretty but then violent death rarely is.

Merissa was surrounded with cops by the time I got there. Someone had untied her from the corpse and she was leaning against a large, good-looking uniform. Discriminating even in a crisis, that's Merissa. She bleated when she saw me, then toppled into my arms.

The cops were considerate, kept the wrap-up brief. It was still too long. We went into the house and someone made coffee. When we finished that pot someone made another. Merissa drank herb tea and whispered. Even after they left she whispered.

"Help me to bed, Kat."

"Okay."

"You'll stay, won't you?" Her whispered voice was tight and anxious. I nodded. After she went to bed I went into her study.

Call it curiosity. No, it was more. I wanted to see what a man had held someone hostage for, then died for. It took me all night to piece it together, to figure it out.

In the morning I was at the kitchen table drinking coffee when Merissa stumbled in.

"Good morning." She smiled weakly. I didn't smile at all. "Oh, you made coffee." I nodded. "Thanks."

"I figured it out, Merissa."

She smiled weakly again. "Coffee machines aren't that tough, Kat, but congratulations." She poured a cup of coffee.

"You weren't the hostage, he was." She sat down heavily, spilled coffee on her robe. "I found the pictures of Patty." I'd grown up with Patty, Merissa's little sister, too. "I didn't realize that Howard was the lawyer for Patty's alleged rapist."

"Not alleged; he did it."

"He was acquitted."

"Because of Howard."

"So you decided to off him, a one woman posse bent on vigilante justice."

"But justice at last."

"And I was the fall guy, the dummy, the loyal friend standing around with blinders on who would, and did, swear that you were threatened and terrified, that the phone calls, the threats, the lipstick on the mirror were all real. I fell for it."

She looked at me without moving, her eyes dark and unreadable like gun barrels at high noon in a grade-B melodrama.

"I loved her."

"Loved? Past tense?"

"The Patty I loved is dead. They killed her."

"They?"

"Mostly the rapist, of course. But then it was the whole official process; it was so hard for her. But she did it; she was very brave. And then he got off. He was guilty, everyone knew it, and he got off."

"That was seven years ago."

"Yes. I was bitter but I could live with it. Almost. I assumed it had been a fair trial. Then, doing the article, I uncovered new information. He got off, not because Howard is a great trial lawyer but because he intimidated and scared away witnesses, witnesses who had seen the rapist's car, even gotten the license number, and who would have made a solid case against him. He had a mask on, you see, and the jury wasn't convinced by Patty's ID. That's how he got off."

"There's an answer for that."

"Yes." She nodded.

"Not your answer."

She ignored my comment. "You see, at first I thought it would be enough to expose him in my article, that there would be justice then, for Patty, for me, for all the others. That was naïve of me. The exposure probably would have brought him more business. People want guaranteed outcomes. They care about that; they care more about that than justice, due process, and the law.''

I didn't answer right away. I was afraid maybe she was right.

"So you got him to come over here?''

She nodded. "It was easy. The man has an ego the size of Rhode Island. I played up to it and he came.''

"You did a nice job, Merissa: the Tahoe setup, the lipstick threat. Did he really make the phone calls?''

"Oh yes, he made them, but he didn't threaten my life. And I edited the tapes.''

I nodded. "Very nice. It's not easy to get cops to kill someone for you.'' She stared at me. "He didn't have a gun either, but you knew that. It's not easy to get cops to kill an unarmed man either.'' I took a sip of my coffee. It was cold. "What if he'd been captured instead?''

"They wouldn't have believed him; they'd have believed me. I have pages and pages of information proving he's a liar. They won't believe you either, Kat.'' She said it matter-of-factly. "He deserved to die.'' Her voice was pleading with me now.

"Please understand.'' Her voice was soft, sad, siren. "He deserved to die.''

"Maybe. Not that way. Not without a trial.''

"He deserved it. Even that wasn't enough. I wanted him to pay the way Patty paid, is still paying.''

"He paid with his life.''

"Yes. And it's not enough. Just like it was not enough that Nazi war criminals were executed simply and cleanly. They should suffer, all of them, as their victims did. Do,'' she corrected.

"Merissa, look at what you're saying. Howard isn't the only one playing God with people's lives.''

She stood up, went to the refrigerator, pulled out a bottle of champagne, wrestled with the cork and poured two glasses. I shook my head when she handed me one. Not because it was before breakfast either.

"Drink, please. In celebration of life, of love. The other is done. I hope now I can turn my back on death, vengeance and hatred. I'll never finish that article. I'm doing another one, one on a woman who takes in children off the streets—children no one wants—and gives them love. Please drink.''

I drank. It was better champagne than I was used to and it tasted bitter, sour.

"More?" I shook my head. She poured it anyway. "It's behind us, Kat," she said softly. "Let's forget it."

I couldn't forget it. I wasn't an accessory to the crime, but it was close enough. That was one reason. There were others. Too many of them.

And was it behind us? Hatred takes longer than love to dissolve.

Three days later I bumped into Riley. Literally. He frowned, muttered, backed off.

"Hey, Riley," I said cheerfully.

"Kat?" The question mark was clear.

"It's two-fifteen," I said. He looked at me, puzzled, and I smiled. I don't wear a watch and had no idea what time it was but I knew that I could give Riley the time of day now, knew that I didn't want to hate anymore.

I didn't know about the rest yet.

Portland resident Gabrielle Kraft knows Hollywood from the inside: among her Tinseltown credits she lists stints as executive story editor at Universal Studios and story analyst for Warner Brothers. Her books, featuring Jerry Zalman ". . . who practices the art of the deal in Beverly Hills, CA, and is one of the fortunate few who realizes that (in Hollywood) the Emperor isn't wearing any clothes . . ." include Bullshot *(1988 Edgar nominee),* Screwdriver, Let's Rob Roy, *and* Bloody Mary.

In "Wow Finish," the desperate ambition of a Hollywood hopeful comes to a head on one fateful day.

WOW FINISH

by Gabrielle Kraft

HERE'S HOW IT happened. I'd been hanging around this town for a few years, trying to shoehorn my way into a glamour spot at one of the studios, but the best I'd managed was a job at a newly formed production company with a suite of offices off Ventura Boulevard in the Valley. A mediocre office with used furniture. No secretary.

I'd been there two months when Nick Tully, an ex-studio executive who'd gone independent after he'd been bounced in a shake-up, stuck his head into my office one morning.

"Tom," he said. "Good news for you."

"Nick, sit down, sit down," I said, jovial as a Salvation Army Santa sweating out a heat wave. Whatever Tully had to say to me, I knew it wasn't good news.

"Bill's no longer with us," he said as he took off his glasses and rubbed his hand across his eyes. Tully has a habit of wrinkling his forehead all the way up his scalp, which makes him look forlorn. Kinda like "Gee, kids, anybody here seen my puppy?"

"He's not. Hmmm." Big surprise. Bill's office is next to mine and I know his project's going nowhere with the major studios, plus I heard yelling in there Friday night. One plus one equals no more Billy boy.

"But the good news for you is," Tully goes on, "I want you to take over anything he had current. Go through that pile of scripts in his office. Tom . . ." Tully wrinkles up again. "I'm counting on you to help us out. We need a hot project to grease the wheels around here."

"I'll get right on it, Nick," I say, smile-smile-smile on the outside. Inside, I'm dying. What Tully is telling me is that if I don't squeeze some blood out of the rocks lying around Bill's empty office, my noggin's next on the block. Not what you like to hear when you just financed a nearly new BMW and you're charged to the max on your gold card.

But because I was clever, I fancied I was ruthless, and a week later I came up with a great possibility. As Lord Tully commanded, I'd combed through the pile of screenplays poor ol' fired Bill left behind and an astonishing thing happened. I found a good script.

It was a little gem. Hard, bitter, sex, violence, the whole nine yards. There was only one thing wrong with it: the end was no good. It needed, as we say, a wow finish. But I knew just what to do, how to slot in a big explosion, the best friend dies to save the hero, blah blah blah, layer the end of the story with all the lies dreams are made of, the lies that would make it big box office.

The writer's name was Ed Faraday and he was a middle-aged guy with kids. He'd been around since the year one, written a few novels, one or two arty screenplays, nothing you could take to the bank. He was just a writer and he was clinging tight to the frayed rope of hope, praying that this deal would make it all happen. I got on the phone and Faraday told me that his little tale of lost ethics in the munitions factory was high art and he wouldn't change a comma on its chinny chin chin. I listened, I was sympathetic, but I knew he had another think coming and I believed that I'd be able to wrench the script away from him, can all the talk-talk and tack on that big wow finish.

I didn't tell him this right away; I wasn't dumb enough to kill the writer who laid the golden oeuvre or bust his boyish dreams. My reasoning was that if I told him up front that his script had to be changed, it would only upset him. Better to wait, take it slow until the bright green smell of studio money was floating in the air. But I knew I had to give Faraday a taste now, just to get him on the hook, so I met him for breakfast, dug deep into my own pocket and took a short, very low money option on the thing without mentioning it to Nick Tully. I was hoping I could get away with this unethical twist of the knife into Tully's gut and praying that I could recoup when I made my big sale to one of the majors. Nothing ventured, right?

So, in order to marry a writer I didn't control to a deal I wasn't sure I could make, I began to court a young executive I knew from my Saturday softball game over at the park. I played second base for the Indies; Barry Gorman was right field for the Majors. We'd played often and most of the time we beat the pants off the Majors, which I attributed to the fact that we Indies had to play a lot harder just to keep up.

I only knew Barry Gorman by sight. He was thin and fit and had expensive clothes and he wasn't a very good ballplayer but he hacked away and every two or three games he made an amazing catch.

My plan was that after Barry and I became fast friends we would Vaseline my script—I was already thinking of it as *my* script—onto the studio's production schedule, thus catapulting Barry into the role of exec in charge. And me? Well, you don't want to mid-level it all your life and I had sparkly visions of deserting Tully, becoming a producer or worming my way into Barry's job at the studio when he took that next step up the golden ladder. Musical careers is what I had in mind.

But first Barry Gorman and I had to become buddies. I put Barry on the list for a screening my company was having at an independent projection room on the Strip and he came. Why not? We were both ballplayers even though we were on different teams. We waved across the room at each other; I was alone, he was with a skyscraper blonde I thought I recognized and I took it as a good sign that they stayed for the whole picture and didn't walk out halfway through.

After the movie, we went over to the Hamburger Hamlet and I nodded and told him his comments about the picture were astute. I played it studious and said he was film-wise. I was polite to the blonde, who turned out to be a big-time model, drove a Bentley, and probably made more than Barry and I put together.

Next Saturday after the game, I made sure that Barry and I ran into each other.

"What did you think of Betsy?" he asked me as we shook hands. He acted like he was glad to see me.

"Seems like a nice lady," I said, very noncommittal.

"Oh, she is," he agreed. "She's sincere, all right, but she lacks substance." He sighed. "It's hard to meet women with character in this town. They all want to be actresses."

I laughed and we agreed to get together for dinner next week.

I felt my friendship with Barry Gorman was up on its feet, and to tell the truth I was surprised that getting next to him was so easy. After all, he was much more important than I was in the baroque hierarchy that exists in this town, and he'd really opened up to me, told me about his problems and his personal life. I figured he was a rarity, a nice guy, and his interest in me was genuine.

Over dinner at La Masia, he offered a few helpful insights about Life With Tully and said he'd put me on the list for screenings at the studio. Barry was happy to tell me everything I wanted to know about himself, his thoughts, his ideas, his plans, the wonderful world of Barry Gorman, all the yimmy-yammy you hear every day of your life. But I listened, nodding, being thoughtful. In order to get my script off the ground, I needed Barry Gorman.

Meanwhile, like most would-be producers I'd quickly managed to erase the writer from my mind, but old Ed Faraday didn't want to be erased. The fool.

He kept showing up in my office unannounced, wanting me to stroke his ego, wanting to know how things were going, what they said, what I said. Poor Ed was a complete jerk, except he had a beautiful script hidden in his pocket and I was the only one who knew it was in there. He was a big guy, about my size, and he'd been a Marine. He had that protruding jaw that made me think of all those storybook pictures of pre-historic man toasting a slab of dino burger on the barbie. Didn't look like a writer is what I'm saying here. Looked like a Death Row inmate, if you want to know the truth.

So here's this mutant who keeps staggering into my office wanting to share, and all I want to do is suck his brain dry with a straw and heave his desiccated body out the window. But no, I'm too smart for that. I nod and listen to him rant about the multinationals, tell me how this script is going to be a breakthrough, the *Citizen Kane* of our time. . . . I nod, tell him what he wants to hear but the more Ed tells me, the more I hear, the worse I feel.

See, at first I thought that Ed the jerk would jump at the sign of real money; now I'm not so sure. Unlike me, unlike Barry or Tully, the poor writer's a true believer. He actually thinks his script is more than scribbled cannon fodder for those of us who toil on the battle lines of the media. He thinks that if the deal gets made and the picture gets made and the reviews are good and the folks get to see it, it would make a difference. The world would have to take notice of Ed Faraday and he'd finally get to make concerned statements about society's ills on *Nightline*. Me, I knew that all it would mean would be that Vanna would give us another spin of the Wheel of Fortune. Maybe the gods would be kind and we'd all get a free vowel.

But I ignored my misgivings and when the time was right I showed Ed's script to Barry. He gave it a fast read over the weekend and first thing Monday morning we had a meeting.

Barry had a big corner office in a shiny glass building right in the middle of the lot and he had it all tricked out with pastel design elements, including a set of Elvis plates behind his desk just to prove he was a humorous guy.

"No calls," he snapped as I came in. "Tom, I like it. Sure, it needs work . . ."

"Needs a wow finish," I said.

He laughed and nodded in agreement. "Right. I can get it made. Now tell me your end."

I settled back into his Barcelona chair, enjoying the view of the scrub oak on the mountain behind the sound stages that lay spread out under his window. "Since we're being honest"—I smiled—"here's the net-net. I have an option, but Tully doesn't know about it. I went under the table, used my own money."

"Taking chances, aren't you, pally?" he said, toying with a fat black pen I knew was a Montblanc.

"You're a lone wolf, you take chances," I told him. "But sad to say, the wolf's cash is short and my option's about to expire." I figured I had to tell Barry the truth, but I also figured that we were friends, we were on the same side. We could work together. "Can we make a deal that'll make us both happy?"

"Sure we can." He grinned.

By the end of our meeting we'd decided that once we had control of the script, we'd throw poor Ed Faraday out on his ass and do what we wanted. Oh, our prehistoric friend would come in for a nice share of the buckskis, no doubt about it. But we would have control.

I drove back to my dingy office and wrote Barry a long editorial memo explaining my plans for the script. As soon as possible we'd put another writer on it, sharpen up Ed's dialogue and tack on that big exploding wow finish I was dreaming about.

So Barry liked my memo, loved the changes, he was crazy about the whole enchilada. I was euphoric; visions of afternoons by the pool nipped at my brain like piranhas. By now Barry and I were pretty pleased with ourselves and we agreed that the studio would pick up the option and I would recoup my investment as soon as they worked out a deal with Faraday's agent. Of course, I would get a spot on the picture, probably executive producer. We hadn't worked out the nuts and bolts yet, but Barry assured me it was in the bag.

I'd been out celebrating at Morton's the night before, so I got into my dreary office later than usual the next morning and who do I find when I get in?

Ed Faraday, waiting for me. He was shifting uneasily back and forth on the chair outside my door like a sixth-grader waiting for the principal. Except Ed didn't look like a sixth-grader, he looked like an old, tired man, running his big paws through his thinning hair, picking lint off the dirty chinos he always wore.

He followed me inside without a word. "I hear you're setting up a deal with Barry Gorman," he said.

"Where'd you hear that?" I sidestepped.

"Friend of my wife's reads for Gorman," he said. Very flat, toneless, like a young gun at the big shoot-out. "She's a good friend. She saw the memo you wrote Gorman, outlining your ideas for changes. I told you a long time ago, no changes, Tom."

He's silent, standing behind the red chair across from my desk, his big hands kneading the cracked leather like it was dried dough.

I smiled at him, a benign smile that I hoped would comfort him. A bad stroke of luck, I thought ruefully. You forget that this is a small, small town. "No problem, Ed," I told him.

"What are you talking about, no problem," he said. "No problem for you, is that what you mean? Huh? Listen to me, Tom. It's a problem. You change my script, it's a problem. I'm not selling it to Gorman." Hands still crunching the red leather chair, now he's making burgers. His face is twisted and filled with controlled anger.

"Ed, look," I started. All of a sudden I remember what a big guy he is, plus he used to be a Marine. He's also blocking the door, so let's not rile the varmint. "Ed, you're a professional," I said, appealing to his ego. "You always knew the thing wasn't a shooting script. Come on, this deal can give your career the boost you've needed for years. Let's just get the deal, don't you see that? We'll tell 'em what they want to hear. . . ." I adopted a paternal tone, you and me, Ed, we're in this thing together, buddy. All boys together. "We both knew it wasn't going down to the wire without a little tinkering. Tap tap here, tap tap there? Nothing big, don't worry about it. Drink?" I'm still being benign so I stroll past him to the little walnut smoking cabinet where I keep a bottle of Chivas for emergencies.

"Tom," he said, shaking his head, "what are you doing this for? I saw your damn memo. My wife's friend photocopied it, brought it over last night. I told you, no changes. You were gonna screw me, man!"

I shrugged, hoping I looked more apologetic than I felt. I mean, you have to understand how things work in this town. The deal is everything; nothing exists but the deal, and in order to make the deal, I needed the script. But Ed was wrong, I wasn't going to screw him, far from it. He was going to get a lot of money out of this picture, a big credit. All I was going to get was a leg up.

"So don't lie to me," he said. "Pay me that courtesy. Just don't lie to me."

I almost laughed in his face. Don't lie to me. This prehistoric moron is saying don't lie to me. In this town, saying don't lie to me is like saying don't breathe, don't drive, don't live. He saw my mouth twist up as I tried to stifle my laughter and it really popped his cork.

"You little creep," he said. "How'd you get so creepy so fast, huh? I first met you, I thought you were okay. Gorman, everybody knows that guy's a sleazeball. He says yes to everything, tells everybody what he thinks they want to hear, then he porks 'em from behind. Everybody knows that's the kind of guy he is. I know he's trouble, but I thought you were solid. Whaddaya think, I've hung around all these years and I still don't know what's playing, huh?" he said viciously. "Whaddaya think, I'm gonna roll over, let you and Gorman pork me and walk away with my script? Wrong, my friend. Not gonna happen."

I blinked and knew it was all slipping away. Happy days by the pool, a better job, buy a house, a big office . . . My dreams for a new life were crumbling like stale wedding cake under a bored bride's pillow. If I lost control now, if the script slipped away from me now, the deal would die.

"Ed," I said, still paternal, but backing off a little on the pressure. "Nothing bad's going to happen. I wouldn't let anything bad happen to your script. Barry and I—"

"You dumb schmuck," he said. "He's gonna cut you out, too. Think about it, schmucko. What does he need you for? He's gonna pick up the option and cut you out. He's offered me serious money if I make the changes. Serious money, Tom. Why should he give you an allowance? He was just trying to get next to you, see if you had anything he could steal. That's the kind of guy he is, that's the way it works. You're a schmuck and you're deadweight."

Deadweight? A schmuck? Gorman was trying to get next to me? Me! I'd been trying to get next to him! I blinked again; the tidal wave was upon me. "What?" I said stupidly.

"Oh yeah," he laughed as he saw it on my face. For once, he was telling me something I didn't know. "You're out. You didn't know that?" Ed smiled, a little too ferocious with joy. "Gorman does this all the time. Everybody in town is on to him, everybody but you, schmucko."

He laughed and all the fight whooshed out of him as he sank down on the arm of the couch I'd appropriated when the guy in the office next door got canned. Now Ed's giggling at me. Giggling like a Girl Scout.

"You think Gorman got where he is in this town by carrying deadweight like you?" he asked me.

"Shut up," I told him. Very original comment, I realized. "I'm trying to think."

"You know, Tom," Ed said thoughtfully. "All of a sudden I feel a lot better. Now that I know Gorman screwed you, I feel positively happy. Maybe I've changed my mind about the script," he said slowly. "Maybe I'll just go ahead and let Gorman have it, maybe I don't give a damn anymore. I'd like to sit back and watch you shrivel. And I'll tell Tully you optioned the script with your own money, undercut him. Not very ethical, Tom," he said, wagging a big finger at me like I was a bad dog. "Time to think about going into another line of work. You're not tough enough for this dodge. Now me, I'm a writer, this isn't the end of the line for me. I can write another script. But you? You try to duke it out with Gorman, he'll rip your head off, no doubt about it. And Tully'll badmouth you all over town. But the worst part is, I'm gonna make sure everybody knows Gorman suckered you on this deal. You fell for it, schmuck. I'll enjoy watching you struggle." Faraday jumped up off the couch, Magic Johnson in his K mart sneakers, waved me a jaunty toodle-oo and left.

I sat stupidly in my office for a few long minutes, thinking about my new persona as a schmuck. All this work, down the drain. I could handle failure, after all, a deal goes bad on you, there's always hope. But I couldn't handle Ed Faraday's vision of me as a schmuck or my brilliant movie career shredded by laughter. I felt anger flooding across my eyeballs.

Then, who do you think calls? Barry Gorman, Mr. Sunshine, wanting to know if we're on for batting practice this evening.

"Sounds great," I said, a mechanical grin in my voice. "I got a six o'clock meeting. Seven good for you?"

"Seven is great," he says.

I go home and sleep.

I woke up with a headache The dull orange air felt thick and hard on my skin as I got into my next-door-to-new BMW and drove over to the park. Early evening here is strange, the heavy air, jagged palm leaves gnashing their teeth, harsh colored lights glittering off the shining chrome grilles in the sea of cars sweeping down the freeway, the end of the day ripping your skin apart like a thousand glass needles. I pulled into the parking lot, took my gear from under the seat of the car and went out to the diamond to meet Barry Gorman.

I saw Barry across the grass and as I walked toward him I knew that this was the movie I'd been born to make. I felt myself fluid and smooth as I walked in slow motion, saw Barry coming over to me, smiling, his hand out, wanting to shake hands with me. I lifted my shining red aluminum bat, felt its warm, pleasant weight in my hand and brought it down dead center into the middle of Barry Gorman's grinning skull. Wow finish.

Janet La Pierre's Unquiet Grave, *a Macavity award nominee,
introduced readers to the fictional town of Port Silva, California, and to Police Chief Vince Gutierrez and high-school
teacher Meg Halloran; both characters return in* Children's
Games *and* The Cruel Mother. *Janet explains that her fiction
explores themes such as manipulation, seduction, and growing up—or not—in contemporary America. As an example,
she refers to singer Rosalie Sorrels, who says that growing
up is hard, and that after age fifty, she quit trying.*

*In "The Man Who Loved His Wife," Chief Gutierrez and
Officer Alma Linhares confront a man who loved perhaps not
wisely but too well.*

THE MAN WHO LOVED HIS WIFE

by Janet LaPierre

"OFF!" THE DOG hesitated, growling softly, and Alma
Linhares kept her right hand on her holstered revolver
while she considered the options. She didn't want to
blow away somebody's pet, even one this ugly, should have
kept her butt in the car except that boredom and curiosity had
gotten to her.

"Nice doggy," she muttered, and was not surprised to get
another, deeper growl in response. Okay, when the chief sent
her to keep an eye on the son of a bitch who apparently owned
this mutt, he didn't exactly say it had to be from cover. "Mr.
Berquist?" she sang out. "Could you call off your dog please?"

The front door of the house opened, and a tall figure clad in
Levi's and a white T-shirt shambled out onto the porch. "Caesar!" He shaded his eyes with one hand as he peered down
into the yard. "Caesar, go to your house."

The dog, a leggy, grizzled beast with German shepherd
somewhere in its ancestry, lowered head and tail and slunk off.
"Sorry," Arnold Berquist called. "He's confused, he misses
Celia and the kids." Moving across the porch and down the

steps, Berquist carried his gaunt frame with hunched caution, as if a misstep might awaken a pain somewhere. His face was haggard and unshaven, colorless except for reddened eyelids. Hand half extended, he stopped and frowned at her. "I don't know you, do I?"

"No, sir. I'm Officer Linhares, Alma Linhares." She had never met the man, but the Berquists kept having troubles of the kind that brought them to public notice. A gust of wind pushed his smell at her, sweat and booze. Grief might be a good excuse for hitting the bottle, but guilt was just as likely; and she personally wasn't convinced that Celia Berquist had committed suicide.

"Ah." He looked at her, and then past her, toward the chain-link fence and the thick stand of brush that screened his property, five acres as she recalled, from the road. Behind him, the narrow two-story house showed no lights although this late October afternoon was darkly overcast.

"So." He focused on her once again, with a nod and a grimace probably meant as a smile. "Everything is straightened out, and I can proceed with arrangements."

"No, sir, not yet. Chief Gutierrez asked me to stop by, since you don't have a phone. He had to go to Ukiah this afternoon. He should be back before long and he'll come straight here."

"Don't you people care that you're driving me crazy?" He lifted clenched fists and hammered them down against empty air, nearly losing his balance with the force of the gesture. "There can't be any doubt about what happened, it was . . . it's Celia's family, isn't it? Trying to make trouble?"

"I don't really know, sir." Alma saw the shine of sweat on his forehead, saw him shiver. So far as she knew, she was out here as a kind of baby-sitter, and the chief would probably be seriously pissed if she let the baby catch pneumonia. "Could we go inside? The wind is getting real sharp might even be an early rain on the way."

"Oh. Yes, of course." He nodded and reached out as if to take her elbow; Alma stepped aside and gestured for him to precede her. Always a good idea to make clear who was in charge, and besides, she didn't want his hand on her.

It was an old house, pinched and charmless, as if its builder had grudged every board and pane of glass. But the paint was fresh, the narrow staircase and the living-dining room thickly carpeted against noise and drafts. Sofa, several stuffed chairs, a rocker, tables. Pictures on the walls, flowers and landscapes. Big television set, and a spinet piano against the far wall. Most of the furniture sat askew, and flat surfaces bore a thick film of dust.

"Sit down, please. I'm sorry. . . ." He looked around the room and shrugged. "I've never been much of a housekeeper. And to be honest, Celia pretty much gave up this past year on anything but the kids and that committee."

A brick fireplace was centered on the outer wall to the left, its maw filled now by a black iron stove. Alma went to inspect a row of framed photographs on the mantel and found Celia Berquist: cheerleader, cornsilk hair and sky-blue eyes and sexy pout; bride, wide-eyed and ethereal; madonna from a church painting, round-bellied and demure.

Then Celia the mother, holding a baby, trailing a toddler, supervising a crowded sandbox. In the last frame, thinner now with hair dimmed to light brown, Celia stood with two freckled little boys and a skinny girl, holding on her hip the baby of a year or so that had to be poor Amy. The photos were clearly the work of a loving amateur with a steady hand and a good camera, probably Berquist; remembering similar displays in the homes of her sisters, Alma thought it odd that there were no separate shots of the kids.

"In a way I do blame myself." Berquist's voice was rough, as if his throat hurt. "I was thirty . . . aah, no, that's a lie. I'd been teaching for twelve years and I was thirty-five years old. Celia was seventeen and beautiful as a sunrise, she made my whole world glow." As he turned to smile at Alma, she caught behind the lank grey-streaked hair and bleary eyes a glimpse of the man who'd been able to charm the socks . . . or anyway the pants . . . off that gorgeous girl.

"Seventeen," she said, and stopped just short of saying that she, too, had been crazy in love at seventeen with a teacher, a man she hadn't thought of in years. Mr. Corey, who told her she had beautiful eyes and five feet seven wasn't too tall and someday a nice man would love her as much as he, Mr. Corey, loved his wife. Too bad Celia hadn't encountered a Mr. Corey.

Berquist's eyes narrowed and his mouth made a grim down-curve. "Some people, the woman I'd been going out with for instance, saw Celia as a randy teenage girl seducing an older man for the challenge. Girls do that sort of thing, you know; any male teacher who's reasonably young and attractive could tell you endless tales.

"Then of course others—most people, including Celia's family—insisted I'd either brainwashed her or more likely raped her, right there in the classroom."

Alma made a little murmur, something between shock and sympathy, and he shrugged. "So the principal fired me and assured me that I'd never teach again in a California public school. Celia's parents tried to force her to leave me, to have the baby and give it up for adoption. But we loved each other. We knew God meant us to be together forever."

He swung away from the mantel abruptly, dropped to the couch and put his head in his hands. "I'm sorry. I've been alone out here going quietly nuts, nobody to talk to or . . . Could I ask you, Miss . . ."

"Linhares. Alma."

"Ah. A pretty name, is it Spanish?" He lifted his head to look at her.

"Portuguese."

"Alma, I haven't had a decent cup of coffee in days; I can't seem to make it come out right. Would you mind making a pot?"

"Okay." And you owe me one, Chief Gutierrez, she told her boss silently. Probably turn out to be more than one. Berquist stayed where he was, hunched forward over his knees. As Alma turned away, she found there was a picture inside her own head that belonged there on the mantel: Celia one day at the police station, right after her loving husband had beat the shit out of her.

The kitchen, an awkward square of a room with too few windows, contained all kinds of nice shiny appliances, including a Krups coffee maker. Alma located an open can of coffee and set the machine to work. Big garden outside the back door, most of it dried up now or gone to seed. A shed and run for chickens beyond the garden, looking empty. Sinkful of dirty dishes, more dishes littering the table against the wall. A couple of cardboard boxes under the table, and a telephone, not connected. She pulled open a flap on the nearest box, to find a stack of flyers: "Find the Children."

The coffee maker spat and sputtered to a finish; she poured a mugful and carried it in to set it on the low table before the couch.

"Thank you." He sat up, blinked hard and squared his shoulders. "Aren't you having some?"

"I'm not much of a coffee drinker," she lied, preferring to keep her hands free. As he lifted the mug to his mouth, she sat down in the rocker. Her survey of the lower floor had revealed no toy trucks or dolls or sports gear, no children's books or crayoned drawings from school; perhaps Celia's kids had spent all their time upstairs. Or perhaps they had taken along, to their grandparents' home where they were staying, everything they owned.

"Something wrong with the coffee?" she asked as Berquist set the mug down after two swallows.

"Just . . . needs a little something." He lurched to his feet and set off toward the kitchen. Back door, she thought, and got up quickly to follow. His truck was out back, and a lot of open country; if he got away or maybe even killed himself, Chief Gutierrez would eat her alive and spit out the bones. Berquist reached not for the door but for a cupboard high over the sink, to retrieve a bottle; Alma released held-in breath, returned to her chair and sat there watching him top off his coffee with bourbon. Jim Beam, from a 750-milliliter bottle now down slightly more than half.

"So what brought you and Celia to Port Silva?" she asked him. Wife-killer or not, he clearly liked to talk, and it might slow the drinking.

"You ever been to Yuba City?" He didn't wait for an answer. "Hot as hell, dusty, only job I could find was in my Uncle Earl's plumbing shop where I'd worked summers during high school and college. We had this stuffy little apartment, and Celia was sick practically the whole nine months; I think that's when her depression really began. And her mother and sisters and about a dozen cousins were always hanging around. We needed to get away, get ourselves some privacy."

This was private, all right. Five acres of scrubland at the very edge of a chilly north-coast town. Half a mile to the nearest neighbor, five or six to the grocery store.

"So I found a job here, Mazzini's Plumbing. And I bought this place. Room for a garden, chickens, we got a calf to raise. Celia was safe here, and she could send the kids outside to play without worrying that they'd get run over." He reached for the bottle and poured more bourbon into his cup.

"You said her depression began years ago," Alma remarked. "Did she ever see anybody, a doctor, about that?"

"No. We aren't—weren't—believers in psychologists and therapists and that lot. We believe in hard work, and prayer, and trusting in God. And in talking to your pastor; I know Celia drew great comfort from her visits with Pastor Kilgren."

Alma had met Pastor Kilgren of Port Silva Southern Baptist
and had found him well-meaning if sanctimonious, and not
very smart. Put her on the battle lines, she'd a whole lot rather
have Father Lucchesi beside her. On most issues, anyway. "Mr.
Berquist, excuse me for asking this, but I come from a big
family, brothers and sisters and nieces and nephews. I know
kids can really wear you down. Didn't Celia ever want to do
something else for a change—get a job, maybe?"

He sat up and glared at her. "She had a job, right here. Oh,
she wanted to help out, she tried part-time stuff a couple of
times. But James and Ellen hated day care, and the baby got
sick, and I developed an ulcer. We needed her at home."

Celia had her fourth child at, let's see, twenty-four years of age.
Alma suppressed a shudder and reminded herself that her own
mother had had five children by the age of thirty. God. She sighed,
got slowly to her feet and stretched—to ease tight muscles and to
cast a glance out the front window. Dusk coming quickly up to
dark, no traffic. Where was the chief, anyway?

"So we were just fine," Berquist went on mournfully. "Celia
got a small inheritance from her grandmother and I let her buy
a little car. Before that she'd been getting up early to drive me
to work on days she wanted to keep the truck. Besides, she
was pregnant again and the truck wasn't big enough anymore,
not in bad weather."

He took a big mouthful from the mug, set it down, and
reached for the bottle.

"Let me get you more coffee." She snatched up the mug
before he could protest, carried it to the kitchen and filled it.

"Well. Thank you." He took a gulp that must have burned
his mouth, took a second and then tipped in whiskey to the
brim. "Anyway, pretty soon Amy was born and things were
just fine for, oh, quite a while, a couple years."

Alma, shoulder-propped beside the mantel, kept her eyes
down and her whole body still, in a tension that apparently
communicated itself across the room.

"Of course you know about that, the police know. The time
I lost my temper and that's why I'm being treated this way
now, I understand that." Berquist's speech was losing its crisp
edge to the whiskey; he licked his lips and spoke more slowly.

"You see, my wife, my wife didn't talk to me about it, or
to her pastor either. She just drove herself to Santa Rosa and

went to a clinic and had an abortion. Without her husband's permission, I didn't think a wife could do that. I was upset.''

And Celia filed a complaint and then withdrew it the next day. Like any poor dumb broad would who had no education, no job and four kids.

''I never hit her again,'' Berquist said hoarsely. ''I argued with her, and I tried to make her understand that I loved her and wanted her with me, that kids need a full-time mother. But as God is my witness, I never again laid a hand on her in anger. Not even last year, when she went off and left me, left us.''

This was all a matter of sad record. Celia Berquist had hired a baby-sitter, a woman recommended by a church friend. Celia had then set off for a three-week study conference at the University of California at Santa Cruz, a program intended to prepare women for a second chance at higher education. While Celia was away, three-year-old Amy disappeared and was never seen again. The baby-sitter, an illegal from Central America, had disappeared as well.

''She just never got over losing Amy.'' Berquist sniffed and wiped a forearm across his eyes. ''I said we should have another baby. I let her work with that lost-children committee until she wore herself out, then I made her quit for her own good. Took the phone out, told those other people to leave her alone. I loved her. I never blamed her for Amy, she thought I did but I didn't.

''Hey.'' He wiped his eyes again and peered up at her owlishly. ''If you don't drink coffee, how about a little bourbon? No, that's right,'' he said as she shook her head. ''Cops don't drink on duty, huh? Especially not lady cops, I bet. What do you suppose has happened to that boss of yours?''

''I expect him any minute.''

''And what did he send you here for, anyway? To shoot me if I try to run away?''

''You're not under arrest, Mr. Berquist. I think he was worried about you, out here all by yourself.''

''And he sent me company. What a friendly fellow he is. Listen to me!'' He planted his feet and thrust his head forward. Gaunt and grey, he still had an impressive breadth of shoulder, and corded muscles ridged his forearms.

''I swear to God I did not kill my wife, my wife that I loved more than anything on earth.'' His lips trembled, and tears began to spill from his eyes in a slow trickle that he ignored. ''Three days ago my beautiful Celia took the kids to a friend from church.

Then she got into a bathtub full of water and cut her wrists. When I got home from work I found her there floating in her own blood, and I found the note that said she was just too tired to go on. *Shit*, why am I even talking to you?"

"Mr. Berquist, I'm not here to upset you. If you want me to, I'll leave."

"Sure you will, and you'll go about as far as the end of the driveway. A suicide watch, is that it? Listen, I loved my wife, but I'm not going to kill myself." He sank to the couch, stretched his long legs out wearily and took a gulp from the mug. After perhaps ten seconds of silence, he said, "Pretty."

"I beg your pardon?"

"I said you're pretty, a pretty girl. Thick shiny black hair, beautiful eyes." He drank again. "Nice big boobs under that ugly brown shirt, make your husband happy, feed your babies. Pretty girl like you shouldn't walk around with a badge and a gun."

Sure, asshole. Alma kept her breathing even and hoped her anger did not color her face. Sure, spend my days cleaning up after some prick like you, my nights making babies. Probably poor Celia *was* just tired to death, thought suicide looked like a good long rest.

"Almost as pretty as Celia. I didn't kill my Celia." He pulled his legs close, planted his feet with care and rose. "Pretty lady, soft pretty lady. Believe me?"

Actually, she did. "Yes, I believe you," Alma assured him as she began to back toward the door. She couldn't shoot this weeping drunk, and she wasn't confident that she could take him out any other way, not in this narrow, furniture-cluttered room. Not when he had about seven inches on her and those long arms. Let's get this out-of-doors.

He came slowly around the table, swaying slightly, arms wide as if to embrace her. She moved sideways, felt the door handle behind her, pulled the door open and backed around it.

"Officer Linhares?"

"Jesus!" She'd backed right into Gutierrez, practically knocked him down. "Sorry, Chief. I was just . . . trying to defuse the situation."

"Good." Gutierrez stepped into the room. Alma followed close on his heels. Berquist looked blearily at them, nodded, backed up and sat down.

"Chief. Chief Gutierrez, I'm glad to see you. I bet you have the coroner's report, and the handwriting report, and all that stuff, right?"

"Right."

"So you know that I did not kill my wife. I didn't kill Celia."

"Correct, I know that. But what about Amy?"

Berquist squinted, opened his mouth, closed it and swallowed. "I don't understand."

"Before killing herself, Celia Berquist wrote a note."

"I know *that*. I found it for God's sake."

"Another note, more of a letter. She wrote a letter to the Port Silva Police Department, to me, and went out and mailed it and then came home and climbed in the bathtub."

"No."

Alma watched Berquist shrink into himself, shoulders high and tight and quivering, bent knees up close like a barricade to hide behind. She turned to look at the man beside her and flinched. Gutierrez's dark face was hard as a clenched fist, his lips drawn tight in a white-toothed snarl. Alma took a quick step sideways.

"Listen. 'Dear Chief Gutierrez. My husband Arnold Berquist killed our daughter Amy Berquist, age three. I am sure about this, I worked it out from things he has been saying to me recently.' "

Jesus, Mary and Joseph. Alma put one hand across her mouth, the other on the butt of her revolver.

"That's not true." Berquist shook his head. "Absolutely not true. Celia was depressed, suicidal. She kept having terrible nightmares about Amy, and she came to see them as real."

"There's more. 'I have tried to think where he put her after killing her, and the only place would be his fishing place, up near the Lost Coast on a creek called Usal Creek. I have never been there, but one of the men he works with has, Peter Benoit. I believe you will find my daughter Amy Berquist buried there. Thank you for your help. Celia Berquist.' "

"I got the letter this morning," said Gutierrez. "Peter Benoit took me to the place on Usal Creek. I found Amy."

Alma, feeling her lateish lunch rise to press at the back of her throat, turned from Gutierrez's frozen face to stare at the man who loved his wife.

Berquist frowned into space, let his shoulders slump and his hands fall loose. "But I had to show her what terrible things could happen if she left us."

Meg O'Brien's new series featuring Jessica James, investigative reporter, is set in Rochester, New York, where Meg once lived. Introduced in The Daphne Decisions, *skeptical, irreverent Jesse and her cohorts—a homicide detective, a yuppie mob leader, and a guru named Samved—return in* Salmon in the Soup *and* Hare Today, Gone Tomorrow.

In "Kill the Woman and Child," Jesse's ability to hit the mark helps her score a bull's-eye at a holiday bash.

KILL THE WOMAN AND CHILD

by Meg O'Brien

"COME IN, OUTLAW. Over." The low voice issued from a two-way radio attached to my belt. It was accompanied by a crackle of static.

Outlaw. The name, much as I despised it, seemed appropriate enough. My mom had labeled me Jessica when she was still in and out of the ether and Pop was on a drunk. It never even occurred to her that with a last name like James, I'd be known as Jesse by third grade. When I was twelve I hung out with boys, and I wanted to change my handle to Spike, or Bugs, or something equally amusing, but Mom wouldn't allow it. Just as well. In Rochester, New York, in my neighborhood, changing your name was the sort of thing you did when getting married, or (same difference) on the way to jail.

I pulled the radio from my belt and punched the talk button. "This is Outlaw. Come in, over."

"Judas is heading in your direction. He's wearing a black leather windbreaker, work boots, brown cords . . ." I knew the rest of the description well enough: thirty-seven, six feet tall, light hair. A nasty scar running straight down the middle of his cheek. "He's armed with a Wolfe 134 automatic rifle, and he knows we're here. Don't blow it this time."

I clicked off without saying "Over." My mouth was too dry. I shifted the weight of my own rifle and raised it to shoulder level, peering through the sight and scanning the quiet street.

It was a small town, colonial in style like so many in New York State. An ordinary village, except that a child killer, a sniper—code name Judas—stalked its streets.

The temperature, I thought, must be in the nineties. The time was 2:07 P.M. We were too far inland from Lake Ontario to get a breeze, but every now and then a truck rumbled by, raising dust in the air. My black sleeveless tee stuck to my back, and my long brown hair, tucked inside a fatigue cap, bled sweat onto my forehead.

I leaned my back against the brick siding of the town hall and tried to relax. Breathe in. Breathe out. Don't let your nerves take over.

The crackle again. "Outlaw? He should reach you in less than ten seconds. He should be in your view. Over."

I snaked a look around the building. I didn't see him anywhere. Nor did I hear any sounds. No birds, no dogs, and even the traffic had quit. I felt like the abandoned marshal in some Wild West movie. Was everybody hiding indoors, like in *High Noon*, that old Gary Cooper flick? And what would I do when Judas appeared? Would I step out, cool and brave as Coop, and shoot him dead? Or would I turn tail and run?

I had blown it yesterday. I couldn't fail again.

My hands shook. The rifle slipped from my grip. I caught it before it hit the ground.

I didn't want to do this. I hate guns. I hate killing. To me, heaven is a place where people leave people alone. But my job was to make sure Judas was killed. "It shouldn't be that difficult," they had said in the briefing. "The man is a monster. He deserves to be killed."

Keep telling yourself that, Jess. He deserves to be killed.

A sound, like that of a twig snapping. A grunt a short distance away. The hairs rose on the back of my neck. *Behind me.* I swung around. *Judas. Killer. Monster.* He stepped out from the shelter of a mom-and-pop grocery store less than thirty feet away, his weapon raised to shoot. I jerked back and felt my legs turn to liquid as bullets ricocheted above my head. From other areas I heard loud reports begin. Someone was covering me, drawing his fire their way. Maybe they'd get him first.

I closed my eyes, willing myself far away in Florida, the Caribbean, Duluth—anywhere but here.

At some point, the gunfire settled down. I took a deep breath and dared a look at the store again. A gun barrel glinted in the sunlight. It was pointed directly at me. I yanked my rifle up. Sweat blurred my eyes, and I had to pull back and hurriedly wipe them. I sighted into the sun again.

That quickly, Judas disappeared. Where the hell *was* he? One moment he was there, and the next—

Shit! Movement only ten feet away now—across the street by the bank. Judas? I couldn't be sure. Then something metallic clicked, so close that it almost stopped my heart. There was no doubt in my mind it was Judas. I whirled sideways and aimed my rifle as a projectile slammed into the ground at my feet, spraying pieces of asphalt everywhere. I wasn't thinking, suddenly, about how I hated killing. I pulled the trigger without thought, in a knee-jerk response to fear. The rifle bucked, slamming into my shoulder, almost knocking me down. The sound split my eardrums. I realized I hadn't put the automatic on, and I closed my eyes and squeezed the trigger over and over, not wanting to see the bullets strike their mark.

I heard a baby cry.

My eyes flew open, and with horror I saw that where Judas should have been, there stood instead a light-haired woman holding a baby. In my mind, a look of terror crossed her innocent face. (You understand, I tell this now from hindsight. It all happened simultaneously that day. The woman. The baby's cry. My finger squeezing the trigger.)

My bullets struck and the woman fell, clutching her child. They lay motionless in the dust.

I dropped the rifle as pain enveloped my heart. *I couldn't do anything right.* I heard Pop saying that over and over: "You always do everything wrong, Jesse . . . never do anything right." He'd say it in a drunken stupor most of the time, but that didn't change the fact that I believed every word. Even at thirty, I was still hearing it—a family recipe, handed down from one drunken Irish generation to the other: *You'll never amount to anything good.*

I stumbled the few feet across the street and stood above the woman and baby. Her chest, her face, the baby's entire body, were riddled with holes. Shaking with rage, I kicked the woman. She flopped a little, but otherwise, she didn't move. I kicked the baby. I stomped on his face. "God damn you both," I yelled.

Then, turning my back on the painted plywood target, I left the Davies School of Defense for Executive Bodyguards. I never wanted to see the goddamned place again.

I stopped in at a bar on the way home. Not Harrigan's, where the bartenders knew me and knew I'd been to a treatment program recently. A dreary little joint called Jack's, somewhere along the river. It had rotting green window shades and was dense with smoke. Factory workers were drinking their lunch with sides of Polish sausages and pickled eggs.

I ordered a Genesee Screw—Genesee beer over sliced oranges, my old favorite from drinking days. I had to tell the bartender how to make it, and when I specified Genesee, he lifted a scraggly gray brow. Genesee is usually only ordered hereabouts by merchant marines, mass murderers, and embittered reporters like me.

When it came, I stared at it a while. While I stared, I remembered how I'd gotten into this mess.

Marcus Andrelli, head of an elite branch of the mob in Western New York, had offered me a job as his bodyguard. This is the New Mob, you understand—no drugs, prostitution, or ordinary street crime will ever tarnish its smooth white cuffs. A cabal of Harvard-type business grads, Marcus's group is dedicated to the proposition that all men are created to move money and land with the least amount of legalities and the highest level of profit possible.

I make no excuses for the fact that Marcus is my friend and sometime lover. The reasons are unclear, even to me, but have something to do—I suspect—with that old adage about moth to the flame. As for the offer of a job as bodyguard, being a reporter has its frustrations, and I guess Marcus noticed I had sort of burned out. I love writing (as Peter DeVries, I think, has said); what I can't stand is the paperwork. Marcus, on the other hand, offered $60,000 a year, a company Beamer, and travel to foreign countries.

You probably think that as a woman with very little cash in her pocket, a '68 car with bad karma, and a job I hate, I jumped at the chance.

Are you *crazy*? Me, Jesse James, work for (wait a minute now, what's that euphemism?) the *organization*? Become an outlaw for *real*? My ingrained sense of guilt would never allow it.

Take the woman and baby, for instance. I will carry that moment of stupidity around with me all my life. The problem being: What if they'd been real? That, of course, was the whole point of the Davies exercise, and why it had played havoc with my nerves. As the kid of an alcoholic, I'd learned early on that more often than not, I fail.

So I could never work at a job that required I carry a gun. I opted instead for doing a little independent study at Davies School of Defense—research for a story on exotic vocations. I'd felt sure I could free-lance it if the *Herald* didn't bite.

I pushed my cap back on my head and shivered as the air-conditioning finally had its way with my sunburned arms. I fiddled with the frosted glass of the Genesee Screw, but didn't drink. I kept seeing that target—that woman and child. The damned thing was like Swiss cheese. How had it gotten that way?

In the classes at Davies—before you go out on the exercise field—they teach you to stop shooting when you hear the baby's cry. It's the first clue you've blown it: an automatic wail issuing from a speaker high above the grounds once you hit the woman and child. The target is then picked up by an instructor and assessed as a kind of "report card." A new, unblemished hunk of plywood takes its place.

But the target I'd hit was already riddled with holes. My rifle hadn't been on automatic; a few splinters should have been the extent of the damage from me—provided I'd struck it at all. And I'd been the first student out on the field that day.

Someone practicing in the night, then? An instructor, say—and he'd forgotten to change the target before the day's run? Whoever, he was one mean son of a bitch. A crazy who didn't like women and kids at all. It gave me the creeps, and I wondered what kind of checks they ran on people before letting them teach at those schools.

I finally left the beer untouched and went in search of a phone. The wall around it was decorated with graffiti, and among its many offerings—the Salvation Army, Travelers' Aid, 1-800-HERPES2—was an AA number. I ignored it, of course. Since drying out at St. Avery's three months ago, I'd been seeing a New Age shrink in Pittsford named Samved. He and I had concluded there was nothing worse than imprinting a belief on one's consciousness like: *I am an alcoholic.* I mean, when you've already got a bad self-image, where do you go from there? I much prefer Samved's approach: *You have a problem with drinking on this plane, today. In reality, however, you are a perfect child of God. Children of God can be healed.*

I eyed my beer, back there on the bar. Wet my lips.

Uh-huh.

I clunked in a quarter and dialed Marcus Andrelli's private line.

Marcus, dressed in gray sweats and an old pair of white Converse running shoes, was still on the phone when I arrived. His black hair was damp and curling from a recent workout. His desk, a field of glass the size of a small hockey rink, was piled high with newspapers, *Wall Street Journal*s, real-estate dailies and files on every major politician in the country. A computer blinked, a fax was busy spewing forth reams of paper, and two additional phones were ringing.

Behind Marcus, sheer blue curtains stretched over wall-to-wall glass. When the curtains are pulled back they reveal the entire city of Rochester beneath one's feet—and a fine place for the city of Rochester to be, if you ask me.

I paced, only half hearing a series of sentences involving words like *foreclosure . . . bankrupt . . . takeover.* I thought how much alike—and unalike—Marcus and I are. In his work, he manipulates and cons people, just like me. But I'm embarrassed when I do it, and immediately thereafter comes the guilt.

Marcus, on the other hand, considers his antics a skill. He learned to live with himself years ago, and hasn't always got a whole lot of patience with angst like mine. Why I burden him with it, I don't profess to know.

"Jess . . ." Marcus said as he hung up. He rose from his desk, a tall, well-exercised figure at forty-two, with hard, even features. His brown, nearly black eyes were tinged with caution most of the time, warranted or not. Marcus ordinarily doesn't turn that expression on me, for which I am glad. "You look—"

"Dusty," said an amused voice from the other end of the room.

I hadn't even seen Tark there. For a big hulk of a guy, he

manages to kind of inconspicuously hang around. He was leaning against the back of a sofa, arms folded, legs crossed nonchalantly at the ankle.

Tark is Marcus's bodyguard and has been his friend since childhood. More Diogenes in latter days than Dillinger, Tark's fondest wish is to go on a backpacking trip in the Himalayas. He was hoping I'd take Marcus up on his offer of a job and sub for him while he was gone.

"Go ahead, laugh," I grumbled. "I'd like to see *you* out at that not so funny farm, crawling under barbed wire in one of those imported silk suits of yours."

He grinned.

I turned to Marcus. "I need a drink."

His dark brow lifted almost as much as the bartender's at Jack's, but for different reasons. And even though he knew damn well what I meant, Marcus headed for the bar where he'd already fixed a pitcher of something cold and almost assuredly virgin. He poured me a glass.

"Try this," he said.

I tasted the honey-laced pineapple crap and swore something unpleasant under my breath. Marcus could be damned aggravating when it came to helping me stay sober. Two Saturdays ago, for instance, I'd headed out to his cabin at Irondequoit, thinking it'd be a great day to sit on his yacht down on the water, drink a little, catch some rays. (I'd plotted the part about "drinking a little" for three solid days in advance.)

Instead, there never was time, somehow, to sit on the *SeaStar* and fall from grace. We'd sanded and painted, scoured and scraped, and even ridden a fallen tree down an estuary of the bay, planning to use it for the mast of the Tancook Whaler that Marcus was building from scratch. I couldn't walk for days afterward, my muscles were that sore. I stayed sober, though. It wasn't until the weekend was over that I realized Marcus had planned it that way. Marcus Andrelli could be sneaky. Never saying a word, but ahead of me all the way.

"They've got all these targets," I began now without preamble, pacing. The cap was jammed down over my eyes, and my hair was falling out of it in long sweaty strings. Despite the juice, I could taste grit in my mouth, feel it on my face, and I looked, I suppose, about as stunning as I ever do.

"One minute," I complained, "it's a genuine bad guy popping out at you. The next, it's Rebecca of Sunnybrook Farm.

And the place is booby-trapped, fake bullets exploding all
around, but you forget they're fake—you have to psych yourself
up to kill or they wash you out, you *fail* . . .'' I faltered over
the word and turned away, picking up a small bronze figurine
and staring at it blindly. "You have to learn to think fast, because in real life there's no time to think. The problem is, I'm
not fast." I slammed the object down. "I shot the woman and
the goddamned baby."

Marcus sat on the edge of his desk. "You agonize too much.
It was only a target, Jess."

But Tark understood. "The thing that's bothering Jess is what
bothers me all the time: what if, in the heat of action, your
instincts are wrong?" He stood with his broad back to the
windows, hands stuck in the pockets of his expensive black
summer-weight suit. His dark hair, tinged with gray, was short
and brushed straight back, his features worked over but not
otherwise bad. "The thing you've got to remember, Jess, is
that you haven't had the kind of training that others take before
that particular exercise. I gave you—what?—six hours on a
practice range, just so you could hold a weapon with some
authority? You couldn't expect to do any better than you did."

"Dammit, it doesn't matter. I made the wrong decision, I
always do—"

"You always take on more than you should," Marcus said
impatiently. "You throw yourself into hot water over and over,
then ask yourself why you keep getting burned."

I gulped down more juice and stared longingly at the bottles
on the bar. A little rum in this stuff would taste real good. I
sneaked a glance at Marcus. He seemed unconcerned, but that
didn't fool me. If I reached for the rum he'd break my arm.

"Listen, I don't mean to make more of this than it is." I
managed a smile. "I've got my story, after all. Hell, I've got
a better story than I'd expected: SCREW-UP REPORTER SHOOTS
WOMAN AND BABY. I can see the headlines now."

Marcus and Tark didn't say anything. They just gave each
other that look I'd come, lately, to know: *Jess is on the edge.
How much longer can it be?* Any minute now Marcus would
be saying, "Jess, have you noticed how much you're swearing
today?" (He worries about the old-fashioned Italian Catholic
things like that. And for somebody who likes to be her own
boss, this quaint, protective attitude toward women is per-
versely endearing to me.)

But I ranted on, unable to stop, I was so wired. "What I can't get out of my mind is that shredded target. You'd think they were training the bad guys there, not the good ones."

Tark murmured, "Now there's a thought," and turned to gaze out the window, looking thoughtful.

"Speaking of mercenaries," Marcus said, "will you be covering the Eastman bash tomorrow?"

"Ah, the definition of mercenary . . . corrupt, unprincipled, scheming . . . it fits our city's financial fathers to a T."

The occasion tomorrow, according to the news releases, was a celebration of the remodeling of the George Eastman mansion. In actuality, the town's financial fathers had chosen this particular date because of the international peace talks taking place in the Thousand Islands this week. It was the perfect time to draw in foreign dignitaries, make business contacts 'round the globe.

"What about you, Marcus? You planning to cash in on this little opportunity too?"

"Got to keep ahead of the game," he said, and shrugged.

The secret to Marcus Andrelli's success, in business and with people—always be ahead of the game.

He slid off the desk, put an arm behind my back, and drew me outside to a small terrace. I heard the apartment door close softly and knew that Tark had left us alone.

We stood looking out over Rochester: Marcus, who had made the leap from the wrong side of the tracks to owning maybe half of what he saw, and me—somewhere on the tracks themselves, wondering when, if ever, the train would come wooshing along and run me down.

Marcus said, "We make choices in life, Jess. Year to year, moment to moment—once a path is set, a decision made, you can't go back and question everything. You could become paralyzed that way."

I pushed back my cap. "Look, no offense, but Christ, Marcus—how can you live that way?"

"For me, there are no more choices. I can't change what I do."

"Well, damn it all, anyway—"

He pushed a dusty tangle of hair from my face. "Have you noticed you're swearing a lot lately?" my sometime lover said.

* * *

I had time on my hands after that, so I checked in at the *Herald* for the first time in a week, got yelled at by Charles Nicks, my editor, and ambushed by Becky Anderson—who had followed me here from the *Weston Free Press*. She did this to annoy me, I'm convinced. It's her Life Purpose to keep reminding me that I'm not up to code in my dress, manners, or style.

Charlie rubbed his bald little pate irritably with ink-stained fingers and yelled through his glass cubicle, "Don't disappear on me again, James! I need you covering that Eastman crap tomorrow. You and Anderson. Keep an eye on that prince, that what's-'is-name. You know, the one those nuts tried to kill last month."

Prince Rasir of Senadon. Only nineteen years old, an assassination attempt had been made against him in his own country less than four weeks ago. Some hullabaloo over his wanting to enter into an arms agreement with the U.S. Not everyone in the South China Sea was happy about this state of affairs. He now traveled with an extra contingent of bodyguards. I doubted there would be much action with all that muscle around. Some assignment. I started to grouse under my breath.

Becky interrupted. She smoothed a hand over her raw-silk skirt and said primly, "Jesse, it would be nice if you'd dress tomorrow. Since we'll be there together, I mean."

"Not to worry." I dusted off my jeans while thumbing through papers in my IN box. "I'll clean these up."

She coughed delicately. "Jesse."

"Huh?"

"There will be visiting dignitaries there. I had in mind a dress and heels."

I looked up. Becky's every shining blond hair, as always, was lacquered into place. Well, hell, she edits the Lifestyle section. She has to look neat for all those teas and Barbie Doll stuff.

I jammed my hands on my hips and stuck my chin out, narrowing my eyes to nasty green slits. Daring her to say one more word about my clothes.

"Of course, if that's all you have . . ." she mumbled quickly.

I knew she'd back down. The woman has no balls.

When I got home to my apartment on Genesee Park Boulevard, Mrs. Binty was on the front porch, rocking and shelling peas. She's been cooking lately for Mr. Garson, across the street. He used to come over and help her prune the rosebushes, but Mr. Garson's been in mourning since his wife died three months ago. Now he even forgets to eat unless you put the idea in his mind. So Mrs. Binty (my landlady) sits beneath her wisteria like some tiny little white-haired fairy-tale lady with an enameled blue bowl on her lap, shelling away. She entices Mr. Garson over with those fresh sweet peas like the old witch in "Hansel and Gretel," luring the children with bits of cake.

"I let your nice friend Grady North in," she warbled as I stepped out of my '68 Campbell's soup can, a rusted red-and-white Karmann Ghia. "He's been chipping off that old paint while he waits for you. That way, we can start redoing the window frames."

Sure enough, there through the tree leaves was Grady North above me on the porch roof, chipping away. I sighed. Just what every girl needs to come home to on a hot summer day. A cop.

"It was only a plywood target," I said after we'd gotten some iced tea and gone back out on the roof. "But I felt those bullets hit *me*." (Samved says if we listen to ourselves, we can know how much something's bothering us by how often we bring it up.) Grady and I sat with our backs against the windows, shaded from the evening sun by the branches of Mrs. Binty's oak trees.

Difficult as ever, my friend the cop stretched out his long legs and opined: "You will always have problems over moral issues so long as you insist on living half your life outside the law."

I gave him a nasty look and noted that in a cotton preppy shirt, pleated khaki pants, and sneakers, he looked better, as usual, than me. Thank God for the paint chips in his sandy hair. They reduced his handsome quotient—despite his nice, tight ass—by at least ten degrees.

"Let's not get into the foibles of my personality," I muttered.

"Everything you do, you do ass backwards."

"Now you sound like my mother."

"You know it's true. You look around, ask yourself what's legal, then do the exact opposite."

"Usually, the opposite is best."

"And I wonder just where you picked up an idea like that."

"Leave Marcus out of this or I'm going inside."

He swore under his breath.

"You're even testier than usual," I observed. "What's going on?"

He didn't answer directly, but broke a thin twig off the tree and bent it back and forth with one hand with so much nervous tension, it splintered in half. "You covering the Eastman celebration tomorrow?"

"Yeah."

"You heard any rumors?"

"About what?"

"Anything. Anything at all."

"Sure. The president of IBM will be there with his three mistresses, one of whom has two heads. Tom Selleck may show . . . or was that Rex Reed? Hard to remember, there's so much shit floating around."

"Never mind!" he exploded, getting to his feet. "If you ever took two minutes to be serious—"

"Crimin*ee*. Take it easy, will you?"

My phone rang. I unwound my aching limbs and went in to answer it. It was the police commissioner's office, for Grady. He stood behind me, grabbing the phone before the words *It's for you* were even out of my mouth.

"Yeah? Yeah, okay. Right. Will do." He paced back and forth, tugging at the phone line impatiently as he talked.

Grady's a detective in Homicide, but he works with the commissioner's office in planning security when important events take place. You wouldn't exactly say that Rochester is a hotbed of political ferment, but historically, it has been a center for activism. The major terminal for the Underground Railway in the north was here; it's the place of Susan B. Anthony's birth and early feminist years; and during Vietnam the town was littered with marching priests and nuns—many of them my old teachers from Mercy High, in boots, miniskirts with fringe, and carrying guitars. (Mention this now and they look a little wistful . . . or simply blank.)

Aside from that, we're an important business town. Western Union was founded here, as was Eastman-Kodak, Bausch & Lomb, Xerox. And all of these companies, along with several others, were hosting the event this weekend at the George Eastman House.

"I'll be there," Grady said. He slammed the phone down.

"What's wrong? What going on?"

He rolled down his shirt sleeves and buttoned his cuffs. Despite an attempt to be casual, there was a look on his face I recognized something that's only there when things have gone quite wrong. "Goddamn foreign politicians," he said angrily. "They bring families and wander all over, let down their guard. I just wish they'd held this damn thing in Toronto."

I couldn't get any more out of him. After he left I went over the list of VIPs I'd picked up at the *Herald*, the ones who would be at the Kodak Festival the next day. I could see Grady's problem with security. Aside from famous artists, photographers, and the usual sprinkling of politicians and business leaders, several heads of state from the peace talks had been invited. Further, it was summer; as Grady had said, they'd bring their families and combine the trip with a vacation. Rochester, with Lake Ontario and the Genesee River—lots of water, trees, flowers, and clean blue sky—isn't a bad place at all to visit. If you catch us on a good day, in fact—one of the two or three between winter and summer—you might never want to go home.

The thought of trying to secure the Eastman grounds, however, with its hidden nooks and crannies, made me shudder.

I sipped my iced tea, going over and over the list. Memorizing details to add to my notes the next day. Now and then I could hear the buzz of Mrs. Binty's conversation with Mr. Garson. There didn't seem to be much pizzazz in his tone. Strange, I thought, the way life stops for the survivor when someone dies. They cease functioning for a while.

Functionaries . . .

The thought stuck, but didn't go any further just then.

The George Eastman House has exhibits ranging from the first snapshot one hundred years ago, to Lewis Carroll, Julia Margaret Cameron, and Ansel Adams today. The grounds are composed of stone walls and gardens with high shrubs and trees. The mansion—fifty rooms or so—is Georgian, with mellowed brick, huge ivy-covered chimneys, and stone porches. Ordinarily, this is a quiet, peaceful place to wander and regroup.

Today, however, there was a black cloud of tension in the air. Grady North stalked by at one point—dressed for the occasion like a man on his way up, but obviously working—and I tried to get his attention. He glared and kept on stalking. I assumed he'd been working through the night setting up security. Besides the many Three-Piece Suits that looked like executive security types, there was a sprinkling of cops throughout the grounds. Grady had them arrayed in spiffy dress blues, their black shoes polished to a glassy sheen. They managed to look impressive rather than unnerving, sort of like the British Royal Guard.

I was standing with Becky Anderson beside a bed of periwinkle and herbs. It stated just that on the little metal sign stuck in the ground: PERIWINKLE AND HERBS. In deference to Becky's sensibilities, I had worn my white cotton slacks, a red silk blouse, and flats. I had even combed my hair. There were sweat stains already beneath the armpits of the blouse, but looking at Becky, I didn't feel too bad. It had rained during the night, and the ground was still damp. Becky's high white heels had been sinking up to the hilt since we arrived, unintentionally aerating the grass. Following behind her, I had tried not to laugh, but she'd caught me.

"You've always intimidated me," she said now.

I didn't hear her at first. I was busy watching the wife of Rasir, the young Prince of Senadon. No more than a girl herself, she was chasing after her three-year-old son. Her long teal-blue dress, shot through with gold thread, was coming undone in the chase. She grabbed at it with one hand while the other hid a bubbling laugh. A tall nun in white habit—à la Mother Teresa—had been taken by surprise as the ruler's son snatched her long white skirt in passing. The nun pushed with frantic modesty to keep her skirt down. She wasn't quick enough. The kid's pass revealed bare legs above white socks with tennis shoes. The ruler's wife caught up with her child at last and, giggling, swooped him high off the ground. The nun jammed her hands into her full sleeves irritably and turned away.

Even Becky laughed, and that's when I realized what she had just said: "You've always intimidated me."

I faced her and said belatedly, "I intimidate *you*?"

She flushed. "You seem so sure of yourself. The way you dress and act, like you couldn't care less what people think."

I should have felt good. I'd never known my nemesis felt that way about me. Underneath all the bravado, I was intimidated by *her*.

For a brief moment I wanted to tell her so. Then I was

distracted by the sight of Marcus talking with one of the country's top political photographers, along with a man I recognized from the papers as a VP from Xerox, and the mayor. Nobody ever said Marcus doesn't mingle well.

He was looking sharp: three-piece summer gray suit, white shirt, blue tie. A slight breeze lifted his black hair as he stood with one hand in a pocket, the other punctuating his conversation. He seemed attentive to the group, but never once stopped scanning the crowd. On one pass he saw me. Becky caught the message that passed between us and cast me a scathing look.

"I'll see you in a while," I said. "I have to talk to someone."

Her mouth thinned out. "We're supposed to be covering the prince."

"Jeez! Becky—" I bit my tongue. "You go. I'll be with you in a minute, okay?"

She aerated the ground some more and flounced away.

I wandered off to a side garden, where there were fewer people milling around than out front. After a few minutes, Marcus joined me. We stood a few feet apart and gazed in different directions, talking in low, casual tones as if commenting on the weather or the state of periwinkles in July. (Maintaining a low profile in public, we call it.) Marcus still surveyed the grounds.

"You look unusually vigilant," I noted.

"With good reason." He glanced at his watch. "When are you leaving?"

"Leaving here? After the fireworks, I guess. Whenever this shindig is over. Why?"

"It seems your friend Grady North has been more than usually busy since last night. Beefing up security, bringing in out-of-town help."

"I noticed. What do you think's going on?"

"Tark has been hanging out with the bodyguard contingent. Apparently, there's been an assassination threat."

I had a sinking feeling. "Don't tell me. Rasir." Christ, I'd just sent Becky Anderson off alone to cover the story of the year.

Marcus nodded. "Could be a false alarm, of course. A scare to throw a monkey wrench into his Washington trip."

Rasir's country, Senadon, was one of the largest and richest island countries south of China. Rasir was said to be nervous about the recent unrest there. He was scheduled to fly to Washington after the peace talks in the Thousand Islands, to sign an alliance that would arm his country and help him to build its first army. A small opposing faction in the South China Sea was said to have been behind the attempt on Rasir's life last month.

I looked around at the Eastman grounds, thinking that I'd been stupid to disregard the likelihood of another attempt here. It was true that Rasir was protected now by a virtual wall of bodyguards—a fact I'd confirmed upon arriving. Yet, access to these grounds was relatively easy. And there were over three hundred guests milling about; a large turnaround crowd. People kept coming and going.

I could see why our friends in Toronto had passed up the chance to hold this little clambake over there.

"I wonder why Grady doesn't just shut the whole thing down. Send everybody home."

Marcus began to speak but paused as his eyes lit on a cop who had just entered the West Garden. The cop's glance slid over us, then away.

"From a purely pragmatic viewpoint," Marcus said quietly, "North is faced with a sticky diplomatic problem. There's a lot of potential wealth here today, and more at stake than the life of one prince from one small country. I'd hate to be in his shoes."

He was right. Half the people here were from Fortune 500 companies, their hopeful fingers in the government tills of other lands. Grady's orders from high up almost certainly would have been to bring in all the help he needed—but to handle things.

Marcus was still looking at the cop. "There's something . . ." He shook his head. "Let's walk."

When we were beyond the crowd, on the other side of a high stand of shrubs, he faced me and folded his arms. His chin went up in that cocky don't-argue-with-me manner I knew so well.

"I've arranged for Tark to take you home."

"Excuse me?"

"Don't argue, Jess. I don't want you hurt."

"Marcus, it's my job to cover the prince. I can't walk out on that now. Besides, I won't be hurt—"

"If there's trouble around, you find it. Jess, you look to be hurt."

Now, that really did hurt. It was good for another ten minutes of dialogue, in fact. I revved up for it—but then I remembered a lesson from crafty old Samved on passive resistance: *Don't be afraid to go with the program now and then. If nothing else, it quells suspicion.*

I didn't give in too easily. I appeared to think about it. Then I shrugged. "Where is Tark?"

"By the refreshment tent, waiting for you."

"I have to use the rest room. I'll meet him there."

A pause while Marcus considered the efficacy of leaving me on my own. Finally he nodded, although his mouth held a slight worried smile. The small white scar beneath his left eye stood out in relief; a sign of tension. He tilted my chin up with one finger. "Thank you, Jess. I know how you loathe being taken care of."

I gave him a warm look. I even met his eyes. "By anyone but you," I said.

I swung my tote to my shoulder and headed in the direction of the rest rooms, which were near the refreshment tent. Once out of Marcus's sight, however, I turned without a qualm the opposite way.

There's another thing my guru/shrink is wont to say (paraphrasing Shelley): *Obedience is the bane of all genius. It makes slaves of men.*

That's what I love about Samved. He's got a quote for everything.

The thing is (and aside from the fact that Marcus had become too damned protective of late), I needed a story. More particularly, I needed something different from all the rest. Charlie Nicks had been on my back about being out of the office too much, and I'd been fired from one too many jobs in the past few years. "You just don't know how to follow orders," was the most common complaint. It was true. So to make up for that failing, I try harder. And when I come up with something brilliant, some story they can't possibly turn down, I buy myself another week, another month, before I'm out the door.

The key word, however, is *brilliant*. Things have to have a twist—something my fellow scribes don't click into, at least until the story's out on the wires under my name. And it had occurred to me, listening to Marcus, that there just might be one hell of a twist going on here today.

Casting back in memory, I dredged up everything I'd read about the chain of command in Senadon. The man who would replace Rasir, should he die, was his brother. From all reports, they thought alike. He would presumably carry out Rasir's quest for arms.

An assassination, therefore, would do nothing to stop an alliance. It might, in fact, hasten one. It seemed to me the opposing faction would realize that eventually, and realize, too, that the alternative way to bring a country—or a political talk— to a halt is to see to it the functionaries stop functioning.

Which is exactly what might happen if Rasir were thrown into mourning.

I have to admit I didn't think this up out of a clear blue sky. It occurred to me only because I'd been haunted since the night before by the image of Mrs. Binty's friend, Mr. Garson—and the malaise he'd suffered since his wife died. For three solid months now, the man had barely been able to tie his own shoes.

How, then, would a nineteen-year-old boy, albeit prince, cope with the death of that bubbly young girl and their toddler son?

It took me less than five minutes to locate the princess again. She and her child were in the East Garden, watching a puppet show from the last row behind a small group of mothers and kids. Two foreign-looking bodyguard types, in black suits, stood behind them. I remembered that they had been on the periphery earlier, when the princess was chasing her son. The cop I'd seen in the West Garden was here now, too, clearly keeping an eye on things.

The princess still seemed unconcerned, however. I realized that she must not have been told about this latest threat. The prince, possibly to keep any danger from touching her and the child, was as far away as he could be—involved in talks with various business leaders at the front of the mansion. I'd left Becky Anderson to keep an eye on him there, which was either the smartest or dumbest thing I'd ever done in my life. Becky might wind up with the hottest story of her fluff-filled career, while I'd be out of a job.

I'd never seen anyone so jumpy as Rasir. His complexion was pale, and he rubbed constantly at a small mole on his homely, boyish face, looking about nervously as he waited for the blow to fall.

I wandered behind the audience at the puppet show a few minutes, but then I worried about being seen by Marcus or Tark and carted off to someplace safe and banal. There was a natural grouping of shrubs and trees along one wall, and I eased back into it. I could still see most of the garden through a screen of delicate vines. Twenty minutes later, when nothing had happened, I began to feel stupid lurking in the shrubs that way. The air was hotter and thicker than mustard in hell, and I half expected to look sideways and see, peering back through the greenery, a fellow wretch from the *National Enquirer*.

Bored, I stretched prone on the ground, cleared another space to see, and propped my chin on my hands. All sorts of organisms rose from the ground to attack my nose. I swallowed a sneeze. Birds chirped and insects buzzed. From the front lawn came the strains of the Navy Band as it played Sousa marches and light pop. Wiping my eyes clear of sweat (I hate summer; have I said that yet?), I focused on the young princess—

And then I saw that nun again. The one who'd been so angry at having her skirts hiked up by the royals' son. On such a hot day, in that habit, why was she even hanging around? Was she a glutton for punishment? A secret exhibitionist? Was she hoping for another thrill?

One way or another, something about her was off.

The puppet show continued, and the nun made a slow circuit of the garden. She appeared to read from a small black book. Now and then she'd stoop to touch a flower. And although I'll admit to a suspicious nature, it seemed to me, after watching her at this for a while, that she was in fact checking out the young mother and her son.

Interestingly, the cop had a close eye on the good sister too. As did the black-suited bodyguards.

It was one of those times, when the nun bent to read a tag on a rosebush, that her sleeve caught on a thorn and was pulled back. She was about ten feet away from me then, and I saw a gleam of chunky gold on her wrist. She pulled the sleeve down quickly, but not before I saw that the gold was a watch.

A gold watch? I thought curiously. On a nun? Times had changed.

But well, come on . . . vow of poverty or not, if nuns could wear miniskirts in the seventies, why not gold watches in the nineties? Think of it: yuppism, alive and well and living in a convent in Rochester, New York.

While I was mulling all this over, the puppet show ended. The audience of children and mothers began to wander from the garden to the front of the mansion. The sky was growing dark; it was nearly nine P.M.

The nun, approaching from the left, began to walk slowly toward the princess—who, with her son, followed by their bodyguards, was trailing the rest of the crowd. As the princess picked up her pace, the nun did too. The distance between them closed, and the nun's hand reached into the deep folds of her habit. She seemed to pat something, as if reassuring herself it was there.

My own hand, which had curled around a narrow branch of shrubbery, tightened. My skin prickled. I had never carried a gun in my life before last week, but the first, most important lesson at the Davies School had been: Be aware of your weapon at all times. Know where it is, be sure it's in good order and accessible. Time after time I had made that patting gesture myself—out of nerves, more than anything.

The nun, of course, could have been patting a rosary. Or maybe she had a pastrami sandwich tucked away in there.

At that instant, a loud boom sounded—almost stopping my heart. But the princess laughed and picked up her child, pointing to the sky as it bloomed with red and gold. The fireworks had begun. Her son squealed with delight, then buried his head in her shoulder—frightened, no doubt, by the rapid noises that followed.

I looked up at the fireworks, too, an automatic reaction . . . and when I looked back into the growing gloom, I saw with a start that the bodyguards were gone. So was the cop. Christ, they had left the princess and her son alone.

Further, the young mother's journey toward the front of the house had been effectively cut off by the nun. The princess looked startled at the nun's hastening approach. She took a step back, an anxious question (I thought) in her eyes. It was so much like my experience the day before at the Davies School, with the innocent woman, the expression of alarm, the child—

The nun reached into her habit again, and I moved.

I stumbled to my feet, my legs stiff and protesting. Shoving the vines aside, I tore across the grass. As the nun—whose back was to me—took another step toward the princess, I reached her and grabbed her by the shoulder.

She turned, her dark eyes flaring with anger.

"It's Saturday. Confession time," I said.

The hand came out of the nun's habit, and in it was a gun.

The young mother screamed. Her son began to cry. She clutched him tighter and backed away.

I held my hands up, palm out. "Don't shoot. Take it easy." I was scared out of my wits. My legs were weak, and my jaw felt like it was wired; it barely moved. I edged around, trying to position myself between the two royals and the nun.

The nun raised her weapon, pointing it at me.

"Look, don't do this," I pleaded. And again, it was like Davies—in slow motion, everything happening at once. "I've got a friend on his way—a cop—he's armed—"

I can't even begin to explain the chaos that followed. The fireworks were exploding above us in rapid bursts of light. One of them whistled, like those old bombs in World War II movies. The garden flickered with white, then dark, and from the shadows behind the nun came a cool, familiar voice.

"Well, what have we here?"

It was Marcus. Tark moved in beside him, yanking his Magnum from its holster. The nun whirled to face them, and as she did, Marcus grabbed her arm and, with a quick, hard twist, relieved her of her weapon.

"Get Jess out of here," he ordered Tark, holding the nun at bay. "Get her out . . . now."

Meanwhile, the cop from earlier came racing across the garden, revolver drawn. He came to a halt several feet away, legs spread. "Drop your weapons!" he yelled nervously. "Stand back!"

There was an explosion then from the front of the mansion, unlike that of the fireworks. It rocked the ground beneath our feet. Screams and the crash of breaking glass. It sounded as if the whole George Eastman House had been bombed.

The princess, squeezing her baby to her breast, cried, "My husband!"

We all froze, like a da Vinci tableau, to stare in that direction. Then the princess made a move as if to run to the front of the mansion. Marcus grabbed her. He thrust her at the cop, who was still in firing stance, yelled, "Watch her!" and took off running toward the sound of the screams.

Tark glanced at the young cop, who seemed frozen by the events except for a tremor in the hands that held his gun. The poor guy looked like he'd never been faced with having to shoot anyone before. "Christ," Tark muttered, "rookies." He shoved his Magnum into my hand. "Take care of things." He ran after Marcus. I stood there with the heavy weapon hanging like an unpleasant fish from the end of my hand.

My stomach coiled. "Get out of here, Princess." I jerked my head in the direction of the museum buildings behind the mansion, where I thought she'd be safe. "Go, *now*."

"Wait." That from the cop, whose hand was moving on his revolver.

And while he was focused on us, the nun reached into her full white sleeve and pulled out a second weapon, its silver casing no more than a wink in the darkening night. In one smooth movement she brought it up, aimed at the cop, and shot. Blood spurted from the cop's neck. He fell. Almost without thinking, I raised Tark's Magnum and gripped it with both hands. The nun's pistol was leveled at me now.

"Police!" the nun yelled. "Drop it!"

Police?

I wavered, confused.

The cop, still on the ground, grabbed up his fallen revolver and shot the nun, who staggered back, dropping her weapon, her hand flying to her shoulder. Fireworks went off like strobe lights, and in their flash I saw that blood had spattered the cop's uniform and brown shoes.

Brown shoes—Jesus, God, I thought inanely, *the cop has brown shoes.*

But then it was dark once more, and I wasn't sure what I had seen.

"Shoot him," the nun cried, reaching for, but unable to grasp, her weapon.

But the nun was not a nun. She was someone claiming to be a cop—while the cop had turned his revolver on me.

My finger closed on the trigger of Tark's Magnum as I vacillated half seconds between the nun and the cop, then back to the nun again. I broke into a cold sweat. *Christ Almighty, help,* I prayed. *Don't let me fail this time.* My own reasoning voice came back, clear as a bell: *The nun is a terrorist, Jess, the nun is lying . . . shoot the nun, shoot the nun, Shoot—*

So I goddamned shot the cop.

* * *

That was last week, and things have quieted down a bit since
then. Even the weather's cooled off, and I'm sitting out here
on the roof of Mrs. Binty's porch, in an evening breeze off
Lake Ontario, trying to put my thoughts on paper.

I guess the first thing to clear up is that I made the right
decision for a change—although, either way, things would've
worked out okay.

The "cop" was a hired assassin, and no wonder he was
nervous: the princess was his first paying job. He had slipped
onto the grounds and gone unnoticed during Grady's last-
minute pull-in of out-of-town help.

"Rasir's enemies in Senadon," Grady told me, "knew they'd
never get to him. He's too heavily guarded. They hired the
assassin to stall the alliance by killing his wife and child."

The Garson Directive, it shall be known as henceforth.

Which leaves us with the "nun." She, it turns out, was one
of Grady's undercover cops. I could have been in deep shit,
getting in her way. But talk about a twist (and saving ass),
what Grady didn't know was that in going through an antiter-
rorist course at Davies, the undercover "nun" met up with a
genuine terrorist who was training there secretly at night. Practicing on the "good-guy" targets to overcome any qualms about
shooting into crowds. Hence the well-ventilated target of the
woman and child.

Anyway, the nun and the terrorist fell in love (how's that for
a movie title?) and the nun turned. While Grady had put her
on the Eastman grounds that day to protect Rasir's family, the
young woman's actual agenda was to kill the princess and her
child.

Her terrorist friend took out the princess's bodyguards during the first boom of fireworks that night, when the rest of us
were distracted. Their bodies were found later in a maintenance shack on the Eastman grounds.

So like I said, I could've shot either the nun or the cop; both
were the bad guys that day. But the cop was the one left pointing a gun—and I wouldn't be alive now if I'd gone the other
way.

Samved claims I was being guided "from another plane,"
given bits and pieces of information to process that helped me
make a right decision in the end. But the only thing I can
remember processing is the fact that Grady North, being the

worst stickler for the rules I've ever known, would not in a million years allow a real cop—on that kind of high-level duty—to wear brown shoes.

I'd appreciate it if you wouldn't tell anyone I even mentioned that. Things are bad enough without the tabloids printing some scuzzy story about how I killed a guy over his Thom McCanns.

The city offered me a medal of "valor" for saving the lives of the princess and her son. (The prince was fine; the bomb a mere distraction. A few windows had to be replaced, but other than that, little harm was done.) I balked and made humble noises about the medal, but then I thought: *What the hell— how else would I ever get pinned?*

Besides, it'll look good on a résumé someday. With my record for being fired from jobs, that's not a minor consideration.

While the crowd applauded and the press took pictures and I stood looking like an idiot in a white suit and Becky Anderson's borrowed new heels, I couldn't help but think how easy it is to con people about these things. Because no matter how I try, I can't get beyond the fact that what I did that day resembled nothing like valor at all.

Sure, I saved the princess—and for that I'll be eternally glad. But I had my own agenda when that gun was in my hand. Most people do, when they kill. For me it was the fear of screwing up again, and according to the "experts," that all goes back to Pop.

I remember him saying once: "Jesse, girl, you . . . your mother . . . you're too much a burden on the heart." This was one night when he was stewed to the gills (otherwise I'd never tell this; you have to understand, Pop was a peace-loving guy at heart, but when the drink was on him, he tended toward morose). Anyway, he was sitting there in his overstuffed chair, still in the tired coveralls he always wore to climb down into those hot, gassy vats at Kodak, although he'd been fired the night before. He was horribly drunk, and holding a gun to his temple. I was ten at the time, and I remember throwing up right there on the living room rug, and then crying until he stopped and put it down.

The world exacts a high price from men who would be poets, who dream of tossing words like silver birds into the sky and wind up shoveling food into the mouths of dependents instead.

Later he said: "Jesse, girl, you couldn't even let me die in peace." He said it heavily, with none of the usual twinkle in his eye, and I've always understood, no matter what anyone since has said—counselors, gurus, or well-meaning friends—that I'd screwed up yet again.

So the circle of guilt goes round and round. Someday, when the prisons are too full to put any more people in them, the courts will assign all miscreants an Irish Catholic father to instill perpetual remorse for their sins. As for me, I grew up with mine, and the only mystery, so far as I can see, is that I haven't yet succumbed this week to an overwhelming desire for a Genesee Screw.

*Sara Paretsky's Chicago provides private investigator V. I.
Warshawski with plenty of tests, but her wit, her agility, and
her toughness prove to be up to the challenges. Named one of
thirteen Women of the Year in 1987 by* Ms. *magazine and a
major force in the establishment of the Sisters in Crime organization, Sara has written six novels, including* Bitter Medicine, Killing Orders, Deadlock, Indemnity Only, Blood Shot
*(winner of a 1989 British Crime Writers Silver Dagger award
and Anthony nominee), and* Burn Marks.*

*In "The Maltese Cat," V. I. develops a pet theory to ex-
plain the disappearance of her client's sister.*

THE MALTESE CAT

by Sara Paretsky

1

Her voice on the phone had been soft and husky, with just a
whiff of the South laid across it like a rare perfume. "I'd rather
come to your office; I don't want people in mine to know I've
hired a detective."

I'd offered to see her at her home in the evening—my Spartan
office doesn't invite client confidences. But she didn't want to
wait until tonight, she wanted to come today, almost at once,
and no, she wouldn't meet me in a restaurant. Far too hard to
talk, and this was extremely personal.

"You know my specialty is financial crime, don't you?" I
asked sharply.

"Yes, that's how I got your name. One o'clock, fourth floor
of the Pulteney, right?" And she'd hung up without telling me
who she was.

An errand at the County building took me longer than I'd
expected; it was close to one-thirty by the time I got back to
the Pulteney. My caller's problem apparently was urgent: she
was waiting outside my office door, tapping one high heel im-

patiently on the floor as I trudged down the hall in my running shoes.

"Ms. Warshawski! I thought you were standing me up."

"No such luck," I grunted, opening my office door for her.

In the dimly lit hall she'd just been a slender silhouette. Under the office lights the set of the shoulders and signature buttons told me her suit had come from the hands of someone at Chanel. Its blue enhanced the cobalt of her eyes. Soft make-up hid her natural skin tones—I couldn't tell if that dark red hair was natural, or merely expertly painted.

She scanned the spare furnishings and picked the cleaner of my two visitor chairs. "My time is valuable, Ms. Warshawski. If I'd known you were going to keep me waiting without a place to sit I would have finished some phone calls before walking over here."

I'd dressed in jeans and a work shirt for a day at the Recorder of Deeds office. Feeling dirty and outclassed made me grumpy. "You hung up without giving me your name or number, so there wasn't much I could do to let you know you'd have to stand around in your pointy little shoes. My time's valuable, too! Why don't you tell me where the fire is so I can start putting it out."

She flushed. When I turn red I look blotchy, but in her it only enhanced her makeup. "It's my sister." The whiff of Southern increased. "Corinne. She's run off to Ja—my ex-husband, and I need someone to tell her to come back."

I made a disgusted face. "I can't believe I raced back from the County Building to listen to this. It's not 1890, you know. She may be making a mistake but presumably she can sort it out for herself."

Her flush darkened. "I'm not being very clear. I'm sorry. I'm not used to having to ask for things. My sister—Corinne— she's only fourteen. She's my ward. I'm sixteen years older than she is. Our parents died three years ago and she's been living with me since then. It's not easy, not easy for either of us. Moving from Mobile to here was just the beginning. When she got here she wanted to run around, do all the things you can't do in Mobile."

She waved a hand to indicate what kinds of things those might be. "She thinks I'm a tough bitch and that I was too hard on my ex-husband. She's known him since she was three and he was a big hero. She couldn't see he'd changed.

Or not changed, just not had the chance to be heroic anymore in public. So when she took off two days ago I assumed she went there. He's not answering his phone or the doorbell. I don't know if they've left town or he's just playing possum or what. I need someone who knows how to get people to open their doors and knows how to talk to people. At least if I could see Corinne I might—I don't know.''

She broke off with a helpless gesture that didn't match her sophisticated looks. Nothing like responsibility for a minor to deflate even the most urbane.

I grimaced more ferociously. ''Why don't we start with your name, and your husband's name and address, and then move on to her friends.''

''Her friends?'' The deep blue eyes widened. ''I'd just as soon this didn't get around. People talk, and even though it's not 1890, it could be hard on her when she gets back to school.''

I suppressed a howl. ''You can't come around demanding my expertise and then tell me what or what not to do. What if she's not with your husband? What if I can't get in touch with you when I've found that out and she's in terrible trouble and her life depends on my turning up some new leads? If you can't bring yourself to divulge a few names—starting with your own—you'd better go find yourself a more pliant detective. I can recommend a couple who have waiting rooms.''

She set her lips tightly: whatever she did she was in command—people didn't talk to her that way and get away with it. For a few seconds it looked as though I might be free to get back to the Recorder of Deeds that afternoon, but then she shook her head and forced a smile to her lips.

''I was told not to mind your abrasiveness because you were the best. I'm Brigitte LeBlanc. My sister's name is Corinne, also LeBlanc. And my ex-husband is Charles Pierce.'' She scooted her chair up to the desk so she could scribble his address on a sheet of paper torn from a memo pad in her bag. She scrawled busily for several minutes, then handed me a list that included Corinne's three closest school friends, along with Pierce's address.

''I'm late for a meeting. I'll call you tonight to see if you've made any progress.'' She got up.

''Not so fast,'' I said. ''I get a retainer. You have to sign a contract. And I need a number where I can reach you.''

"I really am late."

"And I'm really too busy to hunt for your sister. If you have a sister. You can't be that worried if your meeting is more important than she is."

Her scowl would have terrified me if I'd been alone with her in an alley after dark. "I do have a sister. And I spent two days trying to get into my ex-husband's place, and then in tracking down people who could recommend a private detective to me. I can't do anything else to help her except go earn the money to pay your fee."

I pulled a contract from my desk drawer and stuck it in the manual Olivetti that had belonged to my mother—a typewriter so old that I had to order special ribbons for it from Italy. A word processor would be cheaper and more impressive but the wrist action keeps my forearms strong. I got Ms. LeBlanc to give me her address, to sign on the dotted line for $400 a day plus expenses, to write in the name of a guaranteeing financial institution and to hand over a check for two hundred.

When she'd left I wrestled with my office windows, hoping to let some air in to blow her pricey perfume away. Carbon flakes from the el would be better than the lingering scent, but the windows, painted over several hundred times, wouldn't budge. I turned on a desktop fan and frowned sourly at her bold black signature.

What was her ex-husband's real name? She'd bitten off "Ja—" Could be James or Jake, but it sure wasn't Charles. Did she really have a sister? Was this just a ploy to get back at a guy late on his alimony? Although Pierce's address on North Winthrop didn't sound like the place for a man who could afford alimony. Maybe everything went to keep her in Chanel suits while he lived on Skid Row.

She wasn't in the phone book, so I couldn't check her own address on Belden. The operator told me the number was unlisted. I called a friend at the Fort Dearborn Trust, the bank Brigitte had drawn her check on, and was assured that there was plenty more where that came from. My friend told me Brigitte had parlayed the proceeds of a high-priced modeling career into a successful media consulting firm.

"And if you ever read the fashion pages you'd know these things. Get your nose out of the sports section from time to time, Vic—it'll help with your career."

"Thanks, Eva." I hung up with a snap. At least my client

wouldn't turn out to be named something else, always a good beginning to a tawdry case.

I looked in the little mirror perched over my filing cabinet. A dust smudge on my right cheek instead of peach blush was the only distinction between me and Ms. LeBlanc. Since I was dressed appropriately for North Winthrop, I shut up my office and went to retrieve my car.

ll

Charles Pierce lived in a dismal ten-flat built flush onto the Uptown sidewalk. Ragged sheets made haphazard curtains in those windows that weren't boarded over. Empty bottles lined the entryway, but the smell of stale Ripple couldn't begin to mask the stench of fresh urine. If Corinne LeBlanc had run away to this place, life with Brigitte must be unmitigated hell.

My client's ex-husband lived in 3E. I knew that because she'd told me. Those few mailboxes whose doors still shut wisely didn't trumpet their owners' identities. The filthy brass nameplate next to the doorbells was empty and the doorbells didn't work. Pushing open the rickety door to the hall, I wondered again about my client's truthfulness: she told me Ja— hadn't answered his phone or his bell.

A rheumy-eyed woman was sprawled across the bottom of the stairs, sucking at a half-pint. She stared at me malevolently when I asked her to move, but she didn't actively try to trip me when I stepped over her. It was only my foot catching in the folds of her overcoat.

The original building probably held two apartments per floor. At least, on the third floor only two doors at either end looked as though they went back to the massive, elegant construction of the building's beginnings. The other seven were flimsy new-comers that had been hastily installed when an apartment was subdivided. Peering in the dark I found one labeled B and counted off three more to the right to get to E. After knocking on the peeling veneer several times I noticed a button imbedded in the grime on the jamb. When I pushed it I heard a buzz resonate inside. No one came to the door. With my ear against the filthy panel I could hear the faint hum of a television.

I held the buzzer down for five minutes. It's hard on the

finger but harder on the ear. If someone was really in there he should have come boiling to the door by now.

I could go away and come back, but if Pierce was lying doggo to avoid Brigitte, that wouldn't buy me anything. She said she'd tried off and on for two days. The television might be running as a decoy, or—I pushed more lurid ideas from my mind and took out a collection of skeleton keys. The second worked easily in the insubstantial lock. In two minutes I was inside the apartment, looking at an illustration from *House Beautiful in Hell.*

It was a single room with a countertop kitchen on the left side. A tidy person could pull a corrugated screen to shield the room from signs of cooking, but Pierce wasn't tidy. Ten or fifteen stacked pots, festooned with rotting food and roaches, trembled precariously when I shut the door.

Dominating the place was a Murphy bed with a grotesquely fat man sprawled in at an ominous angle. He'd been watching TV when he died. He was wearing frayed, shiny pants with the fly lying carelessly open and a lumberjack shirt that didn't quite cover his enormous belly.

His monstrous size and the horrible angle at which his bald head was tilted made me gag. I forced it down and walked through a pile of stale clothes to the bed. Lifting an arm the size of a tree trunk, I felt for a pulse. Nothing moved in the heavy arm, but the skin, while clammy, was firm. I couldn't bring myself to touch any more of him but stumbled around the perimeter to peer at him from several angles. I didn't see any obvious wounds. Let the medical examiner hunt out the obscure ones.

By the time I was back in the stairwell I was close to fainting. Only the thought of falling into someone else's urine or vomit kept me on my feet. On the way down I tripped in earnest over the rheumy-eyed woman's coat. Sprawled on the floor at the bottom, I couldn't keep from throwing up myself. It didn't make me feel any better.

I dug a water bottle out of the detritus in my trunk and sponged myself off before calling the police. They asked me to stay near the body. I thought the front seat of my car on Winthrop would be close enough.

While I waited for a meat wagon I wondered about my client. Could Brigitte have come here after leaving me, killed him and taken off while I was phoning around checking up on her? If she had, the rheumy-eyed woman in the stairwell would have seen her. Would the bond forged by my tripping over her and vomiting in the hall be enough to get her to talk to me?

I got out of the car, but before I could get back to the entrance the police arrived. When we pushed open the rickety door my friend had evaporated. I didn't bother mentioning her to the boys—and girl—in blue: her description wouldn't stand out in Uptown, and even if they could find her she wouldn't be likely to say much.

We plodded up the stairs in silence. There were four of them. The woman and the youngest of the three men seemed in good shape. The two older men were running sadly to flab. I didn't think they'd be able to budge my client's ex-husband's right leg, let alone his mammoth redwood torso.

"I got a feeling about this," the oldest officer muttered, more to himself than the rest of us. "I got a feeling."

When we got to 3E and he looked across at the mass on the bed he shook his head a couple of times. "Yup. I kind of knew as soon as I heard the call."

"Knew what, Tom?" the woman demanded sharply.

"Jade Pierce," he said. "Knew he lived around here. Been a lot of complaints about him. Thought it might be him when I heard we was due to visit a real big guy."

The woman stopped her brisk march to the bed. The rest of us looked at the behemoth in shared sorrow. Jade. Not James or Jake but Jade. Once the most famous down lineman the Bears had ever fielded. Now . . . I shuddered.

When he played for Alabama some reporter said his bald head was as smooth and cold as a piece of Jade, and went on to spin some tiresome simile relating it to his play. When he signed with the Bears, I was as happy as any other Chicago fan, even though his reputation for off-field violence was pretty unappetizing. No wonder Brigitte LeBlanc hadn't stayed with him, but why hadn't she wanted to tell me who he really was? I wrestled with that while Tom called for reinforcements over his lapel mike.

"So what were you doing here?" he asked me.

"His ex-wife hired me to check up on him." I don't usually tell the cops my clients' business, but I didn't feel like protecting Brigitte. "She wanted to talk to him and he wasn't answering his phone or his door."

"She wanted to check up on him?" the fit younger officer,

a man with high cheekbones and a well-tended mustache, echoed me derisively. "What I hear, that split-up was the biggest fight Jade was ever in. Only big fight he ever lost, too."

I smiled. "She's doing well, he isn't. Wasn't. Maybe her conscience pricked her. Or maybe she wanted to rub his nose in it hard. You'd have to ask her. All I can say is she asked me to try to get in, I did, and I called you guys."

While Tom mulled this over I pulled out a card and handed it to him. "You can find me at this number if you want to talk to me."

He called out after me but I went on down the hall, my footsteps echoing hollowly off the bare walls and ceiling.

III

Brigitte LeBlanc was with a client and couldn't be interrupted. The news that her ex-husband had died couldn't pry her loose. Not even the idea that the cops would be around before long could move her. After a combination of cajoling and heckling, the receptionist leaned across her blond desk and whispered at me confidentially: "The vice president of the United States had come in for some private media coaching." Brigitte had said no interruptions unless it was the president or the pope—two people I wouldn't even leave a dental appointment to see.

When they made me unwelcome on the forty-third floor I rode downstairs and hung around the lobby. At five-thirty a bevy of Secret Service agents swept me out to the street with the other loiterers. Fifteen minutes later the vice president came out, his boyish face set in purposeful lines. Even though this was a private visit the vigilant television crews were waiting for him. He grinned and waved but didn't say anything before climbing into his limo. Brigitte must be really good if she'd persuaded him to shut up.

At seven I went back to the forty-third floor. The double glass doors were locked and the lights turned off. I found a key in my collection that worked the lock, but when I'd prowled through the miles of thick grey plush, explored the secured studios, looked in all the offices, I had to realize my client was smarter than me. She'd left by some back exit.

I gave a high-pitched snarl. I didn't lock the door behind

me. Let someone come in and steal all the video equipment. I didn't care.

I swung by Brigitte's three-story brownstone on Belden. She wasn't in. The housekeeper didn't know when to expect her. She was eating out and had said not to wait up for her.

"How about Corinne?" I asked, sure that the woman would say "Corinne who?"

"She's not here, either."

I slipped inside before she could shut the door on me. "I'm V. I. Warshawski. Brigitte hired me to find her sister, said she'd run off to Jade. I went to his apartment. Corinne wasn't there and Jade was dead. I've been trying to talk to Brigitte ever since but she's been avoiding me. I want to know a few things, like if Corinne really exists, and did she really run away, and could either she or Brigitte have killed Jade."

The housekeeper stared at me for a few minutes, then made a sour face. "You got some ID?"

I showed her my PI license and the contract signed by Brigitte. Her sour look deepened but she gave me a few spare details. Corinne was a fat, unhappy teenager who didn't know how good she had it. Brigitte gave her everything, taught her how to dress, sent her to St. Scholastica, even tried to get her to special diet clinics, but she was never satisfied, always whining about her friends back home in Mobile, trashy friends to whom she shouldn't be giving the time of day. And yes, she had run away, three days ago now, and she, the housekeeper, said good riddance, but Brigitte felt responsible. And she was sorry that Jade was dead, but he was a violent man, Corinne had over-idealized him, she didn't realize what a monster he really was.

"They can't turn it off when they come off the field, you know. As for who killed him, he probably killed himself, drinking too much. I always said it would happen that way. Corinne couldn't have done it, she doesn't have enough oomph to her. And Brigitte doesn't have any call to—she already got him beat six ways from Sunday."

"Maybe she thought he'd molested her sister."

"She'd have taken him to court and enjoyed seeing him humiliated all over again."

What a lovely cast of characters; it filled me with satisfaction to think I'd allied myself to their fates. I persuaded the housekeeper to give me a picture of Corinne before going home. She was indeed an overweight, unhappy-looking child. It must be hard having a picture-perfect older sister trying to turn her into a junior deb. I also got the housekeeper to give me Brigitte's unlisted home phone number by telling her if she didn't, I'd be back every hour all night long ringing the bell.

I didn't turn on the radio going home. I didn't want to hear the ghoulish excitement lying behind the unctuousness the reporters would bring to discussing Jade Pierce's catastrophic fall from grace. A rehashing of his nine seasons with the Bears, from the glory years to the last two where nagging knee and back injuries grew too great even for the painkillers. And then to his harsh retirement, putting seventy or eighty pounds of fat over his playing weight of 310, the barroom fights, the guns fired at other drivers from the front seat of his Ferrari Daytona, then the sale of the Ferrari to pay his legal bills, and finally the three-ring circus that was his divorce. Ending on a Murphy bed in a squalid Uptown apartment.

I shut the Trans Am's door with a viciousness it didn't deserve and stomped up the three flights to my apartment. Fatigue mixed with bitterness dulled the sixth sense that usually warns me of danger. The man had me pinned against my front door with a gun at my throat before I knew he was there.

I held my shoulder bag out to him. "Be my guest. Then leave. I've had a long day and I don't want to spend too much of it with you."

He spat. "I don't want your stupid little wallet."

"You're not going to rape me, so you might as well take my stupid little wallet."

"I'm not interested in your body. Open your apartment. I want to search it."

"Go to hell." I kneed him in the stomach and swept my right arm up to knock his gun hand away. He gagged and bent over. I used my handbag as a clumsy bola and whacked him on the back of the head. He slumped to the floor, unconscious.

I grabbed the gun from his flaccid hand. Feeling gingerly inside his coat, I found a wallet. His driver's license identified him as Joel Sirop, living at a pricey address on Dearborn Parkway. He sported a high-end assortment of credit cards—Bonwit, Neiman-Marcus, an American Express platinum—and a card that said he was a member in good standing of the Feline Breeders Association of North America. I slid the papers back into his billfold and returned it to his breast pocket.

He groaned and opened his eyes. After a few diffuse seconds he focused on me in outrage. "My head. You've broken my head. I'll sue you."

"Go ahead. I'll hang on to your pistol for use in evidence at the trial. I've got your name and address, so if I see you near my place again I'll know where to send the cops. Now leave."

"Not until I've searched your apartment." He was unarmed and sickly but stubborn.

I leaned against my door, out of reach but poised to stomp on him if he got cute. "What are you looking for, Mr. Sirop?"

"It was on the news, how you found Jade. If the cat was there, you must have taken it."

"Rest your soul, there were no cats in that apartment when I got there. Had he stolen yours?"

He shut his eyes, apparently to commune with himself. When he opened them again he said he had no choice but to trust me. I smiled brightly and told him he could always leave so I could have dinner, but he insisted on confiding in me.

"Do you know cats, Ms. Warshawski?"

"Only in a manner of speaking. I have a dog and she knows cats."

He scowled. "This is not a laughing matter. Have you heard of the Maltese?"

"Cat? I guess I've heard of them. They're the ones without tails, right?"

He shuddered. "No. You are thinking of the Manx. The Maltese—they are usually a bluish grey. Very rarely will you see one that is almost blue. Brigitte LeBlanc has—or had— such a cat. Lady Iva of Cairo."

"Great. I presume she got it to match her eyes."

He waved aside my comment as another frivolity. "Her motives do not matter. What matters is that the cat has been very difficult to breed. She has now come into season for only the third time in her four-year life. Brigitte agreed to let me try to mate Lady Iva with my sire, Casper of Valletta. It is imperative that she be sent to stay with him, and soon. But she has disappeared."

It was my turn to look disgusted. "I took a step down from my usual practice to look for a runaway teenager today. I'm damned if I'm going to hunt a missing cat through the streets of Chicago. Your sire will find her faster than I will. Matter of fact, that's my advice. Drive around listening for the yowling of mighty sires and eventually you'll find your Maltese.''

"This runaway teenager, this Corinne, it is probable that she took Lady Iva with her. The kittens, if they are born, if they are purebred, could fetch a thousand or more each. She is not ignorant of that fact. But if Lady Iva is out on the streets and some other sire finds her first, they would be half-breeds, not worth the price of their veterinary care.''

He spoke with the intense passion I usually reserve for discussing Cubs or Bears trades. Keeping myself turned toward him, I unlocked my front door. He hurled himself at the opening with a ferocity that proved his long years with felines had rubbed off on him. I grabbed his jacket as he hurtled past me but he tore himself free.

"I am not leaving until I have searched your premises," he panted.

I rubbed my head tiredly. "Go ahead, then."

I could have called the cops while he hunted around for Lady Iva. Instead I poured myself a whiskey and watched him crawl on his hands and knees, making little whistling sounds—perhaps the mating call of the Maltese. He went through my cupboards, my stove, the refrigerator, even insisted, his eyes wide with fear, that I open the safe in my bedroom closet. I removed the Smith and Wesson I keep there before letting him look.

When he'd inspected the back landing he had to agree that no cats were on the premises. He tried to argue me into going downtown to check my office. At that point my patience ran out.

"I could have you arrested for attempted assault and criminal trespass. So get out now while the going's good. Take your guy down to my office. If she's in there and in heat, he'll start carrying on and you can call the cops. Just don't bother me.'' I hustled him out the front door, ignoring his protests.

I carefully did up all the locks. I didn't want some other deranged cat breeder sneaking up on me in the middle of the night.

IV

It was after midnight when I finally reached Brigitte. Yes, she'd gotten my message about Jade. She was terribly sorry, but since she couldn't do anything to help him now that he was dead, she hadn't bothered to try to reach me.

"We're about to part company, Brigitte. If you didn't know the guy was dead when you sent me up to Winthrop, you're going to have to prove it. Not at me, but to the cops. I'm talking to Lieutenant Mallory at the Central District in the morning to tell him the rigmarole you spun me. They'll also be able to figure out if you were more interested in finding Corinne or your cat."

There was a long silence at the other end. When she finally spoke, the hint of Southern was pronounced. "Can we talk in the morning before you call the police? Maybe I haven't been as frank as I should have. I'd like you to hear the whole story before you do anything rash."

Just say no, just say no, I chanted to myself. "You be at the Belmont Diner at eight, Brigitte. You can lay it out for me but I'm not making any promises."

I got up at seven, ran the dog over to Belmont Harbor and back and took a long shower. I figured even if I put a half hour into grooming myself I wasn't going to look as good as Brigitte, so I just scrambled into jeans and a cotton sweater.

It was almost ten minutes after eight when I got to the diner, but Brigitte hadn't arrived yet. I picked up a *Herald-Star* from the counter and took it over to a booth to read with a cup of coffee. The headline shook me to the bottom of my stomach.

FOOTBALL HERO SURVIVES FATE WORSE
THAN DEATH

Charles "Jade" Pierce, once the smoothest man on the Bears' fearsome defense, eluded offensive blockers once again. This time the stakes were higher than a touchdown, though: the offensive lineman was Death.

I thought Jeremy Logan was overdoing it by a wide margin but I read the story to the end. The standard procedure with a body is to take it to a hospital for a death certificate before it goes to the morgue. The patrol team hauled Jade to Beth Israel for a perfunctory exam. There the intern, noticing a slight sweat on Jade's neck and hands, dug deeper for a pulse than I'd been willing to go. She'd found faint but unmistakable signs of life buried deep in the mountain of flesh and had brought him back to consciousness.

> Jade, who's had substance abuse problems since leaving the Bears, had mainlined a potent mixture of ether and hydrochloric acid before drinking a quart of bourbon. When he came to his first words were characteristic: "Get the f--- out of my face."

Logan then concluded with the obligatory run-down on Jade's career and its demise, with a pious sniff about the use and abuse of sports heroes left to die in the gutter when they could no longer please the crowd. I read it through twice, including the fulsome last line, before Brigitte arrived.

"You see, Jade's still alive, so I couldn't have killed him," she announced, sweeping into the booth in a cloud of Chanel.

"Did you know he was in a coma when you came to see me yesterday?"

She raised plucked eyebrows in hauteur. "Are you questioning my word?"

One of the waitresses chugged over to take our order. "You want your fruit and yogurt, right, Vic? And what else?"

"Green pepper and cheese omelet with rye toast. Thanks, Barbara. What'll yours be, Brigitte?" Dry toast and black coffee, no doubt.

"Is your fruit *really* fresh?" she demanded.

Barbara rolled her eyes. "We don't allow no one to be fresh in here, honey, regardless of sex preference. You want some or not?"

Brigitte set her shoulder—covered today in green broadcloth with black piping—and got ready to do battle. I cut her off before the first "How dare you" rolled to its ugly conclusion.

"This isn't the kind of place where the maitre d' wilts at

your frown and races over to make sure madam is happy. They don't care if you come back or not. In fact, about now they'd be happier if you'd leave. You can check out my fruit when it comes and order some if it tastes right to you."

"I'll just have wheat toast and black coffee," she said icily. "And make sure they don't put any butter on it."

"Right," Barbara said. "Wheat toast, margarine instead of butter. Just kidding, hon," she added as Brigitte started to tear into her again. "You gotta learn to take it if you want to dish it out."

"Did you bring me here to be insulted?" Brigitte demanded when Barbara had left.

"I brought you here to talk. It didn't occur to me that you wouldn't know diner etiquette. We can fight if you want to. Or you can tell me about Jade and Corinne. And your cat. I had a visit from Joel Sirop last night."

She swallowed some coffee and made a face. "They should rinse the pots with vinegar."

"Well, keep it to yourself. They won't pay you a consulting fee for telling them about it. Joel tell you he'd come around hunting Lady Iva?"

She frowned at me over the rim of the coffee cup, then nodded fractionally.

"Why didn't you tell me about the damned cat when you were in my office yesterday?"

Her poise deserted her for a moment; she looked briefly ashamed. "I thought you'd look for Corinne. I didn't think I could persuade you to hunt down my cat. Anyway, Corinne must have taken Iva with her, so I thought if you found her you'd find the cat, too."

"Which one do you really want back?"

She started to bristle again, then suddenly laughed. It took ten years from her face. "You wouldn't ask that if you'd ever lived with a teenager. And Corinne's always been a stranger to me. She was eighteen months old when I left for college and I only saw her a week or two at a time on vacations. She used to worship me. When she moved in with me I thought it would be a piece of cake: I'd get her fixed up with the right crowd and the right school, she'd do her best to be like me, and the system would run itself. Instead, she put on a lot of weight, won't listen to me about her eating, slouches around with the kids in the neighborhood when my back is turned, the whole nine yards. Jade's influence. It creeps through every now and then when I'm not thinking.''

She looked at my blueberries. I offered them to her and she helped herself to a generous spoonful.

"And that was the other thing. Jade. We got together when I was an Alabama cheerleader and he was the biggest hero in town. I thought I'd really caught me a prize, my yes, a big prize. But the first, last and only thing in a marriage with a football player is football. And him, of course, how many sacks he made, how many yards he allowed, all that boring crap. And if he has to sit out a game, or he gives up a touchdown, or he doesn't get the glory, watch out. Jade was mean. He was mean on the field, he was mean off it. He broke my arm once.''

Her voice was level but her hand shook a little as she lifted the coffee cup to her mouth. "I got me a gun and shot him in the leg the next time he came at me. They put it down as a hunting accident in the papers, but he never tried anything on me after that—not physical, I mean. Until his career ended. Then he got real, real ugly. The papers crucified me for abandoning him when his career was over. They never had to live with him.''

She was panting with emotion by the time she finished. "And Corinne shared the papers' views?'' I asked gently.

She nodded. "We had a bad fight on Sunday. She wanted to go to a sleepover at one of the girls' in the neighborhood. I don't like that girl and I said no. We had a gale-force battle after that. When I got home from work on Monday she'd taken off. First I figured she'd gone to this girl's place. They hadn't seen her, though, and she hadn't shown up at school. So I figured she'd run off to Jade. Now . . . I don't know. I would truly appreciate it if you'd keep looking, though.''

Just say no, Vic, I chanted to myself. "I'll need a thousand up front. And more names and addresses of friends, including people in Mobile. I'll check in with Jade at the hospital. She might have gone to him, you know, and he sent her on someplace else.''

"I stopped by there this morning. They said no visitors.''

I grinned. "I've got friends in high places.'' I signaled Barbara for the check. "Speaking of which, how was the vice president?''

She looked as though she were going to give me one of her stiff rebuttals, but then she curled her lip and drawled, "Just like every other good old boy, honey, just like every other good old boy.''

V

Lotty Herschel, an obstetrician associated with Beth Israel, arranged for me to see Jade Pierce. "They tell me he's been difficult. Don't stand next to the bed unless you're wearing a padded jacket."

"You want him, you can have him," the floor head told me. "He's going home tomorrow morning. Frankly, since he won't let anyone near him, they ought to release him right now."

My palms felt sweaty when I pushed open the door to Jade's room. He didn't throw anything when I came in, didn't even turn his head to stare through the restraining rails surrounding the bed. His mountain of flesh poured through them, ebbing away from a rounded summit in the middle. The back of his head, smooth and shiny as a piece of polished jade, reflected the ceiling light into my eyes.

"I don't need any goddamned ministering angels, so get the fuck out of here," he growled to the window.

"That's a relief. My angel act never really got going."

He turned his head at that. His black eyes were mean, narrow slits. If I were a quarterback I'd hand him the ball and head for the showers.

"What are you, the goddamned social worker?"

"Nope. I'm the goddamned detective who found you yesterday before you slipped off to the great huddle in the sky."

"Come on over then, so I can kiss your ass," he spat venomously.

I leaned against the wall and crossed my arms. "I didn't mean to save your life: I tried getting them to send you to the morgue. The meat wagon crew double-crossed me."

The mountain shook and rumbled. It took me a few seconds to realize he was laughing. "You're right, detective: you ain't no angel. So what do you want? True confessions on why I was such a bad boy? The name of the guy who got me the stuff?"

"As long as you're not hurting anyone but yourself I don't

care what you do or where you get your shit. I'm here because Brigitte hired me to find Corinne.''

His face set in ugly lines again. "Get out."

I didn't move.

"I said get out!" He raised his voice to a bellow.

"Just because I mentioned Brigitte's name?"

"Just because if you're pally with that broad, you're a snake by definition."

"I'm not pally with her. I met her yesterday. She's paying me to find her sister." It took an effort not to yell back at him.

"Corinne's better off without her," he growled, turning the back of his head to me again.

I didn't say anything, just stood there. Five minutes passed. Finally he jeered, without looking at me. "Did the sweet little martyr tell you I broke her arm?"

"She mentioned it, yes."

"She tell you how that happened?"

"Please don't tell me how badly she misunderstood you. I don't want to throw up my breakfast."

At that he swung his gigantic face around toward me again. "Com'ere."

When I didn't move, he sighed and patted the bedrail. "I'm not going to slug you, honest. If we're going to talk, you gotta get close enough for me to see your face."

I went over to the bed and straddled the chair, resting my arms on its back. Jade studied me in silence, then grunted as if to say I'd passed some minimal test.

"I won't tell you Brigitte didn't understand me. Broad had my number from day one. I didn't break her arm, though: that was B. B. Wilder. Old Gunshot. Thought he was my best friend on the club, but it turned out he was Brigitte's. And then, when I come home early from a hunting trip and found her in bed with him, we all got carried away. She loved the excitement of big men fighting. It's what made her a football groupie to begin with down in Alabama."

I tried to imagine ice-cold Brigitte flushed with excitement while the Bears' right tackle and defensive end fought over her. It didn't seem impossible.

"So B. B. broke her arm but I agreed to take the rap. Her little old modeling career was just getting off the ground and she didn't want her good name sullied. And besides that, she kept hoping for a reconciliation with her folks, at least with their wad, and they'd never fork over if she got herself some ugly publicity committing violent adultery. And me, I was just the baddest boy the Bears ever fielded; one more mark didn't make that much difference to me.'' The jeering note returned to his voice.

"She told me it was when you retired that things deteriorated between you.''

"Things deteriorated—what a way to put it. Look, detective what did you say your name was? V. I., that's a hell of a name for a girl. What did your mamma call you?''

"Victoria,'' I said grudgingly. "And no one calls me Vicki, so don't even think about it.'' I prefer not to be called a girl, either, much less a broad, but Jade didn't seem like the person to discuss that particular issue with.

"Victoria, huh? Things deteriorated, yeah, like they was a picnic starting out. I was born dumb and I didn't get smarter for making five hundred big ones a year. But I wouldn't hit a broad, even one like Brigitte who could get me going just looking at me. I broke a lot of furniture, though, and that got on her nerves.''

I couldn't help laughing. "Yeah, I can see that. It'd bother me, too.''

He gave a grudging smile. "See, the trouble is, I grew up poor. I mean, dirt poor. I used to go to the projects here with some of the black guys on the squad, you know, Christmas appearances, shit like that. Those kids live in squalor, but I didn't own a pair of shorts to cover my ass until the county social worker come 'round to see why I wasn't in school.''

"So you broke furniture because you grew up without it and didn't know what else to do with it?''

"Don't be a wiseass, Victoria. I'm sure your mamma wouldn't like it.''

I made a face—he was right about that.

"You know the LeBlancs, right? Oh, you're a Yankee, Yankees don't know shit if they haven't stepped in it themselves. LeBlanc Gas, they're one of the biggest names on the Gulf Coast. They're a long, *long* way from the Pierces of Florette.

"I muscled my way into college, played football for Old Bear Bryant, met Brigitte. She liked raw meat, and mine was just about the rawest in the South, so she latched on to me. When she decided to marry me she took me down to Mobile for Christmas. There I was, the Hulk, in Miz Effie's lace and crystal palace. They hated me, knew I was trash, told Brigitte they'd cut her out of everything if she married me. She figured she could sweet-talk her daddy into anything. We got married and it didn't work, not even when I was a national superstar. To them I was still the dirt I used to wipe my ass with.''

"So she divorced you to get back in their will?''

He shrugged, a movement that set a tidal wave going down the mountain. "Oh, that had something to do with it, sure, it had something. But I was a wreck and I was hell to live with. Even if she'd been halfway normal to begin with, it would have gone bust, 'cause I didn't know how to live with losing football. I just didn't care about anyone or anything.''

"Not even the Daytona,'' I couldn't help saying.

His black eyes disappeared into tiny dots. "Don't you go lecturing me just when we're starting to get on. I'm not asking you to cry over my sad jock story. I'm just trying to give you a little different look at sweet, beautiful Brigitte.''

"Sorry. It's just . . . I'll never do anything to be able to afford a Ferrari Daytona. It pisses me to see someone throw one away.''

He snorted. "If I'd known you five years ago I'd of given it to you. Too late now. Anyway, Brigitte waited too long to jump ship. She was still in negotiations with old man LeBlanc when he and Miz Effie dropped into the Gulf of Mexico with the remains of their little Cessna. Everything that wasn't tied down went to Corinne. Brigitte, being her guardian, gets a chunk for looking after her, but you ask me, if Corinne's gone missing it's the best thing she could do. I'll bet you . . . well, I don't have anything left to bet. I'll hack off my big toe and give it to you if Brigitte's after anything but the money.''

He thought for a minute. "No. She probably likes Corinne some. Or would like her if she'd lose thirty pounds, dress like a Mobile debutante and hang around with a crowd of snot-noses. I'll hack off my toe if the money ain't number one in her heart, that's all.''

I eyed him steadily, wondering how much of his story to believe. It's why I stay away from domestic crime: everyone has a story, and it wears you out trying to match all the different pieces together. I could check the LeBlancs' will to see if they'd left their fortune the way Jade reported it. Or if they had a fortune at all. Maybe he was making it all up.

"Did Corinne talk to you before she took off on Monday?''

His black eyes darted around the room. "I haven't laid eyes on her in months. She used to come around, but Brigitte got a peace bond on me, I get arrested if I'm within thirty feet of Corinne."

"I believe you, Jade," I said steadily. "I believe you haven't seen her. But did she talk to you? Like on the phone, maybe."

The ugly look returned to his face, then the mountain shook again as he laughed. "You don't miss many signals, do you, Victoria? You oughta run a training camp. Yeah, Corinne calls me Monday morning. 'Why don't you have your cute little ass in school?' I says. 'Even with all your family dough that's the only way to get ahead—they'll ream you six ways from Sunday if you don't get your education so you can check out what all your advisers are up to.' "

He shook his head broodingly. "I know what I'm talking about, believe me. The lawyers and agents and financial advisers, they all made out like hogs at feeding time when I was in the money, but come trouble, it wasn't them, it was me hung out like a slab of pork belly to dry on my own."

"So what did Corinne say to your good advice?" I prompted, trying not to sound impatient: I could well be the first sober person to listen to him in a decade.

"Oh, she's crying, she can't stand it, why can't she just run home to Mobile? And I tell her 'cause she's underage and rich, the cops will all be looking for her and just haul her butt back to Chicago. And when she keeps talking wilder and wilder I tell her they'll be bound to blame me if something happens to her and does she really need to run away so bad that I go to jail or something. So I thought that calmed her down. 'Think of it like rookie camp,' I told her. 'They put you through the worst shit but if you survive it you own them.' I thought she figured it out and was staying."

He shut his eyes. "I'm tired, detective. I can't tell you nothing else. You go away and detect."

"If she went back to Mobile who would she stay with?"

"Wouldn't nobody down there keep her without calling Brigitte. Too many of them owe their jobs to LeBlanc Gas." He didn't open his eyes.

"And up here?"

He shrugged, a movement like an earthquake that rattled the bedrails. "You might try the neighbors. Seems to me Corinne mentioned a Miz Hellman who had a bit of a soft spot for her.'' He opened his eyes. ''Maybe Corinne'll talk to you. You got a good ear.''

''Thanks.'' I got up. ''What about this famous Maltese cat?''

''What about it?''

''It went missing along with Corinne. Think she'd hurt it to get back at Brigitte?''

''How the hell should I know? Those LeBlancs would do anything to anyone. Even Corinne. Now get the fuck out so I can get my beauty rest.'' He shut his eyes again.

''Yeah, you're beautiful all right, Jade. Why don't you use some of your old connections and get yourself going at something? It's really pathetic seeing you like this.''

''You wanna save me along with the Daytona?'' The ugly jeer returned to his voice. ''Don't go all do-gooder on me now, Victoria. My daddy died at forty from too much moonshine. They tell me I'm his spitting image. I know where I'm going.''

''It's trite, Jade. Lots of people have done it. They'll make a movie about you and little kids will cry over your sad story. But if they make it honest they'll show that you're just plain selfish.''

I wanted to slam the door but the hydraulic stop took the impact out of the gesture. ''Goddamned motherfucking waste,'' I snapped as I stomped down the corridor.

The floor head heard me. ''Jade Pierce? You're right about that.''

VI

The Hellmans lived in an apartment above the TV repair shop they ran on Halsted. Mrs. Hellman greeted me with some relief.

''I promised Corinne I wouldn't tell her sister as long as she stayed here instead of trying to hitchhike back to Mobile. But I've been pretty worried. It's just that . . . to Brigitte LeBlanc I don't exist. My daughter Lily is trash that she doesn't want Corinne associated with, so it never even occurred to her that Corinne might be here.''

She took me through the back of the shop and up the stairs to the apartment. ''It's only five rooms, but we're glad to have her as long as she wants to stay. I'm more worried about the cat: she doesn't like being cooped up in here. She got out Tuesday night and we had a terrible time hunting her down."

I grinned to myself: So much for the thoroughbred descendants pined for by Joel Sirop.

Mrs. Hellman took me into the living room where they had a sofabed that Corinne was using. "This here is a detective, Corinne. I think you'd better talk to her."

Corinne was hunched in front of the television, an outsize console model far too large for the tiny room. In her man's white shirt and tattered blue jeans she didn't look at all like her svelte sister. Her complexion was a muddy color that matched her lank, straight hair. She clutched Lady Iva of Cairo close in her arms. Both of them looked at me angrily.

"If you think you can make me go back to that cold-assed bitch, you'd better think again."

Mrs. Hellman tried to protest her language.

"It's okay," I said. "She learned it from Jade. But Jade lost every fight he ever was in with Brigitte, Corinne. Maybe you ought to try a different method."

"Brigitte hated Jade. She hates anyone who doesn't do stuff just the way she wants it. So if you're working for Brigitte you don't know shit about anything."

I responded to the first part of her comments. "Is that why you took the cat? So you could keep her from having purebred kittens like Brigitte wants her to?"

A ghost of a smile twitched around her unhappy mouth. All she said was "They wouldn't let me bring my dogs or my horse up north. Iva's kind of a snoot but she's better than nothing."

"Jade thinks Brigitte's jealous because you got the LeBlanc fortune and she didn't."

She made a disgusted noise. "Jade worries too much about all that shit. Yeah, Daddy left me a big fat wad. But the company went to Daddy's cousin Miles. You can't inherit LeBlanc Gas if you're a girl and Brigitte knew that, same as me. I mean, they told both of us growing up so we wouldn't have our hearts set on it. The money they left me, Brigitte makes that amount every year in her business. She doesn't care about the money."

"And you? Does it bother you that the company went to your cousin?"

She gave a long ugly sniff—no doubt another of Jade's expressions. "Who wants a company that doesn't do anything but pollute the Gulf and ream the people who work for them?"

I considered that. At fourteen it was probably genuine bravado. "So what do you care about?"

She looked at me with sulky dark eyes. For a minute I
thought she was going to tell me to mind my own goddamned
business and go to hell, but she suddenly blurted, "It's my
horse. They left the house to Miles along with my horse. They
didn't think about it, just said the house and all the stuff that
wasn't left special to someone else went to him and they didn't
even think to leave me my own horse."

The last sentence came out as a wail and her angry young
face dissolved into sobs. I didn't think she'd welcome a friendly
pat on the shoulder. I just let the tears run their course. She
finally wiped her nose on a frayed cuff and shot me a fierce
look to see if I cared.

"If I could persuade Brigitte to buy your horse from Miles
and stable him up here, would you be willing to go back to her
until you're of age?"

"You never would. Nobody ever could make that bitch
change her mind."

"But if I could?"

Her lower lip was hanging out. "Maybe. If I could have my
horse and go to school with Lily instead of fucking St. Scholastica."

"I'll do my best." I got to my feet. "In return maybe you
could work on Jade to stop drugging himself to death. It isn't
romantic, you know: it's horrible, painful, about the ugliest
thing in the world."

She only glowered at me. It's hard work being an angel. No
one takes at all kindly to it.

VII

Brigitte was furious. Her cheeks flamed with natural color and
her cobalt eyes glittered. I couldn't help wondering if this was
how she looked when Jade and B. B. Wilder were fighting over
her.

"So he knew all along where she was! I ought to have him
sent over for that. Can't I charge him with contributing to her
delinquency?"

"Not if you're planning on using me as a witness you can't,"
I snapped.

She ignored me. "And her, too. Taking Lady Iva off like
that. Mating her with some alley cat."

As if on cue, Casper of Valletta squawked loudly and started
clawing the deep silver plush covering Brigitte's living room
floor. Joel Sirop picked up the tom and spoke soothingly to
him.

"It is bad, Brigitte, very bad. Maybe you should let the girl
go back to Mobile if she wants to so badly. After three days,
you know, it's too late to give Lady Iva a shot. And Corinne
is so wild, so uncontrollable—what would stop her the next
time Lady Iva comes into season?"

Brigitte's nostrils flared. "I should send her to reform school.
Show her what discipline is really like."

"Why in hell do you even want custody over Corinne if all
you can think about is revenge?" I interrupted.

She stopped swirling around her living room and turned to
frown at me. "Why, I love her, of course. She is my sister,
you know."

"Concentrate on that. Keep saying it to yourself. She's not
a cat that you can breed and mold to suit your fancy."

"I just want her to be happy when she's older. She won't be
if she can't learn to control herself. Look at what happened
when she started hanging around trash like that Lily Hellman.
She would never have let Lady Iva breed with an alley cat if
she hadn't made that kind of friend."

I ground my teeth. "Just because Lily lives in five rooms
over a store doesn't make her trash. Look, Brigitte. You wanted
to lead your own life. I expect your parents tried keeping you
on a short leash. Hell, maybe they even threatened you with
reform school. So you started fucking every hulk you could
get your hands on. Are you so angry about that that you have
to treat Corinne the same way?"

She gaped at me. Her jaw worked but she couldn't find any
words. Finally she went over to a burled oak cabinet that concealed a bar. She pulled out a chilled bottle of Sancerre and
poured herself a glass. When she'd gulped it down she sat at
her desk.

"Is it that obvious? Why I went after Jade and B. B. and all
those boys?"

I hunched a shoulder. "It was just a guess, Brigitte. A guess based on what I've learned about you and your sister and Jade the last two days. He's not such an awful guy, you know, but he clearly was an awful guy for you. And Corinne's lonely and miserable and needs someone to love her. She figures her horse for the job.''

"And me?'' Her cobalt eyes glittered again. "What do I need? The embraces of my cat?''

"To shed some of those porcupine quills so someone can love you, too. You could've offered me a glass of wine, for example.''

She started an ugly retort, then went over to the liquor cabinet and got out a glass for me. "So I bring Flitcraft up to Chicago and stable her. I put Corinne into the filthy public high school. And then we'll all live happily ever after.''

"She might graduate.'' I swallowed some of the wine. It was cold and crisp and eased some of the tension the LeBlancs and Pierces were putting into my throat. "And in another year she won't run away to Lily's, but she'll go off to Mobile or hit the streets. Now's your chance.''

"Oh, all right,'' she snapped. "You're some kind of saint, I know, who never said a bad word to anyone. You can tell Corinne I'll cut a deal with her. But if it goes wrong you can be the one to stay up at night worrying about her.''

I rubbed my head. "Send her back to Mobile, Brigitte. There must be a grandmother or aunt or nanny or someone who really cares about her. With your attitude, life with Corinne is just going to be a bomb waiting for the fuse to blow.''

"You can say that again, detective.'' It was Jade, his bulk filling the double doors to the living room.

Behind him we could hear the housekeeper without being able to see her. "I tried to keep him out, Brigitte, but Corinne let him in. You want me to call the cops, get them to exercise that peace bond?''

"I have a right to ask whoever I want into my own house,'' came Corinne's muffled shriek.

Squawking and yowling, Casper broke from Joel Sirop's hold. He hurtled himself at the doorway and stuffed his body through the gap between Jade's feet. On the other side of the barricade we could hear Lady Iva's answering yodel and a scream from Corinne—presumably she'd been clawed.

"Why don't you move, Jade, so we can see the action?'' I suggested.

He lumbered into the living room and perched his bulk on the edge of a pale grey sofa. Corinne stumbled in behind him and sat next to him. Her muddy skin and lank hair looked worse against the sleek modern lines of Brigitte's furniture than they had in Mrs. Hellman's crowded sitting room.

Brigitte watched the blood drip from Corinne's right hand to the rug and jerked her head at the housekeeper hovering in the doorway. "Can you clean that up for me, Grace?"

When the housekeeper left, she turned to her sister. "Next time you're that angry at me take it out on me, not the cat. Did you really have to let her breed in a back alley?"

"It's all one to Iva," Corinne muttered sulkily. "Just as long as she's getting some she don't care who's giving it to her. Just like you."

Brigitte marched to the couch. Jade caught her hand as she was preparing to smack Corinne.

"Now look here, Brigitte," he said. "You two girls don't belong together. You know that as well as I do. Maybe you think you owe it to your public image to be a mamma to Corinne, but you're not the mamma type. Never have been. Why should you try now?"

Brigitte glared at him. "And you're Mister Wonderful who can sit in judgment on everyone else?"

He shook his massive jade dome. "Nope. I won't claim that. But maybe Corinne here would like to come live with me." He held up a massive palm as Brigitte started to protest. "Not in Uptown. I can get me a place close to here. Corinne can have her horse and see you when you feel calm enough. And when your pure little old cat has her half-breed kittens they can come live with us."

"On Corinne's money," Brigitte spat.

Jade nodded. "She'd have to put up the stake. But I know some guys who'd back me to get started in somethin'. Commodities, somethin' like that."

"You'd be drunk or doped up all the time. And then you'd rape her—" She broke off as he did his ugly-black-slit number with his eyes.

"You'd better not say anything else, Brigitte LeBlanc. Damned well better not say anything. You want me to get up in the congregation and yell that I never touched a piece of ass that shoved itself in my nose, I ain't going to. But you know better'n anyone that I never in my life laid hands on a girl to hurt her. As for the rest . . ." His eyes returned to normal and he put a redwood branch around Corinne's shoulders. "First time I'm drunk or shooting somethin' Corinne comes right back here. We can try it for six months, Brigitte. Just a trial. Rookie camp, you know how it goes."

The football analogy brought her own mean look to Brigitte's face. Before she could say anything Joel bleated in the background, "It sounds like a good idea to me, Brigitte. Really. You ought to give it a try. Lady Iva's nerves will never be stable with the fighting that goes on around her when Corinne is here."

"No one asked you," Brigitte snapped.

"And no one asked me, either," Corinne said. "If you don't agree, I—I'm going to take Lady Iva and run away to New York. And send you pictures of her with litter after litter of alley cats."

The threat, uttered with all the venom she could muster, made me choke with laughter. I swallowed some Sancerre to try to control myself, but I couldn't stop laughing. Jade's mountain rumbled and shook as he joined in. Joel gasped in horror. Only the two LeBlanc women remained unmoved, glaring at each other.

"What I ought to do, I ought to send you to reform school, Corinne Alton LeBlanc."

"What you ought to do is cool out," I advised, putting my glass down on a chrome table. "It's a good offer. Take it. If you don't, she'll only run away."

Brigitte tightened her mouth in a narrow line. "I didn't hire you to have you turn on me, you know."

"Yeah, well, you hired me. You didn't buy me. My job is to help you resolve a difficult problem. And this looks like the best solution you're going to be offered."

"Oh, very well," she snapped pettishly, pouring herself another drink. "For six months. And if her grades start slipping, or I hear she's drinking or doping or anything like that, she comes back here."

I got up to go. Corinne followed me to the door.

"I'm sorry I was rude to you over at Lily's," she muttered shyly. "When the kittens are born you can have the one you like best."

I gulped and tried to smile. "That's very generous of you,

Corinne. But I don't think my dog would take too well to a kitten.''

"Don't you like cats?" The big brown eyes stared at me poignantly. "Really, cats and dogs get along very well unless their owners expect them not to."

"Like LeBlancs and Pierces, huh?"

She bit her lip and turned her head, then said in a startled voice, "You're teasing me, aren't you?"

"Just teasing you, Corinne. You take it easy. Things are going to work out for you. And if they don't, give me a call before you do anything too rash, okay?"

"And you will take a kitten?"

Just say no, Vic, just say no, I chanted to myself. "Let me think about it. I've got to run now." I fled the house before she could break my resolve any further.

Barbara Paul, with a doctorate in theater history and criticism, straddles two fictional worlds: she writes both science fiction (An Exercise for Madmen, The Three-Minute Universe, and three others) and mysteries (The Renewable Virgin, A Cadenza for Caruso, Prima Donna At Large, Good King Sauerkraut, and eight others). Her love of the theater is evident not only in her choice of that setting for many of her novels but also in her ability to coax readers to suspend their disbelief willingly.

In "Appetites," a near-future society chews on some familiar problems and it's up to individuals to cook up solutions.

APPETITES

by Barbara Paul

MR. KOUROS COULDN'T open his shop Monday morning, because a dead man was blocking the door. Middle-aged man, stick-thin, probably hadn't eaten for days But that wasn't what killed him. Mr. Kouros bent over until he could see the metal implant in the man's hand. He hurried down to the public phone on the corner and punched in the number that every "clean" resident of the city had memorized months ago.

"Disposal," an androgynous voice answered.

"OD needs picking up," Mr. Kouros said. "Fourteen-ten Detweiler Street."

The voice repeated the address. "Right, thanks for calling it in."

Mr. Kouros walked back to his shop and waited, keeping his eyes averted from the pitiful figure in the shop doorway. *You'd think I'd be used to it by now,* he thought dully.

Within five minutes the high bleating of the mobile disposal unit reached his ears; in the larger places like New York or Los Angeles he'd have had to wait as long as an hour. The blue-and-silver van pulled up to the curb. Mr. Kouros watched impersonally as two muscular young men and an older one piled out of the back and proceeded to zip up the corpse in a body bag. They moved quickly and efficiently; no waste motion. Mr. Kouros liked that. "Will they do an autopsy?" he asked.

The older man laughed shortly. "What for?" He shook his head at Mr. Kouros, and then they were gone.

Neat. No fuss. No questions.

Mr. Kouros unlocked the door and went into his shop. Shelves filled with gourmet foods gleamed in the artificial light, as did tables displaying shamefully overpriced designer kitchen utensils. Racks of lovingly chosen wines lined one wall, samples from the larger stock in the temperature-controlled basement. Mr. Kouros glanced at his watch: ten-fifteen. The dead man had made him fifteen minutes late opening up. And his assistant was late this morning. Again.

Speak of the—"Morning, Mr. Kouros," a cheery young voice called out. "Bus was late."

Mr. Kouros grunted and went back to his office to start the coffee. Colombian Supremo today. Roger, his assistant, began checking the cheese display case to see what needed to be replaced. A woman came in and bought two smoked pheasants.

By the time she was gone, the coffee was ready. Mr. Kouros carefully cut two slices of pineapple-and-macadamia-nut cake. Roger came into the office, took his customary chair in the corner, and sipped at the coffee. "Sumatra Mandheling?"

"Good heavens, no—Colombian Supremo." It was a game they played. Every day Mr. Kouros would brew a different kind of coffee, and every day Roger would try to identify it. He was right about half the time.

Mr. Kouros had almost finished his cup before he noticed Roger's right hand. Something new there, a round metal implant of the sort he'd already seen once that morning. "Roger?" He couldn't believe it. "You're a doper?"

Roger waved the hand with the implant airily. "Don't worry, Mr. K. I can handle it."

Dear God. "You can *handle* it. Roger, this morning I found an OD curled up against the door here. That man must have thought *he* could 'handle' it."

Roger was taken aback. "This morning?"

"This morning. Is that the way you want to end up—zipped into a plastic bag and hauled off to a morgue like a piece of meat scraped up off the sidewalk? You die with that thing in your hand and you're just a statistic. Even if you're hit by a truck—nobody investigates, nobody does an autopsy. You're a registered doper now, Roger. You're labeled."

The young man cleared his throat nervously. "I hear they're going back to doing autopsies. Most of the hard cases have already overdosed—the police are going to have time to investigate again."

"That should be a great comfort to you," Mr. Kouros remarked dryly.

"Look, it's only recreational drugs with me. I'm not an addict—it's just once in a while."

Silently Mr. Kouros pointed to Roger's right hand.

"Because it's the only way you can get the stuff now!" Roger laughed. "You can't buy it on the street anymore, not since the government started handing it out free. Besides, why should I pay when everybody else is getting it for nothing?"

"You're killing yourself."

"No, I'm not, Mr. Kouros, honestly. All I do is smoke a little pot. I don't do the hard stuff more than two, three times a year. It's nothing to worry about." They both heard the shop door open, and Roger jumped up in relief. "I'll get it."

Mr. Kouros stood in the office doorway and watched his assistant. Roger had registered with one of the Federal Dispensing Centers and had been implanted with the required identification disc, but he showed no signs of being addicted. Yet. His walk was steady and his voice clear and cheerful as he spoke to the customer.

The customer was a young woman who looked as if she couldn't really afford the forty-two dollars she plunked down for the hazelnut cheesecake she'd asked for. Important dinner tonight, then; trying to impress someone. Her boss? Her husband's boss? His parents? Something of a purist, Mr. Kouros didn't approve of hazelnut cheesecake. But he sold it anyway.

Then without warning the shop was busy. A business executive wanting four bottles of Château Pétrus. A middle-aged couple indulging themselves at the cheese display. A college student who took ten minutes deciding between two moderately priced burgundies. An old man who came in every Monday morning to buy Australian apricots. Two youngsters looking for something that would make a nice gift. Repeat customers, newcomers—a wave of them, all at once. The mail carrier came.

When the rush was over, Mr. Kouros went back to his office to look through the morning's mail. He skimmed through the catalogs from a couple of his suppliers before opening the letters and bills, nibbling from a plate of cheese and olives as he read. He looked at his watch: eleven-thirty. An hour and a half before he met the others.

A little over an hour later he told Roger he wouldn't be back directly after lunch; he had a doctor's appointment. Roger politely expressed the hope that nothing was wrong. No, said Mr. Kouros, just his annual checkup. He had to account for his absence that afternoon some way.

But lunch first. Only seven blocks to the restaurant; plenty of time. He passed a Federal Dispensing Center two doors away from his shop. Only one or two "customers" inside; when the place had first opened, there'd been lines all the way up the block. Perhaps they could shut down before long.

The fall weather was just beginning to turn nippy, exactly the way Mr. Kouros liked it. Up until a year ago he'd have had to fight lunchtime crowds all the way to Mrs. DeMarco's restaurant, but not now. Already overpopulation had stopped being a pressing problem.

Mr. Kouros hurried his step, beginning to feel a little anxious. His route took him past a large record-and-tape outlet; the tune floating from the speaker over the door was soft and catchy, inviting the listener to hum along. That was something else that was changing—the music. Pop music didn't seem to *pound* at him the way it once had done.

Mrs. DeMarco's restaurant had a deceptively modest facade. Inside, the decor was as luxurious as the cuisine that attracted diners from all over the state. The maître d' nodded pleasantly and allowed Mr. Kouros to proceed unescorted to Mrs. DeMarco's private table; Mr. Kouros preferred it that way.

The restaurant's owner was looking older and more worried than he'd ever seen her before, but she mustered up a tight little smile for him. "Hello, Mr. Kouros. The third member of our group isn't here yet—we'll have time to try this new pâté."

Mr. Kouros murmured something appropriate as he slid into the booth next to her. The man they were waiting for had frequently and loudly proclaimed that pâté was a practical joke some culinary ne'er-do-well had foisted off on the unwary. Mr. Kouros tasted the new pâté; it was delicious. He cleared his throat and said, "We still have time to change our minds."

"Second thoughts?"

"No. I was wondering about you."

Mrs. DeMarco shook her head. "I've been paying off that bastard for eight years. But no more. I've reached my limit."

Mr. Kouros pursed his lips. He'd been paying only five years, but even that was unconscionably long. It had to stop. "We could just wait," he said, playing devil's advocate. "He'll kill himself eventually."

"That could take years. Besides, all dopers don't OD. Ziegler's one of the indestructible ones. He won't stop until somebody stops him."

Mr. Kouros felt a familiar rush of anger. "God, how I hate that man!"

"I know the feeling," Mrs. DeMarco said sadly. "He was here this morning."

"Here? What did he want?"

"He wanted to show me a jar of cockroaches he'd collected." She didn't have to explain further. Ziegler was a county health inspector who had the power to shut down both their businesses. The first time Ziegler had come into Mr. Kouros's shop, he'd pretended to find a jar of marmalade that had the remains of a dead fly in it. Mr. Kouros had been slow to catch on; he'd checked his inventory and insisted the jar wasn't part of his stock. Ziegler kept the marmalade for "evidence" and returned every day to uncover some new imaginary health violation until Mr. Kouros finally did catch on. In Mrs. DeMarco's case, Ziegler had simply dropped a dead mouse into a simmering pot of béchamel sauce.

So they'd both paid, month after month, for the privilege of staying open. Ziegler jotted down every payment—cash only, please—in a small spiral notebook that was never out of his possession. *Wouldn't want to cheat you*, he'd smirk. Mr. Kouros and Mrs. DeMarco conferred frequently but could find no way to slip from their extortionist's grasp. Their resentment bubbled and seethed until it began to poison them. But still they did nothing; the impetus for action had come from the third member of their group.

"Here's Mr. Furneaux now," Mrs. DeMarco said.

Mr. Kouros watched the other man make his entrance. Mr. Furneaux was, as usual, dressed in clothing that stopped just short of being flamboyant—a large man wearing his avoirdupois like a carefully chosen accessory. He was a successful wine merchant, a wealthy man, and he looked the part. The other two bought their wines exclusively from him, and the three of them had been dining together off and on for years. Mr. Furneaux had listened sympathetically as Mrs. DeMarco and Mr. Kouros complained bitterly about the health inspector's extortion racket; but now the wine merchant's life also had been contaminated by the noxious Ziegler, and in a far more personal way than theirs.

"Am I late?" Mr. Furneaux asked, looking at his watch. "No, I'm not late. Has today seemed shorter to you than most Mondays? The bird of time is on the wing and all that." He sat down. "Well. He's at his cabin at the lake. He's taken the week off from his job."

"When does your daughter plan to join him?"

"Tomorrow. So we can't put it off."

Mr. Kouros felt honor-bound to make one more attempt. "Ziegler's a hophead. The problem may take care of itself."

"*Your* problem may take care of itself," Mr. Furneaux said, "but Diane is so besotted with that man that she'll do anything he tells her. A week alone with him and she'll come back with one of those charming little metal discs implanted in her hand. I can't afford to wait. You're not backing out, are you, Mr. Kouros?"

"No, I'm in." He just wanted to make sure of the other two.

"Let's order," Mrs. DeMarco suggested.

Ordinarily the two men would quiz her about such matters as whether the white asparagus or the artichoke hearts were a better choice that day, but this time they made their selections quickly and without discussion. Mr. Furneaux bit into a canapé and didn't notice it was pâté. "He doesn't give a damn about her, you know," he said, still thinking of his daughter. "At first he just wanted her as a bed partner, but then he found out how much money I have." Ziegler had proposed marriage to young Diane Furneaux at about the same time he'd notified

Mr. Kouros and Mrs. DeMarco that their monthly payments were going to be raised.

Mr. Kouros didn't know about Mrs. DeMarco, but the high payments were putting a strain on his business. "How old is your daughter?" he asked Mr. Furneaux.

"Nineteen. Old enough to know better."

Mrs. DeMarco laughed humorlessly. "At that age a girl can fall in love with a werewolf. I don't mean to be indelicate, Mr. Furneaux, but this is probably her first intense sexual relationship. That can blind you to everything else."

"She's certainly acting like a blind woman," Mr. Furneaux growled. "I've even shown her pictures of Ziegler with other women, nuzzling their necks . . . once even fondling a woman's breast in public. So what does dear little Diane do? She accuses me of faking the photographs!" Mr. Furneaux shifted his considerable weight and scowled. "*I don't want to hear about it, I don't want to talk about it*—she's been like that her entire life. And she hasn't been overprotected. Her mother and I have honestly tried to make her understand something of the way of the world. But she just closes her eyes and covers her ears every time she runs up against something even remotely unpleasant."

"She sounds like a very frightened girl," Mrs. DeMarco said quietly.

Mr. Furneaux shot her a sharp glance. "Whatever the reason, she simply refused to believe Ziegler's still seeing other women after they became engaged. He never *stops* seeing other women—every day, one or two different ones! The man is insatiable. Biggest case of satyriasis I've ever come across. He can't see a woman without trying to bed her."

"I know," Mrs. DeMarco said dryly. "He even tried with me."

Mr. Furneaux raised both eyebrows. "Dear me. Although I don't know why I'm surprised. That certainly is in character."

Mr. Kouros was worried. "You say you daughter isn't planning to join him until tomorrow? What if he has another woman with him at the cabin—right now, today?"

The wine merchant frowned. "I've been thinking about that. If there is a woman with him, we'll have to find some way to get her out of the cabin."

"Some way? Shouldn't we have a plan?"

"How can we? We don't know where they'll be in the cabin or what they'll be doing. We'll have to wait until we get there."

Their food arrived. Mr. Kouros barely tasted the sorrel soup as they all ate silently, all three caught up in their own thoughts. He didn't like the possibility of a last-minute complication in the form of some unknown woman in the company of their prey. But he couldn't think what to do about it. "Maybe we should wait and let him kill himself," he said again, this time meaning it a little more.

Mr. Furneaux sighed. "He's not going to overdose. The Free Drugs Program has been in effect . . . how long now? A year? All the hopeless cases are already dead. Anyone who's survived this long isn't likely to OD now. When was the last time you saw a dead body in the street?"

"This morning. I found one by the shop entrance when I came in."

Mr. Furneaux made a moue. "Oh dear—how unpleasant for you. But remember what it was like the first month the Federal Dispensing Centers opened? Crazies all over the place, dopers dropping like flies, corpses lying there on the sidewalks, disposal teams working around the clock. Remember how *awful* it was?"

"Desperate situations call for desperate remedies," Mrs. DeMarco said, repeating the incumbent president's campaign slogan.

"But it's not like that now," Mr. Furneaux went on. "The surviving dopers are doing just that—surviving. Ziegler's too sex-crazy and too money-hungry to let his taste for that white powder be anything more than just another indulgence in his pampered life. Mr. Kouros, *we can't wait*."

Mr. Kouros raised no further objection.

They finished lunch and waited a few moments at the front entrance while the valet brought Mr. Furneaux's Mercedes around. Mrs. DeMarco slid into the front while Mr. Kouros climbed in the back. The front seat had been pushed all the way back, to allow room for Mr. Furneaux's portly figure to fit behind the steering wheel.

"It's about an hour to the lake," Mrs. DeMarco said. "If everything goes according to plan, we should be back here before six."

If. All the way to the lake they talked *what if.* What if Ziegler and a woman were in the bedroom, what if they were in the kitchen, what if they had gone out. They considered every possibility they could think of.

"Are you absolutely certain autopsies are still not being performed on dopers?" Mr. Kouros asked Mrs. DeMarco.

"Not unless he has a bullet in his head or a knife sticking out of his chest," she said, "and sometimes not even then. The number of deaths has eased up,. true—but the medical examiner's office just doesn't have the time or the facilities to perform all those autopsies. They still have their regular work to do, you know. The overdosers are automatically separated from all other deaths and, well, summarily disposed of."

"My assistant heard they were going to start doing autopsies again."

Mr. Furneaux snorted impatiently. "I've been hearing that rumor for the past six months. There's nothing to it. As long as these idiots keep registering with the government's Free Drug Program, the police are going to continue to sack 'em, tag 'em, and burn 'em. A boon for the crematories."

Mrs. DeMarco winced.

"Excuse the crudity of my expression, dear Mrs. De-Marco," Mr. Furneaux apologized. "I simply find it impossible to feel sorry for the fools. I firmly believe that everyone has the right to kill himself any way he wants. But the police are still pushing the bodies through, assembly-line style. I had dinner with one of the deputy police commissioners on Saturday, and he made it quite clear that the special division responsible for collecting dopers' bodies still regard their work as garbage disposal."

Mr. Kouros grunted, satisfied. It was a crucial point. Without the guarantee that their deed would go uninvestigated, not one of the three would have found the courage to undertake an act of murder. *Give them as much as they want as often as they want it*—that was the present administration's answer to a problem that had long since escaped all rational control. *Let them kill themselves off.* And the nation's addicts had cooperated by dying by the thousands, unknowingly providing Mr. Kouros, Mr. Furneaux, and Mrs. DeMarco with the smoke screen that they needed.

About a fourth of the lakefront had been cleared and turned into a resort area, but around the rest of the lake the woods ran down almost to the waterline. It was in the wooded section that Ziegler had bought a cabin, accessible only by a narrow dirt road and isolated from the resort condominiums. Mr. Furneaux parked the Mercedes off the road among the trees, muttering about his paint job. The three of them picked their way through the undergrowth to Ziegler's cabin, which had been built before the resort area was developed and was now beginning to show its age. Terrified of being caught, the three conspirators crept around the outside, looking in through the windows.

They found Ziegler. He was lying naked on a bed, either asleep or zonked out. With a woman lying on each side of him.

Two women. That was one *what if* they hadn't thought of.

"Where does he *find* them?" Mr. Furneaux whispered in exasperation. "Now what do we do?"

Mrs. DeMarco was looking through the window again. "There's a syringe on the bedside table," she said, "and a spoon and some other paraphernalia. Did you know he was freebasing now? The women, too, probably."

They found an open window in the kitchen; Mr. Kouros climbed through and opened the back door to let the others in. At the bedroom door, they hesitated. One of the women on the bed with Ziegler had long red hair—naturally red, her state of undress made clear. The other woman was younger; her blond hair was close-cropped and her body slim as a boy's. All three lay like leaden things; only shallow chest movement as they breathed indicated they were alive.

Mrs. DeMarco tiptoed up to the side of the bed. She lifted the arm of the red-haired woman and let it drop heavily; no response. She tried it with Ziegler and the other woman; they too failed to respond. "Out like a light."

Mr. Kouros and Mr. Furneaux and Mrs. DeMarco stood looking at one another for a long moment, mouths suddenly dry and hands involuntarily twitching. This was it.

Ziegler was younger and presumably stronger than they, so the plan had been for the two men to restrain him while Mrs. DeMarco held a pillow over his face. But Ziegler was offering no resistance. So all three of them pressed the pillow down— and held it.

And held it.

One of Ziegler's hands made a feeble movement—his only response. Soon, even that stopped. Still they held the pillow in place. Bearing down hard, avoiding one another's eyes.

After an eternity, they took the pillow away. Breathing heavily, Mr. Kouros felt for a pulse but couldn't find one. Then he put his ear to Ziegler's chest, listening for a heartbeat that wasn't there. Mrs. DeMarco took a mirror from her purse and held it to Ziegler's lips. The mirror didn't fog. Mr. Furneaux pulled back an eyelid and looked at one dead eye.

Neither of the two women on the bed had so much as moved a muscle. "It's going to be a shock for them," Mrs. DeMarco said, "coming out of it and finding him like that."

"Better them than my daughter," Mr. Furneaux muttered.

They didn't linger. The drive back to town was mostly a silent one. They wouldn't know until the following morning whether they had gotten away with it or not. Every day the newspaper printed a list of new deaths from routine overdosing; if Ziegler's name showed up on tomorrow's list, they were home free.

Mr. Furneaux dropped Mrs. DeMarco two blocks from her restaurant and Mr. Kouros an equal distance from his shop. No one said anything. Mr. Kouros checked the time: a few minutes before six. He hurried to his shop.

"Well, it's about time!" Roger greeted him explosively. "I was beginning to think you'd never come back!"

Mr. Kouros examined his assistant's eyes. The pupils looked all right; Roger was just tired and feeling put upon. "It took longer than I thought."

"Mr. Kouros, we need somebody else in here," Roger said earnestly. "It's too much for just two people to handle. And when you're gone all afternoon . . . urgh, they had me running in circles! We need some help—even part-time would be an improvement. You can afford part-time help, can't you?"

"Mm, perhaps I can." *Now I can.*

"That's great! Oh, by the way, somebody from the police was here earlier—about that guy you found in the doorway this morning? I told him you called it in."

Mr. Kouros waited until he could feel his heart beating again. "They're investigating . . . an OD?"

"Yep. I told you they were going to start again. Did you know the guy?"

"No." He had trouble swallowing. "You go on home, Roger. I'll close up." Roger threw both arms over his head, cheered heartily, and left.

Mr. Kouros went into his office, sank into the chair behind

his desk, and dropped his head into trembling hands. All the way back from the lake he'd held in his panic, and now he let it out in wave after wave of shuddering. His stomach heaved.

After a while, when he had emptied himself of his tension, he began to think rationally again. He reached for the telephone.

"I don't understand it," Mr. Furneaux bleated, the fear in his voice sharp and jagged. "Saturday they were not investigating overdoses, Monday they are." He pressed down on the accelerator. "I don't understand it," he repeated.

"Obviously your source of information isn't as reliable as you thought," Mr. Kouros remarked sharply from the backseat.

"A deputy police commissioner!" Mr. Furneaux protested. "Who would know better than someone from the commissioner's office?"

"You misunderstood him," Mr. Kouros snapped.

Mrs. DeMarco sighed and said, "Please—don't argue. Not now. Can you drive any faster, Mr. Furneaux?"

"I'm over the limit now. The last thing we need is to get stopped for speeding."

"It's a chance we'll have to take," she said. "We may already be too late."

"We *are* too late," Mr. Kouros muttered. "Those two women must have come to by now."

"Perhaps not," Mr. Furneaux said nervously. He floored the accelerator. "Or if they did come to, maybe they just went away and left him there. Maybe they didn't call for a disposal unit."

"Why would they do that?" Mrs. DeMarco asked curiously.

"I don't know why!" Mr. Furneaux's voice went up a key. "But if the police do an autopsy and discover he died of asphyxiation, they'll investigate and find out he was marrying my daughter as well as extorting money from you two!"

"We know that, Mr. Furneaux."

"He's *got* to be there!" Desperate.

Mr. Kouros was trying to think ahead. "If he is, the obvious thing to do is dump him in the lake. Weight him down good. Did he have a boat?"

"I don't know," Mr. Furneaux said. "If he didn't, we'll just have to steal one."

Mrs. DeMarco sighed again. "I wonder if that's as easy as it sounds."

They finished the rest of the drive in silence. Night had fallen by the time they reached the lake; Mr. Furneaux stopped the car in the same place in the dark woods where he'd parked earlier in the day. He took a flashlight from the glove compartment and let the beam play over the ground. For the second time that day the three murderers picked their way carefully to Ziegler's cabin.

The place was dark. Mr. Kouros could hear Mr. Furneaux's labored breathing and he caught a whiff of Mrs. DeMarco's perfume, but he couldn't make out either face. "What now?"

"Shine the light into the bedroom," Mrs. DeMarco suggested.

They felt their way around the cabin until they reached the bedroom window. Mr. Furneaux hesitated and then carefully raised his flashlight. The beam fell on an empty bed.

They were too late.

The drive back to the city was a morose one. Mr. Kouros pointed out that Ziegler had been extorting money from victims other than themselves, that the police would find other suspects listed in Ziegler's spiral notebook. The thought brought little comfort to any of them.

The first thing Mr. Kouros did the following morning was check the newspaper listings of the previous day's routine deaths from overdosing. There was no Ziegler on the list.

Mr. Furneaux telephoned, panic-stricken. Mr. Kouros did his best to calm the other man, suggesting that the police had listed Ziegler's death too late to make the morning editions. Mrs. DeMarco called, saying they'd better meet for lunch again today.

The two phone calls made him late. By the time Mr. Kouros arrived at his shop, Roger was waiting impatiently by the locked door, along with a youngish man of Oriental extraction who introduced himself as Sergeant Wong of the police. Mr. Kouros fumbled with the lock and let them in; he took the police sergeant back to his office while Roger began his daily check of the cheese display.

Mr. Kouros absentmindedly started making the morning coffee. "I wasn't aware the police had begun investigating routine overdoses, Sergeant," he said tentatively.

"We haven't," Wong replied, dropping into the chair facing Mr. Kouros's desk. "That's not gonna happen for a while yet.

I'm here because the man you found in your doorway was wanted for armed robbery. The crime rate's way down now, since the users don't have to steal to support their habits anymore. But there'll always be *some* crime. Did this guy ever come into your shop?''

Mr. Kouros wanted to kiss Sergeant Wong; he had to concentrate hard on not letting his elation show. ''I don't believe so,'' he answered carefully.

Wong fished a photograph out of his pocket. ''Take another look.''

Mr. Kouros studied the morgue photo of the dead man. ''No, I'm sure I've never seen him before. You might ask my assistant, though. Armed robbery, you say? You mean he was here to rob me?''

''Unlikely. He and a buddy had just held up a savings and loan—it's the buddy we're looking for. No, dopers occasionally have lucid spells when they remember they have to have food to stay alive . . . and you sell food. He had money in his pocket. He probably just wanted to buy something. Would you ask your assistant to step in here, please?''

Roger, when summoned, looked at the photo and shook his head. ''I don't know him.''

''He might have come in with another man—it would have been recently.''

''Sorry, Sergeant. I just don't remember ever seeing that man, and I've got a pretty good memory for customers' faces.''

Wong gave a resigned shrug. ''Well, it was a long shot. The buddy'll probably end up in somebody else's doorway before long anyway. They were both dopers.''

Roger slid his right hand behind his back.

''Dreadful way to die,'' Mr. Kouros murmured conventionally.

''It was withdrawal that killed him,'' Wong said, standing up. ''Neither one of them dared go into a Dispensing Center for their daily fix, not after they'd been identified as the ones who held up the savings and loan. The feds are real good about helping out that way.''

Mr. Kouros cast around for something to say. ''Would you like some coffee, Sergeant?'' He opened a tin of Scottish shortbread and laid out a dozen pieces on a plate.

''Smells good. But I got eighty-seven places I gotta be before noon. Thanks anyway.'' He nodded goodbye to both of them and left.

We're safe, we're safe, we're safe, Mr. Kouros sang silently to himself. Roger was chattering away about something or other; Mr. Kouros kept his back turned until he was sure he had his face under control. He poured the coffee and handed his assistant a cup.

Roger went over to his usual chair in the corner before tasting the coffee. ''Colombian Supremo,'' he said in surprise. ''The same kind you made yesterday!''

''Oh?'' He hadn't noticed.

''Ha! You tried to trick me!'' Roger grinned at him.

Mr. Kouros smiled back. ''You're getting too sharp for me, Roger.'' He sat drinking coffee and half listening to his assistant talk, inwardly shouting with pleasure over the good news Sergeant Wong inadvertently had brought him. Ziegler's name would be in tomorrow's newspaper list; his death was not being investigated. They'd panicked over nothing.

When Roger finished his coffee and went back out into the shop, Mr. Kouros reached for the phone to let his friends know— but then stopped. He'd be seeing them in a few hours at Mrs. DeMarco's restaurant; he'd tell them in person. Mr. Kouros chuckled in anticipation of the expressions on their faces.

In the shop, four customers were being kept waiting while Roger patiently explained to a belligerent-looking man that the rice crackers he'd bought yesterday were not stale, they were *supposed* to taste that way. Mr. Kouros went out and helped. When the last of the waiting customers had been taken care of, he headed back toward his office just as the shop door opened again. He glanced over his shoulder to see two women coming in.

One woman had an abundant head of hair that Mr. Kouros knew was naturally red. The other woman was younger, with close-cropped blond hair and a body as slim as a boy's.

He stood paralyzed as the two women said something to Roger, who nodded and gestured toward the office. They took their time approaching, looking Mr. Kouros over from head to toe.

''Well?'' the redhead asked her companion.

The blond nodded, eyes gleaming. ''He's one of them.''

The redhead turned a slow, dazzling smile on him. ''Perhaps we could go into your office, Mr. ah . . .''—she consulted a small spiral notebook—''Mr. Kouros? We need to talk in private.''

Stunned, Mr. Kouros followed them into his office and closed the door. He stood for a moment staring at the two women he'd seen for the first time only yesterday and then backed away toward his chair, putting the desk between him and them. The redhead sat in the chair facing his desk and the blond took Roger's chair in the corner. "What do you want?" Mr. Kouros asked hoarsely.

The redhead held up the spiral notebook. "Do you know what this is, Mr. Kouros?"

He blinked, didn't answer. It was Ziegler's record of Kouros's payoffs.

"I see that you do," the woman went on. "What you don't know is that my friend here was awake yesterday afternoon."

He glanced at the blond, who nodded. "You and a dark-haired woman and a fat man," she said. "I watched you kill him. You held a pillow over his face until he suffocated."

Mr. Kouros couldn't have answered her if he'd wanted to.

"You frightened her, you know," the redhead said reproachfully. "She didn't know what to do—so she played dead. And kept her eyes open a slit. Just enough to make sure she could identify all three of you."

Mr. Kouros worked his mouth, said nothing.

"I'll bet you were worried when his name didn't show up in the papers this morning, weren't you?" the redhead went on conversationally. "Well, the police don't know anything about him. We took care of that for you, Mr. Kouros."

He had to swallow twice before he could speak. "Where is he?"

"In the lake. In a spot only my friend and I can locate. Do you want us to tell the police where it is?" She smiled lazily, playing with him.

"What do you want?" he asked leadenly.

"Oh, I think you know what we want." She held up the notebook for him to see one more time and then dropped it into her purse. "We knew he'd been ripping people off for ages, and now we know who they are. So we thought we'd go through the names in his notebook until we found the three my friend saw yesterday. You're the first. I don't suppose you'd care to save us some time and tell us who your friends are?"

He glared at her wordlessly.

She gave a mock sigh. "Ah well, we'll find them sooner or later. Now." She leaned forward in her chair. "My friend and I will be around the first of each month to collect. Same arrangement—cash only. You understand?"

Mr. Kouros fought down a wave of nausea and stammered, "I—I'm to pay you now instead of him. I'm right back where I started."

"Well, not exactly," the redhead said apologetically. "You're to pay the same amount—but to each of us. Double payments from now on, Mr. Kouros. That's what you get for being naughty." The blond in the corner giggled.

"Double payments? I can't make double payments!"

"Sure you can," the redhead said easily. "You'll find a way. And remember, if you ever think of *not* paying, all we have to do is let the police know where they can find a certain water-logged corpse." She stood up; so did her friend. "It's the middle of the month now. We'll be back in a couple of weeks. So you see, you'll have some time to figure out where to get the extra money." She opened the door but paused to add, "If you run into your two friends in the meantime, tell them we'll be around to see them before long." She gave him her dazzling smile once again and left, followed by the blond, who looked back and winked at him.

Mr. Kouros sat for a long time staring at nothing. Double payments! Where was he going to get the money? He'd been better off with Ziegler. He didn't even know these women's names or where they could be found. They'd be back in two weeks, they said.

It was intolerable. His financial bondage to Ziegler had driven him to an act of desperation he'd never thought himself capable of—but instead of solving his problem, it had left him in deeper than ever. How could he get rid of these two women? He couldn't kill again. He knew he couldn't kill again. He thought he couldn't kill again.

Two weeks. They had two weeks in which to come up with a plan. Absently he picked up a piece of the Scottish shortbread and took a bite.

Mr. Kouros glanced at his watch and saw it was time to leave for Mrs. DeMarco's restaurant. Two weeks wasn't very long. They'd have to start working on a plan immediately, right now. And this time there couldn't be any mistakes.

He told Roger he'd be taking a longer lunch than usual and left, wondering how to find the right words to tell his friends what they were going to have to do.

Gillian Roberts says that ". . . Humor is my weapon of choice . . ." and she uses it with great skill. Caught Dead in Philadelphia, *a 1988 Anthony winner, introduced schoolteacher-sleuth Amanda Pepper and police officer C. K. Mackenzie, whose adventures continue in* Philly Stakes. *Roberts is the* nom de mystère *of mainstream writer Judith Greber, whose* Easy Answers, The Silent Partner, *and* Mendocino *demonstrate the same grace of language and compassion for the human condition as her Amanda Pepper series.*

In "Fury Duty," twelve women scorn the justice system to mete out a verdict of their own.

FURY DUTY

by Gillian Roberts

IT WASN'T MY favorite night even before Celia became the bearer of bad news.

I was already failing to cope with several other problems.

Item: all the sinks in the house were backed up and the plumber's estimate was twice my bank balance.

Item: my dog had impregnated a hapless bitch whose owner demanded that I harvest Fido's wild oats.

Major item: the manuscript my editor expected in two days had no ending. Actually, there was an obligatory final scene. All impediments removed, my couple would marry. That is generally considered a happy ending, although I can't imagine why. Nonetheless, my problem was how to get my characters to the altar without retracing paths taken in my earlier books.

I write both romance and horror novels. They aren't all that different, when you think about it, so I considered solving my problem by switching genres. My hero could become a werewolf. I'd make him look like my passionate dog and then I'd kill him off.

My women's group was due in a matter of minutes, and I

slapped icing on a mess of cake that I'd been too rushed to leave in the oven long enough. I decided that *Sweet Savage Steppes* shouldn't be about werewolves. Maybe its brooding Slavic hero—thank heavens for glasnost!—was sufficiently unique. Mikhail could say and do the exact same thing an Iowa farmer did in my last book and nobody would notice.

The cake looked like a relief map of Switzerland. Once upon a time, when cooking was still a female form of arm wrestling, this would have caused an anxiety attack. But my women's group had been around too long to have its members lose face through mediocre handling of flour and sugar.

The group started at the dawn of time, the era before the ERA, to coin a phrase. We were all married then, and Julia Child, not Gloria Steinem, was our guru. If we wanted to get out at night without husbands, it was cooking lessons, a Tupperware party, or a book club. We chose books—with a little food on the side.

In the sixties, when we began, we ate fruit suspended in Jell-O and talked about best-sellers, babies, color schemes and couples. In the seventies we ate whole grains, read feminist tracts and talked about ourselves. In the eighties, everybody went on her own special diet, read only business and professional articles (or in my case, my alter ego, Alexa Fury's romantic gush) and talked about disappointments—children, jobs, sex and husbands, our own exes and the recycled ones we date.

In just a few minutes, we were going to eat undercooked cake and discuss an obscure South American novel I hadn't had time to open, thanks to the miseries of Mikhail and Ariel.

I began cleaning up, but before I'd made a dent, the doorbell rang. My premature guest was Celia Arnold, toting the veggies and low-cal dip she always brings. Celia has spent the last twenty-five years trying to lose ten, then twenty, now thirty pounds.

"Something horrible's happened, Dee," she said, plunking her vegetables onto the kitchen table. "I saw the archfornicator."

"Who?" Hard to believe, but I thought she meant a guy—an intriguing-sounding one at that.

"The netsuke—Laurel's netsuke! The one with the woman and three men. You always talked about it!"

Automatically, I looked out the kitchen window toward the charred remains of the house where Laurel Tobias once lived.

It's been on the market for two years now. Nobody wants the half-burned scene of a murder.

Maybe you've read about Jackson Tobias? The man who shot his estranged wife so he could get their valuable collection of Japanese carvings? He'd bashed in a cabinet to get the figures, and he tried to hide the fact by burning the house and the cabinet to cinders, but I saw the fire and reported it in time for the evidence of his crime still to be intact.

They only found one netsuke—in his apartment. He insisted Laurel had given it to him a week earlier. The same night he'd given her his gun to ease her fears. He said. Everybody knew he'd taken the netsukes all and hidden them.

Except now two years later, Celia had found a second netsuke.

"Jackson's in prison," I said. "He must have an accomplice selling off the pieces. Maybe that redheaded tramp he was seeing?"

Celia sat down on a kitchen chair. "Wrong," she whispered.

"Cut the drama, would you?" I heard a wet plop as icing slopped off my ski slope of a cake. Why we served desserts when everybody wanted to lose weight escaped me. I glared at the cake, but it did no good, so I scowled instead at Celia.

"I saw it last week," she said. "At an Open Spaces meeting. The hostess heard me gasp and thought I was a prude. She rushed to explain that netsukes were used by the Japanese to close their money bags, that this one was centuries old, ivory and very finely carved. Actually, we had a lot of fun checking exactly what each of the three men was doing to that woman. Did you ever realize that one of them was—"

"Celia, get to the point!"

"Okay. The fornicator was a fiftieth birthday gift to her husband. From a cousin, a year ago. I couldn't figure out how. I mean Jackson was arrested two years ago, the morning after he—the morning after the fire."

I kept my hands steady spooning decaf into the coffee maker.

Celia twiddled a carrot stick. "It made me sick to think of him making a profit from murder. Besides, any netsuke money belongs to Laurel's estate, not his."

Maybe. The dispute had never been settled. Laurel had claimed that her father, a merchant seaman, collected the netsukes years earlier. Jackson insisted he'd bought them on his own travels. Whatever.

"I told this woman I was a collector and I'd never seen one like this."

Next to my ex-husband, Celia is the worst storyteller I know. "Yes, yes," I prompted. "Did she know *where* the cousin found the figure?" Maybe pornographic money-bag closers had been a Japanese fad two hundred years ago. Maybe there are thousands of teeny tiny orgy carvings. Maybe that woman owned somebody else's archfornicator.

Celia pouted. I was spoiling her fun.

"The group'll be here any minute," I said, to placate her.

She sighed loudly. "I called the cousin and *finally*, he gave me the name of a dealer. I think maybe this guy is not completely on the up-and-up."

"The cousin?"

"The art dealer. How would I know about the cousin? I never even met—"

"*Celia!*"

"I left twelve messages in four days before the dealer returned my call. He gave me the name of an auction house. Where I again left message after message."

"You should have called me. I would have found ways to speed things up."

"You always take charge. I wanted to do this myself."

The coffee maker made the bubbly digestive noises I generally find comforting, but this time they weren't enough.

"The auction house was in Chicago, Dee. *Chicago*. Why? There are places here in town." She leaned closer. "I drove there today because they wouldn't talk on the phone. But when I marched in and said I had questions to do with a dead friend and that maybe I'd call the police, they came around. I was so scared! What if they'd really made me call the cops!"

"Celia? The records?"

"They told me who'd brought in the figures. *Figures*, Dee not just one. Two dozen netsukes." She leaned back and smiled smugly.

"You're driving me crazy!"

"Okay. They were brought in *two years ago*. In October. One entire month before Laurel died. And they were brought in by a woman." Her smile faded. "I've been sick since I heard. We've done a terrible thing! Jackson didn't steal anything that night, and if Jackson didn't steal anything, then maybe he didn't—"

I stood up, too charged to stay in place. "Don't rush to conclusions. First of all, you said two dozen pieces, but Laurel had over thirty. What about the rest?"

"Maybe she placed her figures at more than one auction house."

"Second, we could be talking about somebody else altogether, not Laurel. Somebody else could have owned an archfornicator as part of a collection. Did the auctioneer tell you the name of the woman who sold them?"

Celia nodded.

"*Yes?* Well?"

"You'll never guess."

I resisted the urge to bang her infuriating head against the wall.

"It wasn't Laurel Tobias," Celia finally said.

"Then this whole thing is a tempest in a—"

"Erin S. Tisiphone brought them in."

I gasped. It had been a joke among the three of us. During the seventies, when our consciousness rose, our collective husbands fled. Mine packed and departed first. Celia's waited, then took off with their baby-sitter, who, he claimed, was still "a real woman."

Jackson seemed to believe this was a phase we were going through, and he didn't budge. Instead, he labeled us "The Three Furies." In fact, that's how I acquired my pen name. Deedee Blatt isn't either romantic or horrifying, so I became Alexa—as close as I could come to Alecto the Implacable—Fury. In the wake of the womanly baby-sitter, Celia picked Megaera, the Jealous One, and the meek Laurel accepted third and last choice, Tisiphone, the Avenger of Blood. But it was a mouthful, so she played with the Greek name for the Furies, *Erinyes*, and became Erin S.

"What'll we do?" Celia wailed. "We testified that the netsukes were in her house, which meant that Jackson stole them. We convicted him."

"The cabinet, remember? It was smashed."

Celia shrugged. "Maybe she did it. Maybe she was angry, or it was a coincidence, an accident, or somebody else altogether murdered her."

"With Jackson's gun?" I shook my head. "And who else had a key? There wasn't any break-in, and the door was locked."

"She killed herself," Celia said. "He probably really did give his gun to her, like he said. We thought she told us everything, but she didn't. We didn't know she'd sold the netsukes. Why didn't she tell us she needed money instead of going all the way to Chicago out of shame?"

"Maybe that wasn't why she went." I spoke slowly and deliberately. "Everything makes sense if Laurel wanted to frame Jackson. Make her suicide look like murder. And maybe Erin S. Tisiphone was a message for us if we ever found out—to remember friends and Furies and not go soft."

Celia's normally pink skin blanched. "But even so, if Jackson didn't do it—what did we do?"

We had done plenty. Celia and I had testified on behalf of Laurel. And the entire book group had taken off from work and gone to court every single day to sit like a second, silent jury, condemning Jackson Tobias. The fact is, we convicted the man. The fact is, he deserved it.

But now Celia seemed ready to run to the police and recant. I had to talk her out of making a terrible mistake, but there was no time or opportunity, because the bell rang.

"The women!" Celia said. "They'll know what to do. After all," she asked plaintively, "what are friends for?"

Typically, Celia took forever retelling her story, but for once, I was grateful, because it gave me time to think. By the time she was near the close, we were deeply into the evening, finished with lasagna and salad, through everybody's decision to cheat on their diets "just this once" and into friendly reassurances that my cake was okay. "Pudding-ish, but more delicious than it looks—like us," someone quipped. Women of a certain age make jokes.

We sat in a homey, rough circle in the living room. It gave me pleasure to watch the firelight flicker over the timeworn faces. It had been hard as hell keeping this house after my divorce, but when my friends gathered in it, it seemed well worth it.

When Celia finally stopped, there was a chorus of reactions. Nobody was overly shocked that depressed Laurel had committed suicide, only that she had made her own death look like murder. I listened to the exclamations. "Timid Laurel framed her husband!" "Who would have thought it of her?" "It's hard to believe that Jackson's innocent."

I recognized my cue. "Maybe Jackson isn't innocent," I said. "Even if he isn't guilty of pulling the trigger or stealing the netsukes."

"I hate the word games." Janet, the newest member, was young enough and still-married enough to believe in absolutes. "Either Jackson Tobias killed his wife or he didn't."

I gentled them toward the idea. "Perhaps the question is *when* he killed her, not whether." I waited until they'd absorbed that, then I continued. "Since there are so many ways to destroy someone, and so many steps to the process, why only be concerned with the last one—the issue of whose finger pulled the trigger or lit that match? Why do we endlessly debate when life begins and never consider when death begins?"

"What are you getting at, Dee?"

"There are more crimes than there are laws. Surprising as Celia's discovery may be, I think the issue is not whether Jackson shot Laurel, but whether he murdered her."

The firelight played against the walls while the women digested my cake and my words.

"Listen, we're"—Janet counted—"twelve ordinary women who—"

"A jury," another woman said. "We're a jury."

"Not really. We aren't the law." Janet was so disgustingly young and sincere, I had been against admitting her, and now I was convinced I'd been right.

"There are lots of systems of law," a woman who'd been part of the group all twenty-five years said. "Erin S. Tisiphone is a reminder that the furies had their own ways of handling injustice."

There was a long silence. I refilled coffee cups and wineglasses and watched our shadows paint the walls.

"I say we put Jackson back on trial," someone finally decided. "Tonight. Here. Now."

"For what, precisely?" Janet snapped. She was feisty, I'll give her that. Eleven women versus her, and she held her ground.

"For murder. By legal methods."

One woman hunched over her coffee cup, as if seeing visions in it. "Like, do you remember when she was finally able to stop helping—for no pay—with the business and the kids were launched and she went back to her painting? How he said that only immature children deluded themselves about their so-called talent.''

"How about," a second voice added, "when she had her first show and he bought all her work before the opening—to spare her humiliation, he said?"

"And then he never hung a one of them up," Celia murmured.

"He was so stingy. She made the girls' clothing and Halloween costumes and the curtains and drapes and could barely afford paintbrushes while he whooped it up on business expenses and—"

"Remember his white-glove inspections? And jokes about wishing he could afford the servants Laurel so obviously needed?"

"I'm not sure I like where this is going," Janet said. "You're talking about leaving an innocent man in prison!"

"Not forever. He's in for manslaughter and he'll be out in seven years."

"Which is a shorter sentence than Laurel served!"

"But still!" Even in the flickering light, I could see Janet's jaw set in righteous indignation. "You don't imprison a man because of an unpleasant domestic life or—"

"We're talking about justice," someone countered. "The man eroded her self-esteem, broke her spirit and destroyed her before she put a gun into her mouth. *That isn't innocence!*"

"You didn't know him, Janet," an older member said. "You didn't know her, either. You never saw any of it."

"Like how, whenever she said anything, he'd get a patient, patronizing expression, like she was a cute but stupid pet."

"Or how about the food? In front of whoever was there—clients, his friends, us—he'd poke his fork, purse his lips, question ingredients, apologize to guests, saying poor Laurel had tried so hard and he was so proud, anyway. She withered in front of our eyes."

"Once, when I was away on vacation and Laurel thought Jackson was away on business, I saw him and a young woman in a very unbusinesslike embrace."

"Well, I saw him right here in town with a real bimbo—wild red hair and skirt that looked painted on, and that was the same day Laurel was—the day she died! It was disgusting how they were carrying on. Poor Laurel, hoping and hoping he'd come back. I'm glad Dee convinced me not to tell Laurel right away or I'd feel responsible for her suicide, now that I think of it."

"Jackson once came on to me," a new voice said, "and when I squawked that Laurel was my friend, he made a sad face and said she was his friend, too, but he wanted a *woman*."

"Husbands," somebody hissed. The fire crackled and flared. Several women looked at their hands as if studying the imprints that marriage and time and maybe too much giving had made. Then they looked up, confused. I recognized that look from years and years of meetings. We were all waiting for someone to make sense of what happened between women and men.

"You know how people embezzle money?" I said. "That's how Jackson embezzled Laurel's life. He pretended it was still in her account, but little by little, he transferred it to his own. And finally, she was bankrupt." I rather liked that. A little flowery, perhaps, and heavy on the metaphor, but not bad. In fact, Alexa Fury could use it to break the gridlock. Mikhail, out in the cold, could take Ariel's hand and say, "Boris has embezzled your happiness."

"Jackson crushed the life out of Laurel," Celia said.

"Then she was too crushable!" Again it was Janet, the believer. "Women can be party to their own—"

"She was an artist, not a Valkyrie!" Celia said.

"And he was a bully!"

"But it's the end of the twentieth century! We're in charge of our own lives!" Janet's strength, or bullheadedness, was awesome. But then, she'd been raised on a different kind of food than the rest of us, nourished by what we'd painfully scraped up from below the surface of our lives.

"Laurel was brainwashed," somebody said.

"Even so, what a pathetic revenge—killing herself to make a point. If he were mine, I'd kill *him*!"

"Not if you were so destroyed you had no more strength," someone reminded her. "That's the whole point."

There was a long pause. Nobody had more to add. My turn, then. "Time for a verdict." I ripped paper into twelve slips and each woman searched her purse for pens and pencils.

"I—I abstain," Janet said. She scrambled to her feet and headed for the door. "I won't stop you, but I can't agree. Who made us jury and judge? You're not being fair." And she disappeared into the night.

Fair. I shrugged. Our view of justice was obscured by marital scar tissue, but we did try to be fair.

As fair as Furies can be.

The vote was "guilty." Unanimous—except for Janet's abstention.

"We have our verdict," I said. "What's the sentence?"

"Erin S. Tisiphone, rest in peace," our oldest member said. "And let your betraying bastard of a husband rot where he is."

There were no objections.

So the group now worships Saint Laurel, clever martyr of the war between the sexes.

I consider Laurel's sanctification my most inventive fiction, because, of course, she was not bright or brave enough to frame Jackson.

Laurel lived and died a coward. When Jackson didn't pay support after their separation, she should have dragged him into court. But she wanted him back, so to avoid harassing him, she decided to sell the netsukes.

I discouraged the idea. I suggested that it wasn't legal to dispose of assets she and Jackson held in common.

In reality, my motives were less about law and more about myself. At the time, I still believed that anything that cost Jackson, cost me.

It didn't matter. As is obvious, she only pretended to listen to me, and she covered her tracks very well with the trip to Chicago and the pseudonym.

I assume that with some invented excuse for the windfall, she gave her kids the netsuke money while she was alive.

One thing. I am a fair woman, so let's set the record straight. Jackson wasn't a villain. You've heard the evidence. He wasn't much worse than any other man. Certainly better than my poor excuse of a husband had been. Jackson even had moments of decency, like when he gave Laurel his gun. I warned him not to. She was drinking so much by then, she could have blasted anybody who entered the house, including me.

As it turned out, Laurel didn't shoot anybody but herself. But in her own dim way, she managed to do me in, and I resent her for it. After a quarter century of Laurel—and flings with other airheads—Jackson's system couldn't tolerate a strong woman.

So the bastard dumped me for a redheaded, tight-assed, brainless bimbo he flashed all over town. At least we had behaved like adults. We had been discreet. Even after he moved out of his house, we kept a profile lower than a mole's. Not even Laurel suspected. To this day, nobody does.

But what our discretion boils down to is this: Jackson never took me anywhere or bought me so much as a restaurant meal, let alone jewels or anything else of value. I could have used a financial gift or two. I churn out book after book, but it's never enough. I've come to understand that romance doesn't pay.

Anyway, given our secretiveness, I hadn't a clue he was cheating on me until that woman in my book group rushed over to describe, in horrible detail, the passionate scene she'd witnessed between Jackson and the redheaded slut.

And all I could hear her saying was that I had absolutely nothing left. No Jackson, no husband, no youth, no money, no pride, no hope of anything good ever happening to me again. I hunted Jackson down and we had quite a scene. I humiliated myself, but the man was scum. He kept checking his watch, because his tootsie was waiting.

When you understand how shabbily Jackson treated me, I'm sure you see why he had to be punished, no matter what he did or didn't do to Laurel.

Anyway, that day, after the fight with Jackson, I needed to be with a woman friend, and I figured Laurel understood man troubles. Don't misunderstand. I wasn't going to say that it was her husband who'd done me wrong. I just figured we could cry in our beers—her beers—together.

Except, midway between our houses, I heard the noise. It wasn't like in the movies or TV. It was massive and definitely final.

I ran to her door and knocked and rang—then I looked through the living room window. Laurel, or what was left of her, was on the couch. There was a gun on the floor, below her dangling hand. She had taken the coward's way out.

It was awful. Worse than any horror story. I made it back to my place gagging and retching. I intended to call emergency, even though I could tell it was all over for Laurel.

And that was when I realized that it didn't have to be all over for me. Why waste the material at hand? With all due modesty, I must say I came up with a concept that was beautiful in its simplicity. But, after all, that is my profession.

Longtime neighbors like we were have each other's house keys. I let myself into Laurel's back door, picked up a chair and bashed in the locked netsuke cabinet. That's when I found our Laurel hadn't listened to me. She'd sold all but six of her netsukes. I nearly cried. My imagined profits had just evaporated, but I reminded myself that money wasn't the main point.

Still, money would have made it sweeter, and lots of money would have made it indescribably delectable, but I had no such luck. In fact, I eventually had to sell my six netsukes cheap in the black market because the murder case made too many headlines for reputable dealers to touch the things. My paltry take in no way compensated for the grief Jackson had caused me. In any case, as a secret netsuke seller myself, you can understand why I nearly had heart failure when Celia decided to play sleuth. Who knows which netsukes and which sales slips she might have unearthed?

Anyway, that evening, I stuffed the tiny carvings in a grocery bag I'd brought because I'd been expecting the full three dozen. Then I lit a cigarette and put it and another lit match on the floor, near where Laurel's hand dangled. When the rug caught, I left by the back door and was in my house in a minute.

And that was that. Except for calling the fire department once I could see flames from my house. And except for my imaginative testimony, which, I can safely say, was my finest hour of storytelling. Besides, I had a willing audience. The cops were young and male. I was middle-aged and female, which is to say, a sexless, unthreatening, powerless and grand-motherly figure in their eyes. They automatically trusted me.

I told them Laurel had told me Jackson was coming over that evening. And I told them Laurel was so pathologically afraid of guns she'd never allow one in the house. And I told them Jackson and Laurel had fought about the netsukes so much that she'd locked them up and hidden the key.

They thanked me for being such a good citizen.

Obviously, it isn't true that all the world loves a lover. The lover's former lover certainly doesn't.

Poor Jackson. He didn't know that. He didn't know anything. He never read the classics and didn't understand what he was saying when he called me a Fury. The fact is, he didn't even understand nonclassical, garden-variety fury.

The kind hell hath none like.

Live and learn.

Sarah Shankman, writing as Alice Storey, introduced readers to investigative reporter Samantha Adams in First Kill All the Lawyers. *An affectionate yet independent Atlanta expatriate who returns to her roots, Samantha continues to examine the social foibles of the New South in* Then Hang All the Liars. *With* Now Let's Talk of Graves, *Samantha visits New Orleans and Shankman drops her pen name. Other Shankman novels include* Impersonal Attractions *and* Keeping Secrets.

In "Say You're Sorry," a long-simmering resentment flares up during a Fourth of July heat wave.

SAY YOU'RE SORRY

by Sarah Shankman

DOWN IN BATON Rouge darkness had fallen, and the official State of Louisiana fireworks display could finally begin. An expectant, sunburned crowd filled the Capitol lawn. Children sat on their fathers' shoulders dribbling half-eaten ice-cream cones down their backs. Teenaged couples held hands, willing their palms not to sweat. Then, for the fifth time that day, the Capital City High School Marching Bank struck up the opening notes of "The Star-Spangled Banner" and everyone rose, some more proud than others to be Americans in this summer whose television stars included Senator Sam Ervin and the whole panoply of Watergate crooks.

As the crowd sang the words *bombs bursting in air*, red, white, and blue rockets shrieked across the clear evening sky, exploding into mushrooms of light that reflected in the clear eyes of children and then floated, trailing off into vapor. The fireworks would continue for half an hour, each barrage of sound and light more spectacular than the one before, punctuations of *oohs* and *ahs* joining the growing roar until the grand finale that smothered all reverberations except its thunderous self, reminding more than one Vietnam veteran, who leaned against a crutch or sat in a wheelchair, of sounds he'd just as soon forget, but couldn't.

Across town from the Capitol lawn on a narrow street that intersected Front, Loubella Simms sat alone on her porch steps and watched the lights above the treetops. She lighted one long cigarette off another and sipped iced tea from a sweating glass.

Inside the darkened living room, her battered hi-fi repeated the same record over and over, Sweet Emma and her band from the New Orleans Preservation Hall playing Dixieland. Slideman, a trombone player and one of Loubella's friends and admirers, had brought her the record, which was now worn scratchy, but she didn't mind. It didn't have all that much further to go.

With that thought, she ran a hand inside her faded pink seersucker housecoat and trailed her fingers across her pendulous left breast.

The sweet man named Isaac was the one who had found the spot first.

Now who was Isaac? He was the one who bought the River City Hotel (read "whorehouse") from the sheriff who had bought it from Blanche, the former mistress of River City and the woman who, out of misplaced jealousy, had had Loubella locked up.

"Honey," Isaac'd said to her one night when they were lying in bed together, nothing serious, just sipping bourbon and messing around. "Honey, I . . ." And then he'd hesitated as he'd realized he was about to drop a stone into waters whose circles might never stop.

"What?"

"I think I feel something here."

" 'Course you do, sugar. You feel what you always feel when you get the mood on you."

"No I don't." His voice had become serious so that Loubella had sat up in bed and switched on the light.

She'd put her hand atop his, and together their hands moved in a slow circle.

Then she'd slipped her fingers beneath, and she, too, felt what he was talking about. The lump was about the size of her smallest fingernail, but round like an egg yolk.

She took a deep breath, and when she let it out the lie came

with it: "Oh, that's been there for a long time. I get them all
the time, little old lumps like chicken fat."

"That's not true, Loubella. You know it's not."

She'd waved off his words and pulled him to her, smothering
his worrying with her mouth.

But after he'd gone, after he'd looked her straight in the eye
and ordered her to see a doctor the very next day, and after
she'd nodded that she would, she'd lain awake for a long time
tracing her fingertips over and over the spot.

It wasn't gone the next morning or the one after that. In fact,
it grew larger all the time, as if it were a child inside her
doubling and redoubling until it could draw its own breath.

"The doctor said nothing, it's nothing, just as I told you,"
she answered her lover when he asked her about it.

Actually the doctor had said nothing because she had never
gone to see him. A couple of times she had picked up the
phone to call for an appointment, but then had dropped it back
into its black cradle as if it were a snake.

There was no way that she was going to let anyone cut off
her breast.

Why, she said to herself this Fourth of July night as she
watched the fireworks explode into the air, she'd be so lopsided
she'd fall off the sidewalk into the street. And she managed a
crooked smile at the thought of that.

When she'd been a young girl and these ridiculous things
had sprouted themselves like ever larger fruit—oranges, canta-
loupes, then finally watermelons—on her chest, she'd been
ashamed. The boys had opened their legs as she'd passed,
touched themselves, and sniffed after her as if she were a dog
permanently in heat. But then when she'd seen that her breasts
were to be her meal ticket, as no other opportunity had presented itself, she'd said "So be it." She'd never loved her bos-
oms even though she'd named them Lou and Bella and had
pretended that she appreciated the men who looked at her chest.
But in time she'd grown used to her bounty, and parting with
half of it was something that she simply couldn't bring herself
to do.

She knew the consequences. She didn't need a doctor to tell
her that. And before long she could feel the sickness growing,
reaching out beneath her armpits, putting feelers into her groin.
Now there was no call to remove her breast; it was already too
late.

Loubella leaned her back against the step and lit another cigarette, watching the smoke curl into the night air. In a moment she'd get up and flip the record to the other side and put on a pot of water. It was too hot a night for coffee, but she wanted it anyway—sweet and black, the perfect end to a perfect day.

And she couldn't imagine one more perfect. Isaac had come over about noon and they'd had a long, gentle time in bed. Then they'd taken a cool shower together and she'd spread out their holiday dinner: fried chicken, potato salad with sour cream (her secret ingredient), baked beans, and pineapple upside-down cake.

"Honey," Isaac had said, "you should have been a cook."

"I should have been lots of things. But I'm stuck with what I've been. It's a little too late."

"It's never too late, Loubella."

But she'd seen the look in his eyes, and she knew he could see what looked back at her from her mirror these days. She could smell it too. They both knew she was already holding hands with a bad-breathed lover, Mr. Death.

Then they'd sat for a while on the porch playing gin rummy, right out in the open, not caring who came by. Not that Isaac had ever been big on sneaking and hiding, but in some ways he was circumspect. Not this day. Not this Fourth of July, which was also Loubella's birthday. She was forty-six.

"Lordy, lordy, who'd of thought I'd be getting so old?"

"And so beautiful." He'd kissed her and placed among the cards before them a little jeweler's box.

Inside was a diamond solitaire, a big sparkling beauty of an engagement ring.

They smiled at each other, Loubella's gold tooth shining like a ray of sunlight. They smiled, for they both understood the symbolism and yet knew that in that sense the ring didn't mean a goddamned thing.

For her lover was married, a Baton Rouge businessman who carried considerable weight, and he wasn't about to toss over everything to marry a retired whore. Not that they would have had time to do that anyway, even though divorces could be had now in only six months. Both of them knew that Loubella didn't have that much time left.

She held her hand out before her now that he was gone, watching the diamond catch the fireworks' light, admiring the token of his love like a sixteen-year-old girl. She savored both it and the favor she'd asked of him, which he'd granted—making the phone call without missing a beat.

Loubella, she said to herself now, *all in all you've had a good life.*

The whoring hadn't gotten her, nor the drugs, nor the time in jail. She'd risen above them all like cream coming to the top. And these last few years with Isaac, tending her little house and the bar in his now respectable River City, they'd been all she'd ever hoped for, more than she'd ever dreamed.

And in just a little while it would be over. For Loubella was not waiting for Mr. Death to name the time. She would do that herself. Not for her the long hoping and the slow snipping, a breast here, a womb there, all her hair falling out, what was left of her fading beauty gone, till there was nothing left but the tubes and high hospital bed and the drugs dripping into her veins, the drugs that didn't quite smother the smells or the pain.

She heard the big car coming even before she saw its head-lights. She sat up straight and a tingle ran right down the back of her neck.

Oh, it had been such a while since she'd seen her enemy's face. This time was going to be so sweet.

Now the heavy door of the Cadillac slammed, just once, which meant Blanche hadn't brought her husband Aces with her. Well, it would have been nice to have them both, but Aces didn't really matter. Blanche had been the hand behind the hand that turned the key that locked the door that kept her imprisoned eleven and a half years, almost one quarter of her life.

"Evening, Blanche," Loubella called from the steps. She had been sitting there for a while growing cats' eyes and could see into the night.

"Loubella?" Blanche stopped dead still as she recognized the voice.

"Sure 'nuff. Come on in."

Blanche came closer now. Good Lord have mercy, how she'd aged! The golden girl was gone. And here in her place stood a middle-aged pouty pigeon in a blue dress that was too tight, stretched across the bulging stomach and the spreading butt. Ah, beautiful Blanche, Loubella thought, has all that barbecue caught up with you at last?

"Isaac called and gave me this address. Said he wanted to talk some business." Blanche's voice was wary.

"He does."

"Well, where is he?" Blanche stood uneasily, shifting her considerable weight.

"Inside." Loubella gestured up toward the porch, pointing at a wicker chair. "But why don't you sit out here with me for a minute first 'fore you go in? Give yourself a rest."

Loubella watched Blanche's mouth open and close. No, not a pouty pigeon. Now she reminded Loubella of a chicken, an old rusty hen, ready for the pot.

"Would you like some coffee?" Loubella kept her voice ever so light.

"Why, yes," said Blanche, smoothing her dress across her stomach with nervous little hands. She hadn't seen Loubella since before she'd been sent away. "I guess I would. Yes, that would be awfully nice."

Loubella smiled her still-pretty smile, full lips pulled back from teeth that were perfect and white except for that one spot of gold, which was nothing but vanity. Then she disappeared into the house.

Blanche fidgeted in the wicker chair. She smoothed and re-smoothed her lap, adjusted her rings, tried to find a place to plant her twisting feet. Though age had slowed her down, now she felt fourteen again, flighty as a bird just this moment locked in a cage. She hadn't expected Loubella gliding toward her now, carrying a tray with two pretty china cups, so delicate that, between the pattern of violets, they were translucent.

"Oh," Loubella said then, just as her rear end touched her chair. "I forgot the cake. Would you like some?"

"No, I just couldn't. Thank you." Blanche listened to herself playacting that she wasn't unnerved. *Woman,* she thought, *butter wouldn't melt in your mouth.*

"Sure you could." Loubella smiled. "Have some cake."

Blanche wondered if the other woman were mocking her little jelly rolls of fat. She really must go on a diet, but then it always had been hard for her to deny herself anything she wanted to put in her mouth.

"You've got to have some of my birthday cake."

"Your *birthday*. Why, of course it is. The Fourth. I'd forgotten."

And she had, but she remembered now.

When they were girls, even though Loubella was almost ten years younger than she, she'd never missed Loubella's birthday party. It was *the* event of the summer. Loubella's grandmother, who was her entire family, had taken her in when everyone else, for one reason or another, had disappeared, would churn peach ice cream for the whole neighborhood, spread tables with ham and chicken, once even saved to pay a three-piece band who'd played for dancing in the street beneath Japanese lanterns until the last pair of happy feet stopped. After that night Blanche had said to her mother that Loubella was going to grow up thinking the entire country celebrated *her* birthday, not knowing it belonged to the whole United States.

"That little girl has no family but her Mamaw, Blanche, who gives her this one day. Begrudging her that, child, you ought to be ashamed." And Blanche had been. She'd tried to make up for her jealousy by pretending to be the big sister Loubella had never had.

She remembered holding Loubella, a dark-haired little girl, a doll baby, balancing her on her knees while she divided her hair into sections and braided her pigtails. She taught her to swim at the edge of the river, along with a couple of other little kids. She'd baptized them first, pouring water over their heads with a handleless cup, making up the words as she went along.

"And the Baby Jesus watch over you and carry your little soul straight to heaven without no detours if you drown," she'd said. Loubella's brown eyes had grown wide like saucers plopped into her face.

Yes, there'd been a long time when she'd truly loved the girl Loubella, had mothered her and smiled proudly at the mention of her name.

Now, from atop her coffee cup, she slid a look toward the woman and felt a flash of regret, then shame. How fragile friendship could be. How was it you spent years with some-one—your minds so interwined you didn't even need to pick up the phone but could just transmit thoughts—laughed to-gether, loved each other, and then things changed? There was a misunderstanding, an angry word that grew into a great wrong as you carried it around in your hand, blowing on it to give it life until, like a flame, it had a will of its own. But it had been more than a cross word, hadn't it, that thing that had turned her love for Loubella to hate?

It had begun one July when Parnell, then Blanche's husband

and owner of River City, decided to pick up where Loubella's
mamaw had left off and in a fit of flamboyance treated his girls
to a trip on a paddleboat all the way down the river to New
Orleans. He'd said that his girls didn't have to work on the
Fourth, but Blanche had known that that was just his excuse to
throw a party for Loubella.

Before that, when Blanche had come back to Baton Rouge
to marry Parnell and had found Loubella in his stable of
whores, it had made her sad for a bit, but then a woman had
to do what she had to do. For a while she and Loubella had
carried on together like they had when they were girls. They'd
run into each other on the back stairs, Loubella in a yellow
silk wrapper that glowed like fireflies, and then they'd sit right
down on the steps, their legs tucked back against them within
their encircling arms, gossiping and giggling with no mind for
the passing hours, reaching their hands out and patting one
another on a knee or a shoulder, little butterflies of affection,
easy, easy, old love.

But Parnell had noticed, and he hadn't liked it, not one bit.

"You don't need that whore teaching you tricks, Blanche,"
he said. "Unless you planning on turning pro."

"Parnell! You know Lou and I've been friends since we were
girls!"

"I know what you been. You think I didn't grow up in this
very same neighborhood? But Loubella *works* for me, woman.
She's my whore. Just 'cause she don't punch no time clock
don't mean she ain't on salary. And the lady of the house don't
fraternize with the help."

Well. Blanche hadn't believed a word of that. She knew there
was something more tiptoeing around in Parnell's big head.
She also knew that he sampled the goods from time to time,
like a moonshiner sipping his own whiskey, and she guessed
that included Loubella too. But then, she enjoyed a taste of
other sweetmeat her own self now and again, so she wasn't
about to be calling the kettle black.

And every once in a while, like naughty children ignoring
all warnings, she and Loubella still slipped off to have a good
visit, and whatever quick and dirty passed between her husband and her friend was no part of that.

But then there'd been Loubella's Fourth of July birthday and
the paddleboat and—worse than catching them in bed together,
because what would that mean, after all, a little roll in the hay

between two people who trafficked in flesh—she'd seen their eyes meet.

Again and again throughout that afternoon, she'd watched that connection between them, as simple and direct as plugging in a lamp. Their glances crossed and caught and held, and Blanche had to turn her gaze away, for if Parnell had leaned over and slowly licked Loubella's naked eyeball, the act could not have been more intimate. Everything else in the entire world, including her, oh yes, including her, fell away. And Blanche, who had never had that kind of communion with another human being in her whole life but recognized it when she saw it, hated Loubella from that very afternoon to this.

So she'd punished her, hadn't she, she'd punished her good. Planted a load of dope in her room, then called the cops to raid her own joint. It was hers by then, Aces having already pulled the trigger that morning so long ago, pulled the trigger that had blasted Parnell's head and sent it rolling and tumbling like a child's ball down Front. She'd married Aces right after that, before they sent him up for a little stay in Angola.

Now she looked up at Loubella from the edge of her violet-sprigged coffee cup and all the years fell away. There before her was the face of the little girl with birthday candles shining in her eyes, the little girl she'd loved as her own. Parnell had been dead for so many years, and he hadn't been worth shaking a stick at, anyway. What had all that been about? Blanche wondered what would happen if she reached out and patted Loubella's cheek and said, "I'm sorry I was so mean." Would Loubella understand that if she could do it all over again she'd do it differently?

Loubella caught her look and that old communion of spirits that ran between them straighter than the string of a child's tin-can telephone told her what Blanche was thinking.

She smiled and her gold tooth twinkled. Blanche's heart lurched. That tooth had always reminded her of Parnell's with his diamond, but no, no, forget Parnell. He was what had brought her to this pass in the first place. Maybe *that* had been her problem all along, paying attention to men, my God, there had been so many of them, when there were other folks, plenty of other folks, her family, her children, all those women who could have been her sisters, sitting right there in her face big as life—hell, maybe they *were* life—and she had looked right through them like they were water, past them to whatever man was waggling his dick like it was a magic wand that would turn her into a fairy princess with its touch. *Well, you been touched by them wands plenty times, ain't you, woman, and you ain't no princess yet.* But here was Loubella smiling at her. Maybe it wasn't too late.

"You gonna come in the house and sample some of my cake or not?" Loubella was asking.

"Why, I'd be proud to," Blanche answered, rising from her chair and feeling like she was floating. Something had been released in her, and she felt light and wispy as a pink cloud. "And by the way, happy birthday, Miss Loubella."

"Thank you, Miss Blanche." Loubella ducked her head as if she were suddenly shy. Why, yes, Blanche thought. The little girl is still there. We can start over. It's not too late.

Blanche watched Loubella bustling around her neat kitchen, and suddenly the two girls of long ago had swapped places. Now Loubella was the momma, the momma Blanche had never really been to anyone. For the small acts of mothering Blanche had practiced on Loubella had not followed her into adulthood. Now that she thought about it, she couldn't remember ever plaiting her own daughters' hair, though she must have. And she'd certainly never taught Jesse to swim. Who had done all those things—washed their clothes, cooked the countless meals her children must have eaten—because indeed they had grown up. It all seemed like such a blur now, those years of their childhood. She remembered a few snatches, but the pictures in her mind were duplicates of the pictures she'd pasted in a photo album. The kids standing in front of one of her new Cadillacs. All three of them lined up on the porch of River City. Jesse in a new white suit for one of her weddings, she couldn't remember which.

But there were no photographs of the three children sitting with Blanche reading or storytelling or fixing a hem. Did their grandmother Lucretia have pictures like that in her photo album? she wondered. Did people take pictures of a woman serving dinner to her family?

Well, they ought to. Not that she would ever be caught dead in one, but look now, here, at Loubella putting food on the table in front of her. Those sturdy hands carefully placing the little violet-sprigged dessert plate that matched the cup and saucer, they were delivering more than a piece of cake, more like a gift of love.

"Loubella!" Blanche exclaimed suddenly, for her eye had finally caught the diamond sparkler upon Loubella's left hand, and her mind quickly jumped from its maternal meditation back to the more familiar territory of earthy goods. "Good Lord have mercy, where did you get that pretty thing?" And in an instant Blanche, with an eye accustomed to weighing and assessing, had its value appraised as precisely as if she'd examined it with a scale and a jeweler's loupe.

"Isaac." Loubella smiled. "It's Isaac's birthday present to me."

With that, Blanche remembered why she'd come in the first place.

"Where *is* Isaac?" she asked, looking around the room as if he might be hiding behind the sugar canister or underneath the table with its plastic lace tablecloth.

"Oh, he slipped out the back to get some Scotch. Said we ought to have a proper celebration and I'd just run clean out. But I've got some bourbon. Could I sweeten your coffee with a little nip?" And before Blanche could answer, Loubella had poured her a generous dollop, filling her coffee cup to the brim.

"But I thought you said he was here, inside. Didn't you say that a little while ago?"

"He was. He'll be right back. Go ahead, Blanche, drink up."

Blanche took a sip and then another. The dark, sweet coffee and the alcohol warmed her blood even hotter on this July delta night. She could feel it coursing right down to her toes. And the warmth distracted her for a moment from the other questions that had popped into her mind. Like, what did Isaac want? What was the deal he had mentioned? Why had he given her Loubella's address? And what was it between them, anyway, his giving Loubella a diamond as if she were a decent woman?

Loubella answered that last one even before Blanche threw it out.

"That Isaac, he is the sweetest man. We've been keeping company, you know, for quite some time."

"Well, I swear. I never knew that."

"Honey, there's lots of things you don't know about Loubella. It's not exactly as if we been in touch."

Blanche lowered her gaze then. Here it comes. This wasn't going to be as easy as she'd thought.

But in a moment all was calm again. She'd mistaken a passing

cloud for a storm gathering. And before she knew it, Loubella
was sweetening up her coffee again, and they were leaned back
in their chairs, Loubella tucking her feet up, her legs in the circle
of her arms, and it was like they were back on the service steps
of River City gossiping about folks like Parnell had never come
between them, as if his head had never rolled down Front.

"Tell me 'bout your children. What's Jesse up to?"

"Well, I guess he's doing all right. Married. Uh-huh." She
paused a moment, thinking about that. And then with pride in
her voice said, "He called me today just to say hello."

"He lives in California, doesn't he? They come and visit
you?"

"Uh-huh. Once. Stopped by my house." She put her cup
down, and this time Loubella didn't even bother with the coffee, just filled it with bourbon, straight up. "Why, I think that
day they said they'd been by to see you too."

"That's right."

"Can't say as I thought much of her."

"Why not?"

Blanche just shrugged. You'd have to be mother to a son to
understand that.

Loubella rose then, steady as a rock, for no alcohol had
passed her lips, just coffee and a few bites of cake. As she
skirted the back door, she reached out and tested it, just to
make sure. Before Blanche came, she had locked that dead
bolt from the inside and dropped the key in her garbage sack.
Of course, Blanche didn't know that.

"Way things are these days, you can never be too safe,"
Loubella said.

Blanche nodded. "Ain't that the truth. Why, just last week,
I was reading in the paper about some crazy boys downtown
grabbed a woman on her way home, arms full of groceries
and . . ."

Loubella wasn't listening, except to a plan she'd run through
her mind so many times that it had become a script. She
couldn't hear Blanche because she was following that script.
Now she read the line that said, "Excuse yourself," and she
did.

"Bathroom," she said.

"Sure, honey. Me too, after you."

Loubella closed the kitchen door behind her and headed
down a little hall to her bedroom where she picked up the red

five-gallon can of gasoline she'd earlier placed inside. She tipped the nozzle, splashed the bed, and began a damp trail that followed her as if to her mamaw's house. In the living room she locked the front door from the inside and hid that key, too, beneath a cushion of her favorite chair. Then she doused the chair, the sofa, the faded Persian rug. After that she did what she'd said, went into the bathroom and relieved herself. For she wanted to be perfectly at ease for this last best part, the cherry on her ice cream sundae.

Then she rejoined Blanche, who had been sitting there drinking another couple of fingers of bourbon that she didn't need. Loubella frowned. She wanted Blanche slowed, but not so drunk that she missed a moment of the impending horror show.

"Honey, I been thinking about what I said about Jesse and that girl, his wife, uh . . ."

"Lily," Loubella said.

"That's right, Lily, and then I was thinking about you and Isaac. You did say—" And then she stopped. "Jesus Christ, Loubella, what *is* that smell?"

Loubella settled herself back at the table and plopped down the can she was still holding, planted it on the floor.

"Gas," she answered.

Blanche jumped up, holding a hand to her breast. "The line's busted!" She reached for Loubella's arm. "Come on, honey, we got to get out of here!"

Loubella smiled at her as serenely as if she'd just gotten up off her knees from prayer and knew beyond a shadow of a doubt that her supplication had been answered.

Blanche saw that and suddenly her blood ran cold.

Well, forget Loubella. She was getting out of here. She pushed past her to the back door and jerked at it. It didn't open. She jerked again. "The door's locked!" she screamed.

Already she was hysterical. This was better than Loubella had even dreamed. She just kept on watching as if Blanche were a picture show, a movie she had waited a long time to see.

"Aren't you going to do something? You just going to sit there?" Blanche's voice shrilled with terror and disbelief.

Of course, Blanche had always thought that nothing very bad was going to happen to her, and up until now, she'd been right.

As if in answer, though without saying a word, Loubella stood, picked up the gasoline can, which until now Blanche hadn't spotted, and heaved it toward her, splattering Blanche's baby-blue dress.

Blanche screamed. She stood in one place with her hands in fists atop her head and screamed. You would have thought she could already feel the flames.

"*What* are you doing?"

"What does it look like, Blanche?" Loubella's words were slow and calm. "I'm killing you. Actually, I'm killing us both." And with that she reached over into a cabinet drawer and pulled out a revolver and placed it before her among the violet-sprigged china and the near-empty bottle of bourbon and the remains of birthday cake. The gun didn't look very much at home.

Blanche was jumping around now as if a fire were licking at her underpants. She whirled and raced out of the room. Loubella could hear her battering at the front door.

"It ain't no use, Blanche," she called. "The doors are locked, and Isaac put bars on the windows last year. You might as well come on back in here."

Blanche blundered around a while longer before she did as she was told.

She was whimpering. Big tears were rolling down her face. "No, no, no," she whispered over and over.

"You think you can always get your own way, don't you, Miss Blanche? Well, this time you can't."

"Why?" Blanche wailed.

"Why what?"

"Why are you doing this to me?"

"Why, Blanche, I can't believe you don't know how *much* I hate your guts."

Blanche reeled around the room, scrabbling at the things on the kitchen cabinet, grabbed a dish towel, and dabbed at the front of her dress.

"Don't worry about it being stained, honey. Ain't nothing of it going to be left."

Blanche began to scream again. Someone would hear her. Surely someone would.

But it was the night of July Fourth. Hardly anyone was home. And those who were, were mostly drunk. Besides, nobody ever paid much attention to a woman screaming in this neighborhood. They figured whoever she was she was getting what she deserved, and if she didn't, she either ought to get the hell out or pick up a skillet and show the man what for.

"I didn't mean any of it, Loubella, I'm sorry." And she started to cry again, not paying any attention to her dripping nose. "I was gonna tell you tonight, just a while ago, that if I had to do it all over, I'd do it different, I swear."

"That may be true, but those years are already long gone."

"Oh, Loubella." Blanche fell to her knees, scratching on the floor at Loubella's feet. "Please, don't do this."

"Remember when you baptized me in the river?" asked Loubella in a faraway, dreamy voice.

"Yes." Blanche was sobbing, her face buried in Loubella's knees.

"Remember how you prayed that if we drowned, the Baby Jesus would take us straight to heaven with no stops in between?"

"Yes." Blanche's answer was muffled. But in it was just a whisper of hope. Maybe if Loubella could remember those days, when Blanche had been kind, she could find a bit of mercy in her heart.

"Remember how you poured the water over our heads with that old broken cup?"

Blanche nodded. And with that she felt liquid pour all over her hair, dribble down her neck.

But it wasn't river water. It was gasoline—high test.

Blanche jumped up and screamed. And screamed. And screamed. She couldn't stop now. Liquid ran down her legs too. Gasoline and urine mixed together, for Blanche had completely lost control of herself.

"You never should have done what you did, Blanche. Parnell may have loved me, but he married you. He would have given you anything on earth you wanted."

"I know. I know," Blanche moaned.

"He was too good for you, bitch. You know, you're the one who was the whore. I did it 'cause I had to. You did it 'cause you liked it. 'Cause you wanted *everything*. You always was a greedy gut, even as a girl. 'That's *mine*,' you'd say. Licking a biscuit so nobody else would touch it. '*Mine*,' no matter what."

Blanche kept on moaning. She had stopped twitching around the room and had fallen back in her chair as if she'd returned for another cup of coffee, another drink, except that her head was down on the table buried in her arms, and the liquid running down her face was a mixture of gasoline and tears.

"And Parnell was yours. But those years you took from me—

those eleven years, six months, and nine days—that quarter of my life I spent in jail, those wasn't yours to take. *Those* were *mine*."

"I know. I know."

"Say you're sorry, Blanche." Loubella's voice was very soft and very cold.

Blanche's head snapped up.

"I *am* sorry."

"But not as sorry as you're gonna be."

At that, Loubella reached into her wrapper pocket and pulled out a box of wooden kitchen matches. She struck one and dropped it. The floor burst into licking tongues of red and yellow.

In that moment, Blanche saw her chance. Quick as a snake, her hand grabbed the revolver sitting on the table and she fired it without thinking, striking Loubella in the breast.

Loubella reeled backward. Laughter poured from her throat while crimson pumped from a hole in the pale pink wrapper, from right near the spot where her cancer was now cheated from its slower march toward death.

"Thank you, Blanche," Loubella whispered, and even as she died, she struck and dropped another match.

It was then that Blanche realized, too late, far too late, that she had shot the wrong person. She should have shot herself. For a bullet through the brain was much quicker—why, it hardly compared to burning to death.

The gas can exploded then, and flames engulfed her dress, her hair, her face.

She reached one twisting hand toward the revolver, where she'd dropped it on the table. Maybe it still wasn't too late. But it was. For Loubella had loaded only one bullet in the chamber. She'd known that whether she fired it or Blanche did, one was all she'd want or need.

The curtains were on fire now, the rugs, the sofa, the bed, the walls, the floor. And in the midst of it, caroming from one small room to another, from door to window to door, was the fireball that was Blanche. That didn't last very long, though. Soon she dropped and writhed, white teeth showing and glimmers of bone, as beautiful Blanche, blackened like a redfish, fried and crisped and barbecued to a turn, just a little before midnight on this evening of July the Fourth.

Shelley Singer, who covered fashion shows, spelling bees, and Cook County's death row during her stint as a journalist, introduced poker-playing unlicensed investigator Jake Samson and his carpenter friend Rosie Vicente in Samson's Deal. *The pair, who live in Oakland and are involved in cases that allow them to explore the cultural diversity and beauty of northern California, returned in* Free Draw, Full House, Spit in the Ocean, *and* Suicide King.

In "Heart Attack," a woman finds she has a disturbing situation well in hand.

HEART ATTACK

by Shelley Singer

THE MAHIMAHI WAS $11.95 a pound. She didn't want to pay that much. The shark was $7.95 but she didn't feel like shark. She didn't feel like cooking. It wasn't fun to cook for just herself. The woman behind the counter asked if she could help her. Barbara shook her head and left the fish market, stopping instead at the deli next door.

She was wondering about the calamari salad when she heard a bright, familiar voice say, "The pâté's terrific," and turned to see her old friend Judy Brachman grinning at her. "Got a few minutes for a cup of coffee? I haven't seen you in months."

Was that true? Months? It was. Had Judy called her during that time? She didn't think so. And she knew she hadn't called anyone. She didn't know why. She'd just felt like spending time alone since she'd stopped seeing Jay.

They strolled to the café at the corner. Judy went inside to get the coffee while Barbara staked their claim on a sidewalk table. She sat facing the Rockridge BART station, diagonally across College Avenue. A commuter train—she glanced at her watch: four o'clock—slid by on its elevated track, heading east

to the bedroom communities on the other, warmer side of the
hills. Bedroom communities. She'd always found that an odd
expression. Like one vast whorehouse. Judy came out again,
carrying two enormous bran muffins as well as the coffee. Judy
had a tendency to gain weight, had, in fact, gained some since
Barbara had seen her last. But between binges of obsessed
dieting, she affected a kind of amused despair and ate what she
damned pleased. That was one of the things Barbara liked best
about Judy. Her amused despair.

"So, Barbara. What's new?" Several passersby glanced at
Judy, their attention drawn by her loud, crowing, completely
unselfconscious voice.

"Nothing. How's Paul?"

"Fine. He hates his job, but he always hates his job."

"And the kids?"

"Great. Angela's starting Stanford in the fall, isn't that
amazing? But what about you? The last time I saw you, you
were going out with some UC Berkeley professor."

"Jay. Yes. He licked his fingers when he ate. Excessively.
In public."

"I take it you're not seeing him anymore."

Barbara smiled. "Not for about five months now."

Judy sipped her coffee. "Too bad." A muscular young man
rode by on a mountain bike. Judy watched his tight buns di-
minishing toward Berkeley. "I suppose you've heard about
Barry."

Barry was Barbara's ex-husband, ex by seven years.

"No. I haven't heard anything about Barry." She nibbled an
edge off her muffin. Did it really taste like dust or was it the
mention of Barry's name that had created that effect?

"He had a heart attack." Barbara let her muffin fall to the
table; it rolled off and dropped to the sidewalk. Her friend
watched its progress. "I should have called you."

Judy was part of a widely extended circle of friends that
included a number of people who had been trying half heart-
edly to avoid each other for years, including Barry and Barbara. Their marriage had not ended easily, with mutual respect
and by mutual agreement, the way so many people liked to
pretend a marriage could end. He'd been cheating for months
with a woman she knew. A year after their divorce he had
married again, a third woman entirely. Barbara had moved out
of North Berkeley—although only just across the Oakland bor-

der—in an attempt to escape some of the more abrasive memories. But she couldn't escape Berkeley, and she didn't really want to. "Berkeley" includes the parts of neighboring cities and towns that behave like Berkeley, and the urban East Bay is a very small place in a lot of ways. Barbara and her dates ran into Barry and his wife from time to time, at movies, at plays, at the symphony. Even once at a jazz club in her own neighborhood. This was always difficult for Barbara, because she was still very angry with Barry. And because she'd been unable to find anyone she wanted as much as she'd wanted him. Had wanted him, that is, until she'd started hating him.

A heart attack. He could have died and she never would have seen him again.

"How bad was it?"

"It was pretty bad, but it happened a week ago and he's alive."

Alive but damaged. A scar on his heart.

Barbara felt a touch, Judy's hand on hers. "Barbara? I'm sorry. I didn't know it would hit you this hard."

Barbara squeezed her friend's hand, then squeezed a laugh out of herself. "I didn't either."

"Barbara," he said. "This is really sweet of you."

"I asked a nurse to find a vase," she said, negligently waving the bouquet of jonquils.

"They're beautiful. I love jonquils. They're so cheerful."

"And yellow." She had, of course, remembered that he liked yellow flowers. He had always bought her yellow flowers, even though she preferred red ones.

"So you heard I had a little setback."

"Judy Brachman. I ran into her at Rockridge Market Hall. In the deli. In front of the calamari salad."

He laughed. He had always enjoyed the way she talked, understood it better than any other man had.

"How are you feeling, Barry?"

"Not too bad. I should be out of here in a couple of weeks. I'll be fine. Just have to watch the old stress, take it easier for a while."

"Will you take some time off from work?"

"Oh, maybe a little. But I love to work, you know that. I'd die if I didn't sell real estate." He caught himself, laughed nervously. "It wasn't the job that did it. It's my genes. And don't tell me to get a new pair." They both laughed.

"But what about your work?" he asked. "How's it going? I've seen a couple of your shows around town. You're going in some interesting directions."

Barbara was touched that he'd noticed. Her painting was changing, had changed and grown tremendously in the years they'd been apart.

"I've got a one-woman show next month at the Albany Gallery."

"Well, I'm impressed. Very impressed. You deserve it."

He looked tired. He still wore an oxygen tube; it rested on his upper lip like a transparent mustache.

The man in the other bed coughed. For the first time, she looked at him. Very old and thin, leashed to an IV bottle. His eyes were closed.

"I can only stay a few minutes," Barbara said.

Barry looked genuinely disappointed. "But you'll come back? Barbara . . . I've missed you."

She hadn't expected him to say anything like that, but she understood that it must be his illness talking. He was scared, lying there in that hospital bed with a tube in his nose. He could have died. She would have lost him forever.

"I can come back tomorrow, Boo." It was her pet name for him. It had just slipped out. But he was very tired. He didn't seem to notice.

"Yes, please," he said. "Come back tomorrow." He closed his eyes.

The next day, she canceled an appointment with a gallery owner to arrive at the beginning of visiting hours. Barry's wife was there. Her name was Jeanine. She actually said—Barbara couldn't believe it—"How nice to meet you. I've heard so much about you."

After a few minutes of chat about who knew whom and who was doing what and living where, Jeanine said she was dying for a cup of coffee, that she wanted to stretch her legs, and that she'd be back in an hour or so—"Since you're here to watch over him, Barbara." She gave Barry a peck on the cheek, smiled brightly at Barbara, and strolled out the door.

"She does know that I'm your first wife, doesn't she, Barry?" Barbara was puzzled by the woman's casual, good-humored response to her presence.

"Oh, yes. I think so. How could she not?"

Oh well, Barbara thought, if she wasn't jealous she wasn't jealous. And Barbara had an hour to be with Barry. Alone. In fact, completely alone. The other bed was now empty. She didn't ask about the old man because she didn't want to know.

She plumped Barry's pillows, smoothed his covers, talked about her work, asked about the new condos in El Cerrito, the block of Victorians in Oakland. Once, he took her hand, looked into her eyes, started to speak, shook his head, let her hand drop again.

Until she had seen him hurt, sick, vulnerable—and didn't he seem lonely?—she truly had had no idea she still loved him. She had hoped she'd gone past hate to indifference, that they could even be friends at some point. But the heart attack had told her the truth. If he'd died, she never would have seen him again, his dark, gray-streaked hair, his beautiful blue eyes, his strong hands with their long expressive fingers. His soft, deep voice.

"Barbara, I'm so glad you came to visit me. After all these years, just to see you again, talk with you—it means so much. I don't know . . ."

She knew. She took his hand, patted it, held it. She knew. It was all very dreamlike, a circle completed, a past reclaimed to make right again.

That night when she got home, there was a message on her machine from Judy. "Hi, have you seen Barry? How's he doing? Give me a call, will you?"

Barbara poured herself a glass of wine, lay down on her bed with the phone, and dialed Judy's number.

"I saw him last night and tonight," she told her friend. "He looks all right, but he's still pretty weak."

"Tell me exactly how he looks."

Barbara hesitated. How could she describe him? "Why don't you go visit him?"

"I did, just a couple of days after he got sick. But they weren't letting anyone in but his wife then. Tell me how he looks."

Barbara gave a mental shrug. Why not? She certainly had recorded every detail of his appearance in her mind.

The next day, again, Barbara arrived at the beginning of visiting hours. She thought he was looking a little better, had a bit more color.

His wife wasn't there. The other bed was still empty. She
took his hand.

"Oh, Barbara. What would I do without you?" He sighed
and shook his head. She touched his cheek. He kissed her
hand. This was not, she knew, the best time to talk to him
about his obviously chilly marriage. It could wait. It could all
wait until he was completely well.

The phone rang and he picked up the receiver.

"Oh! Hello. Yes. How nice of you to call."

Barbara had been sitting close to him. She couldn't miss that
loud, crowing voice.

"No. I don't think that would be a good idea, actually. . . .
No. I can't. I'll be out in a week, the doctors say. . . . Yes,
isn't that terrific?" He glanced at Barbara, an elaborately blank
look on his face. The look was a familiar one. "Listen, I'll
talk to you later, okay? Right. Good-bye."

He knew that Judy was a friend of hers, but he hadn't said
"Barbara's here" during their brief conversation, and he said
nothing now about the call having been from Judy.

A nurse came into the room. "Sorry to interrupt your visit,"
she barked, "but Barry, here, has to take a walk through the
halls."

"I don't want to take a walk."

The nurse was already hauling him to his feet. Barbara had
forgotten what skinny little calves he had. The nurse wrapped
his robe around him.

"You have to take a walk. We have to keep the lungs clear."
She marched him out into the hall.

The only flowers in the room were from her and from his
coworkers. But Judy wouldn't have sent him flowers. Barbara
thought back seven years and remembered that he never threw
his mail away, not even his love notes. She'd found some then.

She pulled open the drawer of his bedside stand. Sure
enough. A card. One of those with a watercolor on the front
and the unprinted interior.

And inside the card: "I miss you terribly. I want to be with
you now. Please let me visit you. Judy."

When Barry and the nurse came back, Jeanine was with
them. She was holding his arm, stroking it. He was leaning
against her. He said, "Sweet Jeanine. My Rock of Gibraltar."

Then, as if suddenly noticing Barbara's presence, as if he

had not remembered she was there, he said, "Look who's here, Jeanine. Barbara!"

The son of a bitch had done it to her again. Over and over again, through the night, the words kept pounding at her. "The son of a bitch has done it to me again."

The next morning, she couldn't eat breakfast, didn't even want coffee. And she couldn't work. Her whole body ached. She did a hundred strokes on her rowing machine, as fast as she could. She worked up a sweat, but she was still quivering with tension. She took some balls and a tennis racquet and drove over to Ho Chi Minh Park—she never remembered what its real name was, it had been Ho Chi Minh since the sixties— and hit some balls against the backboard.

She put the racquet and the balls back in her car and ran around the park.

After that, she sat in the car and cried with rage and frustration. It was no use. His life was an ongoing insult to her. She had to do something about the man, finally.

The gun was still in the trunk at the foot of her bed, wrapped in flannel. A .32 she had bought early in her life as a divorced woman, on the advice of a man she had dated for a month, a man who believed that a woman living alone should have a gun and should know how to use it. He had scared her with his certainty, convinced her with his display of protectiveness.

She wasn't actually going to use the gun. She had never planned on using it, even against an intruder. The plan had been, then, to point it at the man and watch him run away.

The plan now was to point it at the man and scare the shit out of him. Scare some decency and remorse into him. And if she happened to scare him to death, this weakened victim of a recent heart attack, to cause a second, fatal attack, that was all right too. In fact, it sounded like a damned good idea.

Jeanine was there, her purse and jacket flung across the still unoccupied bed next to Barry's. She was reading a magazine, which she added to her pile of personal debris when Barbara walked in. Once again, she was friendly and chatty, but this time, Barbara was having trouble with the small talk. Sweat kept breaking out on her forehead. Even though she tried hard to set her shoulder bag casually on the floor, she couldn't seem to let go of it; she clutched the strap in a sweaty fist. She could feel Jeanine watching her, but she didn't dare meet her eyes.

Again, in a few minutes, Jeanine announced that she was going to get some coffee, stretch her legs.

When Jeanine left, Barbara said, "Do I seem nervous to you, Barry?"

He gazed at her, frowning. "No. Or at least I hadn't noticed. You look lovely as always."

"Do I seem the same as always?"

"Of course." He gazed at her earnestly. "Barbara, I'm a little tired. I don't understand what you're getting at."

She stood and, holding her bag tightly against her side, walked to the door of the room and closed it.

He smiled at her. "Barbara," he said teasingly, "I don't know what you have in mind, but—"

She smiled back at him, approached his bed, pulled the gun out of her bag and pointed it at him.

She didn't say anything. She just kept smiling at him.

He gulped, choking on his own spittle, staring at the gun.

He tried to yell and managed only a loud croak.

The door swung open and Jeanine came in. She looked at the gun, looked at Barbara.

The gun jerked in Barbara's hand, away from Barry, toward the ceiling. "I wasn't really going to shoot!" she said.

Jeanine stared at her for a second, reached back to close the door and, in three strides, was beside Barbara, snatching at her raised gun hand.

But she didn't do what Barbara expected, didn't take the weapon away from her.

Jeanine pulled down on Barbara's hand, leveled the gun, sighted along the barrel, squeezed Barbara's trigger finger, and shot her husband.

"Thanks, Barbara," she said. "I really appreciate this."

*Susan Trott's novels (*Pursued by the Crooked Man, Sightings, The Housewife and the Assassin, The Exception, *and three others) offer her readers engaging, quirky characters involved in situations that shimmer with the magic and the mystery of life. She claims that she has not held down any job for more than two weeks but that she ". . . has won a coveted black shirt in the Dipsea Race, raised three children, published seven novels, and in all her wanderings has never been arrested for vagrancy."*

In "Sensational Solution," a woman senses the answer to a puzzling question.

SENSATIONAL SOLUTION

by Susan Trott

GREG FOUND ME bailing out my sports car: a twelve-year-old Alfa Romeo Spider. Its top was down when an unseasonal rainstorm slammed out of the sky and filled it to the gunnels. I was off on a run at the time.

The water mostly collected in the wells behind the seats, and while I was bailing I was cleaning them out from the accumulated debris of maps, paperbacks, a can of sardines, leaves, cones, berries: sundry droppings from trees and birds.

Greg parked his impeccable Chrysler LeBaron, then joined me, his handsome face dark and scowling, turned gargoylish by his revved-up spleen. He'd obviously come from his wife.

I was on the regret side of my affair with Greg, having peaked out on the elation side in record time. Once again, enchanted by a pretty face, a good mind, a passable wit, I hadn't waited to know the inner man. Now I did, and it was an angry one, possibly a downright mean one. Currently his wife was the butt of his anger, but I bet something or someone always was and would be. I'd been sympathetic at first. She'd taken up with another man, kicked him out, was suing for divorce and wanted all he had plus half of what he didn't.

He leaned his long elegant length against a tree and watched me with scorn.

"I didn't know it was going to rain," I said needlessly, putting the bailing can aside and taking up the sponge.

"Look at that mess. Probably the first time you've cleaned it this year."

I flushed. "You can criticize my housekeeping but not my carkeeping. I take very good care of my car. I love it." I squeezed out the sponge. It was fun. It had been a long time since I'd sponged. It was sexy.

"Then why don't you ever put it in your perfectly good garage instead of exposing it to all the weather—not to mention all the animals and insects."

"I like the spiderwebs."

"And paw prints?"

"It's not everyone has opossum prints on their car," I said proudly.

"Sardines, yet. Not that you'd have any way of opening them. You probably have a can of Campbell's soup down there too."

Those sardines had been in my car about a year and a half. I'd sort of resigned myself to their being there. I hadn't wanted to throw them away because, after all, they're food, but I suppose I could have moved them to my kitchen. Still, what business was it of his? I longed to present more bizarre objects to baffle and infuriate him further: refried beans, a dozen roses, two parakeets, a set of graduated sockets (there *was* a socket-wrench ratchet handle) because all this was not lighthearted raillery on Greg's part, it was just this side of nasty.

So, not to be cowed, to express my utter freedom of movement, I tossed the can back into the well. "My lucky sardines," I explained, smiling. He was acting like a husband of ten years instead of a lover of a month. Happily we'd made no promises and I could easily end it. No time like the present.

"I think it's all over with us, Greg. It was a mistake. We're not right for each other."

"What? Just because I criticize your carkeeping?" He smiled, trying to joke. Too late.

"That and the look in your eye for the last ten minutes. I don't go out with guys who look at me like that."

"Oh, hell, Sandy, I've just been with Janet and she's being

so completely unreasonable, so greedy and vicious, I really thought I was still looking at her. I'm sorry I took it out on you. Really I am. I should have cooled down before I came over. Forgive me?"

I almost melted. But I wasn't fooled. The words were good but the feeling was spurious.

"There's nothing to forgive. You have a right to feel the way you do. You're going through a hard time. I think you need to work it out by yourself. What I'm looking for in a lover, not unreasonably, is love, not hate. You're feeling a lot of hate. I'm sorry."

The look he gave me then was enough to make me involuntarily grab hold of the socket-wrench ratchet handle, but he didn't hit me, didn't even speak; he just went to his car and pulled out of the driveway without another word. I gazed with interest at my white knuckles, then pocketed the tool. I would put it on my mantel and see if anyone claimed it. The rest of the debris I bagged and threw in the garbage.

I gazed at the sky. I looked at my "perfectly good garage" but decided to leave the car out as usual. If the car was out then friends driving by could tell I was home and stop by and say hello. I liked that. Also, it would need hours in the sun to dry properly, and even though there wasn't any sun just now, there would be tomorrow or the next day. Also, I didn't want to dispossess the nocturnal creatures of their playpen, didn't want them to think I was turning into a hardass just because I'd gone out with one for a month.

That was a mistake. Because the next thing that happened to the dear old car was a horrible smell. But before that, something horrible happened to me. I was accused of murder.

"We'd like to ask you some questions," the lieutenant said when I answered the door. This was three days later. "My name's Mack Scher." He showed me his I.D. "This is Joe. Okay if we come in?"

"Sure." He was short and thin, with a receding hairline that he admirably combed back, not forward. "You can call a lawyer if you want."

"I wouldn't dream of it. I don't even let lawyers call me." If a cop could possibly have a twinkle in his eye, he seemed to.

"Nice house."

"Thanks."

It was almost noon and the sun was streaming in the many windows. The wooden floors gleamed, and all the furniture looked colorful and friendly. Mack and I sat. Joe sort of stood around looking for criminals.

"Where were you yesterday between five and six?"

"On a run. That's my running time. I come home from work, change, and go."

"Alone?"

"Yes."

"Anyone see you?"

"I suppose someone did somewhere along the course. Why?"

"Janet Hale was murdered around five-thirty."

When I looked blank, he said, "Mrs. Gregory Hale."

"Oh."

"Your boyfriend's wife."

"Ex-boyfriend," I said crisply.

"It was a drive-by shooting, as she was climbing the steps to her house. Your car."

I sat up from my lolling position as if to spring to the defense of the Alfa, as if my car were being accused, not I. "I'm sure mine isn't the only silver Alfa Romeo in the area."

"It's the only one that has a license-plate holder that says 'Death Before Dishonor.' Strange sentiment for a woman to have on her car."

"Not in the least. It's a noble sentiment. It's from Homer's *Iliad*, by the way, not from the Hell's Angels."

He murmured something that sounded like "Big deal."

"What's at issue here," he said, "is not where the quote came from, it's where the bullet came from. Your car."

"Obviously someone borrowed my car, the rat, someone who hated both of us."

"Did Mr. Hale ever use your car? Could he have made a key?"

"No," I answered honestly, "he never did." I wondered if he'd be able to overcome his fastidiousness in order to pin a murder rap on me. Probably not if it meant risking getting bird droppings on his pants or spiderwebs on his sleeve.

"But I often leave the keys in it." Mack Scher looked highly disapproving of this practice. "I'm easygoing about my car. It's like a pet that I trust not to stray."

"We're going to fingerprint it. Have you driven it today?"

"Yes. Saturday morning I always drive up the mountain to run the trails, so if it was wiped clean last night, my fingerprints will be there." I wished I could resay the sentence. It sounded as if I'd left fingerprints on the mountain. "Of course," I added, "*he* knows my schedule."

"He being Gregory Hale?"

"Yes, he being him."

While Joe fingerprinted me Mack said, "It doesn't look good. You've got motive, no alibi, and your car was spotted leaving the crime scene."

"Wait a minute. Why wasn't *I* spotted? Was the top up?"

"Yes."

"Aha! Proof! I never have the top up during summertime."

He snorted. "Some proof."

"Well, fingerprint the latches," I urged him, ashamed to hear anxiety in my voice. Anyone who believes in death before dishonor should laugh in the face of an obvious frame, not whimper.

The fingerprints on the car were all mine, although there were none on the latches, which I thought was extremely telling. Mack didn't.

I said, "If the top was put up and then down last night, there should be someone's fingerprints on the latches unless someone wiped them, right?"

"For proof you need fingerprints, not a lack of fingerprints, and so far we only have yours." He wrinkled his nose. "Kind of a bad smell in there," he commented.

"I know. I noticed it driving back from my run. It's almost as if it's expressing shame at its involvement in the poor woman's death, a stigmatic scent, emblematic of its disgrace."

"Let's not get fanciful here."

"Okay, it's cat urine."

"Stronger than that," Mack said. I went over and sniffed. It had gotten more powerful and pervasive. Say it had been peed on last night. Why, if it was out in the sun and open air all morning, would it be getting stronger? "Maybe possum urine," I said. "I've a possum that lives under the house, comes out at night."

"Could be," he said. "Never smelled possum urine, myself." He paused, sniffed, nodded. "Possumbly."

Oh, Mack! I stared at him consideringly. Was this murder case in good hands?

"I'm not arresting you yet," he said. "But don't leave town. I recommend finding someone who saw you on your run last night."

"Does *he* have an alibi?"

"Yes."

I spent the rest of the weekend out on the bike path looking for a familiar face from Friday's run and not finding one. I was feeling depressed, not because of the murder rap hanging over me but because I'd spent time with a rat like Greg. Had I always been such a bad judge of character? I figured I'd cheer up once Greg was arrested, but what if he wasn't? We were dealing with an extremely careful man who'd wiped not only the wheel, the key, the shift, the door, and the seats, but the latches that secured the top.

Meanwhile, old Greg was portraying me to the lieutenant as a villainess of the deepest dye whose license-plate holder didn't mean I'd die rather than commit a dishonorable act but meant I'd kill anyone who got in my way. And Janet was in my way. Plus, said he, I was a wildly jealous, passionate person who'd been known to follow him when he went to see Janet, then go into ungovernable rages. He cited the ratchet handle incident, only he made it sound like it was part of boxful of tools that had been flung at him instead of a lone one I'd held a bit tightly, scared by the look in his eye.

"I'm not saying I believe him," Mack said when he told me all this on Sunday, "but he is a fairly distinguished person, whereas you've got a reputation for being, let's say, unconventional, a little wild."

"I should hope so. I'd hate to have my tombstone read 'She had a good reputation.' "

"How would you like it to read?"

She liked fast cars and good-looking men, I thought but didn't say. Anyhow it wasn't true anymore. It could stand only if I excised *looking*, and changed *fast* to *smelly*.

On Monday after work, I was asked to come down to the station for further questioning along with Greg. As I approached the car I could smell it from a distance. It seemed enveloped in a vile miasma. Getting in, I gagged. The possum urine scent had gotten much worse. I couldn't figure it out. Suppose—worst case—he'd peed on the seat that had a rip in it and the urine had gotten into the foam, wouldn't it still begin to dissipate by now? Why would it be getting worse? And why would a possum pee in a car, anyhow, with all the trees and bushes around? Also, the surprise rain two days before the murder had washed the finish and there hadn't been paw prints on the car that Saturday morning, as far as I could remember. He could have leapt in over the door, but possums were slow, plodders not leapers.

The smell was better as I jammed along the road, but when I parked at the station it hit me again. I was about to scurry from the car because my tendency from the start had been to run from the odor rather than investigate it. Instead, I sat there, thinking, sniffing, looking about, and I suddenly thought, fish. It's actually a sort of fish smell. And then, naturally, I remembered the sardines. But could canned sardines smell?

Yes. Canned sardines could.

Then I knew I had Greg nailed.

I ran into the station crying, "Proof! I've got proof Greg did it. Real proof! Follow me."

"Now hold on a minute," Mack said, but he followed me, and so did a couple of uniforms, and so, of course, did Greg, Mr. Tall, Mean, And Handsome, Mr. Too Perfect to Kill. But his tallness was going to be his undoing!

I looked at Greg gleefully. He was cool and unruffled.

"I haven't touched anything," I said, leading them all to the vaporous vehicle. "I only realized when I got here, and then I just ran in to get you to come and see."

At the car, they all held their noses and looked put upon. "Mack, don't ask me why, but there's a can of sardines in the well behind my seat. Remember the sardines?" I asked Greg, laughing a little, actually sort of cackling.

"Yes I do," he said dryly. "So?"

"So they're about to inform against you. It's going to be curtains for Greg 'Killer' Hale."

I opened the door, reached down behind the driver's seat, and picked out the can. Sure enough, there was an open gash in it. "You see. This is what was causing the car to stink ever since Saturday night, and every day of the sun shining on it made it worse. How do you guys think it got that gash? Mack? Greg?"

I waited for the light to dawn. "He had to push the seat back when he drove the car," said Mack, "because his legs are longer. And the metal rail sliced it open. When he returned the seat to its former position, it left the can exposed."

"Right!" I crowed. "And I'll bet you he was so busy re-membering to wipe the top latches that he forgot to wipe his fingerprints off the lever under the seat."

At this Greg turned pale, staggered, and actually began to faint. Of course it might have been the smell, too, that put him under. We were none of us looking too well.

"My lucky sardines," I sang. "My trusty old Alfa."

Mack looked at the car with admiration. "Scentsational," he said. The man was impossumble.

Greg was being led away, sort of half dragged because of his weakened state, and the fingerprint man, lying half in, half out of the car, was going to work on the lever. Someone came and placed the sardines in a plastic bag. I hated to think how they'd be by trial time, the wheels of justice grinding so slow. Exhibit A would empty the court.

Suddenly I panicked. Maybe that was Exhibit B and my car was A. "You're not going to impound my car, are you? It's an open-air kind of car. It's never even been garaged, let alone imprisoned. And after all, it solved the murder!"

"I'll see what I can do," Mack said. "Maybe it will be enough if it promises not to leave town. Meanwhile, don't leave the keys in it, okay?"

"I'll try to remember, but maybe you should come by every so often to check."

He smiled. "Maybe I should."

I drove home for my evening run. There was a very nice spiderweb underway on the dash, in the corner where it met the window. Life was sweet. So was the air.

Marilyn Wallace, former English teacher and pastry chef, has featured homicide detectives Jay Goldstein and Carlos Cruz, as well as a "guest protagonist" in her novels. In A Case of Loyalties *(a Macavity award winner), the third character was a painter whose daughter is a murder suspect; in* Primary Target *(an Anthony nominee), the detectives meet the first woman to make a serious bid for the U.S. presidency. In* A Single Stone, *the "guest" is a woman accused of murdering her own child.*

In "A Tale of Two Pretties" (with apologies to Dickens), two women decide to turn the worst of times into the best of times.

A TALE OF TWO PRETTIES

by Marilyn Wallace

Part the First: True Confessions

Body Heat

He rolled onto his back and she traced the lines of definition along his triceps. "Only a little while before you check into the drug treatment center. Six o'clock. Three hours. I'm scared, Mickey. What am I gonna do without you?"

"You'll be fine. Vinnie promised me he'd keep an eye on you." He ran a finger along her cheek. "You don't want me wired and wasted, or strung out and wrung out, right? This is a no-fail program, babe. It'll work for me."

Cindy smiled and slid her fingers down the valley of his breastbone. "Twelve weeks apart. At least we'll have plenty of time to think up some proper rewards. For both of us."

Through the venetian blinds, afternoon sun fell in slats across his chest. How stupid she had been to think that if they moved from Chicago to San Francisco, his problems would disappear.

He had found new connections within twelve hours and was back on the same damn roller coaster: cocaine as long as the sun was shining, some kind of downer to get him through the night until it was time to start again. A good residential rehab program was Mickey's last chance to get clean.

Fifty thousand dollars worth of clean.

Picking up and leaving Chicago and coming all the way out here and now living without him for three months would be worth it if it worked. A whole year of him nodding out and falling asleep or being jittery and angry, a whole year of bad sex or no sex . . . Finally, he had agreed; he didn't want to live like that forever.

She jumped off the bed, paced to the window, looked down on a couple dressed all in black as they strolled, arms linked, toward Haight Street. San Francisco was such a dismal city, gray and chilly, not like the sunny California she'd expected. They'd arrived a month ago, at ten minutes to midnight, New Year's Eve, and found a dim and quiet tavern in which to toast new beginnings. The next day the sun had shone for a total of twenty minutes.

She had gotten her bearings quickly—it never took her long to scope out the Right Neighborhood, the Right People—and they started working the insurance scam. Choosing the fanciest homes, telling housekeepers that she was sent to take pictures for insurance purposes. Mickey timed it so that he rang the bell ten minutes after she arrived; when the maid answered the door, Cindy lifted something—a silver this, a gold that—and put it in her camera bag.

It wasn't a bad scam but she hated having to deal with Vinnie. Her contacts in Chicago told her that Vinnie could fence anything, but something about his ferret eyes made her uneasy and contributed to her worries about the immediate future. She'd have to figure a way to work without Mickey. A queasy feeling twisted her stomach at the thought: *without Mickey*. Restless, she reached for the *Chronicle* and scanned the headlines, her gaze lingering on the picture on page three.

Maybe the woman in this picture was the answer. Maybe she could capitalize on the resemblance . . .

"Next time we should get Vinnie involved sooner." Mickey came up from behind her and pulled her against him. "He said he'd help us figure out the best places to hit. What do you think?"

Cindy moaned and slid Mickey's hand down from the waistband of her jeans. "Can't we talk about that some other time, sweetie?" she said as she wriggled closer to him. "There are other things to do now, better things."

Mickey was breathing faster now, pressing up against her. If only she could get him to forget Vinnie—she would handle *him*. He had a soft spot—or was it a hard one? she laughed to herself—for her since that afternoon in the warehouse. She hadn't known *how* making it with Vinnie was going to come in handy; she knew she'd figure it out when the time came. It had been easy enough, afterwards, to convince him to pay her thirty cents on the dollar and to tell Mickey it was only twenty. The extra she put in a separate account; together with the diamond pendant she'd kept back from the last job, they'd have enough when Mickey got out.

"Oh, Mickey, honey, it'll be so nice when you're back." Cindy unbuttoned her blouse and held Mickey's hand up to her breast. "It'll really be like starting fresh."

Breathless

Charlotte Durning stopped at the landing to catch her breath. "But why me, Ed? I don't deserve all this public scrutiny, these stories about my shelties and my claustrophobia. Now my *picture* is showing up in the *Chronicle*. On page three." She pressed a slim, manicured hand to her bosom. "Why am I the scapegoat? It's terribly unfair. All I did was pass on the name of an excellent contractor to a city official who was dissatisifed with the other bids he'd gotten."

His expensively vested chest heaving with exertion, Ed Partridge patted his upper lip and replaced the folded handerkerchief in his pocket. "I wish you would try an elevator again. Maybe you've outgrown your difficulty."

Even the thought of an elevator—doors closing, four walls and floor and ceiling all pressing in on her—brought a sheen of cold sweat to her face. She took another breath, waited for the wave of darkness to pass, whispered a simple, "No, Ed. We'll walk."

He nodded and followed as she started up the stairs again. "Charlotte, my dear, the contractor happens to be an executive of a public corporation in which you are a majority stockholder. The city official has jurisdiction to rule that you can add a penthouse despite the local building height ordinance. Last year, it would have made no splash. This year, San Francisco is on an ethical government campaign and the self-righteous bastards are out to nail you.''

Charlotte Durning didn't like the tone of his voice, not one bit. He was her lawyer. She was paying him three hundred dollars an hour, more for court fees and expenses, thousands of dollars in telephone calls. But it would all be worth it if they won.

She *couldn't* go to jail. She'd die.

She'd never last a day. Even in her own home, closed doors and small spaces terrified her. Flying was a trial to which she subjected herself, heavily sedated, twice a year only—for the spring couture showings in Paris and then in December for opening night at La Scala. She never drank anything before or during a flight: those tiny closets they called bathrooms on the planes were the worst. She refused to stay in hotels unless she could have a suite. It wasn't an indulgence so much as a form of self-preservation, she had explained to her accountant.

Jail was unthinkable.

Her throat would swell with fear; she'd choke and die. Charlotte Durning, widow and sole beneficiary of the estate of Preston Durning III (which she surely deserved after putting up with the randy old fart through her best years—all of her twenties, part of her thirties), simply couldn't go to jail. She was counting on Ed Partridge to get her off.

''I used up all my peremptory challenges on single women with children, but I'm still not happy with the jury.'' An unhealthy red glow mottled his pasty cheeks and a fine line of perspiration sprouted again on his upper lip. ''Jury of your peers—hardly any of those around. They're all wintering in Biarritz or Aspen or Cabo.''

Well, she couldn't help it if she was blond, slim, and rich, could she? Surely they'd understand that she had gotten involved in this ugly mess out of pure disinterest. She had seen how two needs complemented each other and she'd brought them together. If that was a crime . . .

How much would it take—a thousand each? Ten thousand? Twelve people on a jury, that would make a hundred and twenty thousand, which would hardly put a dent in her resources. But, really, one juror was all she needed to delay things long enough for the political climate in this fickle city to become more hospitable. Unless she got caught . . .

"I want you to be prepared. A year ago, the same facts and the same defense would have worked. Today—" When Ed shrugged, his starched collar rose on his wattled neck—"I think we ought to consider the prosecutor's deal. The DA offered to reduce the charge. You'd do three months in a minimum security facility and then it would be over."

Three months in jail? She'd never survive.

Part the Second: The Birds

Vertigo

Her soup was just the way she liked it. Charlotte Durning dipped her spoon into the steamy saffron-scented liquid and tasted it, then sucked up a long swallow of champagne, blinking away the fizz as she let her gaze wander through the room.

That woman, two tables away—what was it about her? She had an oval face, a not-bad straight brown bob; her green eyes never even looked up from the book she was reading until her salad arrived. When the woman smiled at the waitress, a pang of excitement lapped at Charlotte's tummy, a little flicker she didn't quite understand.

Charlotte brought the spoon to her mouth. Maybe she could cut back to three aerobics classes a week, now that soup was the only thing she could manage to get down. Except for champagne, of course, and coffee. They were getting her through her days and nights. Today was Wednesday, two days after her picture first hit the local papers, and she had reached a desperate conclusion. A straw, maybe, but today she would suggest to Ed that the nice plumber on the jury, the one who—

The woman two tables away pushed her salad plate to the center of the table, reached for her book, leaned back in her chair. She swept her hair behind her left ear. Charlotte stared.

If her hair was blond . . .

If it curled toward her face a bit more . . .

If her foundation makeup was more pink, less peachy . . .

A quick inventory: nondescript black slacks and gray

sweater. Turquoise-and-silver ring. Shoes and purse showing signs of wear. Her posture was good; she looked the right shape.

"Charlotte, dear, did you hear me at all?" Ed scooped up a caper and speared a flaky chunk of salmon, stared at his fork, then popped it all in his mouth.

She could hardly catch her breath. A rapture, like the sound of angels singing, filled her heart.

"You must consider your options. The DA is willing to take the reduced charge until court opens day after tomorrow. No later." Ed Partridge's milky white fingers reached for her hand. "I'm your lawyer. I'm the best in the state. But we're losing this one. That's three years instead of three months, and it won't be at the minimum security facility. I strongly advise . . ."

But his words faded. In the past sixty seconds, Charlotte Durning had come to see hope where none existed before.

She stared. The woman was getting up, plucking her scuffed black purse from the chair.

Thank God, she thought as the woman walked toward the rear of the dining room. *She's going to the rest room. Mustn't scare her.* Charlotte measured the woman's height; surely Providence was looking after her once again. "I'm going to the little girls', Ed."

She didn't wait for a nod or a smile from her attorney but scurried out of her seat, following the woman's straight-backed march past the dessert trolley to the rear of the restaurant. The rest room door swung shut; Charlotte sniffed the air before she walked in. *Charlie.* Good, the right sort, the kind who might be open to a proposition.

The toilet flushed; an eddy of fear whirled in the bottom of Charlotte's stomach. She reached into her purse and pulled out a comb and a tube of lipstick. The stall door latch squeaked. Charlotte forced herself to peer into the mirror, forced her hand to bring the comb to the crown of her head.

Footsteps.

Charlotte stepped back to allow the other woman access to the sink. Water splashed; the sweet smell of pink liquid soap wafted through the air.

The other woman, hands still dripping into the rust-stained sink, lifted her head and looked in the mirror.

Charlotte gasped. "My God, it's incredible," she said, her voice a hoarse whisper. She took a step forward.

Staring into the stranger's eyes in the mirror, the heat from their shoulders flicking across the narrow space that separated them, Charlotte felt giddy. The other woman's mouth opened; her lips were moist, her eyes shining with excitement. Charlotte was rocked by a sudden desire to kiss the woman on her identical mouth, to make the difference between self and other disappear. She shuddered, reached over, and brushed the other woman's hair toward her face, noting the tiny lines that netted the outer corners of the woman's eyes. Age was right, too.

"Wow! That's amazing." The other woman leaned closer, then moved out of Charlotte's reach. "Spooky."

There was no wretched regional accent but her voice was thin, a little high. Well, they'd chalk that up to nervousness. Anyone would be nervous going in to plead guilty to bribing a public official. "My name is Charlotte Durning."

"Cindy Carson. Like Kit." Water dripped from her hands into a puddle on the tile floor.

She'd need a good set of acrylic nails—you never knew what those vultures hungry for the beating heart of a public figure would notice.

The woman reached for a paper towel; three fluttered to the floor. As Cindy Carson and Charlotte Durning knelt to retrieve the towels, their heads bumped lightly.

"Sorry," they said at the same time.

Eyes crinkling, Cindy stood slowly; then she laughed, shaking her brown hair. "This is *so* strange. Gotta run or I'll miss my appointment. Bye."

Don't freeze up now, Charlotte thought as she fought a clutch of fear. *She's your only chance and all the signs are right.*

Cindy Carson pulled away from the hold of Charlotte's gaze and reached for the door.

"Wait." Charlotte's eyes teared with relief that she'd finally broken her own silence. "I need to talk to you later. Please. Tell me how I can reach you." She glanced at her watch. She had to be back in court in less than five minutes.

"I, uh . . ." Cindy's quaver trailed off. "Look, you're scaring me." She started for the door again.

"Please. I need your help. And I have a lot of money to pay for it." She reached into her purse and pulled five hundred-dollar bills from her wallet.

Cindy stared at the money but didn't move.

"Meet me at Macy's. Tomorrow at noon. I'm talking about a lot of money. Enough so that, if you were smart, you wouldn't have to worry for the rest of your life."

The faucet dripped noisily. Beyond the rest room walls, the roar of lunchtime conversation rose and fell at the restaurant tables.

"Linens? Sportswear? Electronics?" Cindy frowned and reached for the bills, folded them in half, then jammed them into the pocket of her slacks.

"Beauty salon." She could have spared herself those moments of fright by taking out the cash sooner; Charlotte felt better already. "Fourth floor."

The Lady Vanishes

Charlotte squinted and shook her head. "Look," she said, fluffing the hair toward Cindy's face. "Mine falls forward. Hers keeps curling the wrong way. Can't you do something about it?"

The stylist stepped back. She should have known—anyone who would wear a terrible brown cardigan over that yellow polyester uniform wouldn't have the necessary panache to pull it off. But she couldn't very well have waltzed into her own Union Street salon and directed Bijou to recreate Cindy Carson in her image. Makeup and clothes would have to take care of the rest.

A gnawing fear nibbled at her stomach. How silly to be afraid now, she chided herself. This was going to work to everyone's advantage.

If by some miracle the case went her way or was thrown out of court, then Cindy would keep the $30,000 she'd already been given for her troubles.

But if things went as she expected, Charlotte would deposit $250,000 each month into a Swiss bank account; the bank would print a coded message in the *Chronicle* to let Cindy know that everything was okay. And while Cindy took her place in the facility, Charlotte would live in Cindy's Fillmore Street apartment. When the three months were up, they'd each resume their lives.

"This is better, don't you think?" Cindy flicked a curl down toward her cheek, raised an eyebrow, sat back with her shoulders squared and her neck stretching.

Do I really look like that? Charlotte wondered as she squinted through her dark glasses. *Do I really appear to be so cold and distant? No wonder I have no friends.*

Now the effect was so nearly right she gasped. The sleek blond hair curled into a gentle frame around the Cindy/Charlotte oval face.

Charlotte tried not to watch as Cindy, who had spent ten minutes practicing just before they'd entered the beauty salon, scrawled a signature on the charge slip. The receptionist nodded, tore up the carbons, and went back to her *TV Guide*. Cindy and Charlotte hurried out of the department store onto the crowded street, jostled by the crush of midday shoppers, and started walking.

Three blocks later, they still had said nothing to each other. Cindy stopped in front of Gump's window. "I don't know about this whole trip."

"What do you mean?" Charlotte untied her scarf and let it fall to her shoulders. She pulled the dark glasses away from her face.

Cindy frowned. "Oh, shit. I don't know."

"Oh, *dear*," Charlotte corrected, her forehead wrinkling in disapproval. "Charlotte Durning would never say 'Oh, shit' in so public a setting. And prison, don't forget, is a public setting. Oh, dear; oh, my; oh, Lord. Any of these. But not 'Oh, shit.' Okay?"

Cindy nodded. "Just a little nervous, I guess. I'm ready for the rest. I'm really hungry, though. You want to pick up some lunch on the way over to my place? Pizza, or maybe some take-out bagels and lox?"

Charlotte's stomach fluttered. "I forgot to tell you. I'm allergic to smoked things. Something in the curing process, I don't know. No bacon. No lox, even though most of it isn't smoked but pickled. No ham. No barbecue."

An annoyed scowl flitted across Cindy's face and Charlotte shivered. Instead of the giggle she expected, Cindy's right eyebrow and the right corner of her mouth rose. She was good, this woman, maybe too good. Charlotte shivered again. She felt inhabited—no, that wasn't quite right. She felt replaced.

Well, that was what she wanted, wasn't it?

Cindy sighed. "That's gonna be a bummer. What *do* you

eat for breakfast? I know about the cholesterol rap, but I've been eating bacon and eggs five days a week all my life.'' She giggled, then frowned. ''And the other two days it's bagels and cream cheese and lox.''

This whole thing *couldn't* fall apart over the breakfast menu. ''Three months of cornflakes and milk—you can put up with that for three quarters of a million dollars. I'll bring some with me tomorrow morning so you can try it.'' For a minute, she couldn't read the expression on Cindy's face. Then she laughed as she realized that the cant of the head, the pursed mouth, were her own gestures when she was making a difficult decision.

Damn, the woman really had her down cold. Was she so transparent, so easy to mimic?

What did all this identity stuff matter, anyway? She wouldn't be going to jail; that was all that counted.

Rear Window

''Here, I'll take the box of cornflakes. I want you to practice opening the door with this key. It's a little tricky.''

Charlotte took the key and looked up as a tan-and-brown pigeon settled on a second-story windowsill. Would there be an elevator? She had forgotten to ask; her throat filled with bile and a cold fist squeezed the air out of her lungs.

''You okay?'' Cindy laid a warm hand on Charlotte's bare arm.

''What floor?'' Charlotte finally managed to say.

Cindy held up her hand, her fingers spread in the victory sign. ''Second. One flight of stairs. You can make it.''

Charlotte nodded at Cindy's grin and followed her up the wooden stairs. Cindy's Fillmore Street apartment was in what Ed Partridge would call a marginal neighborhood, with yuppies and upscale restaurants moving the blacks and Hispanics farther into the Mission District or the Western Addition.

Weekends would be noisy. Evenings would be nothing like the cloistered quiet of home, where the back rooms looked out over the lights of the Golden Gate Bridge and the jewellike twinkle of cars crossing the bay.

But it wouldn't be jail, she thought as she wiggled the key in the lock.

"Pull down on the knob and pull the key out just a tiny bit," Cindy directed.

Charlotte jiggled the key but nothing happened. It wouldn't turn. "Oh, shit," she muttered.

"Good." Cindy grinned. "You're getting it now."

The key suddenly felt right; the lock turned, the door opened, and they clattered inside.

Ordinary.

That was the first word that came to Charlotte Durning's mind.

Blessedly ordinary. A Haitian cotton love seat. A pair of rattan chairs with rose-colored cushions. An imitation Oriental on the dull wood floors and lots of green plants in clay pots.

She followed Cindy down the hall. They passed an oval mirror with a carved oak frame. Charlotte pulled Cindy's sleeve.

"What?" She looked annoyed and shrugged out of Charlotte's grasp.

Without saying anything, Charlotte turned Cindy's shoulders so that they both faced into the mirror. It was too unbelievable, not knowing which of the images reflected her own face and which was the other's. Finally, Cindy broke away and hustled to the kitchen.

"The top element of the toaster oven is dead so you have to toast one side first and then turn your bread to toast the other side." She yanked the refrigerator door open, pulled out a package of bacon. "Oh, shi— oh, dear. I think I'll just fry this up and have it all. Before I get in that taxi."

She tossed the package onto the counter and stood a moment too long, hands on hips. Her eyes narrowed. "You never been printed, have you? By the cops. Fingerprints, I mean."

Charlotte raised her eyebrows. "Of course not."

"We'll be okay then. Now sit down and let's turn you into a brunette."

Charlotte watched in fascination as Cindy moved about the tidy kitchen. Maybe she'd learn to cook in these three months. And catch up on her reading and learn to sew or knit. She could do lots of things, without the distraction of board luncheons where the primary objective was to show off how thin you were and how many good deeds you could buy for your good name. No days wasted after late-night parties in which she'd have to fish for questions to ask a fiercely dull diplomat or a boorishly crass manufacturer so that she could be rewarded with the excruciating details of their daily lives.

"What do you do all day? When you aren't looking for work, I mean." Charlotte breathed the ammonia fumes of Miss Clairol Golden Chestnut #390 and squeezed her eyes shut as Cindy dabbed the thick stuff on her head. She could practically hear the other woman shrug and screw up her nose.

"Not much," the voice behind her said. "Whoops. Dripping. Keep your eyes closed."

Charlotte obeyed; the cool touch of the damp cotton swab as it mopped up the hair dye felt . . . what? Sisterly? She didn't have a sister. Her fastidious mother had decided after Charlotte's birth that one such messy event was enough. Charlotte opened her eyes, marveling at the growing embryo of affection she felt for Cindy Carson.

Cindy secured a plastic cap on Charlotte's head with a clip; she set the timer and sat down at the chair across the table.

"I'm a crossword puzzle freak. And I have an herb garden back here. See?" Cindy threw open the window; four wooden boxes filled with lacy greens formed a rectangle on the fire escape outside the kitchen. Sun kissed the soil and sparkled on a white enamel watering can. "Just water them twice a week. Snip the tops of these and use them in omelets. Should be strong and fully grown when I get back."

Charlotte felt a tingle of anticipation.

She would help those brave little seedlings struggle to full fragrant growth. She would do something constructive.

"Mostly," Cindy said as she picked a dried tomato seed from the counter, "I walk. This is a great city for walking. Great bookstores. Places that sell handmade stuff. Cafés. I really like just strolling around and looking in the windows of other people's houses, you know?" She was silent for a moment, her eyes clouded and far away. "You're sure it's going to be three months max? Any more than that—I don't know if it's worth it. Mickey really needs to hear from me—for support, you know. I'm counting on you to mail the letters. To this address." She tapped the yellow note under the plastic sushi magnet on the refrigerator.

"I'm very reliable; of course I'll mail your letters. Look, my attorney says three months. No more, no less."

A siren screamed down Fillmore toward Church Street. She wouldn't back out now, would she? There was no time to do anything else, no chance to make other arrangements. Cindy Carson simply had to honor her commitment.

The timer jangled through Charlotte's thoughts.

"Okay, wrap this towel around your neck and bend over the sink." Cindy tested the water, turned down the hot. "There."

Charlotte closed her eyes. The ammonia smell was awful but the water was soothing. Charlotte gave herself up to the warm water and the light massage of Cindy's fingers on her scalp.

"All done." Cindy wrapped Charlotte's dripping head in a towel. "Here, wash the makeup off your face and we'll go in the bedroom. Light's better in there. You can show me how you do your eyeliner and I'll show you how to use the blusher along your cheekbones."

"*Our* cheekbones." Charlotte beamed. Of course this was going to work. She washed her face, scrunched her drying hair with her fingers, and tiptoed through the living room toward the open bedroom door. Cindy was struggling with the back of the white silk blouse.

My God, she was perfect.

It was like watching a videotape of a former self . . . outside, able to see what other people see, the filters of sensation and internal memory removed.

She was beautiful, with a cool dignity that would keep people at a distance. Charlotte stepped behind her and buttoned the buttons, then stood waiting, silent, solemn.

Again, they both stared at the image in the mirror; for a moment Charlotte felt the dreamy disorientation of a too sudden awakening.

Cindy tittered and they fell into fits of helpless giggles, sliding down to the floor where they swiped at the tears on their own faces and ended by almost drowning in each other's eyes.

Charlotte pulled away first.

Part the Third: The Long Good-bye

The Big Sleep

Two days left—thank God. All the romantic rot she'd told herself about growing herbs and learning to embroider and discovering the quaint niches of the city—how stupid she had been. After a week in Cindy Carson's squalid little apartment, she had missed her sheets being changed twice a week, had longed for just one dinner at Masa's, had cursed as one by one her nails broke. She had forborne the comments of the men as she walked down Church Street. Somehow, between daytime quiz shows and a few Danielle Steel novels, she had managed to pass the time. The best she could say was that it was almost over.

Charlotte put the cornflakes in the cupboard and crushed the empty milk carton before she tossed it in the garbage. As though it had been waiting for her attention, the sun broke through the fog and the street below shimmered in the dappled late morning light. She sprang from the chair and threw the window open.

Must be the dampness that keeps these herbs so green, she thought as she pinched off a leaf. *Certainly nothing I did.* A licorice smell drifted to her—basil? Cindy had planted the seeds and as they grew, she had faded into an insubstantial memory. Charlotte nibbled a corner of the leaf and wondered how accepting someone else's identity would alter her life, beyond this boring familiarity with the ordinary.

Cindy's closet had taught her nothing, had, in fact, been a disappointment. The colors were overdone, ranging from a too-cheery rose blouse to the brightest jewel-green jacket to florals that bloomed with garden hues. And her bookcase: Marques next to Lessing, Tyler beside Hardy, Oliver Sacks and Daphne DuMaurier and Dashiell Hammett. The girl didn't seem to be able to settle down.

Her collection of records was another example of her flightiness. Charlotte had made three purchases and now she ambled to the bedroom, put on her Johnny Mathis album, and settled into the rocking chair to enjoy the classic sounds.

Two more days. If she was careful she'd be able to string the last fifty pages of the book, a story of three orphaned sisters, to the end of her time. She'd resume life as Charlotte Durning—no jail, no cell, no throat filled with fear.

A noise from the front of the apartment startled her. A door squeaked and she heard voices. Heart pounding, she sat still, afraid that any movement might alert the intruder to her presence.

"Cindy?" a voice called out.

A male voice. Someone else had a key to this apartment, someone Cindy never told her about. She would say she was Cindy's sister . . . unless the person who was out there happened to be Cindy's brother or cousin or someone who would know better.

"She's not here. I told you—she usually goes out walking in the afternoon." A different voice, also male.

Johnny Mathis warbled on. Doors slammed, objects clattered to the floor.

"Hey, Vinnie, you don't have to make a mess." The second voice again.

Charlotte finally started breathing again. She hadn't closed the window; the fire escape, while not her favorite means of egress, would do. At least it was open, no small enclosed box. She stood up, held the rocker to keep it from slapping back and forth on the wood floor, and tiptoed to the window.

"No way, Cindy."

She could hardly breathe. A hand grabbed her shoulder, spun her around. She was looking into the narrow face of a small, sharp man with beady eyes.

"I, uh . . ." Maybe she could talk him out of . . . What did he want, anyway? He didn't look like he was related to Cindy; she'd try the sister bit. "Cindy's not here. I mean, I'm her—"

"Look, Cindy," the man growled, "all I want is that diamond pendant that you lifted from the Emerson mansion. The deal was you give me an exclusive on all your stuff and I give you that extra cut. So when I got a hold of that insurance report, you gotta believe I was mad. No broad holds out on Vinnie." He squeezed her arm; she winced in pain.

"Don't hurt her, man. You promised." Wide-shouldered and tall, the second man swayed and leaned against the door frame for support. He seemed to be having trouble keeping his eyes open. "Just find it and let's get out of here, okay? I gotta meet my connection in fifteen minutes."

She wasn't going to stand here and be roughed up by these thugs, whatever they thought Cindy had done. Charlotte screamed; she stomped her feet on the floor and screamed again, trying to break away from the grip of the man with the ferret eyes.

"Shut the bitch up, Mickey. Or I'm gonna have to."

The man called Mickey drew himself upright. 'Don't talk about her like that. I don't like the way you're treating her, Vinnie. You said all you were gonna do was scare—"

Before Mickey could finish his sentence, Vinnie's hand shot out. Something hard cracked against Mickey's temple and for a moment, eyes open wide, he looked like a little boy whose favorite teddy bear had been torn to shreds. Then his eyes rolled back in his head, he clutched his chest, and he crashed to the floor in an unruly heap.

"Fuck piss shit," muttered the other. He looked around, his hand reaching for the leather belt she'd left on the bed when she changed her jeans. When he moved, she bit his hand and screamed again.

"That's it, Cindy. You asked for this."

He grabbed a thick white sock from the pile of laundry on the floor and stuffed it into her mouth, then secured it with the belt.

She was going to gag; she couldn't breathe. She was going to throw up from the fear. Everything went dark for a minute. She started to slump.

"No way. You're not going to pull that shit on me."

He was stronger than she would have guessed. He tied her hands behind her back and pulled her hair when she tried to resist. He dragged her to the far end of the room.

The closet. It was tiny. He was going to put her in the closet. She could choke. She would die. She wouldn't be able to breathe in there. The walls would close in on her. She would be filled by the blackness, crushed by it.

He shoved her inside. She fell onto the shoe rack and tried to right herself; she pounded on the door with her feet. She heard furniture dragging across the floor; he was putting something big and heavy across the door. She pounded again. The air was too thick. She was thirsty and hot and she couldn't swallow.

"Come on, Mickey. Move your ass. I found the pendant."

No, they weren't going to leave her in here.

"Shit, Mickey, if you're not gonna get up, I'm gonna have to leave you here too." She heard steps, then a pause. "Mickey?" the worried voice called, and then silence.

She tried to scream but the sound swelled in her throat until it blocked off her air passage.

Her last thought before her heart stopped was that she would probably be buried in Cindy's embarrassing magenta wool suit. In an open casket.

Farewell, My Lovely

Cindy shoved away the tray of gravy-covered lumps and tuned out the din of the mess hall. One day to go. She could hardly wait to see Mickey again—his bright, clear eyes; his smooth, delicious skin. She deposited her tray on the pile, walked through the metal detector, and followed two blond ponytails out into the yard.

This hadn't been half bad, really, except for being hit on all the time—but that was nothing new. She found a place on the grass and tilted her face to the sun. Mickey couldn't write to her, of course, but the Rich Bitch had passed on all the news from his letters: the shakes and the sweats and the terror of creepy-crawlies on his skin were over. He was learning how to cope with pressure, how to relax, how to think positively. He was training on computers. He was feeling good and missing her.

A tall woman with close-cropped hair meandered toward her.

Cindy closed her eyes to the sight of the woman cruising her on the grass. *Think about Mickey—clean, hard, smelling of Old Spice after his shower, his hair still wet, his terrific smile,* she ordered herself. *Think about our fresh start.*

"Dreaming about your secret lover?"

Cindy opened her eyes and looked down at the brown loafers planted on the grass inches in front of her. "Mmm-hmm," she answered.

"Found out you can live without him, didn't you?"

Cindy scrambled to her feet, shivering at the sight of the grainy skin on the woman's chin and at the idea of living without Mickey. "Shit, no," she muttered as she walked, slowly and deliberately, toward the door.

The months had dragged, but the rest of the day was going to fly by. The separation was almost over. She smiled and hugged herself, a little in triumph and a little in anticipation of seeing Mickey at the apartment.

Teri White proves that someone from suburban Shaker Heights, Ohio, can write tough and absorbing crime novels. Triangle *won a 1983 Edgar; her Spaceman Kowalski and Blue Maguire, L.A.P.D., novels* Bleeding Hearts *and* Tightrope *have been called ". . . among the best police stories on the market."* Max Trueblood and the Jersey Desperado *and* Faultlines *reflect Teri's interest in the moral ambiguities in contemporary American society and her conviction that ". . . nothing is all black or all white."*

In "Outlaw Blues," a police officer tests the limits of his "deep cover."

OUTLAW BLUES

by Teri White

I T WAS A simple job.

At least, that was the way Mr. Armani put it to him. An easy job, nothing to it, a real shitwork kind of thing, if you wanted to be completely honest about it. Shitwork.

But, Mr. Armani said with a big smile, how many people were willing to give a man just out of the joint *any* kind of a job at all? How much demand was there on the open market for ex-cons?

Well, Roger couldn't argue with that.

And because he needed a job, any job, even if it was just shitwork, Roger didn't point out that the main reason he *was* an ex-con just happened to be because he had kept his mouth shut after the bust. He never breathed one single word about his, meaning Mr. Armani's, part in the whole bungled warehouse heist.

That kind of loyalty should earn a man something, right?

Apparently, in this world, it earned him the kind of job that nobody else wanted.

Well, okay. Roger prided himself on being a man who could

roll with the punches; otherwise, he might not have survived those two very long years in the state correctional facility.

After thinking about it for ten seconds or so, he told Mr. Armani that he would take the job, whatever it was.

Mr. Armani seemed pleased. And why not? He hadn't just spent 730 days and nights behind bars.

The job turned out to be even less than Mr. Armani had suggested. Mostly it consisted of sitting around a warehouse, playing endless poker games with the other lackeys, and keeping a close eye on half a dozen trucks filled with hot merchandise. There didn't seem to be a whole lot of room for advancement, especially since it seemed to Roger that *his* primary qualification for the job seemed to be that Mr. Armani (quite justifiably, in fact) trusted him. Trusted him to keep an eye on the rest of the sleazebags in the warehouse, all of whom would obviously sell their mothers up the river if it suited their purposes.

This, then, was the reward for loyalty.

But just because he did a stretch rather than become a snitch, Roger was no dummy. It didn't take him long to see some hidden possibilities that might be available to the right man. This nothing job, this shitwork reward for services rendered, could be his big break. His chance. Assuming, of course, that he had the balls to grab for the brass ring.

Assuming that he had the balls to fuck with Mr. Armani.

It never rains in California.

Evan didn't know how the hell *that* rumor ever got started. This was the third wet day in a row and he was pretty tired of it. He sighed and pulled up the collar of his old windbreaker as he got ready to make the dash from his car to the front door of the Pelican Cove.

At least tonight he made it without stepping into any puddles.

The usual group was gathered around the bar. "Usual," for the Pelican meant that most of the customers had lengthy rap sheets for everything from petty theft to murder. Those who didn't already have a sheet were working on getting one. But, hell, even bad guys needed a place where they could come to socialize. Maybe the Pelican was a little lacking, fern-wise, and maybe there weren't any trendy white wines offered, but it served many of the same purposes as the yuppiest hangouts.

Evan absently returned a couple of the greetings that were tossed his way. He'd been coming in here so damned long that by now he was just part of the landscape.

Which was the whole point, right?

He took his regular booth and ordered his regular Guinness on tap. The waitress, a cute-enough blonde, hurried to bring it; her eagerness to serve seemed to prove what he had suspected for some time now. She definitely had the hots for him. Problem was, Evan couldn't make up his mind whether or not to pursue the matter. It seemed like a lot of trouble. Everything seemed like a lot of trouble these days. Except just hanging out here at the old Pelican and being one of the guys.

He settled back to drink the stout, stare at the wall, and listen to the ball game on the TV over the bar.

It took him a few moments to realize that someone was standing next to the table. Not, thank God, the horny waitress. The guy looked vaguely familiar, so he was undoubtedly a regular in the bar. That was not the best character reference one could have. "This table's occupied," Evan said.

"You're Gibson, right?"

Being called "Gibson" was so familiar that he wondered, for a fleeting moment, what the hell his real name was, and if he would even respond to it anymore. He'd been Evan Gibson for a very long time; so long, in fact, that he had a sneaking fondness for the coldhearted son of a bitch. "I'm Gibson," he said finally. "What about it?"

"My name is Roger. I thought maybe we should talk."

Evan sipped the dark, foamy Guinness carefully and took a closer look at the intruder. Thirtyish, auburn hair, wearing jeans and a damp denim jacket. "That so? Just what is it you think we should talk about, Roger?"

"Can I sit down?"

"I guess so." If this guy wasn't just recently out of the joint, Evan would eat the battered Dodger cap he was wearing over the short reddish curls. Ex-cons had a look to them, and Roger might as well have been wearing a freaking sign.

"It's like this," Roger said eagerly. "I hear you're always looking for a score." He kept his voice low, at least, didn't announce this to the whole damned place.

"You heard that, did you?" Evan said mildly.

Roger nodded. "I was asking around, looking for a name,

and Mike Torres told me you and him did a couple jobs together.''

There was a pause. Evan set his drink down carefully. "Torres always did have a big mouth," he said. "That's why I don't work with him anymore."

Roger grinned, which made him look like a twelve-year-old ex-con. "Hey, man, I know that. Why the hell do you think I wasn't interested in touting this deal to him?''

Evan nodded but didn't say anything.

"Well, whaddaya think, Gibson? You interested?''

He snorted. "What the fuck? So far the only thing you've given me to be interested in is your pretty blue eyes. Sorry, but love at first sight doesn't mean I'm interested in doing a job with you.''

"But can we talk about it, at least?" Roger said urgently. "Believe me, you won't be sorry. This is the big one we all wait for.''

"Maybe I'm not waiting for a big one," Evan said.

"Then why are you sitting here in the Pelican?" Roger smiled again. "Every motherfucker in here is waiting. I just want to drop the dream right into your lap.''

Evan glanced at his watch. "I can't talk now," he said. "Maybe if you're around tomorrow." That was a little test he used. Nine times out of ten, the talker with the big idea wouldn't even show up the next night.

Roger just nodded, looking disappointed as Evan slid from the booth and walked away.

It was still raining as he headed back to his car.

Evan had been so far under for so damned long that he sometimes had a hard time remembering whether he was a good guy or a bad guy. Not that it mattered very much, of course. In the beginning it had been sort of a shock to realize how easy it was to slip over to the other side. Apparently he had a real knack for it. As time went on, the Department let more and more of the little things he had to do—like the jobs with Torres, for example—go by unnoticed, because all the time he kept getting closer and closer to the big fish they were really after.

It had been almost three months since Evan had last asked to be brought in from the field. They told him to hang in there a little longer. That was what they always said, and he realized suddenly that it was what they would continue to say, so he didn't bother to ask anymore. He figured they just intended to keep him out here until his cover was irretrievably blown or he was dead, whichever came first.

They probably didn't care which it was, and most days he didn't give a damn, either.

It was pretty scary to find out that all the fun he had these days came from being an outlaw and not from being a cop.

Roger skipped the perpetual poker game. Instead, he wandered upstairs and leaned against the balcony rail, lit a cigarette, and thought about his conversation with Evan Gibson. Gibson had impressed him as a man who definitely knew his business, a man smart enough to be cautious. Of course, that meant it wasn't going to be easy to talk him into a deal, no matter how good it sounded. And this was damned good.

Roger took his eyes off the cardplayers below and looked instead at the small office that was located up on this level. Inside the office was the safe. And inside the safe was the answer to all of his dreams. It was also the answer to the dreams of Evan Gibson, he knew, but the only problem was going to be convincing Gibson of that fact.

As soon as he could get away from the warehouse, Roger headed for the Pelican. He had dressed with particular care this time. Neat grey slacks, a brand-new white shirt, and a silk tie. Way overdressed for the Pelican, but it showed he had class.

He walked into the bar and looked around hopefully. There was no sign of Evan Gibson. Damn. What if the guy didn't show up at all? Was there anybody else he would feel comfortable about bringing in on this? The collection of losers gathered around the bar didn't inspire a whole lot of confidence. And even the ones who could probably help bring the deal off, theoretically speaking, had one fatal flaw: he didn't think that any of them could be persuaded to cross Mr. Armani.

Roger picked up his bottle of Stroh's and took it to the same booth where he'd sat to talk with Gibson the night before.

It was clear to him that Evan was different. There was something in his eyes that made Roger think he wouldn't be afraid. Those eyes didn't look scared of anything.

The door opened again and Evan Gibson walked in, dressed

in ratty black jeans and a faded windbreaker. So much for class.

Evan didn't seem to be in any kind of a hurry. He stopped at the bar and spent some time talking to the group gathered there. It seemed to take forever before he picked up his mug of Guinness and strolled back, so damned casually, to where Roger was waiting. He sat down as if they had been meeting like this every night for years.

"Hi," Roger said.

Evan just looked at him with those cool grey eyes and nodded.

"Glad you showed up."

"I'm in here most nights," Evan replied. "By the way, I did a little checking on you. You work for Armani, right?"

"For the moment."

Evan raised a brow.

Roger swallowed some beer. This didn't seem like the time to hold back. "The thing is, I've got this problem with Armani. I did a two-year stretch for that bastard. In return, he gives me shit. Is that fair?"

Evan shrugged. "If you're looking for fairness in life, you're a fool." There was a faint Guinness foam mustache above his upper lip and he licked it off. "Armani is a very big deal around here. Not many people want to cross him."

Roger leaned forward. "Fuck Armani," he said. "I'm not scared of him." He gave a faint, bitter smile. "All my fear must've gotten used up over the last couple of years." He eyed Evan thoughtfully. "And I don't think you're scared of him, either."

Evan didn't say anything.

"I know how we can walk away with two million dollars. Two million of that bastard's dollars. Because he trusts me. Does that interest you?"

"Maybe. Maybe I'm interested."

Roger tried not to sound like some damned eager-beaver type. "I have this feeling, Evan," he said. "I have this feeling that you and me could pull this off."

Evan almost smiled.

"So whaddaya say, Evan?"

"I'll think about it."

"For how long?" Roger pressed.

"For just as long as it takes me to decide." Evan stood and looked down at him. "Where can I reach you?"

Roger decided that he didn't want to seem too easy. "You can reach me right here," he said flatly. "But don't wait too long. An opportunity like this doesn't come along every fucking day."

This time Evan did smile. Then he walked out of the bar.

The meet took place at a grungy little seafood restaurant down on the beach. Evan arrived first, parking around by the back door. He took a table in the corner and ordered oysters on the half shell. He was well into the meal by the time Thomas Lenford showed up.

The tall black man always dressed like he was expecting *Ebony* to show up and snap his photograph for the cover. He saw Evan, came over, and sat down. Before saying anything beyond hello, he perused the greasy menu; with obvious trepidation, he finally ordered a bowl of chowder. Then he settled back and crossed his arms across a massive chest, gazing almost benevolently at Evan. "You're looking good, ahh, Gibson."

He might have just been absolutely doing the right thing and sticking to the cover. He might have, yeah, but Evan had a feeling that the SOB just didn't remember what his real name was. Great.

"Thanks, sir. So are you. Terrific tie."

Lenford was flustered momentarily. "Is there a problem? Why'd you want this rendezvous?"

Evan finished the last oyster and sopped up the buttery juice with a chunk of French bread. "Maybe I just wanted some company," he said. "It can get pretty lonely out here, Lieutenant."

Lenford smiled and wiped the rim of his glass before sipping the iced tea. "You are very highly thought of downtown," he said.

"They know my name down there, do they?"

Lenford let that go by.

Evan was suddenly tired of doing the same old dance. "I may have a line to Armani," he said.

Lenford had just taken his first spoonful of the chowder. He swallowed carefully and set the spoon down. "Armani?" he said quietly.

Evan nodded. "This is the first time I've ever even gotten a nibble from that quarter." The waitress must have gotten bored with the rock music magazine she was reading, because she actually wandered over. He decided to live dangerously and ordered a slice of the lemon meringue pie. When she was gone again, Evan said, "Word on the street is that Armani might be in serious trouble. With the organization, I mean. That true?"

Lenford pursed his lips thoughtfully. "I think that maybe Armani is not within our jurisdiction at the moment."

Evan didn't like the sound of that. "Which means what, exactly? Sir?" He jabbed the tines of the fork into the just arrived pie viciously.

"The feds have been on him hard for over a year. They think that cracks are beginning to appear. Cracks they intend to exploit."

"Uh-huh." Evan wanted to be very careful about what he said here; of course, being careful about what he said was a way of life. "Does that have anything to do with the fact that Armani is moving a whole lot of cash through his outfit these days?"

Lenford shrugged. "He's desperate. The feds figure if he blows this, he's a dead man. They want him to reach bottom. Then he'll be eager to fall into their tender clutches."

"Right."

Lenford had finished his chowder. "You get what I'm saying here, Gibson?"

"Why don't you spell it out for me, sir. Just to be sure there's no misunderstanding."

Lenford dabbed at his lips with a paper napkin. "Perhaps it would be best to let your tip on Armani pass, for the time being."

Evan frowned. "I usually decide what leads to follow up on. That's the way I work. I mean, it's my ass on the line, right?"

"Sure, sure. I understand that. But in this particular case . . . well, a wrong move and not only do the feds get their case blown right out of the water, but chances are we end up with an all-out gang war on our hands."

Evan didn't give a good goddamn about the feds or their case, and he also figured that a gang war was pretty much the Department's worry, not his. What did he care if the bastards killed each other off?

Lenford didn't want to hear that, of course, so Evan didn't

say it. Still, he couldn't quite bring himself to capitulate completely. "Despite all of that, sir," he said with the utmost deference, "I assume that my judgment in the field is still primary?"

It took a moment before the black man answered. "Sure," he said. "Of course. We trust you, Gibson." He glanced at the gold watch on his wrist. "I need to move," he said, tossing a five down onto the table. "You'll keep in touch, of course?"

Evan was eating the pie. "Sure," he said absently. "You'll hear from me."

Alone, he licked sticky lemon pudding from the fork and thought about life.

He called the Pelican and left a message for Roger, telling the other man when and where to meet him at the beach. It was time for them to get away from the crowd. Also, the first test of Roger's brainpower would be if he showed up at the time and place specified.

As Evan sat on a boulder, smoking and staring out at the water, he tried to figure out what was happening. He was feeling restless, just the way he used to feel back in the days when being a cop was fun. The feeling scared him a little, because back in those days he'd done a lot of wild, crazy, exceedingly dangerous things.

Was he going to do something dangerous now?

Right on time, he saw a distant figure trudging across the sand toward him. It was Roger. He reached the boulder and leaned against it to shake the sand from his loafers. "You made it," Evan said.

"I made it." Roger glanced at him sharply. "Why? Did you think I wouldn't?"

Evan just shrugged.

Roger hoisted himself onto the boulder, not saying any more until he had a cigarette going. He exhaled slowly and watched the wave action for a moment. "So? You want to do this thing, Evan, or what?"

"I guess so, yeah. I want to do it."

Roger nodded. "Good. We get two million dollars and fuck Armani at the same time." He sounded pleased with both results.

Evan didn't bother to tell him that they were also going to

be sticking it to the damned feds. "Can I ask you a question?" he said.

"Sure. We're partners now, right? No secrets."

"Where'd a two-bit booster like you get the guts to cross somebody like Armani?"

"I don't know," Roger replied flatly. "Maybe I just got brave during my stretch inside. Once I got over being scared."

"How bad was it?" That was a question he had always wanted to ask somebody.

"You've never done time?"

Evan shook his head. It was, of course, the honest answer, but maybe not the truest one. There were all kinds of prisons.

"Try not to go," Roger said.

"I'll keep that in mind." Evan tossed the cigarette butt out over the sand. "Maybe it's about time you filled me in on this wonderful idea of yours."

"Okay." Roger leaned forward, took a deep breath, and started to talk.

It really wasn't all that wonderful, his grand scheme. Basically, his only notion was that they would go in and take the money. He seemed to dismiss almost casually things like guards and the plastic explosives they would need to get into the vault. Those were details, he said. What was important was the two million dollars. And screwing Armani.

Finished, finally, he reached for yet another cigarette. "Well?" he said, sounding pleased with himself. "Whaddaya think?"

"I think that there are a lot of blanks that need to be filled in," Evan said.

"But we can do it, right?"

Evan was quiet for several moments. Then he smiled. "Yeah," he said. "We can do it."

They went to a bar near the beach to celebrate the decision. This was a much different kind of place from the Pelican. It was the kind of place a couple of millionaires would go to. Evan ordered a bottle of very expensive brandy and they talked about a lot of things. Everything but how they were going to get away with Armani's money.

Roger talked about prison. He even talked about what had happened to him there, the rape, and as he was telling that story, he realized that Evan had the same kind of cold eyes as the con who had done it. The same icy look.

That made him a little nervous, but he pushed it aside. "Evan," he said when they were deep into the brandy, "how come you want to do this?"

Evan swirled the golden liquid in its crystal snifter. Then he looked up. "Because it's something to do," he said. "It's crazy and dangerous."

Roger thought that was a little weird, but he just nodded and reached for the bottle again.

Evan spent a lot of time studying the map of the warehouse that Roger had drawn for him. He also picked up the explosives they would need. The main thing that Roger had to do was just keep acting like nothing was happening. He was a little hyper, but Evan figured that he'd settle down once things started happening.

The day before they were set to go into action, Evan started to feel as if he probably ought to check in with Lenford. He went to a phone booth and called.

Lenford wouldn't even talk to him. The sergeant took the call. "Anything happening with Armani?" Evan asked.

"The lieutenant says that nothing has changed since he spoke to you. He says you know what the score is."

"And that's it?"

"You got a problem with that?" she replied.

Instead of answering, Evan hung up very carefully. To hell with them. This was his caper and the damned Department had nothing to do with it. Let them do or say whatever they wanted when it was all over.

Evan was excited.

The back door of the warehouse was unlocked, just as Roger had promised it would be. Evan slipped in silently and started up the dimly lit corridor. He was surprisingly calm. Crime was really not so difficult, once you got used to it.

The first so-called sentry was just a joke. An overweight asshole nearly asleep in a chair. Evan took him out with a solid blow to the back of his skull.

He reached a doorway and stopped, peering into the vast main room of the warehouse. Roger and four others were gathered around a table. The only sound was the soft slap of the cards as they played poker. Evan waited until the hand was over—Roger won the pot; maybe this was his lucky night—and then he stepped into the room, his gun raised. "It's a raid, boys," he said cheerfully.

Everybody but Roger looked real surprised.

One of them reached toward his pocket, and Evan turned the gun on him instantly. "No, no," he said.

Obviously Armani hired fools. The guy should have stopped; anybody would stop, right? But he didn't. Evan hadn't intended to shoot anybody. That kind of thing was really beyond the scope of his job description. But self-defense was allowed, so when a gun appeared in the fool's hand, Evan pulled the trigger on *his* gun. The idiot fell back and hit the floor with a thunk. Evan looked around the table. "Anybody else want to die a hero?"

Nobody moved. Except Roger, who proceeded to go around the table and disarm everybody else.

"You stupid jack-offs," one of them said. "You know who it is you're fucking with here?"

"We know," Roger said. "So shut up."

As Evan watched, he tied the three and taped their mouths closed, then shoved them into a closet. The door closed with a padlock. When that was all done, he stepped back and looked at Evan.

"Hard part's done," Evan said.

"Long as you don't blow us up," Roger pointed out.

"Trust me," Evan said.

They moved quickly, then went upstairs, and, with very little trouble, got into the office. Roger hummed softly as they worked. "You ever do this before?" he asked at one point.

Evan didn't think this was a very good time to tell him that he'd picked up his knowledge by spending a year on the bomb squad, so he didn't say anything.

The blast was louder than either of them had really expected, and Roger waited until his ears stopped ringing before he approached the vault and pulled the door open. "So that's what two million dollars looks like," he said.

Evan tossed him one of the duffels. "We better move."

They didn't talk anymore as they loaded the bags with stacks of bills, then left the warehouse.

Once in the car, Roger released his breath in a very long sigh. "We did it," he said. His voice held awe. "We fucking did it."

Evan just nodded and started the car.

* * *

The motel they stopped at was way out in the sticks. It seemed like a good place to hole up for a couple days, take stock of the situation, decide what to do next. Funny: Here they were, really rich men now, and the joint they were staying in was a dump.

Roger dumped all the money in the middle of one of the beds and started to count it. He kept saying that he couldn't fucking believe that it was actually over, that they had really fucking done it, that all of this money was fucking theirs.

Evan wasn't quite ready to start celebrating. He kept going to the window and peering out.

"Relax," Roger said finally. "We're away clean."

"Maybe." He bent for another look at the parking lot, and then he dropped the curtain as if it were burning. "Shit," he said. "Oh, shit."

Roger looked up. "What?"

"The fun's over, buddy boy."

A sick look crossed Roger's face. "Armani?"

"Nope. The fucking feds. They must have had the warehouse staked out." He shook his head. "Dammit, I should have thought of that. Christ."

"The feds? You serious?"

"Oh, yeah, I'm very serious, Rog."

"So we're fucked, is that what you're saying?"

"Pretty much." He was quiet for a moment. "You are, anyway."

"What?"

Instead of answering, Evan took out his wallet. Behind all the false ID and other shit was his official identification. Usually, of course, he didn't carry it, but tonight it had seemed like a good idea. "Sorry, Rog," he said. "I'm a cop."

Roger didn't say anything; his face went blank. Then his eyes flickered toward the gun lying on the bed next to the pile of cash.

Evan had his gun out. "Don't," he said softly. "Please don't."

Roger sighed and was smart.

Evan picked the gun up and walked over to the door, opening it slowly. One hand, holding the ID, waved in the air. "I'm a cop," he yelled.

Roger still hadn't said anything.

* * *

He couldn't understand why all of a sudden it felt so damned cold. The temperature had to be in the seventies, but Roger realized that he couldn't stop shivering. He sat on the bed, shaking, and watched everything that was going on around him with a strange kind of detachment. It was like watching a movie.

Maybe he'd been born under a freaking unlucky star or something. No normal person could have so much rotten luck. He actually pulls off the biggest damned job of a lifetime, then finds out he was partnered up with a cop.

Unbelievable.

He couldn't hear what was being said just outside the open door, but it seemed like there was some kind of a disagreement going on. Probably fighting about who, exactly, was going to get to haul his ass back inside. He started to get a real sick feeling in his gut.

Evan came back into the room but didn't say anything. He was carrying a pair of handcuffs, which he snapped on Roger expertly. Then he started shoving the money into the duffels again.

A uniformed patrolman joined him and tagged both the duffels. "You want us to run the perp and the evidence downtown?" he asked.

A man in a grey suit, probably a fed, came into the room and glared at Evan.

Evan shook his head. "It's my collar"—he glanced at the fed—"*my* fucking collar, and I'll do the honors."

"You might as well enjoy the moment, asshole," the fed said. "Because your ass is in a sling. You're finished."

"Uh-huh, sure."

"And you don't move without one of my men going with you."

"Fine." He finally looked directly at Roger. "Get up."

Roger did, and was pushed out of the room and across the parking lot. Evan put him into the front passenger seat. A disgruntled-looking fed climbed into the back. They pulled out of the lot with a squealing of brakes.

Roger studied Evan's profile for a block or so. "I trusted you," he said.

"Right," Evan said. "Well, I did warn you about getting sucked in by a pair of pretty eyes." Then he laughed.

Roger leaned his head against the window.

The fed in the backseat snorted.

After they had gone another few blocks, Evan turned off onto a deserted side street and parked. Roger watched him slip a gun from his jacket pocket. What the hell?

Evan turned and pointed the gun at the fed. "Take your clothes off," he said.

"What?" the man said dumbly.

"Take your clothes off. Everything."

"Are you crazy?"

"Maybe. If I am, you better do what I say, because a crazy man is liable to do anything. Even shoot you."

After an unbelieving pause, the fed started to unbutton his shirt. At each step of the undressing process, he would stop and look at Evan with increasing desperation.

Evan just kept staring at him.

At last the man was naked.

"Take your belt and put your ankles together tightly," Evan ordered.

A naked man didn't object much. He did it.

Evan got out of the car. He searched for and found the fed's handcuffs and used them on him. Next he stuffed a handkerchief into his mouth, tugged him out of the car, and rolled him down the small incline that ran along the street.

Then he got back into the car.

"What's going on?" Roger asked.

Instead of answering, Evan took a key from his pocket and unlocked the cuffs.

Roger rubbed his wrists nervously. "Hey, what's going on?" he said again.

Evan started the car. "What do you think about Mexico?"

Roger took a deep breath. "Mexico is okay, I guess," he said.

"Okay," Evan said. "We'll go to Mexico. You, me, and two fucking million American dollars. Unless you object to that idea?"

Roger shook his head. "I got absolutely no objections to that, Evan," he said, starting to grin.

"Good." After a moment, Evan looked at him. "One of these days," he said, "I'll even tell you what my real name is."

"Okay," Roger said cheerfully, not giving a damn.

Then they both started to laugh.

Chelsea Quinn Yarbro's work reflects her eclectic interests and her versatile talents. President of Horror Writers of America from 1988–1990, two-time Edgar nominee, former vice president of Mystery Writers of America, she has written forty-four mystery, science fiction, horror, and Western novels, including The Saint-Germain Chronicles *and* Floating Illusions. *Creator of the Charlie Moon Series (*Bad Medicine; Music When Sweet Voices Die*), she has also written numerous short stories and four books of nonfiction.*

In "Do I Dare to Eat a Peach?" (nominated for a World Fantasy Award), a man finds he can't swallow everything his captors tell him.

DO I DARE TO EAT A PEACH?

by Chelsea Quinn Yarbro

WEYBRIDGE HAD BEEN burgled: someone—some *thing*—had broken in and ransacked his memories, leaving all that was familiar in chaos. It was almost impossible for him to restore order, and so he was not entirely sure how much had been lost.

Malpass offered him sympathy. "Look, David, we know you went through a lot. We know that you'd like the chance to put it all behind you. We want you to have that, but there are a few more things we have to get cleared up. You understand how it is."

"Yes," Weybridge said vaguely, hoping that, by agreeing, he might learn more. "You have your . . . your . . ."

"Responsibilities," Malpass finished for him. "Truth to tell, there are times I wish I didn't have them." He patted David on the shoulder. "You're being great about this. I'll make sure it's in the report."

Weybridge wanted to ask what report it was, and for whom, but he could not bring himself to say the words. He simply nodded, as he had done so many times before. He opened his mouth, once, twice, then made a wave with one hand.

"We know how it is, old man," Malpass said as he scrutinized Weybridge. "They worked you over, David. We know that. We don't blame you for what you did after that."

Weybridge nodded a few more times, his mind on other things. He eventually stared up at the ceiling. He wanted to tell Malpass and the others that he would rather be left alone, simply turned out and ignored, but that wasn't possible. He had hinted at it once, when they had first started talking to him, and the reaction had been incredulity. So Weybridge resigned himself to the long, unproductive wait.

In the evening, when Malpass was gone, Stone took his place. Stone was younger than Malpass, and lacked that air of sympathy the older man appeared to possess. He would stand by the door, his arms folded, his hair perfectly in place, his jaw shaved to shininess, and he would favor Weybridge with a contemptuous stare. Usually he had a few taunting remarks to make before relapsing into his cold, staring silence. Tonight was no different. "They should have left you where they found you. A man like you—you don't deserve to be saved."

Weybridge sighed. It was useless, he knew from experience, to try to tell Stone that he had no memory of the time he was . . . wherever it was he had been. "Why?" he asked wearily, hoping that some word, some revelation, no matter how disgusting, would give him a sense of what he had done.

"You know why. Treating the dead that way. I saw the photos. Men like you aren't worth the trouble to bring back. They should leave you to rot, after what you did." He shook his head. "We're wasting our time with you. Men like you—"

"I know. We should be left alone." He stared up at the glare of the ceiling light. "I agree."

Stone made a barking sound that should have been a laugh but wasn't. "Oh, no. Don't go pious on me now, Weybridge. You're in for a few more questions before they throw you back in the pond. One of these days you're going to get tired of the lies, and you'll tell us what you were doing, and who made you do it."

Weybridge shook his head slowly. His thin, hospital-issue pajamas made him chilly at night, and he found himself shivering. That reminded him of something from the past, a time when he had been cold, trembling, for days on end. But where it had happened and why eluded him. He leaned back on the pillows and tried to make his mind a blank, but still the fragments, disjointed and terrifying, were with him. He huddled under the covers, burrowing his head into the stacked pillows as if seeking for refuge. He wanted to ask Stone to turn the lights down, but he knew the young man would refuse. There was something about nightmares, and screams, but whether they were his own or someone else's, he was not sure.

"You had any rest since you got here, Weybridge?" Stone taunted him. "I'm surprised that you even bother to try. You have no right to sleep."

"Maybe," Weybridge muttered, dragging the sheet around his shoulders. "Maybe you're wrong, though."

"Fat chance," Stone scoffed, and made a point of looking away from him. "Fat fucking chance."

Weybridge lay back on his bed, his eyes half focused on the acoustical tile of the ceiling. If he squinted, he thought he could discern a pattern other than the simple regularity of perforations. There might be a message in the ceiling. There might be a clue.

Stone stayed on duty, silent for most of his shift, but favoring Weybridge with an occasional sneer. He smoked his long, thin, dark cigarettes and dropped the ashes onto the floor. The only time he changed his attitude was when the nurse came in to give Weybridge yet another injection. Then he winked lasciviously and tried to pat her ass as she left the room.

"You shouldn't bother her," Weybridge said, his tongue unwieldy as wet flannel. "She . . . she doesn't want—"

"She doesn't want to have to deal with someone like you," Stone informed him.

Weybridge sighed. "I hope . . ." He stopped, knowing that he had left hope behind, back in the same place his memories were.

Malpass was back soon after Stone left, and he radiated his usual air of sympathy. "We've been going over your early reports, David, and so far, there's nothing . . . irregular about them. Whatever happened must have occurred in the last sixteen months. That's something, isn't it."

"Sure," Weybridge said, waiting for the orderly to bring him his breakfast.

"So we've narrowed down the time. That means we can concentrate on your work in that sixteen-month period, and perhaps get a lead on when you were . . ." He made a gesture of regret and reached out to pat Weybridge on the shoulder.

"When I was turned," Weybridge said harshly. "That's what you're looking for. You want to know how much damage I did before you got me back, don't you?"

"Of course that's a factor," Malpass allowed. "But there are other operatives who might be subjected to the same things that have happened to you. We do know that they were not all pharmacological. There were other aspects involved." He cleared his throat and looked toward the venetian blind that covered the window. It was almost closed, so that very little light from outside penetrated the room.

"That's interesting, I guess," Weybridge said, unable to think of anything else to say.

"It is," Malpass insisted with his unflagging good humor. "You took quite a risk in letting us bring you back. We're pretty sure the other side didn't want you to be . . . recovered."

"Good for me." Weybridge laced his hands behind his head. "And when you find out—*if* you find out—what then? What becomes of me once you dredge up the truth? Or doesn't that matter?"

"Of *course* it matters," Malpass said, his eyes flicking uneasily toward a spot on the wall. "We look after our own, David."

"But I'm not really your own anymore, am I?" He did not bother to look at Malpass, so that the other man would not have to work so hard to lie.

"Deep down, we know you are," Malpass hedged. "You're proving it right now, by your cooperation."

"Cooperation?" Weybridge burst out. "Is that what you think this is? I was dragged back here, tranked out of my mind and hustled from place to place in sealed vans like something smuggled through customs. No one asked me if I wanted to be here, or if I wanted you to unravel whatever is left of my mind. Cut the crap, Malpass. You want to get the last of the marrow before you throw the bones out." It was the most Weybridge had said at one time since his return, and it startled Malpass.

"David, I can understand why you're upset, especially considering all you've gone through. But believe me, I'm deeply interested in your welfare. I certainly wouldn't countenance any more abuse where you're concerned." He smiled, showing his very perfect, very expensive teeth. "Anyone who's been through what you've been through—"

"You don't know what it was. Neither do I," Weybridge reminded him.

"—would have every reason to be bitter. I don't blame you for that," Malpass went on as if nothing had been said. "You know that you have been—"

"No, I don't know!" Weybridge turned on him, half-rising in his bed. "I haven't any idea! That's the problem. I have scraps here and there, but nothing certain, and nothing that's entirely real. You call me David, and that might be my first name, but I don't remember it, and it doesn't sound familiar. For all I know, I'm not home at all, or this might not be my home. For all I know, I never got away from where I was, and this is just another part of the . . . the experiment."

Malpass did not answer at once. He paced the length of the room, then turned and came back toward the head of the bed. "I didn't know you were so troubled," he said finally, his eyes lowered as if in church. "I'll tell your doctors that you need extra care today."

"You mean more drugs," Weybridge sighed. "It might work. Who knows?"

"Listen, David," Malpass said with great sincerity, "we're relying on you in this. We can't get you straight again without your help, and that isn't always easy for you to give, I know."

Weybridge closed his eyes. He had a brief impression of a man in a uniform that he did not recognize, saying something in precisely that same tone of commiseration and concern that Malpass was using now. For some reason, the sound of it made him want to vomit, and his appetite disappeared.

"Is something wrong, David?" Malpass asked, his voice sounding as if he were a very long way off. "David?"

"It's nothing," he muttered, trying to get the other man to go away. "I . . . didn't sleep well."

"The lights?" Malpass guessed, then went on. "We've told you why they're necessary for the time being. Once your memory starts coming back, then you can have the lights off at night. It will be safe then."

"Will it?" Weybridge said. "If you say so."

Malpass assumed a look of long-suffering patience. "You're not being reasonable this morning, David."

"According to your reports, I don't have any reason, period." That much he believed, and wished that he did not. He longed for a sense of his own past, of a childhood and friends and family. What if I am an orphan, or the victim of abuse? he asked himself, and decided that he would rather have such painful memories than none at all.

"What's on your mind, David?" Malpass inquired, still very serious.

"Nothing," he insisted. There were more of the broken images shifting at the back of his mind, most of them senseless, and those that were coherent were terrifying. He had the impression of a man—himself?—kneeling beside a shattered body, pausing to cut off the ears and nose of the corpse. Had he done that? Had he seen someone do that? Had he been told about it? He couldn't be sure, and that was the most frightening thing of all.

"Tell me about it," Malpass offered. "Let me help you, David."

It was all he could do to keep from yelling that his name was not David. But if it was not, what was it? What could he tell them to take the place of David?

"You look terrible. What is it?" Malpass bent over him, his middle-aged features creased with anxiety. "Is there anything you can tell me?"

Weybridge struck out with his arm, narrowly missing Malpass. "Leave me alone!"

"All right. All right." Malpass stepped back, holding up his hand placatingly. "You need rest, David. I'll see that you get it. I'll send someone in to you."

"No!" Weybridge shouted. He did not want any more drugs. There had been too much in his bloodstream already. He had the impression that there had been a time when his veins had been hooked up to tubes, and through the tubes, all sorts of things had run into his body. He thought that he must have been wounded, or . . . A light truck overturned and burst into flame as a few men crawled away from it. Had he been one of the men? Where had the accident occurred? He put his hands to his head and pressed, as if that might force his mind to squeeze out the things he needed to know.

Malpass had retreated to the door and was signaling someone in the hallway. "Just a little while, David. You hang on," he urged Weybridge. "We'll take care of you."

Weybridge pulled one of his pillows over his face in an attempt to blot out what was left there. Gouts of flame, shouts and cries in the night. Bodies riven with bullets. Where were they? *Who* were they? Why did Weybridge remember them, if he did remember them?

Another nurse, this one older and more massive, came barreling through the door, a steel tray in her hand. "You calm down there," she ordered Weybridge so abruptly that his fear grew sharper.

There was a chill on his arm, and a prick that warmed him, and shortly suffused through him, turning his world from hard-edged to soft, and making his memories—what there were of them—as entrancing as the boardwalk attractions of loop-the-loop and the carousel.

Later that day, when Weybridge babbled himself half awake, they brought him food, and did what they could to coax him to eat it.

"You're very thin, Mr. Weybridge," the head nurse said in a tone that was more appropriate for an eight-year-old than a man in his late thirties.

"I'm hungry," Weybridge protested. "I *am*. But . . ." He stared at the plate and had to swallow hard against the bile at the back of his throat. "I don't know what's the matter."

"Sometimes drugs will do this," the head nurse said, disapproval in her tone and posture.

"You're the ones keeping me on drugs," he reminded her nastily. "You don't know what—"

The head nurse paid no attention to him. She continued to bustle about the room, playing at putting things in order. "Now, we're not to lie in bed all day. Doctor says that we can get up this afternoon for a while, and walk a bit."

"Oh, can *we*?" Weybridge asked with spite. "What else can *we* do?"

"Mr. Weybridge," the head nurse reproached him. "We're simply trying to help you. If you just lie there, then there's very little we can do. You can see that, can't you?"

"What happened to the *we* all of a sudden?" he wanted to argue with her, but lacked the energy. It was so useless that he almost wished he could laugh.

"That's better; you'll improve as long as you keep your sense of humor." She came back to the foot of his bed and patted his foot through the thin blankets. "That's the first step, a sense of humor."

"Sure." How hopeless it seemed, and he could not find out why.

By the time Malpass came back, Weybridge had enough control of himself that he was able to take the man's kind solicitations without becoming angry with him.

"You're going to get better, David," Malpass promised. "We'll be able to debrief you and then you can get away from all this. If you cooperate, we'll make sure you'll have all the protections you'll need."

"Why would I need protections?" And what kind of protections? he added to himself.

Malpass hesitated, plainly weighing his answer. "We don't yet know just how much you did while you were with the other side. There are probably men who would like to eliminate you, men from their side as well as ours. If we put you under our protection, then your chances of survival increase, don't you see that?" He stared toward the window. "It would be easier if we could be certain that you're not . . . programmed for anything, but so far, we can't tell what is real memory and what is . . . random."

"That's a nice word for it: random." Weybridge leaned back against the pillows and tried to appear calm. "Do you have any better idea of what happened?"

"You were in prison for a while, or you believe you were in prison, in a very dark cell, apparently with someone, but there's no way to tell who that person was, or if it's your imagination that there was someone there." He coughed. "And we can't be sure that you were in prison at all."

Weybridge sighed.

"You have to understand, David, that when there are such states as yours, we . . . well, we simply have to . . . to sort out so much that sometimes it—"

"—it's impossible," Weybridge finished for him. "Which means that I could be here for the rest of my life. Doesn't it?"

Malpass shrugged. "It's too early to be thinking about that possibility."

"But it *is* a possibility," Weybridge persisted.

"Well, it's remote, but . . . well." He cleared his throat. "When we have a more complete evaluation, we'll talk about it again."

"And in the meantime?"

"Oh," Malpass said with patently false optimism, "we'll continue to carry on the treatment. Speaking of treatment," he went on, deftly avoiding more questions, "I understand you're going to be allowed to walk today. They want you to work up an appetite, and you need the exercise in any case."

"The head nurse said something about that," Weybridge responded in a dampening way.

"Excellent. *Ex*cellent! We'll tell headquarters that you're improving. That will please the Old Man. You know what he can be like when there's trouble with an operative in the field." He rubbed his hands together and looked at Weybridge expectantly.

"No, I don't know anything about the Old Man. I don't know anything about headquarters. I don't recall being an operative. That's what I'm being treated for, remember?" He smashed his left arm against the bed for emphasis, but it made very little sound and most of the impact was absorbed by the softness.

"Calm down, calm down, David," Malpass urged, once again speaking as if to an invalid. "I forgot myself, that's all. Don't let it trouble you, please."

"Why not?" Weybridge demanded suspiciously. "Wouldn't it trouble you if you couldn't remember who you were or what you'd done?"

"Of *course* it would," Malpass said, even more soothingly. "And I'd want to get to the bottom of it as soon as possible."

"And you think I don't?" Weybridge asked, his voice rising.

"David, David, you're overreacting. I didn't mean to imply that you aren't doing everything you can to . . . recover. You're exhausted, that's part of it." He reached out to pat Weybridge's shoulder. "I hear you still aren't eating."

The surge of nausea was so sudden that Weybridge bent violently against it. "No," he panted when he felt it was safe to open his mouth.

"The nurses are worried about you. They can give you more IVs, but they all think you'd do better if you . . ." He smiled, making an effort to encourage Weybridge.

"I . . . can't," Weybridge said thickly, trying not to think of food at all.

"Why?" Malpass asked, sharpness in his tone now. "Can't you tell me why?"

Weybridge shook his head, bewildered. "I don't know. I wish I did." Really? he asked himself. Do you really want to know what it is about food that horrifies you so? Or would you rather remain ignorant? That would be better, perhaps.

"You've got to eat sometime, David," Malpass insisted.

"Not yet," Weybridge said with desperation. "I need time."

"All right," Malpass allowed. "We'll schedule the IV for three more days. But I want you to consent to a few more hours of therapy every day, all right?" He did not wait for an answer. "You have to get to the bottom of this, David. You can't go on this way forever, can you?"

"I suppose not," Weybridge said, fighting an irrational desire to crawl under the bed and huddle there. Where had he done that before? He couldn't remember.

"I'll set it up." Malpass started toward the door. "The Old Man is anxious to find out what happened to you. We have other men who could be in danger."

"I understand," Weybridge said, not entirely certain that he did. What if he was not an agent at all? What if that was a part of his manufactured memories? Or what if he was still in the hands of the other side—what then? The headache that had been lurking at the back of his eyes came around to the front of his head with ferocious intensity.

"We're all watching you, David," Malpass assured him as he let himself out of the white-painted room.

Stone regarded Weybridge with scorn when he heard about the increased therapy sessions. "Taking the easy way, aren't you, you bastard?" He lit a cigarette and glowered at Weybridge.

"It doesn't feel easy to me," Weybridge replied, hoping that he did not sound as cowardly as he feared he did.

"That's a crock of warm piss," Stone declared, folding his arms and directing his gaze at the window. "Anyone does what you did, there's no reason to coddle them."

It was so tempting to beg Stone to tell him what it was he was supposed to have done, but Weybridge could not bring himself to demean himself to that hostile man. "I'm not being coddled."

"According to who?" Stone scoffed, then refused to speak again, blowing smoke toward the ceiling while Weybridge dozed between unrecallable nightmares.

The therapist was a small, olive-skinned gnome named

Cleeve. He visited Weybridge just as the head nurse was trying to coax him out of bed to do his required walking. "Out for your constitutional, eh, Mr. Weybridge?" His eyes were dark and glossy, like fur or crushed velvet.

"We're going to walk twice around the nurses' station," the head nurse answered for him. "It's doctor's orders."

Weybridge teetered on his feet, feeling like a kid on stilts for the first time. Dear God, had he ever walked on stilts? He did not know. The effort of a few steps made him light-headed, and he reached out for Cleeve's shoulder to steady himself. "Sorry," he muttered as he tried to get his balance.

"Think nothing of it, Mr. Weybridge," Cleeve told him in a cordial tone. "All part of the service, I give you my word." He peered up at Weybridge, his features glowing with curiosity. "They've had you on drugs?"

"You know they have," Weybridge said a little wildly. His pulse was starting to hammer in his neck.

Cleeve nodded several times. "It might be as well to take you off some of them. So many drugs can be disorienting, can't they?" He stared at the head nurse. "Who should I speak to about Mr. Weybridge's drugs? I need to know before we start therapy, and perhaps we should arrange a . . . new approach."

The head nurse favored Cleeve with an irritated glance. "You'd have to talk to Mr. Malpass about that."

"Ay, yes, the ubiquitous Mr. Malpass," Cleeve said with relish. "I will do that at once."

Weybridge was concentrating on staying erect as he shuffled first one foot forward, and then the other. His nerves jangled with every move and his feet were as sore as if he were walking on heated gravel. "I don't think I can—"

Both the head nurse and Cleeve turned to Weybridge at once. "Now, don't get discouraged," the head nurse said, smiling triumphantly that she had been able to speak first. "You can take hold of my arm if you think you're going to fall."

Weybridge put all his attention on walking and managed a few more steps; then vertigo overwhelmed him and he collapsed suddenly, mewing as he fell.

"I'll help you up, Mr. Weybridge," Cleeve said, bending down with care. "You appear to be very weak."

"Yes, I suppose I am," Weybridge responded vaguely. He could not rid himself of the conviction that he had to get to cover, that he was too exposed, that there were enemies all

around him who would tear him to pieces if he did not find
cover. Who were the enemies? What was he remembering?

Cleeve took Weybridge by the elbow and started to lever him
into a sitting position, but was stopped by the head nurse.
"Now, we don't want to indulge ourselves, do we? It would
be better if we stood up on our own."

"That's a little unrealistic," Cleeve protested. "Look at him,
woman—he's half starved and spaced out on the chemicals
you've been pouring into him."

Hearing this, Weybridge huddled against the wall, arms and
knees gathered tightly against his chest. He did not want to
think about what had gone into him. The very idea made him
cringe. He swallowed hard twice and fanned his hands to cover
his eyes.

"They're necessary," the head nurse said brusquely. "Until
we know what's happened to this man . . ."

Cleeve shook his head. "You mustn't mistake his condition
for the refusal of an enemy. From what I have been told, this
man is one of our operatives, yet everyone is behaving as if he
were a spy or a traitor." He steadied Weybridge with his arm.
"When it's certain that he's been turned, then we can do what
must be done, but not yet."

The head nurse folded her arms, all of her good humor and
condescension gone. "I have my orders."

"And so do I," Cleeve said mildly. "Mr. Weybridge, I'm
going to help you back to bed, and then I want to arrange to
have a little interview with you. Do you understand what I'm
saying?"

It was an effort to nod, but Weybridge managed it; his head
wobbled on the end of his neck. "I want . . . to talk to . . .
someone." He coughed and felt himself tremble for the
strength it cost him.

"Good. I'll return in an hour or so. Be patient." Cleeve
gave a signal to the head nurse. "Get him back into bed and
arrange for an IV. I don't think he's going to be able to eat
yet."

The head nurse glared at Cleeve. "You'll take responsibility
for him, then? I warn you, I won't be left covering for you if
you're wrong."

What were they arguing about? Weybridge asked himself as
he listened to them wrangle. What was there to be responsible
for? What had he done? Why wouldn't anyone tell him what

he was supposed to have done? He lifted one listless hand. "Please . . ."

Neither Cleeve nor the head nurse paid him any heed. "You'll have to tell Malpass what you're doing. He might not approve."

Cleeve smiled benignly. "I intend to. As I intend to ask for permission to remove Mr. Weybridge from this wing of the hospital. I think we can do more with him in my ward." He turned toward Weybridge. "Don't worry. We'll sort everything out."

"What . . . ?" Weybridge asked, frowning. He felt very tired, and his body ached in every joint. He supposed he was suffering from malnutrition, but there was more to it than that. Even as the questions rose again, his mind shied away from them. There was so much he could not understand, and no one wished to explain it to him. He pulled himself back onto the bed, pressing his face into the pillow, and nearly gagging on the carrion smell that rose in his nostrils. He retched, gasping for air.

"That's enough of that," the head nurse said with unpleasant satisfaction. "When Mr. Malpass takes me off this case, I'll stop giving him drugs, but for the time being, it's sedation as usual. Or do you want to argue about it, Mr. Cleeve?"

Weybridge was sprawled on the bed, his face clammy and his pulse very rapid. His face was gaunt, his body skeletal. He was like something from deep underwater dragged up into the light of day. "I . . . I . . ."

Cleeve sighed. "I'm not going to oppose you, Nurse. Not yet. Once I talk to Mr. Malpass, however—"

The head nurse tossed her head. "We'll see when that happens. Now you leave this patient to me." She gave her attention to Weybridge. "We're too worn out, aren't we?"

Weybridge hated the way she spoke to him but had not strength enough to protest. He waited for the prick in his arm and the warm bliss that came with it. There was that brief respite, between waking and stupor, when he felt all the unknown burdens lifted from his shoulders. That never lasted long—once again, Weybridge felt himself caught in a morass of anguish he did not comprehend.

The walls were thick, slimy stone, and they stank of urine and rats. His own body was filthy and scabbed, his teeth rattled in his head and his hair was falling out. He shambled through the little space, maddened by fear and boredom. Someone else cowered in the darkness, another prisoner—was he a prisoner?—whose?—why?—or someone sent to torment him. He squinted in an effort to see who it was, but it was not possible to penetrate the shadows. He thrashed on his clean, white bed, believing himself in that dreadful cell—if he had been there at all.

Malpass was standing over Weybridge when he woke with a shout. "Something, David? Are you remembering?"

"I . . ." Weybridge shook his head weakly, trying to recapture the images of his dreams, but they eluded him. "You . . ." He had seen Malpass' face in the dream, or a face that was similar. He had no idea if the memory was valid, or the dream.

"We're having a little meeting about you this morning, David," Malpass said heartily. "We're reviewing your case. The Old Man is coming to hear what we have to say."

Weybridge could think of nothing to say. He moved his head up and down, hoping Malpass would go on.

"Cleeve wants you over in his division. He thinks he can get at the truth faster with those suspension tanks of his and the cold wraps. We'd rather keep you here on drugs, at least until you begin to . . . clarify your thoughts. However, it will be up to the Old Man to decide." He gave Weybridge's shoulder another one of his amiable pats. "We'll keep you posted. Don't worry about that. You concentrate on getting your memory in working order."

There was a fleeting impression of another such promise, from another man—or was it Malpass?—that winked and was gone, leaving Weybridge more disoriented than before. Who was the man he had seen, or thought he had seen? What had he done? Or was it simply more of the confusion that he suffered? "How soon will you know?"

"Soon," Malpass said, smiling. "Today, tomorrow. They're going to put you on IV for a while this morning. This evening, they want you to try eating again."

"I can't," Weybridge said at once. "No food." He was sick with hunger; he could not endure the thought of food. "I can't."

"The head nurse will look after you," Malpass went on, blithe as a kindergarten teacher. "We're going to take Stone off for this evening, and Cleeve will stay with you. He wants a chance to talk to you, to study your reactions.''

"Cleeve?'' Weybridge repeated.

"He saw you yesterday,'' Malpass reminded him sympathetically, his face creasing into a mask of good-hearted concern. "You remember speaking with Cleeve, don't you?''

"Yes,'' Weybridge said, ready to weep with vexation. "I haven't forgotten. It's the other things that are gone.''

"Well, possibly,'' Malpass allowed. "You don't seem to recall coming here. Or have you?''

"I . . .'' Had there been an ambulance? A plane? He was pretty sure he had been in a plane, but was it coming here, or had there been a plane earlier, before he had done—whatever it was he had done? Had he flown then? He was certain that he could recall looking down from a great height—that was something. He tried to pursue the image without success.

"Don't work so hard, you only make it more difficult,'' Malpass admonished him. "You don't need that extra stress right now. If you get frustrated, you won't be able to think clearly about your treatment and getting better.''

"I don't think clearly in any case, frustrated or not,'' Weybridge said with great bitterness.

"We're trying to do something about that, aren't we?'' Malpass said, smiling once again. "You're in the best hands, you're getting the finest care. In time, it will come back. You can be sure of that.''

"Can I? And what if it doesn't?'' Weybridge demanded.

"David, David, you mustn't think this way. You'll straighten it all out, one way or another,'' Malpass said, moving away from Weybridge. "I'll drop in later, to see how you're doing. Don't let yourself get depressed, if you can help it. We're all pulling for you.'' With a wave, he was gone, and Weybridge longed for a door he could close, to keep them all out.

There was a new nurse that afternoon, a woman in her midthirties, not too attractive but not too plain, who regarded him with curiosity. She took his temperature, blood pressure and pulse, then offered to give him a sponge bath.

"I'll take a shower, later,'' he lied. He did not like the feeling of water on his skin, though why this should be, he was unable to say. He knew he was a fastidious person and the smell of his unwashed skin was faintly repulsive.

"It might be better if you let me do this for you,'' she said unflappably. "As long as you're hooked up to that IV, you should really keep your arm out of water. It won't take long. And I can give you a massage afterward." She sounded efficient and impersonal, but Weybridge could not bear the thought of her touching him.

"No, thanks," he said, breathing a little faster. What was making him panic?

"Let me give it a try. Dr. Cleeve suggested that we give it a try. What do you think? Can we do your feet? If that's not too bad, we'll try the legs. That's reasonable, isn't it?"

Both of them knew it was, and so he nodded, feeling sweat on his body. "Go slow," he warned her, dreading what she would do. "If I . . ."

She paid no attention to him. "I realize that you're not used to having a women bathe you, but after all, your mother did, and this isn't much different, is it?" She had gone into the bathroom while speaking and was running water into a large, square, stainless-steel bowl. "I'll make it warm but not hot. And I'll use the unscented soap. I've got a real sponge, by the way, and you'll like it. Think about what it can be like with a big, soft sponge and warm water."

The very mention of it made him queasy, but he swallowed hard against the sensation. "Fine," he panted.

The nurse continued to get the water ready for him. "You might not think that you'll like it at first, but you will. I've done work with other . . . troubled patients and in this case, you're easy to deal with. You don't make any unreasonable demands or behave badly." She was coming back to him now, carrying the pan of soapy water. "It won't be so hard. I promise." She flipped back his covers, nodding at his scrawny legs. "Feet first, okay?"

He did not trust himself to answer her; he gestured his resignation.

"Left foot first. That's like marching, isn't it?" She laughed as she reached out, taking his ankle in her hand. "The water is warm, just as I said it would be." She lifted the sponge—it was a real sponge, not one of the plastic ones—and dribbled the water over his foot.

Weybridge shrieked as if he had been scalded, and jerked away from her. "No!"

"What's wrong?" she asked, remaining calm.

"I . . . I can't take it. I don't know why, but I can't." He felt his heart pounding against his ribs as he gasped for air. "I can't," he repeated.

"It's just water, Mr. Weybridge," the nurse pointed out. "With a little soap in it."

"I know," he said, trying to sound as reasonable as possible. "But I can't."

"The way you can't eat, either?" she asked, curious and concerned. "What is it about water? Or food, for that matter?"

"I wish I knew," he sighed, feeling his heartbeat return to a steady, barely discerned thumping.

"Can't you figure it out?" She moved the pan of bathwater aside. "Can you tell me anything about it, Mr. Weybridge?"

He shook his head. "I wish I could. I wish I could tell someone what it was. I might be able to get rid of it if I knew what it was." His eyes filled with tears as he turned away from her in shame.

"Why would food and water do this to you?" she mused, not addressing him directly, yet encouraging him.

"There was . . . something that happened. I don't . . . remember, but it's there. I know that it's there." He brought his hands to his face so that he would not have to let her see his expression. He had a quick vision—perhaps not quite a vision, but an image—of a man with a large knife peeling the skin off someone's—his?—foot, grinning at the screams and maddened profanities his victim hurled at him. Weybridge's skin crawled, and after a short time, he pulled his foot out of the nurse's hand. "I can't," he whispered. "I'm sorry. It's not you. I just can't."

"But . . ." she began, then nodded. "All right, Mr. Weybridge. Maybe we can take care of it another time. It would be sensible to tend to this, don't you think?"

"Sure," he said, relieved that he had postponed the ordeal for a little while.

"What's the matter, though? Can you tell me?" Her expression was curious, without the morbid fascination he had seen in the eyes of Malpass and Cleeve.

"I wish I could. I wish I knew what was happening to me. I wish I . . . I wish it was over, all over." He clasped his hands together as if in desperate prayer. "I've tried and tried and tried to figure it out. I have what are probably memories of doing something terrible, something so ghastly that I don't want to think about it, ever. But I don't know what it was, really, or if it ever really happened, or if it did, if it happened to me. There are times I'm sure it was someone else and that I've merely . . . eavesdropped on it. And other times, I *know* I did it, whatever it is, and . . . there are only bits and pieces left in my mind, but they're enough." It was strangely comforting to say these things to her. "I've heard that murderers want to confess, most of them. I'm willing to confess anything, just to know for sure what happened, and maybe, why."

The nurse looked at him, not critically but with deep compassion. "They're speculating on what's real and what isn't: the doctors and the . . . others here. Some of them think you've blocked out your trauma, and others believe that you're the victim of an induced psychosis. What do you think?"

"I don't know what to think. It's driving me crazy, not knowing." He said this quite calmly, and for that reason, if no other, was all the more convincing.

"Do you want to talk about it—I mean, do you want me to stick around for a while and try to sort out what went on when you were—" She stopped herself suddenly and her face flushed.

"Are you under orders?" Weybridge asked. "Are you doing this because they told you to?"

"Partly," she said after a moment. "I shouldn't tell you anything, but . . . they're all using you, and it troubles me. I want to think that you're doing your best to get to the bottom of your . . . your lapses. I don't like the way that Malpass keeps glad-handing you, or the way Cleeve treats you like a lab animal." She had taken hold of the thin cotton spread and now was twisting the fabric, almost unconsciously.

"Are they doing that?" Weybridge asked, not really surprised to learn it.

"They are," she said.

Weybridge nodded slowly, wondering if this kind nurse was just another ploy on Malpass' or Cleeve's part to try to delve into his missing past. He wavered between resentment and hope, and finally said, "Which of you is supposed to be Rasputin and which is supposed to be the saint? That's the usual way, isn't it? One of you convinces the poor slob you're interrogating that you're on his side and the other one is the bad guy, and by pretending to be the guy's friend, you get him to open up." He slammed his fists down onto the bed, secretly horrified at how little strength he had. "Well, I wish I could open up, to any of you. I wish I could say everything, but I can't. Don't you understand that, any of you? I can't. I don't remember.'' There were only those repugnant, terrifying flashes that came into his mind, never for very long, never with any explanation, but always there, always genuine, and always leaving him so enervated and repelled that he wanted to be sick, and undoubtedly would have been, had he anything left in his stomach to give up. ''God, I don't even know for certain that we're all on the same side.''

''Of course we are, David,'' the nurse protested.

''You'd say that, no matter what,'' Weybridge muttered. ''You'd claim to be my friend, you'd make me want to confide in you, and all the time it would be a setup, and you'd be bleeding me dry, getting ready to put me on the dust heap when you're through with me. Or maybe you want to turn me, or maybe I turned, and you're with my old side, trying to find out how much I revealed to the others. Or maybe you think I was turned, and you're trying to find out.''

''What makes you think you were active in espionage?'' the nurse said to him. ''You're talking like someone who has been an operative. Were you?''

''How the hell do I know?'' Weybridge shot back. ''Everyone here acts as if I was some kind of spy or intelligence agent or something like that. I've been assuming that I was.''

''Suppose you weren't?'' She stared at him. ''Suppose it was something else entirely.''

''Like what?'' Weybridge demanded.

The door opened and Malpass stepped into the room. ''Hello, David. How's it going?''

The nurse gave Malpass a quick, guilty look. ''I was trying to give Mr. Weybridge a massage,'' she said.

''I see,'' Malpass said with sinister cordiality. ''What kind of luck are you having?''

''It seems to bother him, so . . .'' She got off the bed and smoothed the covers over his feet.

''Well.'' Malpass shook his head. ''Tomorrow might be better. There are several things we're going to try to get done this evening, and it would be better if you had a little nap first, David.'' He motioned to the nurse to leave and watched her until she was out of the room. ''Did she bother you, David?''

''She was nice to talk to,'' Weybridge said in a neutral tone, suddenly anxious to keep the nurse out of trouble. Whatever she was, she was the only person he had met who had been genuinely—or appeared to be genuinely—interested in him as a person.

"That's good to know. It's fine that you're talking to someone," Malpass said, smiling more broadly than before.

"You'll make sure she doesn't get in trouble for talking to me, won't you?"

Malpass' eyebrows rose. "Why, David, what makes you think that she'd be in trouble for a thing like that?"

Weybridge frowned. "I don't know. You're all so . . . secretive, and . . . odd about what you want out of me."

"David, David," Malpass said, shaking his head. "You're letting your imagination run away with you. Why would we want to do such a thing to you? You're sounding like you regard us as your jailers, not your doctors. We want you to improve. No one wants that more than we do. But can't you see—your attitude is making everyone's job more difficult, including your own. You're letting your dreams and fears take over, and that causes all sorts of problems for us. If I could find a way to convince you that you're creating chimeras . . ."

"You'd what?" Weybridge asked when Malpass did not go on.

Malpass made a dismissing gesture. "I'd be delighted, for one thing. We all would be." He cocked his head to the side. "You believe me, don't you?"

Weybridge shrugged. "Should I?"

"Of course you should," Malpass assured him. "God, David, you'd think you were being held in prison, the way you're responding. That's not the case at all. You know it's not."

"Do I?"

"Well, think about it, man," Malpass said expansively. "You're being taken care of as thoroughly as we're able. We want you to get better, to get well and be independent. I think everyone here is pulling for you, and . . . well, David, they are all very concerned for you. Everyone hopes that you'll be over this . . . problem soon." He gave Weybridge his most sincere look. "You're a very special case, and we all want to see you get well, entirely well."

"Uh-huh," Weybridge said, looking away from Malpass. "And what will happen to me when I get well? Where will I go?"

"Back home, I would guess," Malpass said, trying to give this assertion an enthusiastic ring.

"Back home," Weybridge echoed. Where was that? What was his home like? "Where do . . . did I live?"

"You mean, you don't remember?" Malpass asked, apparently shocked by this question.

"Not really. I wouldn't be asking if I did," he said testily. "And don't coddle me with your answers. That won't help me at all." He folded his arms, taking care not to press on the IV needle taped just below his elbow.

"Well, you live in a small city about . . . oh, eight hundred miles from here. It's on a river. The countryside is rolling hills. The city has a very large textile industry, and most of the agricultural land in the immediate area is devoted to sheep ranching. There's also a good-sized university. You were an assistant professor there for four years. Do you remember any of this?" Malpass asked. "You're frowning."

Weybridge tried to recall such a place and found nothing in his mind that had anything to do with a small city near a river, or a university. "What did I teach?"

"Physics," was Malpass' swift answer. "Astrophysics. You were lured into the private sector to help develop hardware for space exploration. You were considered to be very good at your work."

"Then, how in hell did I end up here?" Weybridge demanded, his voice shrill with desperation.

"That's what we'd all like to know," Malpass said, doing his best to sound comforting. "Your . . . affliction is a real challenge to us all."

"When did I become an intelligence agent, if I was teaching and then doing space research in industry? What was the name of the university where I taught? What city did I live in? What company did I go to work for? Who was my boss?"

"Whoah there, David," Malpass said, reaching out and placing his thick hand on Weybridge's shoulder. "One thing at a time. First, the Old Man has decided that, for the time being, we're not going to give you too many names. It would be distracting, and you might use the information to create . . . false memories for yourself based on the names instead of your recollections. You can see the sense in that, surely."

"I suppose so," Weybridge said sullenly. "But what the fuck does that leave me?"

"In time, we hope it will restore your memories. We want that to happen, all of us." He gripped a little tighter, giving

Weybridge's shoulder a comradely shake, doing his best to buck his charge up. "When you can name your university, the head of your department, then we'll know we're getting somewhere."

"Why did I become an agent? Or did I?" He had not intended to ask this aloud, but the words were out before he could stop them. "Is this some kind of ruse?"

"Of course not," Malpass declared.

"You'd say that whether it was or not," Weybridge sighed. "And there's not any way I can prove the contrary." He lowered his head. "The bodies. Where were they? Whose were they?"

"What bodies, David?" Malpass asked, becoming even more solicitous.

"The ones I see in my dreams. The ones with . . . pieces missing. There are some in cells and some in . . . trenches, I guess. It's . . . not very clear." He felt the sweat on his body, and smelled his fear.

"Can you tell me more about them?" Malpass urged. "What do you remember?"

Hands on the ground, just hands, with palms mutilated; a torso with the striations of ropes still crossing the chest; a child's body, three days dead and bloated; scraps of skin the color of clay sticking to rusty chains; a man on a wet stone floor, his back and buttocks crosshatched with blood-crusted weals; a woman, hideously mutilated and abused, lying on her side, legs pulled up against her chest, waiting for death: the impressions fled as quickly as they came. "Not very much," Weybridge answered, blinking as if to banish what he had seen.

"Tell me," Malpass insisted. "You've got to tell me, David. The Old Man has been asking about your ordeal, and if I can give him something—anything—he might decide to . . ." He did not go on.

"To what?" Weybridge asked. "Or can't you tell me that, either?"

"I . . . haven't been given permission," Malpass said in an under voice. "I'll need to get it if I'm going to explain what it is the Old Man needs to know."

This was the first time Weybridge had ever seen Malpass display an emotion akin to fear, and in spite of himself, he was curious. "Why should the Old Man care what I remember? He has me where he wants me, doesn't he?"

"Well, sure, but we don't want you to have to remain here indefinitely," Malpass said uneasily, attempting to make a recovery. "We're all . . . doing our best for you."

Weybridge shook his head. "That's not enough, Malpass. You're holding back too much. I don't want to say anything more until you're a little more forthcoming with me." It was exciting to defy Malpass, so Weybridge added, "I want the lights out at night. I need sleep."

"I'll see if it can be arranged," Malpass hedged, moving away from the bed, where Weybridge sat. "I'll let you know what we decide."

What had he said? Weybridge wondered. What had caused the change in the affable Mr. Malpass? He could not find the answer, though it was obvious that something he had triggered disturbed the man profoundly. "Is there something you'd like to tell me, Malpass? You seem distraught."

"I'm . . . fine, David. You're probably tired. I'll let you have a little time to yourself, before they bring you your supper."

Was it Weybridge's imagination, or was there a trace of malice in Malpass' tone of voice? He watched Malpass retreat to the door and hover there, his hand on the latch. "What is it?"

"Nothing," Malpass said fervently.

"I'm interested in what it is the Old Man wants to know. Find out if you can tell me. Maybe we can all work together if you're not so secretive with me." He was almost light-headed with satisfaction as he saw the door close behind Malpass.

The afternoon hours dragged by; Weybridge remained in solitude, the IV unit by his bed his only company. He would have liked to have something to read, but this had been refused when he asked the first time, and Weybridge had not renewed his request. He lay back against the skimpy pillows and stared up at the ceiling, trying to make patterns and pictures of the play of light and shadow there.

About sunset, Dr. Cleeve entered the room, his pursed mouth giving him the look of an overstuffed bag with a hole in it. "I see you are alone," he said.

"Is that unusual?" Weybridge asked angrily. "Did you think someone else would be here?"

"Under the circumstances, yes, I did," Dr. Cleeve said with great meaning. "The Old Man isn't satisfied with your progress. He's about ready to give up on you, and so is Malpass."

"Give up on me? How? Why?" In spite of himself, he felt worried by this announcement.

"You're not telling them what they want to know, what they need to know. They think you've been turned and that you're simply playing with them to gain your new masters some time."

"That's not true!" Weybridge protested, trying to get to his feet. "It's not possible! I don't know what I did, I don't know why I'm here, I don't even know who you are, or who I am. What do I have to do to make you believe that?" His pulse throbbed in his head and his eyes ached. There were the images, the memories of so much horror that he could not bear to look at them directly, but that proved it—didn't it?—that he was not deceiving them.

"Mr. Weybridge," Dr. Cleeve soothed. "You're overwrought. I can understand how that would be, but clearly you can see that you are not on very firm ground." He reached over and patted Weybridge's arm, just below the place where the IV needles were taped. "I see that your veins are holding up fairly well. That's something. A man in your condition should be glad that we do not yet have to cut down for a vein."

"It . . ." There was a fleeting vision of arms and legs, tattered remnants of bodies floating on a sluggish current, catching against river reeds, piling up, then drifting on.

"What is it, Mr. Weybridge?" Dr. Cleeve asked intently. "What is happening to you now?"

Weybridge shook his head. "I . . . it's gone now. It's nothing." He felt the sweat on his forehead and his ribs, and he could smell it, hating the odor for its human aliveness.

"Mr. Weybridge," Dr. Cleeve said, folding his arms and regarding Weybridge through his thick glasses, "are you willing to let me try an . . . experiment?"

"How do you mean, 'an experiment'?" Weybridge asked, suspicious in the depths of his desperation.

"There are ways that we can . . . accelerate your mind. We could find out what has truly happened to you, and what you have done. The danger is that if you have been turned, we will know about it, unquestionably, and you will have to face the consequences of your act, but the waiting would certainly be over." He studied Weybridge with increasing interest. "It would not be difficult to do, simply a bit more risky than what we have been doing up till now."

"And what is the risk?" Weybridge asked, wishing he knew more about Dr. Cleeve—any of them—so that he could judge why the man had made this offer.

"Well, if the suppressed memories are traumatic enough, you could become psychotic." He spread his hands wide in mute appeal. "You could still become psychotic just going on the way you are. It may, in fact, be that you are already psychotic. There's really no way of knowing without taking certain risks, and this, at least, would end the suspense, so to speak." He tried to smile in a way that would reassure Weybridge, but the strange, toothy unpursing of his mouth was not reassuring.

"I'll have to think about it," Weybridge hedged.

"Let me suggest that you do it very quickly. The Old Man is anxious to have your case resolved, and his way would most certainly do you permanent damage." Dr. Cleeve watched Weybridge closely. "If you have not already been done permanent damage."

"And we won't know that until we try one of the techniques, right?" Weybridge ventured, his tone so cynical that even he was startled by the sound of it.

"It is the one sure way." Dr. Cleeve paused a moment. "It may not be that you have any choice."

"And it is really out of my hands in any case, isn't it?" He sighed. "If I say yes to you, or if I wait until the others, the Old Man—whoever he is—makes up his mind to put my brain through the chemical wringer. Which might have been done already. Did you ever think of that?"

"Oh, most certainly we've thought of it. It seems very likely that there has been some . . . tampering. We've said that from the first, as you recall." He smacked his fleshy palms together. "Well. I'll let you have a little time to yourself. But try to reach a decision soon, Mr. Weybridge. The Old Man is impatient, as you may remember."

"I don't know who the Old Man is. He's just a name people keep using around here," Weybridge said, too resigned to object to what Dr. Cleeve said to him.

"You claim that's the case. That's how the Old Man sees it. He thinks that you're buying time, as I said. He thinks that this is all a very clever ploy and that you're doing everything you can to keep us from following up on your case." He shrugged. "I don't know what the truth of the matter is, but I want to find it out. Don't you?" This last was a careful inquiry, the most genuine question the man had asked since he'd come into the room.

"You won't believe it, but I do," Weybridge said, feeling himself grow tired simply with speaking. He had reiterated the same thing so often that it was no longer making much sense to him. "I have to know what really happened to me, and who I am."

"Yes; I can see that," Dr. Cleeve said with an emotion that approached enthusiasm. "You think about it tonight. This isn't the kind of thing to rush into, no matter how urgent it may appear."

As Weybridge leaned back against the pillows, he was feeling slightly faint, and he answered less cautiously than he might have under other circumstances. "If it gets us answers, do whatever you have to do."

"Oh, we will, Mr. Weybridge," Dr. Cleeve assured him as the door closed on him.

There were dreams and fragments of dreams that hounded Weybridge through the night. He was left with eyes that felt as if sand had been rubbed into the lids and a taste in his mouth that drove what little appetite he possessed away from him, replacing it with repugnance.

Malpass did not come to visit him until midday, and when he arrived, he looked uncharacteristically harried. "You're having quite a time with us, aren't you, David?" he asked without his usual friendly preamble.

"I've done easier things, I think." He tried to smile at the other man, but could not force his face to cooperate. "I wish you'd tell me what's going on around here."

"The Old Man wants to take you off the IV unit and see if a few days on no rations will bring you around. I've asked him to give me a few more days with you, but I don't know if he's going to allow it. Three of our operatives were killed yesterday, and he's convinced you can tell him how their covers were blown."

"It wasn't me," Weybridge said firmly, and even as he spoke, he wondered if some of those drastic images stored in his mind where the memories had been might be associated with the loss of other operatives.

"The Old Man doesn't believe that. He thinks you're still following orders." Malpass licked his lips furtively, then forced them into a half smile that reflected goodwill. "You've got to understand, David. The Old Man simply doesn't buy your story. We've all tried to convince him that you're probably nothing more than a pawn, someone who's been set up to distract us, but that isn't making any headway with the Old Man. He's pissed about the other operatives, you see, and he wants someone's head on the block. If it isn't yours, it may have to be mine, and frankly, I'd rather it be yours." This admission came out in a hurry, as if he hoped that in saying it quickly, he would disguise its meaning.

"And you want this over with, don't you, Malpass?" Weybridge asked, feeling much more tired than he thought it was possible to be. "I want it over with too."

"Then, you'll agree? You'll let them question you again, with drugs so we're sure you are telling us the truth?" He sounded as eager as a schoolboy asking for a day without classes.

"Probably," he said. "I have to think it over. You're going to have to muck about in my mind, and that's happened once already. I don't want to be one of those miserable vegetables that you water from time to time."

Malpass laughed as if he thought this caution was very witty. "I don't blame you for thinking it over, David. You're the kind who has to be sure, and that's good, that's good. We'll all be easier in our minds when the questions have been answered."

"Will we? That's assuming you find out what you want to know, and it's still worth your while to keep me alive. There are times I wonder if you're on my side or the other side— whoever my side and the other side may be—and if anything you're telling me is true. If you were on the other side, what better way to get me to spill my guts to you than to convince me that you're on my side and that you're afraid I've been turned. You say you're testing me, but it might not be true."

"David, you're paranoid," Malpass said sternly. "You're letting your fears run away with you. Why would we go through something this elaborate if we weren't on your side? What would be the purpose?"

"Maybe you want to turn me, and this is as good a way as any to do it. Maybe I've got information you haven't been able to get out of me yet. Maybe you're going to program me to work for you, and you started out with privation and torture, and now that I'm all disoriented, you're going to put on the finishing touches with a good scramble of my brain." He sighed. "Or maybe all that has already happened and you're going to see what I wrecked for you. And then what? You might decide that it's too risky to let it be known that you've found out what happened, and so you'll decide to lock me up or turn me into some kind of zombie or just let me die."

"You're getting morbid," Malpass blustered, no longer looking at Weybridge. "I'm going to have to warn the Old Man that you've been brooding."

"Wouldn't you brood, in my position?" Weybridge countered, his face desolate.

"Well, anyone would," Malpass said, reverting to his role as chief sympathizer. "Have you been able to have a meal yet?"

The familiar cold filled him. "No," Weybridge said softly. "I . . . can't."

"That'll be one of the things we'll work on, then," Malpass promised. "There's got to be some reason for it, don't you think? David, you're not going to believe this, but I truly hope that you come through this perfectly."

"No more than I do," Weybridge said without mirth. "I'm tired of all the doubts and secrecy." And the terrible visions of broken and abused bodies, of the panic that gripped him without warning and without reason, of the dread he felt when he saw a plate of food.

"Excellent," Malpass said, rubbing his hands together once, as if warming them. "We'll get ready, so when you make up your mind we can get started."

"You're convinced that I'll consent. Or will you do it no matter what I decide?" Weybridge said recklessly, and saw the flicker in Malpass' eyes. "You're going to do it no matter what, aren't you?"

"I'll talk to you in the morning, David," Malpass said, beating a hasty retreat.

There were dreams that night, hideous, incomplete things with incomprehensible images of the most malicious carnage. Weybridge tossed in his bed, and willed himself awake twice, only to hear the insidious whispers buzz around him more fiercely. His eyes ached and his throat was dry.

Dr. Cleeve was the first to visit him in the morning. He sidled up to Weybridge's bed and poked at him. "Well? Do you think you will be able to help me?"

"If you can help me," Weybridge answered, too exhausted to do much more than nod.

"What about Malpass? Are you going to put him off, or are you going to convince him that my way was the right one?" The tip of his nose moved when he spoke; Weybridge had never noticed that before.

"I . . . I'll have to talk to him." He moved his arms gingerly, taking care to test himself. "I want to do what's best."

"Of course you do," Dr. Cleeve declared. "And we've already discussed that, haven't we?" His eyes gloated, though the tone of his voice remained the same. "You and I will be able to persuade the rest of them. Then you'll be rid of your troubles and you can go about your life again instead of remaining here."

"Will I?" Weybridge had not meant to ask this aloud, but once the words were out, he felt relieved. "Or am I speeding up the end?"

"We won't know that until we know what's been done to you, Mr. Weybridge," said Dr. Cleeve. "I'll have a little talk with Malpass and we'll arrange matters."

"When?" Weybridge asked, dreading the answer.

"Tomorrow morning, I should think," he replied, hitching his shoulders to show his doubt.

"And then?" Weybridge continued.

"We don't know yet, Mr. Weybridge. It will depend on how much you have been . . . interfered with." He was not like Malpass, not inclined to lessen the blow. "If there is extensive damage, it will be difficult to repair it. It's one of the risks you take in techniques like this."

Weybridge nodded, swallowing hard.

"Malpass will doubtless have a few things to say to you about the tests. Keep in mind that he is not a medical expert and his first loyalty is to the Old Man."

"Where is your first loyalty?" Weybridge could not help asking.

"Why, to the country, of course. I am not a political man." He cleared his throat. "I hope you won't repeat this to Malpass; he is suspicious of me as it is."

"Why is that?"

"There are many reasons, most of them personal," Dr. Cleeve said smoothly. "We can discuss them later, if you like, when you're more . . . yourself."

Weybridge closed his eyes. "Shit."

"I have a great deal to do, Mr. Weybridge. Is there anything else you would like to know?" Dr. Cleeve was plainly impatient to be gone.

"One thing: how long have I been here?"

"Oh, five or six weeks, I suppose. I wasn't brought in at first. Only when they realized that they needed my sort of help. . . . That was sixteen days ago, when you had recovered from the worst of your wounds but still could not or would not eat." He waited. "Is that all, Mr. Weybridge?"

"Sure," he sighed.

"Then, we'll make the arrangements," Dr. Cleeve said, closing the door before Weybridge could think of another question.

He was wakened that night—out of a fearful dream that he would not let himself examine too closely—by the nurse who had been kind enough to be interested in him and had tried to rub his feet. He stared at her, trying to make out her features through the last images of the dream, so that at first he had the impression that she had been attacked, her mouth and nostrils torn and her eyes blackened.

"Mr. Weybridge," the nurse whispered again, with greater urgency.

"What is it?" he asked, whispering too, and wondering how much the concealed devices in the room could hear.

"They told me . . . they're planning to try to probe your memory. Did you know that?" The worry in her face was clear to him now that he saw her without the other image superimposed on her face.

"Yes, that's what they've—we've decided."

"You agreed?" She was incredulous.

"What else can I do?" He felt, even as he asked, that he had erred in giving his permission. "Why?"

"They didn't tell you, did they? about the after effects of the drugs, did they? Do you know that you can lose your memory entirely?"

"I've already lost most of it," Weybridge said, trying to make light of her objections.

"It can turn you into a vegetable, something that lies in a bed with machines to make the body work, a thing they bury when it begins to smell bad." She obviously intended to shock him with this statement, and in a way she succeeded.

"You don't know anything about that," Weybridge said heatedly. "You haven't seen bodies lying unburied in an open grave in a field where the humidity makes everything ripe, including the bodies." He coughed, trying to think where that memory came from. "You haven't been locked in a stone-walled room with five other people, no latrine and not enough food to go around."

"Is that what happened to you?" she asked, aghast at what she heard.

"Yes," he said, with less certainty.

"Did it?"

"I think so. I remember it, pieces of it, anyway." He rubbed his face, feeling his beard scratch against the palms of his hands. Under his fingers, his features were gaunt.

"They'll force you to remember it all, if it happened," she warned him. "Don't you understand? They'll throw you away like used tissue paper when they're done. They don't care what happens to you after they find out what you know. Truly, they won't bother to see you're cared for." She reached out and took him by the shoulders. "If you want to stay in one piece, you've got to get away from here before they go to work on you. Otherwise you'll be . . . nothing when they're through with you, and no one will care."

"Does anyone care now?" he wondered aloud. "I don't know of anyone."

"Yours family, your friends, someone must be worried about you. This place is bad enough without thinking that . . ." Her voice trailed off.

"And where is this place? If I got out, where would I be? Don't you see, I have no idea of who these people are, really, or where we are or what it's like outside. No one has told me and I don't remember. Even if I got out, I would have no place to go, and no one to stay with and nothing to offer." His despair returned tenfold as he said these things.

"I'll find someone to take care of you until you remember," she promised him, her eyes fierce with intent.

"And feed me?" he asked ironically. "Do you have a friend with an IV unit?"

"Once you're out of here—" she began.

"Once I'm out of here, I'll be at the mercy of . . . every-thing. Where are we? Where would I have to go for the Old Man—whoever he is—not to find me and bring me back? It might be worse out there." He shivered. "I don't think I can manage. If I could get out, I don't think I'd be able to get very far before they brought me back."

"We're near a river. We're about fifteen miles from the capital, and—"

"What capital is that?" Weybridge inquired politely. "I don't know which capital you mean."

"*Our* capital, of course, " she insisted. "You can get that far, can't you? There are names I could give you, people who would hide you for a while, until you make up your mind what you want to do about . . . everything."

"I don't know about the capital," Weybridge repeated.

"You *lived* there, for heaven's sake. Your records show that you lived there for ten years. You remember that much, don't you?" She was becoming irritated with him. "Don't you have any memory of that time at all?"

"I . . . don't think so." He looked at her strangely. "And for all I know, my records are false. I might not have been here ever, and it could be that I haven't done any of the things I think I have."

"Well, letting them fill you up with chemicals isn't going to help you find. You'll just get used up." She took his hand and pulled on it with force. "Mr. Weybridge, I can't wait forever for you to make up your mind. If they found out I came in to see you and tried to get you to leave, I'd be in a lot of trouble. You understand that, don't you?"

"I can see that it might be possible." He tugged his hand, but she would not release it. "Nurse, I don't want to go away from here, not yet, not until I can get some idea of who I am and what I did. Not until I can *eat*."

"But you will be able to if you leave. You're being manipulated, Mr. Weybridge. David. They're doing things to you so that you can't eat, so you'll have to stay here. If only you'd get away from here, you'd find out fast enough that you're all right. You'd be able to remember what really happened and know what was . . . programmed into you. They don't care what comes of their little experiments, and they're not going to give a damn if you go catatonic or starve to death or anything else. That's the way they've been treating agents that they have questions about." She paused. "I have to leave pretty soon. It's too risky for me to remain here. They'll catch me and they'll . . ." She turned away, her eyes moving nervously toward the door.

Weybridge closed his eyes, but the dreadful images did not fade. There were three naked figures, two of them women, twitching on a stone floor. They were all fouled with blood and vomit and excrement, and the movements and sounds they made were no longer entirely human. "I've been thinking," he said remotely, his throat sour and dry, "that I've been going on the assumption that all the pieces of things I remember, all the horrors, were done to me. But I can't find more than three scars on my body, and if it happened, I'd be crosshatched and maimed. I thought that perhaps I *did* those things to others, that I was the one causing the horror, not its victim. Do you think that's possible? Do you think I finally had enough and wouldn't let myself do anything more?" This time when he pulled on his hand, she let him go.

"I can't say, Weybridge. If you haven't got sense enough to come with me, there's nothing I can do to change your mind. You want to let them do this to you, I can't stop you." She got off his bed, her eyes distraught though she was able to maintain an unruffled expression. "After today, you won't have the chance to change your mind. Remember that."

"Along with everything else." He looked at her steadily. "If you get into trouble because of me, I want you to know that I'm sorry. If I'm right, I've already caused enough grief. I don't know if it's necessary or possible for you to forgive me, but I hope you will."

The nurse edged toward the door, but she made one last try. "They might have given you false memories. They're doing a lot of experiments that way. Or you could be someone else, an agent from the other side, and they're trying to get information out of you before they send you back with a mind like pudding." She folded her arms, her hands straining on her elbows. "You'd be giving in to them for no reason. Hostages, after a while, try to believe that their captors have a good reason to be holding them. That could be what you're feeling right now."

"Nurse, I appreciate everything. I do." He sighed. "But whether you're right or not, it doesn't change anything, does it? I can't manage away from this . . . hospital. I'd be worse than a baby, and anyone who helped me would be putting themselves in danger for nothing. And if you're trying to get me back to the other side, who's to say that I'm one of theirs? Perhaps they want me to do more than has already been done.''

She opened the door a crack and peered out into the hall. ''I've got to leave, Weybridge.''

''I know,'' he said, filled with great tranquillity. ''Be careful.''

''You too,'' she answered. And then she was gone.

Weybridge lay back against the pillows, his emaciated features composed and peaceful as he waited for the needles and the chemicals and oblivion.